World of Midgets

Jeff Gross

To my mother and father

CHAPTER 1

Summoned by the Bureau of Times & Tides, I arrive in Paris in September of 1982. Soon thereafter, a base of operations is provided in a quiet part of the 17th *arrondissement*, Rue Gustave Flaubert. Room 18, a 12 square meter, sixth-floor walkup at the end of the corridor, right across from the Turkish toilet. 500 francs a month. No sooner does the door close than I plug in my typewriter and fire off a missive to American Express, Stockholm, inviting Angel Desperado to join me. The space is tight but so what? Angel, my partner in crime for the last five years, seems like the perfect companion for this latest adventure. We've worked as janitors in Stockholm, we've squeaked by in Berlin, we've done construction in Greece (me surrendering miserably after one day, him hanging in there for months on end), but Paris was always the plan.

Ten days after I settle in to room 18, thirty pounds of books on the shelf, drying line across the window, scavenged pots and pans on the mantelpiece, desk two fingers deep in pigshit and drivel, the round Spanish Concierge knocks on the thin glass of her door to stop me on my way out to the market. Our first contact. The black roots show through her peroxide blonde hair. "Is this you?" she smiles warmly, holding out an envelope with my name on it, Swedish air mail.

"Yeah that's me." I rip open the envelope right then and there and begin to read as I walk out the front door and down the street. Angel is doing just fine, building scaffolding, working black, as they say, his upper lip stuffed with strong *Grov* snuff, like a real Swedish grunt, lifting pipes and planks ten hours a day while teetering six stories above Stockholm. Feeling strong, vital and alive, sleeping five hours a night in a cubby hole at the scaffolding firm, spending the off hours dancing through the never-ending daylight, then retiring to his hole to read and take notes. "Paris? 12 square meters? Yes! Yes! Yes!" Enough time to save $700-$800 and he'll be on his way. Two weeks, a month tops.

In the meantime:

"You are American?" Dressed in slippers and a threadbare brown robe, a black cane in her left hand, Madame Lacombe leans against the wall at the far end of the hall. It has taken her the better part of two weeks to finally give my greetings more than a grunt as we pass in the hallway. "Yes I thought you might be. I like the Americans... Tell me something, you're young *n'est-ce pas?*" Through Madame Lacombe's feeble, 80-year-old, cataract-shrouded eyes, I appear as nothing more than a tall shadow. "Yes I could tell by the voice. Do you intend to stay a long time? Uh hmm, I see. Well then, *au revoir Monsieur.*"

On the sixth floor, the paint, an industrial yellow, is tinted grey by the dust balls which have attached themselves to the walls. The wall-paper, a sort of matching grey oil-cloth, hangs off the corners where it has come unglued. There is a sink in the hall, in which Madame Lacombe, who has no sink, performs some of her ablutions. Right next to it is a sit toilet, a present for Madame Lacombe's 75th birthday, after she could no longer squat in the Turkish toilet. A magic-marker sign inside reads "Please make sure to pull the chain," and another one tacked outside says, "Close the door." On the hall floor, red hexagonal tiles, an indelible black line leads from the stairs to the coal bin outside Number 15, the room in which Madame Lacombe has slept ever since her husband died during the war, 40 years ago. A coffin of a room: felt and foam strips on the window sills to shut out the draft, a blanket on the window-which-never-opens to shut out the light. The coal heater has turned the walls ochre. Brown bags and sagging cardboard boxes cascade from under the rickety bed, piles of old newspapers, junkyards of broken pots, spools and boxes of string-bits, rolls of butcher paper, well-protected mice, grimy memorabilia. On the wall: three suffering Jesuses caked with soot from the heater. Jesuses from the better days when she could still see more than shadows, when her legs were not so atrophied and aching that she could still make her way up and down the six flights, 121 steps, when she wouldn't need someone like Josef Klein to be her eyes and ears on the outside.

"Tell me something, Monsieur," she catches me on the way out, a week after the first real contact. "You take showers don't you?"

"Yes..." I answer warily. It's a strange question.

"Are there still public baths, where you can pay for a shower, or have they torn them down? There are? I see. Tell me something else, *Monsieur. Sans indiscretion.* I hear your machine. It doesn't bother me, no no. But I hear it... Do you have a profession? A writer, you're a writer? I see. I used to love to read when my eyes were still good. Well, you were on your way out. *A bientôt...*"

Walk the streets with your eyes up, and you see them everywhere, thousands of old women just like her haunting the top floors all through Paris, the plastic bags hanging on hooks in the windows, the bits of sagging latex drying on clothes lines of their own, the ghost-like figures propped up on their elbows, waiting for something to happen below. Rent unchanged since 1948: 150 francs a month. Huddled behind the lovely stone facades, with faint nostalgic memories of their dead husbands to warm them. Women nobody remembered to toss a bone to so that they might die happily, or just die period. Living out their misery in pajamas and worn-shiny felt slippers, robes impregnated with the smell of *choucroute*, of onions fried in rancid oil and *camembert* cheese gone sour. Shadows, like Madame Lacombe, peeking a suspicious eye outside their door anytime they hear an unaccustomed sound. Then the hasty retreat back inside their yellowing caves to turn the radio up again. The accordion chords remind them of the days when they used to stroll down the boulevards in their best clothes, when it was still safe to walk in Paris. *"Avant les Arabes."*

For at least the last four years Madame Lacombe has not left the floor of her own will. The legs, the lungs, *"Mon insuffisance pulmonaire."*

"Never mind that," she says, closing her door carefully to keep in the heat as she steps into the hall. By mid-October it has already turned cold, and I can see her breath as she speaks. "As a writer, there are French writers you like, *non?*"

"A few, Cendrars, Flaubert, Céline..." I say, treading carefully, it's a test. "Actually, I'm not that familiar with French literature."

"Céline? You like Céline?" she says, trying, not quite successfully, to hide how pleased she is. It's precisely the opening she'd hoped for. Perfect. "I knew him, you know. His name was really Destouches. He was a doctor at the same hospital as my husband."

"Really!"

"You're surprised. Hmm... *Vous savez,* I was a very cultured woman. I didn't always live like this. I used to play the piano. In 1935 I won first place at the *Conservatoire de Paris.* We used to go out to Meudon to see the Destouches."

"Tell me. What was he like?"

"Oh. There was nothing really special about the man. Except that he had a great big cat which he used to carry everywhere and that he was intelligent. But just to look at him you wouldn't think him to be a remarkable man at all."

"Would you enjoy it if I read you something of his sometime?"

"Yes, very much," she says, a bit too enthusiastically. "But not today. I'm too tired." The American mustn't think she is too eager. "Tomorrow? Around five o'clock?" she suggests, after the pause, as if that is the only possible opening in her very full agenda. All very formal and proper.

The next day, at five o'clock on the tick, she knocks on my door, wearing not one, but two identical brown robes, and a scarf over her head. *"Bonjour Monsieur."*

I offer her the only chair, a hard wooden one that goes with the desk. The bed is softer but also lower and so unstable that I fear she'll tip over. She doesn't seem to mind, she sits with her hands on her knees, regal, like a princess. Up close like this, she looks positively ancient, a face sculpted in copper, a black mustache tinted with strands of grey, a few hairs sprouting from her chin. The rolling radiator doesn't really generate any lasting form of heat, can't quite neutralize the refrigerating effect of the tin roof or the cold wind whistling through the cracks in the window-frame. This doesn't bother me, I don't even use it usually, to save money, but she's so fragile, I'm worried she'll catch her death.

"Tea?"

She shakes her head, she doesn't want to be too much trouble.

"Come on, the water's already boiled. You're going to need it to stay warm. Here, you better take this too." Without asking permission, I drape a blanket around her shoulders. When the tea is ready I sit down opposite her on the bed, open the book and take a sip. *"Voyage au bout de la nuit de Louis Ferdinand Céline..."* Sentence by sentence she concentrates, hunched over, again trying to hide her pleasure, sipping her tea, interrupting every so often to correct the pronunciation, to elucidate the vocabulary, a deliberate, determined attempt to keep the exchange equal. *"La race, ce que tu appelles comme ça, c'est seulement ce grand ramassis de miteux dans mon genre, chassieux, puceux, transis, qui ont échoués ici poursuivis par la faim, la peste, les tumeurs et le froid, venus vaincus des quatre coins du monde. Ils ne pouvaient pas aller plus loin à cause de la mer. C'est ça la France et puis c'est ça les Français."*[1]

She coughs, coming to life like an old diesel engine, then begins to laugh, a rusty, infectious laugh which warms the room, the words accord so with her own view of things. "Ah that was a book, yes. I never told him, but he was never so good again."

I read for an hour, page 30, until my throat is raw from the cold, and my voice begins to fail. "I must retire for my dinner, *Monsieur*," she says, quick to react. "Thank you very much. *Merci, merci beaucoup...*"

I close the door, sit down at the desk and switch on the Smith Corona electric typewriter, a large, clumsy beast which rattles and purrs expectantly. But after reading to Madame Lacombe I am drained, the words are flat, lifeless, they don't even come close to jumping off the page. The unmistakable dull thud of a broomstick banging into the ceiling of the fifth floor below settles it. I've been in enough tenuous living situations in the course of traveling hard over the last few years, that I prefer to remain discreet, invisible, and making enemies right off the bat doesn't seem like a good idea. I shut off the machine, call it a day. Nothing was coming anyway...

I receive a reject slip from the Los Angeles Times for a piece entitled *Fear and Loathing in Rhodes*, about vacation-club Swedes wasted on cheap ouzo reeling drunkenly around Rhodes, dancing the syrtaki to the tune of orchestras playing *Feelings* and the theme to *Zorba the Greek*, piling on the local color in the most cynical way possible. The Times' rejection is brief, polite, matter of fact, "We hope you'll think of us for future submissions," that sort of thing. No mention of what must probably be obvious to anyone with either half-a-brain, or a functioning reality principle: that there is zero chance of a newspaper printing an article about exotic locations where you don't want to go. What would be the point? Unfazed, slightly proud even, confirmation that I am now officially living the life, I tack the envelope on the door, put the note up on the wall by the desk for motivation, and just continue on my rounds, looking for more ideas for travel articles. As for Madame Lacombe, in the days after the reading,

---

[1]"What you call the race is nothing more than a huge pile of moth-eaten sods like me, rheumy, flea-bitten, fear-numbed, who, pursued by hunger, plague, tumors and cold, arrived here vanquished from the four corners of the earth. They couldn't go further because of the ocean. That's your France, and that's the French."

whenever I go out or come in, she listens for my steps on the tiles, the key in my lock. She stands there, right outside her door, her face pleading for the next reading. Her face only, she wouldn't dream of asking.

After a fortnight of such preliminaries she finally breaks down: she is ready to be more familiar. She calls me Monsieur Josef, instead of simply Monsieur. "You don't mind if I call you Monsieur Josef, do you? My helper got your name off the envelope on your door. Monsieur Josef. We could read more Celine, that is if you have the time."

But all of a sudden, there doesn't seem to be any time. Too much to learn, too many café terraces, too many gorgeous women, too many things to observe and study. The Portuguese women prostrating themselves in front of the wax-preserved body of Saint Vincent de Paul, the carp and sailboats in the ponds at the Tuileries, *charcuteries* and cheese shops, the *pétanque* players with their fat stomachs and corn-paper *Gauloises* butts glued to the sides of their mouths, the old guy on Rue Saint Denis playing guitar and singing Brassens songs, the clowns, magicians, fakirs and con-men at Beaubourg or Saint Germain des Près.

"You were gone all day," or "You didn't come home at all last night," she says.

I just shrug my shoulders. The nights put the juice in my legs, the shadows of the buildings conceal a thousand secrets, the ghosts of other visionaries and madmen still lurk around every corner. How to avoid mythical thoughts in a monumental city? Apollo riding the chariot of the sun on the *Grand Palais*, the *Ile de la Cité* and *Notre Dame* seen from the *Pont des Arts*, the tortured wraiths in Rodin's vision of hell, the eleven-layered, two ton casket of Napoleon, the little tyrant, the battles engraved on the *Arc de Triomphe*, a monument floating in blood. What about the unknown soldier, poor bastard, or those anonymous souls who disappeared off the map after the Commune, when Baron Haussmann decided to raze entire sections of Paris to let the light in, and make the streets safe for cannonballs, to remind that no masterpiece is without cost?

"People have been slamming doors up here at night," Madame Lacombe greets me. A change of tactics.

"And who might that be?" I play along, knowing I've been neglecting her.

"I wake up and then I can't get back to sleep..."

I stick my key in the door.

"You're not angry, are you Monsieur Josef? Ask the police, it's against the law to slam doors."

"No don't worry, I'm not angry..." The open door casts a triangle of light into the dark hall. "I'll be more careful. I didn't realize. Well, got to get to work now."

"Yes of course, you must get back to your book." After the reproaches, the charm. "Work well, *à très bientôt.*"

"*Mais sinon, ça va?*" I ask her. "Aside from that, are you OK?"

She takes a long time to answer, cocking her head sideways as if deciding whether I can really be trusted, before finally confiding: "I don't know what stops me from throwing myself out the window."

In her feeble condition, I doubt she could pry the dust-soldered windows open anyway, but I don't mention it. Thoughts to work by.

Below, on the fifth floor, Madame Tournier returns home. Even before she has time to shut her shutters, she hears my electric typewriter. The keys bang down, the letters run down the wooden legs of the desk, pick up speed on the red tiles and crash through the ceiling of her living room. "*Oh non, ooh la la,* this will never do." She runs into the kitchen, grabs a broom and slams it into the ceiling, bang, bang, bang, until the American writer finally concedes and shuts down for the night.

The next morning, when I pop out of the service entrance, the Concierge is deep in conference, a polite-beleaguered smile frozen in place as she wilts under the withering blasts of Madame Tournier's acid tongue. Madame Tournier, hair in a tight bun, severe face, veins full of bile, could be seventy, could be eighty. Sensing my presence behind her, she turns, her face a mask. Hands on her hips, she very deliberately studies me, the wrinkled shirt, the dirty jeans, the used tennis shoes, the disquieting look in the eyes, trying to match her reaction to my caste. "So you're the American with the typewriter!" she says, her tight chicken-butt mouth mustering a polite smile. "Yes, ha ha, you see? My bedroom is right beneath you," she lies. On a roll now, she waves her hand as if to excuse the sin this time, and shakes her head sympathetically. "I don't know how you can live up there. An icebox in winter, an airless furnace in summer... *Invivable,* not even fit for animals. Well I must be going," she adds, turning to exit out the front door, checkmate.

"I'm glad you came," the Concierge says, breathing a sigh of relief as soon as the front door closes. "That woman drives me crazy. I clean her apartment, but she is always stopping here to ask me to come up and drink some wine with her. She drinks two bottles a day. Poor woman, her husband is very sick."

That afternoon, returning home, feeling strong and full of life, I climb the stairs three by three, carrying my provisions for dinner. Just as I arrive on the fifth floor, Mme. Tournier opens her kitchen door to put the garbage down the chute. "Oh hello. Hard walk isn't it? Ah but you're young. I see you've been shopping. Can I offer you a glass of wine?"

"Sure, why not?" She's definitely not my dream date, but in my precarious situation, I can't afford to be making enemies, and there seems no way to turn the offer down without offending.

She washes her hands, wipes them carefully, turns two glasses over on the sink and pulls the cork out of the bottle. "I don't know how you live up there. Simply scandalous!" she says as she pours the wine. She hands me the glass. "*Santé!*" we clink glasses. "How do you say in your country? Cheers? Yes? Well then cheers."

For fifteen minutes she holds me captive in that kitchen. She tells me that the beef liver I have bought is bad for me, bad for the kidneys. She tells me that the seven franc Nicolas wine will destroy my liver, "In France you have to spend 25 francs *minimum* on a bottle of wine." She tells me that too much coffee hardens the spleen, that too many vegetables soften the appendix, that milk makes people too trusting, and beer makes them too aggressive. "Look at the English. And the Germans! *Les Schleus!* You know I was in the resistance. You have heard of Le Vercors? *J'ai fait le Vercors.* July 1944. 3,500 *maquisards*, we held out for two months. The *boches* massacred the villages around us. It was horrible, a blood bath." She downs her wine and slams down her glass, pulls the cork out of the bottle again and pours herself another one. "You must stop by often. It does me good to have someone to talk to."

Reprieved, I give her the smile, shake hands and step out the door, taking the last flight of stairs three by three again, not so much out of vitality this time but out of eagerness to get out of sight. Shaking my head, wondering if I will have enough juice to purge myself of her poison and sit down to write, I turn down the corridor, right, then right again, where Madame Lacombe is leaning against the wall, waiting. "Monsieur Josef, are you sure it is a good idea to leave an envelope with your name on it on the door?"

"Why?"

"Well I wouldn't do it."

I hit the hall light once, twice.

"You know, it doesn't stay on any longer if you hit it twice," she says, nodding her head. "I heard you talking to Mme. Tournier. She is not a good woman, Monsieur Josef."

"She seems a bit lonely. We drank a glass of wine and she told me about the *resistance*..."

"*Le Vercors*, right? Hmm. She drinks too much. You know Monsieur Josef, if all the people in France who said they fought in the Vercors stood on each other's shoulders it still wouldn't be big enough to hold them. They were cowards then, but now, even worse, they are liars. Back then, you know," Madame Lacombe shakes her ancient head slowly, "You could either say no or yes. I didn't say yes, but I didn't say no either. I didn't say anything, I didn't march, I didn't go to meetings. I just kept to myself. *La guerre*... In times of war sometimes you make compromises you would prefer not to make. The others called me a *collabo*. I lost a lot during the war: all my silver, my dishes, my linen, my husband. People don't realize about the suffering back then. It was a time of savagery, *c'était la jungle*, people were animals. I never turned anyone in though. I won't tell you about the French, the denunciations... I knew a policeman who turned in his mother and father. The Germans shot them. People nowadays don't understand that, do you understand that? Is your French good enough?"

Once a day, except Sundays, Madame Lacombe receives a one hour visit from that good Catholic, Madame Jeunet. Jeanette Jeunet with her thicker-than-thick brown-rimmed glasses, her brown coat and blue apron. In case I'm not already awake, she bangs the aluminum pots and pans in the hall sink to bring me outside to talk as she scours away last night's vegetable soup, and cooks Madame Lacombe's lunch, lamb and cabbage. To feel that she is doing her charitable bit for the world, Jeanette Jeunet, the veins in her nose and cheeks broken by spirits, depends on Antoinette Lacombe. And of course, Antoinette Lacombe relies on her for the food, the regular company. Dependency creating bitterness, they torture each other, snipe, then use me as their arbiter.

"I pay her to stay for two hours, but she is gone after one," says Madame Lacombe. "She is awful with me, she steals the grocery money."

"She's such a witch," Mme. Jeunet, her once-a-week black eye partially concealed by the Benedictine-bottle glasses, offers her version. "Nobody else from the agency will take care of her. She always complains. She never compliments me on anything."

A sucker for stories, I nod, listen poker-faced, no way for her to tell what's going on inside, but I don't have much sympathy for the way Mme. Jeunet takes advantage of Madame Lacombe's weak eyesight: the layer of dust in Room 15 is an inch thick and on the move.

Madame Jeunet lives with her pimply son in a dark apartment on the far side of the 17th *arrondissement*. Her husband is no longer alive, she says in such a way as to suggest that he got exactly what he deserved and that at this very moment he is doubtless sweating his too-large balls off shoveling coal for Satan himself.

Six nights a week, she stands with the men at the local bar until closing time. Once a week or so she grows a fresh black eye. The last bruises barely have time to turn yellow before the next ones sprout. It's a mystery. "Oh the brakes failed on my son's *Solex*," she explains, or "I ran into a door, it's nothing." The excuses run in series of fives, increasingly exotic and far-fetched: "A dove, flew right into me, and then another hit the left eye..." She accepts it. The black eyes, the bruises that Madame Lacombe leaves on her: it's all the same, an expected part of life. "She doesn't know how good I am to her," Mme. Jeunet says as she turns off the water in the sink. She complains, a matter of form, but she's powerless to do anything but come back for more.

To me, the remedy seems obvious, a way to help Madame Lacombe slip the chains of her burdensome existence, and to make amends for my inability to read to her. All Madame Lacombe needs is the proper presentation. "I was out in *Parc Monceau*," I broach the subject casually.

"Yes, what is it like now in the park?" Madame Lacombe sits down on the chair next to the coal storage box. She had Mme. Jeunet put the chair out in the hall two days ago. "I haven't been there in almost five years now." She falls right into the trap.

"It's a bit cold, but it's nice. What if we got you a wheelchair? We could wrap you in blankets and I could wheel you out to the park..."

At her end of the corridor, Madame Lacombe pulls her robe tighter over her chest. She sniffles, and her face creases into a frown.

"Sure, I could carry you down to the fifth floor, we could go through Madame Tournier's kitchen, then down the elevator to the street. Wouldn't you like to see the park?"

"*C'est gentil Josef,*" she thanks me for my kindness in a tiny, resigned voice. But she would not think of bothering the collaborator Tournier, of asking for permission to cross her apartment, of being in the hypocrite's debt. Besides, she is quietly positive that if she ventured back onto the streets, long-dormant germs would instantly be magnetized to her from the most bubonic, the most off-white and pestiferous quarters of the new Paris: La Goutte d'Or, Belleville, *Ilôt Chalon, Afrique-sur-Seine.*

"Well if you change your mind..."

"It's the bread, you know." A middle-aged photographer confides to me in a conspiratorial whisper from the next table at Le Weekend, the neighborhood café. "Look at these people! Rats! The hair, safety pins in their noses, cigarettes, dogs, hats. Hats, *nom de dieu!* I'm leaving. Finished, out, finito, kapoot. They stink, and they don't even know it. They don't care. You know what the problem is? You want to know? The problem is that when the flour is stored for too long it gets a parasite. And the parasite, it drives people crazy. Ergotism! *Er-Go-Tisme!* They eat the bread, the bread eats them. The whole city is crazy, minds rotted. *Liberté, égalité, fraternité!* Lunatics praying for the arrival of a demagogue, recreants capable of any act of violence, susceptible, what am I saying: susceptible? Dying for all imaginable follies."

"Is that egotism, or ergotism?" I say as the waitress sets a camembert sandwich down in front of me. A sandwich which the photographer takes as a personal affront, a deliberate, premeditated provocation.

"You don't believe me?" He raises his hands in surrender, angrily zipping and unzipping his camera bag before getting up. "OK fine, you just got here. Eat your sandwich. You'll see." He slams the door as he goes out. Ergotism: why not? Parasites, Parisites.

Back on the sixth floor, after a bit of research at the free library down at the Pompidou Center, I try the notion out on Madame Lacombe. I flap my arms, dance like a mad stork, imitate how it was in the middle ages, when great outbreaks of the ergot poisoning in rye, "*Maladie des Ardents,*" sent whole villages into LSD trips. Peasants ripping out their hair, drowning themselves, jumping to their deaths from haylofts...

"Ergotism?" she chuckles. "Yes, I suppose it's possible..." she sighs and shifts her cane from the left hand to the right. "I don't understand it, Monsieur Josef. Why would someone like you come to Paris, to live here? For me it's different, I don't have a choice. But you, you're young, you have your future."

"Why?" What can I tell her? That I am the spawn of nomads, trailblazers and survivors? That my paternal grandfather, descended from 38 generations of Rabbis renowned for their scholarliness and honor, (including my great-grandfather in Lithuania, known as "The Saint of Tuvrig") decided to flee the yoke of tradition and make his way to Wyoming to become a cowboy? That my maternal great great grandmother was Cherokee, and when she died at a young age, her husband loaded my nine year old great grandmother into the buggy and drove her out to the woods along with her two brothers, 7 and 5, to survive or die, because the new stepmother didn't cotton much to having half-breed children to take care of. What is the right calling for such a mongrel mix, the fruit of a double Diaspora? Where does such a being ever belong? There are a hundred reasons to explain why I am here: predestination for restlessness, a desire to taste every fruit, to escape the religion of happiness in America, to find out what the world is really made of and to hell with the cost, but none of them sound really convincing or anything but youthfully rebellious and naive. And how can anyone else understand them? I don't even understand them myself, really...

"Why am I here Madame Lacombe? Is that what you want to know? I'm here because I've got a motor in my stomach that only feels good when it's going full speed. I'm here because my eyes are full and I feel alive. Have you ever heard of Henry Miller? The American writer?" In the absence of cogent thoughts, the literary angle seems like a good one. "No? Well he came to Paris in the 1930's to become a writer. And he wrote about it. About how he was poor, how he had nothing, but it didn't matter, because inside he was the richest of men. When I started to read his books, for the first time I felt like maybe I wasn't crazy. You know how he described the Americans? He said, 'They walk along like blind geese and the searchlights spray their faces with flecks of ecstasy.'"

Madame Lacombe laughs.

"I felt elation when I read his books. Elation from the force of words which come out when you live a life of devotion, urgency. He made it possible for me to dream, he gave me license to listen to my inner voice, offered me a world I could understand, a view of what a real man was, a man of vision, of harmony, of strength and beauty. He saw it. The richness, the madness, the solution within him, the truth! You might have to suffer, endure hardship, but if you had sufficient purity of heart, if your desire was strong enough, you could find that solution..."

A tiny smile tugs at the corners of Madame Lacombe's mouth, as if she is both charmed by the youthful enthusiasm, and completely certain of the tragic outcome of such a path.

"Let me tell you a story. A few years ago, I found out that Miller was living in California, not far from my home. So I decided I would go to his house, see if I could meet him. I wanted to ask for his blessing, tell him some stories, thank him for giving me life. I wanted to let him know somehow, that whatever regrets he might have at the end of his years, his baton had at least been passed on. I thought some day there will be another young man who will begin to dream, who will discover how much that dream will condemn him to isolation, condemn him to suffering and madness and loneliness. And maybe he will swallow his vision, step in line, denounce his insights, become what he is expected to be because there is no other option. All I hope to do is be there at that point, to write a book which confirms that his view is possible. Just as Henry Miller did for me.

"Well I got to the door, and my legs were shaking. Nervous. Right next to the doorbell was a little typed note on small sheet of paper. It was a quote from Meng-Tse. How did it go... 'When a man...' wait I think I have it written down somewhere." I slip away to my room, dive into my notebooks and find the one with the quote.

"Ah yes, here we go. 'When a man has reached old age and has fulfilled his mission, he has the right to confront the idea of death in peace. He has no need of other men, he knows them already and has seen enough of them. What he needs is peace. It is not seemly to seek out such a man, plague him with chatter, and make him suffer banalities. One should pass by the door of his house as if no one lived there.' Nice no?"

"Hmm," Madame Lacombe snorts. Slowly she hoists herself to her feet. "Maybe I should put up a sign. Keep all the people away. Bah! There wouldn't be anyone to read it anyway. So did you leave him in peace?"

"Well I went away, but I thought it over and came back the next day. I figured the note was for someone else. I never did have much tolerance for closed doors."

"You saw him?"

"I rang the bell, and a tall guy finally opened and asked me what I wanted. He told me if I wanted to, I could write a note to Henry, but to write it big, because he could barely see any more. In my glove box I just happen to have a blank postcard of Cezanne's *The Absinthe Drinkers* from my previous trip to Europe, when I spent many hours in the *Jeu de Paume*. I filled it with huge letters, something about how I wanted to look into eyes that had once blazed fire. I left my phone number, but he never called... What do you want, I was young."

"You're still young. A dreamer. Very young. That's not bad. But my legs hurt, and the doctor says I shouldn't stand up this long."

"Well you wanted to know why I'm here? That's why. I have no choice either."

"It is a nice story, Monsieur Josef, *merci*. But tell me something: when you write your book to save the dreamers, you're not going to write stories that go someplace, are you? They always write stories that end somewhere... In real life, stories don't go anywhere, you know that, don't you? We live a bit, we have some good moments, some bad, but we never go anywhere."

CHAPTER 2

City-Rat crawls through the shadows, a switchblade in his pocket, the fear in his stomach. Got to get high. He sniffs the air for other rats, tucks his long hair back into his wild cap. The baddest motherfucker in Toronto. Five inch platforms: don't fuck with me. He wants to get so high that he won't ever come back. There's a board over his door. The other day, or last month, they came up to his place with a gun. He slammed the door on them but they kicked it down. He pulled his blade out, and stood there, madman, just stared them down until they left. But he's not thinking about that now. He closes the door behind him, sits down on the couch, pulls out his kit and fills the syringe. Ten hits of liquid 25, half the stash. A month ago, sitting there naked, he was trying to find a vein to inject the Meth. Arms? No. No more space between the tracks. Legs? No, too many scars, scabs between the toes. What's left? There, between the legs, why not? He sticks the needle in. Waah! His cock blows up like a balloon. Nearly explodes. Ha!

The needle slides in. The stuff in his veins. He waits. What is this shit? Thirty minutes, an hour, not even a buzz. Thirteen more hits on the table. Why not? City-Rat. He drops them into the syringe, ties his arm off and sends them home. And he waits and he waits.

Back in Germany they would leave him alone. Maybe the last time he was really happy. Nine years old, and he could spend hours by himself, playing with toy soldiers and tanks. "Bang, boom, rat tat tat." Back in Germany his mother used to work in a bar. At four in the morning, when she had finished cleaning up, she would come home. He could hear her voice, and the voice of a drunken man. Another month, another man, anything to plug the loneliness. His father was one of those men, a cabaret actor who came to the *Ruhrgebiet* for a show, charmed and seduced City-Rat's mother and then skipped that coal-mining town. "Your father was a bastard, like all men," that's what his mother had always said. Whore! Fat German cow, he would cry himself to sleep, wishing he had a father like everyone else.

Then she married a Canuck, and they moved to Canada. In school they called him Nazi. The girls wouldn't talk to him, he was short and

17

skinny. He let his hair grow, starting smoking cigarettes, ran with the bad crowd. Made them laugh so they would accept him... Motherfuckers.

"Ahh," it's coming on. He's beginning to fly, to lose control. Feels so good. He rolls a joint, lights it and exhales. There. Wow. His soul rushes through the top of his head and leaps out into space: he feels free, free at last.

Wait! He can't breathe. Throat sealed. He gasps for air. Tries to draw a breath. Bang, back to earth. Help! He crawls over to the window, opens it. Praying to God. He's going to jump. Please God, please. Please help me. Save me, the tears run down his face, his lungs are bursting. He pulls himself to his feet and leans out. Please! A ray of light, sunlight, explodes on his forehead, right on the forehead. K-aah! His throat clears, he can breathe. Breathe...

A sign, City-Rat, a sign, a second chance, wake up boy. Time to clean up your act. What about that time in Ottawa, that man dragging himself along the street with the flow? Stopping against the side of a building, holding his head, unable to convince himself to take another step. Didn't City-Rat see that man and feel his heart fill with love? Didn't he smile at him, imitate him, raise his hands to the sky and yell at God until that man began to smile? Hell he practically glowed with the light City-Rat put in him.

City-Rat never wanted to be an actor, but he can feel his power. It's in the genes, in his blood: he was born to act. He begins to study mime. Impossible not to notice that he has what it takes. After only a year, he's helping the teacher give the classes. In the blood. Nothing left for you here in Canada, the teacher says. Paris, that's the place.

City-Rat gets a loan from the Canadian government, and makes plans to leave. Just before his departure, someone suggests he go see, *Les Enfants du Paradis*, the Marcel Carné film shot during the German occupation in World War II, detailing the rise of the actor Frederic Lemaître, in 1840. The bustling *Boulevard du Crime,* the mime who gets the girl, the poetry that seems to flow from everyone's lips: "*Si tous les gens qui vivent ensemble s'aimaient la terre brillerait comme un soleil.*" If everyone who lived together loved each other, the earth would shine like the sun... He's ready. At the age of 23 he flies to paradise in time for the start of classes at the Le Coq mime school.

"You want to be artists?" Le Coq asks the new students. "I can show you where the door is, but you will have to break it down yourselves."

"OK, all right! Let's go."

They start with the basics of movement. Isolating the joints, loosening the hips, forward, back, side, side; the scales, the vocabulary of mime. Dogs, rabbits, pigs, pigeons, roosters, trees, water, fire, different comic rhythms, *Commedia dell'Arte*: to City-Rat it all comes naturally. While the other students are still struggling to put an imaginary glass on an imaginary shelf, City-Rat has a three course meal cooked, and the dishes washed afterwards as well. When they are supposed to produce their skits together, the other students fumble around, walk in circles, break for coffee, talk, talk, talk. "Is this what you want? Is this it?" City-Rat demonstrates. "Enough coffee!" More, more, more.

City-Rat begins to attend class with the grandfather of mime, Etienne Decroux, the man who taught Marcel Marceau, and Jean-Louis Barrault, the star of *Les Enfants du Paradis*. The school in Boulogne, an unassuming, three-story stone building, is like a temple, every nook and cranny permeated by the master's aura, his ideas, his poetry, his anger, his suffering, his whims. At the age of 80, Decroux, like a legend, like a statue, sits in his office on the ground floor next to the kitchen, barrel chest, and huge hands trained to move with perfect control, putting fountain pen to paper to clarify his notions about movement and theater. Mime: the aristocracy of performing, where the actor has nothing to hide behind, no costume, no set, no words. Mime is suffering, looking at the bad things, the way art looks at the bad things, because pain is most powerful.

It's a different world. Down in the basement, for three months, a half an hour a day, Decroux's assistant puts the new students through the paces of the *Marche Polonaise*, the Polish Walk. A walk Decroux created after being in the infirmary during World War I and watching the Polish soldiers coming back from battle. They had a defeated walk, a defeated stance; every time they took a step they fell to the ground. It seems like the easiest thing to master, but only after two months do the first students begin to get it right. There is a subtle difference between trying to do the walk and actually doing it. The jolt begins to come naturally, and with the jolt comes the emotion of the movement: the sense of despair, exhaustion, the border of life and death, the hollow eyes beyond caring.

After the warm-up, Decroux himself finally comes down to the basement. "*Bonjour tout le monde.*"

"*Bonjour Monsieur.*"

For three months City-Rat learns the rudiments. Resistance; holding the hands correctly; breathing; Eiffel Tower technique: first lesson in movement is how to be immobile; triple design: "First the head, front, back, right and left. Now the chest. Ah, but it's not the same, we cannot move our chests as far backwards as we can forward, so we must remember to keep in measure. We only move the chest as far forward as we can move backward. Symmetry. Now the trunk: hips straight ahead, feel a separation in the points of your back. Separate, lift, and rotate to the right, into the oblique. Right, and back to center, left and back to center. *We always come back to center.*"

Soon enough the newness begins to wear off. Winter is around the corner and the city is turning grey. The girl at the bakery throws his change down on the counter, refuses to put it in his hand, the butcher insults him when he buys his meat. The shoe-maker won't even look at the shoes he brings in for repair, it wouldn't be worth the effort. Stale and defeated, the people drag along the streets, dress, speech, opinions, everything to impress: *la Marche Parisienne.* City-Rat goes to see Jean-Louis Barrault in his theater. Barrault is old, a relic, a fossil, a caricature. "Is this your paradise? You can keep it, and take your children as well." At night City-Rat is tormented by bad dreams. Uncentered, trapped in his tiny room, he watches himself begin to fall apart: impossible to follow two masters.

Feeling very alone, and sporting a scraggly mustache, City-Rat is not yet 24 when he first meets the magician, Robert Sleet. Sleet looks in his eyes, checks out the mustache. "Shave that thing off," he says. "It looks like dirt."

Sleet: the Prophet of The Moment, snap his fingers and the world moves. Six magicians seated around a table at the Café Bonaparte, waiting for their turn to perform in front of the *Deux Magots.* Cards are flying back and forth across the table. Razor blades, coins, scarves, ropes, rings, philosophies materialize out of nowhere then clatter away, vanish. The magicians have spent so much time here that they have hidden tricks in every corner of the bar. They are the center of attention, and it won't be long before the café owner asks them not to come back. Pepe the pickpocket slinks outside to find a wallet fat enough to cover the round. Ten minutes later he slips back in, throws a 500 franc bill down on the table, and orders another *tournée*. To celebrate, Johnny opens his magic bible, which lets loose a ball of fire two feet high.

Sleet talks about Aleister Crowley, Kerouac and Zen, there's fire in his eyes. "Awareness, complete awareness man! That's what it's all about. You got to predict what is going to happen before it happens. Like I was at a magic convention, you know? It was nighttime, after the day's activities, and a half-dozen of us are walking around outside the hall. One of the guys announces that he's going to make the church across the way disappear. Yeah sure. Then he snaps his fingers, and the church vanishes. Too much! Total awareness man, that's it. The guy knew when the church lights were timed to go off."

When it is his turn to perform, Sleet starts the show by making a lit cigarette disappear in someone's jacket. He waves his hand over the jacket, makes that swooshing sound of the wind, and snaps his fingers. Right then a car backfires, a sound so loud that the audience jumps in fright. Awareness: Sleet bows, the way he feels, the way he looks, it seems like the sound came from his fingers, like it wouldn't have happened if he hadn't snapped, there are no coincidences. Amazed, the spectators applaud. The look in Sleet's eyes, the magnetism. That night, City-Rat goes home and shaves off his mustache.

Inspired, invigorated, renewed, City-Rat returns full-time to Le Coq, signing up for the class on clowning. On the first day of class, he sits by himself while the rest of the students, well-dressed, cosmopolitan, faces unmarked, chatter away in the back of the room, waiting for the teacher. The door opens to reveal a man who looks like a fugitive from May, 1968: wild, long, curly hair, a bushy beard, red cheeks that betray a taste for wine, small, round glasses and blue worker's *salopette*. The students look up, then resume their chattering. The man leans on the doorjamb, takes out a pipe, slowly fills the bowl and lights it. He puffs easily, watching the students. After five minutes the pipe goes out. He scrapes the bowl, relights it. Some of the students fall silent, begin to feel uneasy. He puffs away some more, relights the pipe again. By now, ten minutes after he first opened the door, half the class is watching him. Who is this guy? The janitor? Who is it? He cleans his pipe, stares at them some more, takes off his glasses and cleans them. After fifteen minutes, the room is completely still. The students look at each other nervously. Puffing on his pipe, the man in the overalls remains motionless. Another five minutes. The students squirm. Finally he straightens up, closes the door and steps to the front of the class. "*That* was a demonstration of *point fixe*," he says. "It is one of the strongest techniques in theater. My name is Dupont. *I* am the teacher, and *you* are the students. Is this clear?"

"You're Canadian?" Dupont picks on City-Rat. "Get up on stage, Canadian. Do an improvisation for us. You are a *garçon* in a café." Nervously, City-Rat tries his best. "Oh, oh yes, I see, um hmm," he says, falling into character, a stereotype of a Frenchman: beret, baguette, bottle of wine, intolerant, small-minded, *rouspeteur,* nationalistic. "What do they have over there in Canada? Buffaloes? Polar bears? Hockey, *nom de dieu?* That's about all, isn't it? Yes, there are lots of trees in Canada, aren't there? You know what I mean by trees? You know don't you? Wood, stiff. Little branches waving around 'I'm Canadian, I want you to love me.' Now try it again, and a little less Canadian, please!" The whole class screams with laughter as Dupont turns the screws, tries to humiliate, digs to catalyze the student's sensitivity, ("Nobody loves you, *canadien,"*) scrapes away, through terror, through ridicule, the character upon which they, upon which we all, rely in real life. "Stop waving the branches. *Arrêtez de gigoter. Mais arrêtez de gigoter enfin!* You really want to be an actor? You are lousy, you are very lousy. You're not funny! Nobody loves you." On stage, alone behind his clown nose, City-Rat averts his eyes.

"Where are you looking?" Dupont snaps. It is forbidden to look at the floor or the ceiling. City-Rat trembles, a scared kid, vulnerable, defenses blasted away, enduring his destruction by the cynical Frenchman. The way he moves: "*Non!*" The color of his skin: "*Non!*" His style as a mime, "*Non!*" On either side of the clown nose, the tears begin to roll down his cheeks. A sepulchral silence falls over the room, even the other students, the spectators, are too embarrassed. They want to hide, it's unbearable.

Dupont walks up onto the stage, puts his arm around City-Rat, *"C'est bien les arbres. On fait des maisons avec des arbres."* It's not so bad to be a tree... He delivers him. Out of the tears, out of the void, the little mime begins to laugh at his own plight. Tension dissolves, the walls begin to echo with laughter as the rest of the class joins in: relief. Behind his clown nose, City-Rat makes a small gesture, grins, lets another tear drop.

"What matters is the heart: honesty," Dupont explains. "The teacher is here to help you discover your own special way of fucking up. There is nothing we can defend in ourselves. Nothing. We are not Canadian, or American, or tall or ugly, or good lovers or writers or mimes. Are we going to defend the experiences that have made us who we are? No! We are fools abandoned to fate, about to fall on our noses at all times. Only the clown knows this. *"Nous on se dit plein de choses, mais si on les croit, on est con. Il faut reconnaître qu'on est rien que con.[1]"* Once you realize you are *con*, a fool, what can go wrong? A clown cannot conceal who he is. Otherwise people won't laugh."

The money from his loan runs out, but by playing on the street, City-Rat manages to earn enough to move out of his maid's room, and into an apartment on Rue Saint-André-des-Arts, right in the center of the action at Saint Germain. The apartment becomes *the* meeting place. Parties till all hours, climbing to the top of the building and dancing from roof to roof, wine, hash, inspiration, improvisation: they're free, alive.

One afternoon, City-Rat and his two partners suddenly realize they don't have a centime to their name. As if on cue they get up, put their clown noses on, and run downstairs, grabbing a ladder from the entryway as they pass. Up Saint-André-des-Arts they charge, fifty yards to Rue de Seine. There, right in the middle of the road, they plant the ladder. Cars come screeching to a halt. Red clown nose on, a plastic machine gun in his hands, City-Rat climbs the ladder, and puts on his most fearsome gangster face. "Grr, grr, nobody move." Two hundred people, mouths open, watch the spectacle, while one of the guys passes the hat. Backed up cars rev their motors and honk their frustration, doors open just enough so that the drivers, one foot on the pavement, can stand up to see what the commotion is all about. Within two, three minutes the hat holds 250 francs. "OK let's get out of here!" City-Rat whistles and jumps down. Off they dash, splitting through the crowd at full speed, vanishing into the alley next to Le Maso bar. Not really sure that they just saw what they thought they saw, the spectators, now in the hundreds, clap, whistle and cheer.

The street, what a circus! The whole cast of extras from *Les Enfants du*

---

[1] We tell ourselves many stories, but if we believe them we are fools. We must recognize that is what we are, fools.

Paradis: rachitic fire spitters, 40 years old going on 80, jugglers, *saltimbanques,* contortionists, sword-swallowers, whip-crackers, snake-tamers, tubercular fakirs in moth-eaten tights, come straight from the middle ages to grind their faces in glass.

But in addition to them, drawn by the Pompidou Center, by the mime schools, by an accident of fate: a second breed of refugees from the Age of Aquarius, a breed for whom street theater was not only about begging for a few lousy coins. How many times did Sleet throw hats full of money back at the audience if they were not present, not concentrating? And he wasn't the only one.

The street as the artist's stage. The artist, the one who devotes himself completely, whose rigor, whose beauty, whose harmony of movement the spectator cannot miss. The artist: the one who has gone places that the spectator knows he himself would go if only he had the time, the energy, the courage. The spectator responds with applause, with money, because the artist must continue to devote himself, must keep going. His effort keeps beauty alive for all of us, his example shows us what is possible, shows us what we might become, reminds us what it means to be alive.

A few years after the opening of the Pompidou Center: clear plastic facades, Brave New World escalators and blue, white and red external ventilation pipes, an oil refinery dwarfing the old neighborhood of Beaubourg, City-Rat is doing his act at the top of the *plateau* when he sees a new guy down in the corner, dressed in drag, a big floppy straw hat, and carrying a thin purse. On the sloping cobblestoned *plateau,* six acts are working at one time, but everyone stays away from the corner because there used to be a children's playground there, and the street artists continue to regard the space as haunted.

The new guy doesn't seem to know that. Tall, thin as a rail, elastic joints, rubber face covered in white makeup, he's getting a lot of applause, laughter in waves. Straightening his dress, he swishes up to a portly man, smiles and gives him the eye. He pulls a handkerchief out of the purse and drops it on the ground. Chewing a ferocious wad of gum, he nods and whistles for the man to pick it up. The man refuses. The whiteface opens his purse and pulls out a toy gun. He points it at the man, jerks it at the handkerchief and whistles. He doesn't say a word, but the crowd can hear his body say it: "All right asshole, pick up the hankie." They howl. The guy crosses his arms, shakes his head, turns red. "Maybe you don't understand?" The clown pulls off his hat, hits the guy on the shoulder with it, get with it, waves his hand in front of his face: nobody home. Pure energy, coming out in violent spurts.

City-Rat's never seen anything like it. He's wide-eyed, open-mouthed, his heart swells. He's almost offended. Such violence, who does this guy think he is? But it's working. He's telling the world: 'I'm a fucking asshole, you're a fucking asshole, we're all fucking assholes.' He whistles at them because they don't get it, screws his fingers into his head as if they are crazy, hits them with the hat, breaks down the distance between them. Tension and release, tension and release, the whole crowd breathes together. Beaubourg no longer exists, Paris no longer exists, just the anticipation, the puzzle, the laughter. Breathing and releasing, breathing and releasing.

When the show finally comes to a close, the crowd roars. The clown puts his hat on the ground, pulls the gun and points it at the crowd for one last laugh, then stands in the middle of the circle, like a traffic cop, restraining the waves. OK, this side, come forward, no I really don't need your money, go away. OK now come... When they've dropped their coins in, they come even closer, form a circle around him, stare. They want to touch his charisma, to be touched, but they don't dare come too close. "You make your living doing this?" "Where are you from?" "Have you studied mime?" He answers quickly and politely while he stuffs the props back into his suitcase.

"Do you know what you're doing?" City-Rat asks, drawn forward just like the rest, white-face to white-face.

"Yeah, no, I don't know, what am I doing?"

"You're expressing what *everybody* wants to express, you're doing this for everybody. Maybe they don't understand it completely, they just feel this frustration coming out in a very honest form, an art form, the reality... I don't know, wow! My name's City-Rat."

"Strahler." They walk off together for a beer at the *Pinte* café, just above the *plateau*, next to the police station. This is it! Paris, Dupont, life, right here! Another one who understands, the world is great. With ten clowns you could take over this city.

Of course it's not all roses. City-Rat does a show at Saint Germain and the cops stop him. The crowd starts booing, and the first cops call for reinforcements. Five minutes later there are twenty cops surrounding the tiny clown. City-Rat, who is in his Lao-Tzu phase, acts like water, no resistance, water breaks down stone. He has already packed his props into his bag: a plastic bucket, a kazoo, a plastic duck, combs, ice-cream cones, and also a fist-sized ball of wood shavings, which he forms into the shape of a fish as a gag. The head cop throws him up against the paddy-wagon. "So you've been earning *French* francs, haven't you?" he nods his head.

"Well yes, a few..."

"And you've got drugs don't you!" he says. "What's in the bag?" He pulls out ducks, combs, cones, and then removes the ball of wood shavings. "Ah ha! What's this?"

"That sir, is to make a fish," City-Rat explains very meekly, honestly.

"Allez hop," outraged at such insolence, the cop picks him up and throws him into the *panier à salade.*

Dédé, one of the few French acts on the street, devil sticks and rap, has a nice circle going at Saint Michel at the end of Rue Saint André des Arts, when a CRS van pulls up. As the cops get out and straighten their billy clubs, Dédé, who stands no more than 5'4", manages to pry up a sewer grate. He disappears underground, pulling the grate back in place over his head. The men in their summer-SS break into the circle, scrutinize the faces to determine which one is the threat to the public order. The crowd begins to titter, the standard-issue mustaches on the cops begin to twitch and curl. Soon enough the troopers retire, even more red-necked than usual. The van leaves, the grate yawns, and out comes Dédé. Thunderous applause.

Around the city, street artists start dropping like ergot-dazed flies. There are the expected casualties: scarred fakirs and fire-spitters hollowed out by kerosene or burning alcohol, human wrecks. But even the talented ones, the successes, the second breed, begin to forget how to hold it together.

There is a Japanese guy named Koji, who does an ancient Japanese act with twigs, a mask, sword and Japanese costume, Japanese makeup. A ritual dance with the sword. In the middle of Beaubourg, very authentic. One day at Saint Germain des Prés, *Aux Deux Magots*, seven o'clock at night, City-Rat arrives to find Koji standing in front of the terrace, shirt hanging off of his belt, *torse nu*, right hand up in the air breaking at the wrist, head tilted towards his arm, eyes half-closed. Just standing there, not moving, for a *long* time. No one else can play, can get a crowd. The other artists are getting anxious.

"You know this guy," they tell City-Rat, "Tell him to stop it or he's going to get his head beat in."

City-Rat wanders over. A lot of people are watching him, on the terrace and behind. "Koji, how you doing?" he says. Koji doesn't answer.

"Koji, it's City-Rat. What are you doing? How long are you going to play?"

Koji swivels his head, his eyes look dim, almost extinguished. "I am the universe," he says, melted.

"I see..." City-Rat rejoins the others. "I don't know how long he's going to play, he could play like this for a long time, a very long time."

There is another fellow, Duvillard, who makes a tremendous hit just by being immobile. Photo technique: he starts his show with a briefcase, dressed in a '50s suit, very short hair, looking like a bureaucrat. And he just stands there without moving, on the left side of Beaubourg. People start to gather around, unable to take their eyes off him, crowding the balconies on three sides, just watching him not move. He's very neat, glasses, looks like he's going to work. The model citizen, paralyzed. *Point fixe*. They don't know what to make of it, they are transfixed. They can't go anywhere else because he is the most centered, the stillest, the calmest thing anywhere within 50 clicks.

"'What is he really doing Henri?" they're asking themselves, laughing, very uncomfortable. When the crowd is as big as it can get, two thousand people with question marks on top of their heads, prisoners in his strange, immobilized way of thinking, he finally moves. Caught off guard, they are almost shocked.

He walks, sharp corners, paf, paf. And then he stops again. He holds the briefcase out, slightly slanted, he makes circles with the briefcase, in rhythms, one two, one two. And down, paf! And stay there, a very long time, a minute. All of a sudden he cracks the latches on the briefcase, klack-klack! They're laughing, nervous laughter. Inside the briefcase there is a cassette, playing James Bond music. Duvillard takes a gun out and stands: snapshots. He steps outside the circle, falls immobile once again, until the crowd catches on and reforms a circle around him. Then back to the original spot, he looks and smiles.

Then up the stairs in the back, to the railing. He takes out his tie, knots it, then lets it drop onto the railing so that it lays there, just like that. And he stops. And he looks at the guy next to him. A very strange rhythm, two thousand people laughing.

One day, after he hasn't been seen for a while, there is a big circle painted on the ground at Beaubourg, astrological signs, a Star of David, mystical symbols. 11 o'clock in the morning, nobody around. In the middle of the circle, sitting perfectly still in the lotus position: Duvillard, head shaved bald, oblivious to anything else.

"How you doing?" City-Rat asks him. Duvillard doesn't answer.

"OK..." City-Rat just walks away.

Sometimes even City-Rat can't quite hold it together. His woman, a Spanish tango dancer, leaves him. He falls sick, and his partner, his roommate, steals his act, the whole thing. Inconceivable! Then, while he is at Le Coq, someone snatches his bag, so that he has no money left. Weak with hunger, dizzy, he heads down to Beaubourg to do a show. He gets into his patched overalls, his striped shirt, puts on his makeup, his clown nose and the tiny straw hat with a red wire flower sticking out the top. A crowd gathers.

Right then it begins to rain. The last blow, his heart breaks. The crowd disperses, runs for cover under the overhang. "Comedy begins where tragedy ends," didn't Dupont say that? "You get to that point where you either commit suicide, or you laugh..." His feet weigh a ton. Soaked, makeup running, he drags himself to shelter.

They're laughing! They're actually laughing at him. "Waah," he pretends to cry. They laugh some more. "Waaah," he pretends to sob. They're collapsing with laughter, holding on to each other to keep from falling over. Comedy begins in tragedy. He's got them in his hand. He runs out into the middle of the *plateau* at Beaubourg. His right hand raises and his left hand slaps it, cursing the sky. "Stop!" he yells at the rain, at the gods, at his bad luck, at his pain. The rain stops. Comedy begins where tragedy ends.

That summer, City-Rat decides to travel around Europe, playing the streets. He heads up to Amsterdam. One morning he wakes up and his city-rat-grey skin has turned yellow. At the hospital they give him the diagnosis: hepatitis. He checks in. First he shares a room with two dying men, before the nurses take pity on him, and move him to a semi-private room already occupied by a gentle-looking Belgian in his 60s: Jacques. A businessman type, bald head with a fringe of grey around the back from ear to ear, Jacques is recovering from a heart attack.

"On their third day together, Jacques gets up cautiously to make his way to the bathroom. Slowly, painfully, dressed in his ass-length hospital robe, he shuffles across the floor, tubes in his arm, rolling his IV bottles along. He doesn't make it half-way before his bowels suddenly let go, and a pile of shit drops to the floor from under the robe. Frozen, he tries to make sense of his disintegration. His chest heaves, his face goes red, the tears drop to the floor: humiliation, total defeat. 'Come on it's nothing, happens to all of us,' City-Rat tries to comfort him. Jacques stumbles miserably back to his bed, still mortified, and when he lies down the tragedy overwhelms him even more: he sobs uncontrollably. The nurses come in, 'We had a little accident,' City-Rat explains to them.

"'It's all or nothing, all the elements are here,' City-Rat tells himself. Quickly he reaches into his bag for his red clown nose and a mirror. He walks over to the poor man's bed and in one motion slips the nose onto Jacques' face, holds the mirror for him to see. Jacques stops cold. He looks at his drenched, red face, the bald head, the fringe of grey hair on both sides, the clown nose. He can't help but laugh, laugh until it hurts, laugh until City-Rat is afraid he might have another heart attack. Comedy begins in tragedy.

"The next day Jacques's wife comes to the hospital with some jars of marmalade, and various delicacies to cheer him up. 'This is my friend the city rat,' he introduces him. He makes his wife fix sandwiches for City-Rat, makes her give him the marmalade. 'And tomorrow bring him some more. He's my friend...'

CHAPTER 3

On the orders of the Bureau of Times & Tides, in the interest of being even more invisible, and to save the money it would cost to run the water heater, I begin to grow a beard. But so far, after a month and half, no matter how much I pluck and pet, no matter how much I coax the sideburns down, and comb the middleburns up, it still looks ridiculous and moth-eaten, an annoying and very visible attempt by a tall boy to pretend he is a man.

"A beard?" After a month and a half it is finally thick enough for Madame Lacombe to see. She laughs, almost chokes, leaning against the wall to support herself. "*Enfin Antoinette*," Mme. Jeunet scolds her, grabbing her elbow to steer her to her room. "You know you mustn't stay out in the cold."

With the cold weather here to stay, the sixth floor goes into hibernation. Madame Lacombe cuts her appearances down to twice a day, shuttling from her bedroom to Room 2, her television room by the stairs, in the morning, then shuttling even more slowly back to her bedroom in the evening.

"*Ça va*, Madame Lacombe?" I ask.

"*Oh* not really," she answers in a tiny voice, looking at the ground. "*Les courants d'air.* My bones can't take it." Each day the voice comes more feebly than the day before.

In fact, at this point, most of the excitement on the sixth floor is created by Madame Tournier. Invigorated by the hothouse climate of the fifth floor, she marches up the service stairs twice a week to visit her furniture, three maid's rooms full. "It's freezing up here. Scandalous, not even fit for animals," she oozes with empathy. But at night, broomstick in hand, she turns into a different kind of witch. At first the typing cutoff is ten o'clock, then nine, then eight, then seven. Bam, bam, bam.

Fed up, I finally get smart. I rummage through my library, pick out four of the least worthy books, and place them under the wooden legs, so that the desk no longer rests on the red tiles. "OK witch, now let's see you ride that broomstick!" I turn on the typewriter. With the hum of a sewing factory, the massive, graceless Smith-Corona "portable" revs up to full speed. Carefully I hit a key. Then another. Then another. Then whole words, then sentences. Below, all is silent. "7:30. Victory!"

Late the next afternoon when I return from the market, I hear a shrill but incomprehensible assault coming from just inside the Concierge's door: Mme. Tournier. So loud that she isn't even aware of my approach until, from the far wall, a look of tremendous relief washes across the Spanish woman's face. "Wait, I have another letter for you..."

"We'll finish this later," Madame Tournier turns on her heel, walks by me as if I don't even exist, and steps outside. "You saved me," the Concierge laughs as she hands me a letter. German air mail: Angel is in Frankfurt.

"Great!"

"Oh yes, by the way, I guess you were out," the Concierge says. "You're going to be all alone on the sixth floor now. The SAMU came and took Madame Lacombe away. They had to strap her down by force. She was in a coma, but she kept telling them she was OK. Tuberculosis I think."

New shoes, new blue jeans, two weeks in Germany, $200 he gives to a friend in Cologne because she hasn't got a *pfennig* to feed her little girl, the price of a little food and a hotel room in Metz: when Angel Desperado finally arrives in Paris, he has much less in his pocket than the $700 he left Sweden with three weeks earlier. To top it off, he insists on paying two months rent straightaway, "Before I run out," which leaves him with next to nothing to start off this new life, this new adventure on the fringes of video-Christian society. It's not much of a room, true, only four meters by three at the door, two and a half by the window. True, the window is too warped to close, and the north-facing view stretches only as far as the other side of the street. True, the mattress is matted foam and the box spring is a moldy canyon, but there is a hot plate, a radio, even a typewriter and a sink, potentially with hot water. Fortified by the winter in Stockholm two years ago, by his own readings of Henry Miller, and the luxury of having a roof over his head, the 24 year-old Angel has not the slightest concern about the future. Reunited, he slaps his knee with his scaffolding-calloused hands, tilts his head back and roars. Times & Tides: everything works out for those who trust.

From below, a familiar noise, like a banging broomstick initiates him to the sixth floor code of conduct: "The infamous Mme. Tournier..." I laugh. "Got to be a bit more quiet."

The next morning, as Angel and I come out of the service entrance, Mme. Tournier is throwing her hands to the heavens, complaining to the Concierge. "It can't continue like this. I will call the police."

"Sorry about the noise last night," I say. "My friend just arrived..."

"Oh it was nothing," she turns around, instantly all smiles and charm. Angel's wavy blond hair reminds her of a painting at the Louvre. Those cherubs with the golden curls. "Your friend? Interesting..."

By the beginning of December, a month after his arrival, Angel is all but broke. I change $200 at American Express which, thanks to the Reagan-runaway dollar, comes to 1400 francs. After rent, electricity, laundry, and a *Carte Orange* transportation pass, 70 francs for unlimited use of metro and bus, that leaves 20 francs a day, $3, for food, entertainment, coffee, and phone calls. At which rate, with my remaining savings, it should be possible to survive another six months, even if I don't manage to sell a travel article.

Given the situation, the number of windmills to be fought, dragons to be slain, books to be read, and stories to write, far more than six months worth, and given the impossibility, without papers, of finding work, Angel decides that the only logical plan of action is to win the LOTO. A windfall which (only half-joking) he is convinced is all but inevitable as a reward for a life of purity and devotion to the path of seeking truth. Fates sealed: buy the ticket and rake in the loot. He jots seven numbers down on the slip, and, (foregoing coffee for the day) plunks down seven francs for the Wednesday drawing. Thursday morning, back to the bar, the results have been posted. Not good: only two good numbers, not even close.

"Of course!" Angel is undaunted. It wouldn't be right to let him win the first time out. By Sunday, after the proper purification rituals and meditation, he is ready to try again. Another bar this time, the LOTO slips are stacked high, right by the door. "*Deux cafés.*"

"*Deux cafés, deux, ça marche!*" In burgundy vest and black pants the barman pivots on his heel. Like a well-oiled robot, he grabs the handle on the espresso machine, turns it, knocks the old grounds into the waste, gives the grinder two hits to fill the holder with new coffee, slips the handle back into place, pushes the button to start the machine and puts two saucers with spoons on the brass counter. All in one motion. Incredible!

"Roger! One beer, two coffees." They're two deep at the bar, Portuguese and Arab men mostly, filling out *tiercé* forms for the day's horse races, and LOTO slips of their own.

"One beer, two coffees, *ça marche*." It seems like he has dozens of arms. He puts our coffees on the brass counter in front of us, slides the metal sugar bowl at us from the other end of the bar, throws a dozen cups into the sink, grabs a fistful of beer glasses and drops them into the dishwasher.

"Eh Roger, do you make love to your wife like that?" an Arab voice calls out.

"I pissed in your beer, Muhammad, or Anwar, or whatever it is. To my health."

"Three coffees and one *calvados*."

"*Trois cafés, un calva, ça marche*." Hitch, spin, lean, swivel.

"Eh Roger, what happens when the batteries run out?"

" I guess I get your wife to give me yours. *Un ballon de rouge en salle, ça marche*."

"Four beer glasses on the counter," Angel marks the yellow LOTO slips as he talks. "Twenty cups in the sink, seven hitches to get the *café-calva*, three spins to the cash counter..."

The ticket goes in on Tuesday and on Thursday Angel checks the results: four winning numbers, worth 140 francs. "*Ja-wohl!*" Angel whoops. "Ha!" Four winning numbers this time. It can only be a matter of weeks before he manages to count the movements well enough to come up with numbers five and six. "Come on Saint Loto, come on. Move like you know how."

The next Wednesday night, holding the yellow LOTO slip, blowing into his hands to keep warm, he camps in front of a television shop window on the Champs Elysées, waiting for the weekly drawing. Just up the avenue from a legless macrocephalic dwarf selling candies and combs from his wheelchair, one of a multitude of oppressed unfortunates Angel has made a silent vow to assist just as soon as the windfall actually falls.

At 8:30, the picture comes on, forty nine colored balls spinning silently around in a Plexiglas globe. The first number comes out and rolls down the gutter, green number 24. Of course... The second number comes out, purple 42: two for two. Angel winks, a calm sense of destiny warms his body. Then come four balls in a row that haven't the slightest relation to the Saint Loto-approved correct numbers, and *le numéro complémentaire* that practically sneers as it rolls condescendingly into place upside down. A total rout. "Hmm."

Time for a change of tactics. For the next drawing Angel fills out a *bulletin multiple*, eight grills with six numbers apiece. Six grills devoted to the movements of Saint Loto, one a day, just in case the good Saint is trying his faith by throwing in apocryphal swivels, fraudulent coffee cups, misleading hitches and spurious lurches, and the other two grills devoted to counting other things around the city. In a way it's play, an exercise in imagination and artistic frivolity that suits someone, like Angel, functionally, philosophically, unable to take himself seriously. But it's also very serious, not frivolous at all, part of a determined effort to dive in to the richness of life, wholeheartedly, without reservation, the miracle of life with its infinite details, patterns and signs.

Angel is convinced that it is only a matter of time before his perceptions are refined enough. A question of opening the eyes, tuning in, that's all. 41 francs change back from a fifty after buying a grilled pig's foot, a twenty franc note on the ground, six taxis in front of the Crazy Horse at 2 a.m., ten whores asking him to go upstairs on Rue St. Denis, seven francs for a one kilo bag of rice, 14 francs a kilo for steer liver, ten francs a key for chicken gizzards, 13 suckers taken in by the three-card-monte players on Rue St. Denis. 43 people in line for the library at the Pompidou Center at 12, when it opens… so that Angel can get into the language lab to work on his French, and I can roam the mythological world settled into in my usual seat, strategically placed opposite the bookshelves with the Henry Miller books, in case, just in case, a woman with 1001 tales should happen to wander that way.

"Ergotism, sometimes called the Fire of Saint Anthony, is characterized by a slow and eventually gangrenous burning of the extremities which comes from the ingestion of wheat tainted by ergotized or spurred rye. The ergot fungus grows in grain fields, particularly when the weather is wet in spring and then unusually hot in summer. The first reportedly authentic epidemic of ergotism occurred in Paris in the year 945. Many of those afflicted with the plague of fire died, but some of them were saved when they made pilgrimages to Notre Dame and ate the food distributed there. Their belief in the divine nature of the cure was reinforced when they returned home to fall sick once again, only to return to the church and be healed.

"Later, epidemics of ergot poisoning were widely regarded as divine warnings to the people to reassume the ways of peace and justice. Desperate to relieve the burning sensation, the afflicted would sometimes try to cool themselves with holy water. Which apparently neither cooled the fire nor prevented the sudden falling off of feet and hands, but did result in sulfurous clouds thick enough to obscure the sight, an odor noxious beyond description.

"In the year 1105, during one ergotism epidemic in Artois, two jugglers saw the vision of the Virgin Mary ordering them to go pray with the local pastor. After praying all night the Virgin appeared to them at dawn, offered them a candle, saying that all those who believed and would ingest a few drops of wax mixed with water would be healed. She warned that disbelievers would die. A hundred and forty three were immediately saved, just as she promised. The lone person who derisively demanded some wine died miserably at this very moment. One conscientious monk was happy to share the only cure he knew for the fire, which was to amputate the afflicted part. For a hundred years they had been doing it that way at the hospital, and he had a collection of dried out and blackened feet from those hundred years, that resembled exactly those he removed every day."

The cold days turn colder, and at night the wind blows through the warped window. A second draft howls through the crawl-space at the foot of the bed, an even-more-Siberian blast that no amount of insulation brought up by Marie-France, our landlady, no quantities of crumpled newspapers or blankets seem able to harness. Cold water solidarity, Angel grows a mustache, but shaves it off before anyone gets hurt. It's cold enough to hang leftovers inside, cold enough to be able to eat butter. Still no money to run the heater, sleeping in sweatshirts, hoods pulled over the eyes.

An Armenian painter moves in next door, room 19. A small man, dressed in the same suit for a week, blue and greasy, he comes and goes without a word. The Concierge says he works as a dishwasher, but he doesn't even have enough money to get the electricity hooked up. The hideous purple nightmares of genocide he paints every night are done by the light of a candle reflected off a mirror, she wonders if he's a terrorist. But her concern isn't really concern, it's more like light diversion, idle scales to warm up the voice, a welcome break in the obligatory gossip about Madame Tournier and all the other unworthy, mud-tracking, deliberate fingerprint-leaving, disdainfully spiteful bourgeois inhabitants of the building. "I went out to the hospital in Clichy to visit Madame Lacombe. She asked me how you were. She wanted to know why you hadn't come to see her."

Not to be outdone, Marie-France reports that the Concierge goes through our garbage, pores over the crumpled, typed sheets to figure out somehow if Angel and I might not be militant pederasts, international narcotics dealers, or saboteurs. The way Marie-France says this, with a nervous little giggle, she doesn't entirely conceal that she is slightly curious about the situation as well, "Two grown men in such a small room, hahaha..." Monsieur Corsano, the building *syndic* asks how much the rent is, "And don't tell me that you and Marie-France are cousins, nobody has that many relatives." He says that Marie-France is a snake, a wolf in Hermes clothing, that Marie-France mistreats her three children, and that he caught her using the elevator, *incroyable, vraiment,* when she only lives one flight up and they don't even share the expenses for the elevator in their co-op *charges.* Marie-France says Monsieur Corsano is an impotent cretin.

Even after half-a-dozen broomstick warnings, Angel still finds it difficult to rein in his enthusiasm, to remember about Mme. Tournier below. The Armenian comes home at the usual hour, takes out his keys with a clang. Behind the closed door, Angel mimics him as he flips the keys over, opens the top lock, flips them over again, unlocks the bottom lock, jangles them again and opens the middle lock, steps inside and closes the door. "Perfect timing." The ritual cracks Angel up, he slaps his hand on his knee, stomps his feet on the floor. It isn't five seconds before the answer comes from below in broomstick Morse code: "B.i.t.t.e.r & A.n.g.r.y..."

Broomstick Morse becomes an invigorating new game for 80 year-old Mme. Tournier: when will *les américains* next dare tap-dance on her ceiling? Almost overnight she looks a decade younger. She pays the Concierge's husband fifty francs to move her bed right under our floor, so that the living room actually *does* become her bedroom. She waits, broomstick in hand, not wanting to miss a single opportunity to remind us of her existence below.

Vitriol at night, smiles in the morning, the game remains unchanged for a week. Then one day, Madame Tournier learns from the Concierge of Angel's financial situation. She rushes up to her apartment and posts herself in the kitchen, waiting for Angel to pass on the service stairs. She has a job for him. She's no longer strong enough to walk her cancer-stricken husband, Pierre, around the apartment.

"I see." For a month already, between broom beats, the poor man's cries have been eating through the floor: "*Laissez moi mourir, je souffre horriblement,*" he screams, but with a certain dignity, still refined and grammatical in spite of the pain. "Let me die, I'm suffering." If Angel could just spare twenty minutes each afternoon? Terms to be discussed.

Madame introduces Angel to Pierre that very afternoon. Although Pierre is somewhat surprised, he quickly warms to Angel. He tells him stories about his days in Indochina, tells him about the days when there were no cars in Paris, about the Dadaists who used to throw pork chops on stage when they went to the theater, and about the black American jazz musicians who were all the rage in the twenties. When the French music unions forced them to hire French performers, the Americans let them come on stage, but they wouldn't let them play.

Thanks to Angel's daily visits, Pierre too begins to rejuvenate. He no longer begs to die. The lights come back on in his eyes, he can hardly wait for Angel's good cheer each afternoon. Angel walks Pierre from room to room, pulls on his rigid fingers, they talk. So pleased is Pierre to see him, and so sad when he goes, that the sessions, which at first last twenty minutes, after two weeks are running an hour, sometimes two.

Pierre is a sweet old man, but predictably, after breathing the air of that fifth floor apartment for a few weeks, Desperado begins to itch for new horizons, something not quite so flat. The quick and the nearly dead, Angel can feel his own joints begin to stiffen, he regrets the daily constriction. It cuts into his time on the street, it cuts into his good spirits. How did he get into this, how can he get out of it?

To top it off, at the beginning of his fifth week of work, Mme. Tournier suddenly discovers she has no money to pay him after all. She owns a 120 square meter apartment and three maid's rooms of excess furniture. She supports a 150 franc a day wine habit because the cheaper stuff rots the liver, but she has no spare change to cough up to a destitute Angel. And honestly, isn't the ingrate Angel receiving ample compensation in the form of the French lessons he benefits from while pulling on the frozen joints of poor Pierre's perfectly manicured papyrus-skinned fingers. "*Pas trop fort. Il faut que j'aille, il faut que tu ailles.*"

Seeing the look on Angel's face, understanding suddenly as he gets up, the way he says goodbye to Pierre, that Angel will probably not return,

Mme. Tournier wrestles with her conscience as she escorts him through the kitchen to the service stairway. "I was wrong, forgive me, French lessons is not adequate pay after all," she says. Unzipping her tight black sweater, she whips her 80 year-old breast out, and doing a terrible imitation of Lauren Bacall, backs him up against the armored kitchen door.

"No, I couldn't do that to Pierre," Angel says, gulping, French so butchered that it freezes her libido instantly, stops her in her tracks. She doesn't even know how to *begin* to correct him. Which is just distraction enough to help him slip out the door to freedom.

A few days later when he recovers from nearly being taken out in trade, Angel returns once more to try and explain his absence to Pierre, explain that he cannot continue.

"Yes, I understand. You are young. I am an old man," Pierre says. But it's almost too late anyway. Pierre's nights are once again filled with screams. We are auditory witnesses to the whole painful last act, the Doctor's visits, Madame racing through her domain, slamming doors, chiming in with her own soprano arias of suffering until she collapses in tears on her bed at four in the morning. It takes Pierre a good two months to die. They don't make a morphine strong enough to kill even half the pain. Sixty days of agony; no grammatical dignity left as he howls for someone to end his misery, give him a lethal dose, stick his head in the oven. "*Oooh je souffre, tuez moi*, kill me."

Winter. Light grey of sky blends with old grey of stone buildings, and flat grey of sidewalks. Grey, not gray. Gray seems too hopelessly optimistic, ephemeral. Parisian greys are indifferent and eternal. Don't-bother-me-I've-seen-a-thousand-just-like-you grey. Go-ahead-run-around-but-when-you're-done-I'll-still-be-here grey, not-that-I-care.

In the cold, every time it rains, a fat pigeon comes to roost under the eaves, on a ventilation pipe opposite the Turkish toilet. Shifting from foot to foot, he fluffs up his feathers to try and keep warm, wet and miserable but grateful for the overhang. Visible through the tiny window of the toilet, he becomes a consolingly familiar sight, as well as a reliable source of weather information, a poor man's weather vane. Not the shit-on-your-head wrong-side-of-the-tracks type of pigeon, but a good pigeon, a pet.

Winter. Rotting tennis shoes, sweaters with holes in the armpits and holes in the elbows, increasingly grimy windbreakers. Riding the metro just to get warm, noting all the places to thaw out for free, hot air grates on the street, overhead-hot-air blowers in various stores and malls: FNAC, Drugstore...

Money is scarce but always seems to appear when needed. I paint a bathroom, 400 francs. Marie-France, now delighted with us as tenants, ("It's better than having some Portuguese family cooking sardines all day long," she says time and again) asks Angel to wash her windows: 100 francs, then offers him a job painting her kitchen and bathroom in exchange for two months rent. Which leads to another job for both of us, painting a kitchen in the 18ᵗʰ *arrondissement*: 900 francs. Angel finds a 200 franc bill on the ground next to the bar at the American College of Paris, ACP. Angel checks the bulletin board at the American Church, and gets a job baby-sitting for a French couple: 200 francs. Another job, two strong men needed to help an American businessman move from one apartment to the next: 500 francs apiece. I get 600 francs to write a ten-page paper on the Panama Canal for an ACP student. When that one is finished, (B+) a second student offers me 750 francs to write a 20 page sociology paper on drugs, then a third student offers 500 francs for a five page paper about Aeschylus, *The Oresteia* and tragedy, which takes me a week to write.

It's just enough money for a meager diet, long on rice, bread and sautéed onions whose odor permeates the clothing, but so what? It's fuel for adventure, to keep the stomach from growling in between meals provided by any number of generous souls happy to trade food for stories and good cheer, fair exchange. To play their part in this impossible dream, this Henry Miller revival. Moroccan gangsters, Greek crepe makers, Australian ambassadors, Iranian refugees, Brazilian transvestites, Romanian mystics, Spanish nymphomaniacs, American sirens, Lotharios, dancers, street artists and poets... There is nothing intrinsically romantic about the poverty, or the constant need to forage for food. To follow the path, to become a writer, means to wander around, to see and live something new every day, no constraints. To write exceptional books, you must live an exceptional life.

The writer as the conscious manifestation of many lives, many places, with stories his food, his currency. A reality glued together by chance, by the winds, by all that comes free. You're alive because you have to be, if a coin falls on the ground, your foot must be on it before anyone notices, if an opportunity presents itself, if a back door opens, to a concert, a film, a party, you must slip inside before mulling it over. No way to hide from yourself, nothing to buy to help the time pass, no amusement except that which you can create from your own inspirations, your own desires, your own curiosity, your own need to know, to see. To glide through invisibly, observing, leaving things untouched, like Indians. Uncontrollable, almost threatening elation, living according to ideals, a sense of mission to remove the veils. Possibility in the atmosphere, possibility in communication. Elation turning thoughts into action: a canvas in thin air. *"Etendards sanglants élevés."* "Raise the bloody standards!"

Back in Los Angeles, old friends spend $3000 a year just to keep their cars going. They drive to work with the radio rattling their brains ("FM if you please!"), chain themselves to the 40 hour week, come home to TV and beer ("Imported"), then start all over. It just doesn't make sense. Of course, they are all pleased to believe that money makes things easier. But their stories are only of drunken times, of getting loaded and paying for it with expository headaches. When they like things, TV baseball, football, etc... they do so without great joy. New apartments, $1500 a month rent, matching sheets, towels, plates, gruesomely bad paintings hung sideways or upside down, because they fit better that way. How trivial and unremarkable the experiences of daily life. Whole weeks spent without waking up, whole weeks where thoughts are not pursued and examined simply because it isn't important, because there is no need, because that is not the currency there.

Winter. Sprinting through the rain to the *College de France* to hear Michel Foucault's weekly lectures. Inspiring the first week, he talks about *"Parrhesia,"* Plato's notion about the philosopher's, the citizen's, obligation to tell the truth no matter the consequences. Times & Tides! *"Le devoir du dire vrai..."* the disciples jot down every word, miss every word. From the back Angel draws the scene: Foucault's bald head on a platter behind a forest of tape recorders. The machines whir and click off as they run out of tape, while the master talks about how Plato had gone to Sicily and told the truth to the local tyrant, Dionysus. He told him the truth even though he knew that he would end up rowing a galley on the Mediterranean for his trouble. *"La parrhesia, donc,"* each week Foucault starts the lesson the same way. The approach is minute, pedantic; the acolytes, soulless rationalists, martyrs of logic, parrhesites. Their *caca di mosca* devotion seems vulgar, perverse, blind. And they wonder why French culture is moribund, fucked out?

A few weeks later Jorge Luis Borges appears at the *College de France*: a virtual riot to get in the door, the same impassioned acolytes with tape recorders. Blind Borges is a saint: "We cannot write a book that is better than ourselves," he says. "Writing is a means to retain memories. And yet infinite memory, like *The Zahir*, is a curse... Inspiration is far too pretentious a word for me... My subjects seek me, I do not seek them... I have to write them to throw off their spell."

"Is it not possible to write with good sentiment?" someone asks.

"It is just a sentiment like the others," he answers. "We write in order to read books that please us."

Winter. Free karate lessons three times a week courtesy of the American College. Soccer twice a week. Showers afterwards. Enough money coming in to afford one four franc beer a night in the Front Page bar in Les Halles. Run to the 31 bus, timing it to arrive just as *it* does, then off at Etoile. RER down to Les Halles. One beer, maybe two, if someone else is buying, then back on the last RER of the night to Etoile, and a stop at the crepe stand on Avenue Wagram, where Elefteros, a nearly-blind Greek painter from Lesbos, has been making crepes for nearly five years. Such a parade of customers, such a fantastic procession of Brazilian and French transvestites, 400 franc whores in furs, Germans and Japanese, punks and Royalists, the crepe stand is the only entertainment we can afford. In between customers, as we warm our hands over the griddle, discussions about art, perspective, dreams, adventures, and the fraternity of creators, discussions always leavened by a steady supply of crepes which Elefteros, generous to a fault, keeps coming, steadfastly refusing to accept even the most minimal payment. "To do pastels properly, you must squint at the world," Elefteros offers his advice, squinting at the clock above the watch store on the other side of the avenue. "What time is it? 12:15? OK, we close." At the end of the night, Angel tallies the results: 32 crepes with sugar, 20 with chestnut cream, 27 with strawberry jam, 15 with chocolate, 10 with chocolate and grated coconut, 18 with cheese, five *complètes*, ham, cheese and egg.

Winter. A new whore staking out the corner down the block. She smiles at me, says "Ficky-ficky?" then gets a good look at my tennis shoes with the hole in the toe, and turns her face into concrete, so that I become invisible once again. She only takes on guys with cars anyway. They pick her up and park on the side street. The car is easy to track: the one with the tail lights blinking dim-to-bright. She doesn't see me pass by, she has her head in her customer's lap. The john smiles guiltily, starts making motions as if to pretend he's helping her search for dropped keys, or something. When she's done she slams the car door without a look back, lights a cigarette and walks back to her post where she is joined by a *collègue*. The talk doesn't change much, the same comments about the cold, the quirks of the johns, "He was filthy." "Well you know mine, he came in his pants when I unzipped him and he didn't want to pay." In the morning, the previous night's parking spots are marked off by runny balloons.

Winter. On the Champs Elysées: policemen with machine guns protecting the Turkish tourist office, Aeroflot, Syrian Air, Iraqi Air -- the world political situation in a nutshell. I meet an American lass at the American College. For two months we fly through the city so that the streets and monuments become marked by our joy, our delight. Then she goes back to the US for Christmas, and promises to call on Christmas Day at the apartment I am watching for the holidays while Angel's mother visits.

The phone refuses to ring. In Room 18 there is no phone, I'm not used to this, by December 31, I'm going crazy. Finally, at last, I get a letter, from her: "Just woke up from a nap missing you intensely, realizing that the last two months with you have been the happiest of my life. I love you. Back on January 7." No woman has ever said "I love you" to me before, at least not so that it sounded believable; I never believed in love before.

New Year's Eve, in the company of Angel and Mrs. Dolores Desperado, is a most astounding show, a flight on wings of elation. The Champs Elysées filled with people, cars unable to move, firecrackers exploding, Dionysian revelry, the necropolis shuddering, spitting from its bowels a lava stream of passion. Dolores Desperado had pooled all her resources to come to Paris and Angel had walked her everywhere, bubbling with enthusiasm, showing her the spots that have meant so much to a Lumpen-Angel. The grates and benches where he has slept, the free telephones from which he has called her. By New Year's, after three weeks on the Times & Tides tour, she has run down. All she knows is that her son lives in a garret, that she has sore feet, that she still hasn't seen Gene Kelly, and that Paris apparently doesn't give a damn that she has waited all her life to visit.

On the explosion of midnight, men and women kiss, champagne corks pop, women run away, some in tears, others laughing. Dolores takes a swig of burning hot Armagnac from a bottle handed to her by a complete stranger. A distinguished grey-haired man in his fifties approaches her, doffs his cap and says in French, "Excuse me *Madame*, permit me to kiss you." She blushes, they kiss on the cheeks, he bows and then vanishes. It hasn't been such a bad three weeks after all.

On January 7, I ride the train out to the airport three hours early to meet my love upon her return. A week later, weakened by jet-lag, she gives me a cold kiss and says "What's happening to us?" The Paris I have shown her was a nice adventure, a fine interlude, don't-get-me-wrong, but she doesn't really belong, time to move on. Josef Klein in love is a truly pathetic sight, a puppy ripe for euthanasia. And that stupid beard!

Reeling from the pain, I stumble across town, tears running down my cheeks, cross the Alexandre III bridge, look in the Seine for a long time, pick up some paper clips on the sidewalk, then fish a yellow plastic goose out of a garbage can. In a strange way, it seems like the whole thing is happening to someone else. To Josef Klein, identity unknown.

"What's the matter, American? You don't look so good tonight. Your Cadillac break down?" Elefteros says when I walk by.

"No, but love did."

"Why?"

"I don't know."

"Didn't I warn you about American girls?"

"She made me laugh..."

"Forget her. Tonight we fix you two crepes. One cheese. And one sugar. For the pain."

"The pain is in my heart, not my stomach."

"Don't worry. All connected." He hands over the cheese crepe. "In Greek you know the expression *tha yirisei o troxos?* The wheel will turn." He puts the second crepe on the griddle, throws a patty of butter underneath and sprinkles a sugar heart on it before folding. He puts it in a square crepe bag, and wraps it in a half paper towel. "But we also have an expression, '*Tha gamisei o troxos.*' The wheel will fuck you."

Winter. One wall of Room 18 is now almost covered with posters lifted at night from the news kiosks. Temporary fascinations, Nastassja Kinski for Angel, and for me, Princess Grace of Monaco R.I.P. (Le

Meilleur: *"Grace: On N'a Pas Dit Toute La Verité."*) In the euphoria of redecoration, I also stick the latest reject slips up on the wall: LA Times: "Sorry but we lost your article, and then, by the time we found it, it was too late." LA Times: "Thank you for your travel article on Switzerland, 'Between Hell and High Waters.' Unfortunately our travel section is not accepting submissions at this time."

Given my great luck with travel writing, I decide to try my hand at a screenplay tentatively called *Parisites*, about this crazy adventure in Paris, what else? Angel spends his days in the library at Beaubourg, studying the history of Paris, so as to be able to give tours. Above the bed Angel tacks a map of Northern Europe, blindfolds himself and puts his finger on the map: Holland. Holland, why not? When it's time to renew the visa in the passport, it's decided, that's where we will head, hitch-hike from Porte de la Chapelle.

Winter finally seems to end just in time for the May riots. A fine day out, the clouds willing to part and reveal the sun. The cops sitting in the buses playing cards and reveling in the superiority of their weaponry, the solidity of their protections. Still no need to worry, because the students had planned to start the demonstration at 1400 hours and they weren't going to turn their attention to the *Assemblée Nationale* where the *"Loi Savary"* was being debated, until they had marched down the Quai d'Orsay and back through the Invalides. At 1430 the march gets under way, led by a most dignified group of men in red velvet capes and ermine-fringed collars. The professors, on hand to lend their stature to the protest against this law which would require that the medical students be tested after two years in med school to see if they are competent enough to continue. The med students are claiming that this will bring too much competition, to the detriment of their learning to become healers. They suggest that the tests take place after one year, so that those who are not going to make it don't have to waste an extra year before learning that they won't qualify.

"Etudiants en colère," the students chorus, and *"Chaud, chaud, chaud, le printemps sera chaud."* They sound like Arab *merguez* vendors. Some are dressed ready for battle. Bandannas wrapped around their necks to be used in the event of tear gas, motorcycle helmets in hand to ward off the blows of night-sticks, leather gloves to help them pick up and lob back the tear gas grenades. Others look neat and pretty in their very fine fashions and

make-up, lipstick just perfect, mascara not yet smudged. Medical students in white robes with red crosses on them set up first aid stations on the Invalides.

An hour and a half later the cops have ended their card games, and paid their bets. As if playing their parts in some romantic version of 18th century warfare, they line up three-deep across the Quai d'Orsay holding their Plexiglas shields. The sun reflects off the visors of their ugly helmets: it seems like they have no eyes. A first volley of rocks and clots of dirt rains down on them, but they don't move. The ermine-clad professors raise their hands, the leaders of the march shout through their bullhorns and manage to calm the violence. A few of the professors are allowed through the police line to go into the *Assemblée Nationale* and add their opinions to the debate going on inside. A second volley of missiles rains down upon the CRS cop, plastic bags full of pink paint which splatter on the police visors and stain the white ermine collars of the remaining professors. Fights break out among the students, as the pacifists try to calm the more militant. Still most everyone else is just standing around, curious, waiting for something to happen. Legions of photographers, TV.

The battle really starts on *Pont Alexandre III*. A water cannon rumbles up the bridge and begins to spew a mixture of water and soap. The cannon goes limp, a dribble of white foam, the last ejaculated drops coming out of the nozzle, as the truck retreats. Explosions rend the air, now colored yellow by the first barrage of tear gas grenades. The gas rips at the eyes, sucks the oxygen out of the air. Bodies, fleeing bodies, collide blindly trying to hold their breath, then retch and dive to the ground where there is at least a little oxygen.

When the air clears, students run back up the bridge to pelt the CRS, who deflect the missiles with their shields. Then everyone retreats again as the tear gas explodes around and the water cannon comes back up the bridge. A crazy game. The students have no objective other than frustration, they have no weapons other than sticks and rocks and tennis rackets which they use to bat back the tear gas canisters. (The good weather is a cracking good stroke of luck, the gut strings would be simply ruined if it were raining.)

Standing coolly between the cops and students, Angel snaps photos of the folly. *Pont Alexandre III* is littered with rocks and sticks and foam from the water cannon. Dark clouds move in, the wind picks up and rustles the trees. Opinionless, belonging to no party, uninvolved but utterly involved, Angel, raised on dodge ball, war ball, prison ball, dashes in and out of the frenzy dressed in his red windbreaker, a scarf over his mouth. No fool CRS is going to put him out of the game. "Dance cowboy," a volley of pepper gas cans skitters by underfoot, and he hops over them gingerly. A second volley sends a canister into his stomach. The water cannon comes up and then retreats. Angel picks up a clod of dirt and wings it at the cops, just to show them what an ex-Pony League all star can do.

Later that night, in the Latin Quarter, under cover of darkness, the cops get their revenge. Angel is scared to within an inch of his life by a mad, swing-at-anything-that-moves police charge down Rue des Ecoles. He escapes and doubles back. Spectators line the streets. A man in his forties is struck on the head. The blood courses down his forehead and neck, his groceries scatter. "Don't hit me, *je suis du quartier*, I live here!" Bonfires and blue CRS *gyrophares* compete with the nearly full moon to light the night, the students bang their clubs against shop windows, the sirens of store and car alarms fill the air. Bloodied and dazed, some of the students wander through the clouds of gas, choking and crying automatically, emotionless, out of the game. At Place de la Sorbonne, three students run for the safety of a café, but the cops club them badly as they fall into the entrance. An elderly man picks up his bamboo umbrella, reaches through the opening in the café and pokes a cop in the face. Others, outraged, pick up chairs and tables to fight off the keepers of the public order.

With the lingering frustrations of winter safely discharged on the CRS, the trees heavy with fluorescent new leaves, and the terraces of cafés full of people talking, smoking, flirting and soaking up the sun, the city seems to breathe again, to loosen up. A different, slower rhythm, no need to be anywhere, no urgency, it doesn't even get dark until nine p.m. From the fifth floor of the Pompidou Center, the view is exquisite, the whole skyline stretching out under a ceiling of low, puffy clouds: Montmartre, Notre Dame, the Pantheon, the Eiffel Tower. In the Square between Saint Merri and Beaubourg, workmen spread tar in what looks like a shallow swimming pool, but turns out to be a fountain with motorized fiberglass sculptures inspired by Stravinsky's *Firebird*, a bird of fire, a skull, a snake, a hippocampus, an elephant, a hat, a heart and what may or may not be a sea cucumber, spinning and rising and spitting out streams of water.

Now that it's warm enough for audiences to stand around without freezing, the street scene is in full swing. From above, behind the Plexiglas panels of the oil refinery, the *plateau* with its street artists looks like the Middle Ages. Silent, distant, exotic, deformed: *cour des miracles, Boulevard du Crime.*

Akro, a crewcut American clown with big shoes, a red bucket and brown corduroys, stretches a rope trick out to fifteen minutes as the children scream and laugh, French kids reacting to the *guignol*. Above him, and to the left, Mehdi, a Persian gypsy, puts a flea-bitten mongrel through its paces, as the circle yells "*Olé, Olé*." His assistant, a lovely French lass a head taller than he, hands him the props, then opens a box, pulls out a boa constrictor and puts its head in her mouth without blushing. Further up on the flats, Néné, a fakir in a red headband and sagging black tights collects money, his caved-in chest and tattooed arms wrapped in chains. "*Plus que quarante francs, plus que trente-neuf,*" he yells in a hoarse, raspy voice. 40 francs to go, now 39. His woman, Henriette, a used alcoholic with rouged cheeks and a fallen womb, picks up the coins that the spectators, mostly tourists, throw to call his bluff. "*Plus que trente-cinq, trente-trois...allez, allez. Plus que vingt-cinq.*" Three, two, one: "*OK, arrêtez tout. Ar-rêt-ez!*" He raises his hands, concentrates, takes a breath, expands his chest, tenses, then begins to wriggle out of the chains, doing a terrible job of making it look hard. Within thirty seconds the chains lie in a pile on the ground. The audience applauds uncertainly, applauds because it's expected. The fakir whistles, shifts right into his fire-spitting number, and from there he lies down in glass. After twenty minutes of collection, a performance which takes less than ten minutes. When the show is over they applaud again, feeling like they have been conned, but so what, this is Paris. "*C'est pas dans les mains qu'il faut taper, c'est dans les porte-feuilles,*" the fakir's woman screeches at them. Hit your wallets, not your hands. They walk away shaking their heads, small wonder that he collected the money before the performance. Lines of tourists snake over the cobblestones blindly following the raised flags and umbrellas of their tour guides. Occasionally two lines cross, tour guides with the same symbol raised in the air. Japanese tourists follow Danish guides, beer soaked Germans go off with lager-dazed Australians and never know the difference.

Angel's various attempts to sell himself as a guide to Montmartre having come to naught, he is just as broke as ever. No problem, I get a job at the Paris air show, a friend from LA who hires me for ten days to extol the qualities of the Thunder Engine company and its water-cooled V-8 engine, a job paid in Reagan dollars. Thanks to the devaluation of the franc, (three devaluations in the last 20 months) and the hi-jinks of the cowboy's-dollar, ($200=1500 francs) our standard of living, our diet, in other words, improves tremendously. No problem, except for Angel, who feels increasingly diminished by his inability to contribute to the collective, and who begins to shoplift to balance the scales at least a bit.

Around the crepe stand, the familiar characters of the all-starch winter perform their familiar roles. The Portuguese homosexual, so drunk that his lower lip is falling onto his chin, walks around with his cock peeking out of his fly. Laurent, the fat metro driver, his soul banished forever by staring red-eyed for too long down that black hole, is on a rampage because I forgot to shake his hand the night before, cardinal sin. A pimply-faced anencephalic ferret of a waiter, a new guy, comes outside to get a crepe, and for no reason at all begins to lecture me about the glory of Jeanne d'Arc, *la pucelle*. He tells me that if I don't like France I should leave. "Be careful, I know *savate*," he adds.

On the square in front of the Pompidou Center, a stocky African strong man who calls himself Samson pulls four men out of the crowd, defying them to try and pull his arms apart with chains. Then he puts a pitchfork in his belly and challenges them to push on the handle and move him back. They push, they struggle, but he digs in and they can't budge him. He flexes his legs and with a deep grunt sends them flying backwards. The crowd applauds. He removes the pitchfork from his belly, the marks from the tines are deep, spaced between the scars on the rest of his belly.

The tourists are everywhere. Germans in Adidas shoes and purple linen, sandals and socks with blue jeans, standard German van Dyke beards. Italians in packs (there is no such thing as one Italian, Italians come in lots of five), megaphones, down jackets. Dutch rolling cigarettes with Drum tobacco. Swedes with Fjäll Räven day packs, wearing white boat shoes, jeans, looking like bad copies of Americans. American girls wearing white tennis shoes and jeans, wholesome, unmarked, milk-fed complexions, Farrah Fawcett hairdos fresh from the curling irons, nothing to say, but a song on their lips for every occasion, and little noses that wrinkle to warn that they intend to laugh. American boys, eager cannon fodder, printed-T-shirt-wearing studs, who prowl the streets looking for other T-shirts to be friendly with. 3, 25, 10, 4, 22, 21: a most unsymmetrical Loto slip that fails to draw a single winning number.

CHAPTER 4

After five months in the hospital, with winter gone for good, Madame Lacombe returns to the sixth floor as irascible as ever. "You've been telling people I had tuberculosis, haven't you?" she says, glaring from her end of the hall when we cross paths some days later.

"That's what the Concierge told me."

"I didn't have tuberculosis at all," she says as if she's not that kind of woman. *"Il faut pas dire des choses pareilles."* You shouldn't say things like that.

She isn't pleased that I never came to see her in the hospital, she isn't pleased that an Armenian moved on to the floor in her absence, "*Un arménien?*" she isn't pleased that Angel Desperado is here and monopolizing Monsieur Josef's time. "Someone's been using my toilet and not closing the door afterwards."

She begins to cheer up when the Armenian in Number 19 disappears, (the Concierge, ever-faithful source of critical building information, reports that he hadn't paid his 200 franc rent in six months.) and is even happier when Angel, after almost getting caught shoplifting, escaping only thanks to cool nerves and some very quick thinking, leaves for England, where he has been offered a job taming a jungle at the English manor house of the American businessman whose furniture we moved a few months back. When Madame Tournier, who had begun to date an old walrus of a uniformed English admiral, disappears to spend the summer in the United Kingdom, Madame Lacombe turns positively giddy. Not that she lets it show. My good spirits and energy, my optimism, still irk her. Life is not an adventure. Art, generous Greek crepe stand owners, curiosity with no discernible agenda, free meals: Madame Lacombe is convinced it won't last.

"It always comes when you need it, you just have to keep your eyes open," I say.

"Nothing doing," she protests. Eyes open, a lot of rot. "People are horrible." How many friends has she lost in the time since she became too weak to walk down the stairs? How many friends refuse to come around and see her now that she is an invalid, now that she can barely see? Who came to see her at the hospital? Who has visited her on the sixth floor since she came back? "People are horrible, and there's no doubt about it. You don't know how much you're going to need patience. The world's going to get you down. You'll see, the others will try their best to bury you. Josef, listen to an old woman..."

As far as the crepe stand is concerned, Madame Lacombe isn't wrong. So nice and polite with the customers, Elefteros begins to lose touch with his artistic soul. Too many mountains of ergotic white flour perhaps, the only thing he paints in weeks is a new menu, prices raised, with little drawings of strawberries, chocolate bars, chestnuts and Swiss cheese to facilitate the tourists' crepe-ordering process. "One stlawbelly clepa."

"You're losing your edge, Elefteros," I finally tell him. His eyes have turned dull, it's getting serious.

"Hello I love you, won't you tell me your name," he sings, flips another crepe onto the griddle, and slides a spatula of butter under it.

"*Se gamisei o troxos*. The wheel has fucked you. You've got to protect yourself, be harder."

"We don't need no education, we don't need no thought control," he sings, gone completely deaf. He pulls the plastic bucket from under the counter, the iron whisk, and sets to making another bucket of batter. One liter of water, one liter of milk, one kilo of cheap white flour, three packs of vanilla-flavored baking powder...

At 12:30 Elefteros squints at the clock across the street. Time to close. He takes 18 bronze ten franc coins and puts them in a paper crepe bag to hand over to the bar: the rent. He turns off the gas on the griddle, pulls out a spray-bottle of blue ammonia cleaner and begins to wipe down the bowed Plexiglas shelves and windows of the crepe stand, to scrape off the excess batter that has hardened around the griddle. The nerves in his painting hand, the synapses from glaucomatous eyes to fingers are caked in ergot. He counts the rest of the money, 150 francs and change, another lousy night. There's rarely enough left over to make the work worthwhile any more, either he devotes himself to his painting or he dies.

He hands the crepe stand over to another Greek, a pudgy die-hard socialist, staying in Paris to avoid his military service back home. Wearing his face like a bloodhound's while his wife reads the Greek gossip rags, he waits for her to go back to their apartment so that he can turn on the smile, resume with the diversion of casting eyes at all the well-turned ankles that came down the road. The big-shot hypocrite with his olive oil fat-boy paunch: "*Mademoissel.*" And when there are no more ankles, he too begins to sing, but a different tune, "Ahh life is hard. *Diskoli i zoï.*" Going nowhere and knowing it, he sprinkles the crepes with xenophobia and bile, then wraps them in newspaper notions. Too dense to grasp his role in the food chain, he isn't about to offer free crepes to writers with military bases in fair Hellas.

"You see?" says Madame Lacombe.

"No problem," I assure her. "One crepe stand down, so what?"

At the start of summer, the King of Beaubourg, undisputed, is Dorian Strahler. In white face and pointy hat he starts his show, slowly, confidently, walking around, sizing them up, imitating them as he builds the crowd. He stands next to an old lady, lifts his leg and drapes it around her shoulder, he's so limber. The crowd howls at her reaction. A dachshund dragging a leash drifts in to the circle and yaps at the white-face. The mime gets down on hands and knees, crawls after the dog, barking back. The dachshund charges. With exaggerated fear, the clown runs for his life. Another wave of laughter which brings more people to the circle, curious to see what is up. To the left of the circle, which is now 600 strong, someone tries to take his picture with a big shiny Nikon. Delighted, Strahler poses, then he gets an idea. Looking totally innocent he runs over to take the camera, to return the favor and snap a picture of the photographer. Then he runs back to his suitcase, pulls out an old Instamatic, and carries it to the photographer so he can take a picture of the mime with *his* camera. When the photo is snapped, Strahler signals for him to throw the camera back. But the throw is bad, and the camera falls on the ground, shattering into a thousand pieces. The mime looks crushed. Two, three, four, he looks at the expensive camera around his neck; an evil grin spreads across his face. The crowd roars. The camera owner begins to sweat. Strahler takes the camera off his neck and throws it up in the air, once, twice. The audience can't believe the audacity. They're horrified, then greatly amused. Strahler mimics the embarrassed camera owner's terror, his knocking knees. The audience roars with laughter, waiting to see what will happen next. The camera owner is trapped in isometric limbo. He doesn't want to look like an idiot, coming forward to wreck the entertainment, but after all, a thin, uncoordinated-looking man in a clown suit is throwing up 5000 Deutschmarks worth of his equipment. The audience feels for him, tastes the horror of the situation, claps happily, laughs loosely when the photographer finally receives his camera back undamaged.

Twenty more minutes the show lasts, a huge crowd of all nationalities and colors, waves of laughter cascading across the *plateau*. Torrents of laughter like you've never heard anywhere. The rest of the street artists sit off to the side waiting for their turn to perform, trying to dissect the secret of Strahler's magic. Life! Color! Motion! Magnetism! He's in complete control, like a hypnotist, a magician, a demagogue, shaping the circle, wrapping his aura around the crowd so that nobody can leave. Finally, when the show is done, he puts a hat down. Without hesitation the crowd surges forward, but Strahler gives a piercing whistle, puts his hand up, holds them back. Not yet, not yet, not yet. Now. *Ahh!* They pour forward, eager to reward him, and he nods at them, keeping an eye on the hat, just in case. "*Merci*, thank you, *arigato, danke schön.*"

A few minutes later, when he picks the hat up off the cobblestones, good, but not great, for him, the crowd has dispersed mostly. But as he packs his props back into his suitcase, it's the usual, twenty people in a semi-circle just a few paces away. Young people mostly, Scandinavian women, Arab boys, artists and Mormons, not quite willing to let him go yet. Staring but shy, in awe, as if they have never seen a human being like this before and they need to know how such a thing is possible, how such a thing works. "Where you from?" the bolder ones ask, they'd like to be his friend.

"U.S." He tries to be polite even though he is drained, exhausted, his shirt drenched, his makeup running and what he'd like more than anything right now, is just to be left alone.

"Really? Me too. Whereabouts?"

"Boston…"

"*Approchez, approchez!*" The next show starts to set up, Mehdi, the Persian Gypsy laying out chains and whips and trunks with various magic props inside. But none of the other performers stick around. Everyone heads up to *La Pinte*, the old-fashioned café just opposite the *plateau*, a narrow place with heavy wooden tables, plastic Carlsberg ashtrays and benches with springs poking through the sagging red velvet upholstery.

Blackie, a mime dressed in loose-fitting black from head to toe, long braid running down his back, struts in and asks Akro how much he made on his show. "Thirty francs? Ha! Thirty francs," he laughs scornfully.

"Fuck off Blackie. Fucking mime."

"Your circle's all wrong. It's too loose. Your energy is dispersing."

"Man, don't you get it? Nobody wants your advice."

"I don't know what it is today," says an English magician, "They're sleeping man."

"And that's Robert Sleet, delivering *his* favorite line," Akro says.

Strahler comes in, drops his suitcase and orders a beer.

"Eh Strahler, good hat?" Akro calls out.

"I don't know, 600?"

"Shit."

"It's not great today is it?"

"Man, get out of here, 600 francs? Not great. Give me a fucking break."

"I am getting out of here. One more week and I'm off to Israel. Ten day contract at an amusement park in Tel Aviv."

Angel writes from Great Mongeham, Kent. "This then is the beginning of my fourth week here. While the garden shows a drastic change, my notebook shows little. Instead, my hide is the cheap canvas I'm using, and how badly it retains ideas, emotional changes. I feel a profound state now and again, but a drink or one hour too many outside will corrupt it.

"It's a 20 minute bike ride into Deal, where I go once in a blue moon to gawk at the few people walking around. What a crazy screwed up race of people. Perversion must flower here. Every little ember of twisted sexuality must be well fanned. Men and women have absolutely no grace amongst themselves in this most civilized and disciplined nation. Girls look odd, the way they mangle French fashion with the Princess Di fashion and look every bit the human complement to the brown brick buildings that blacken the land. You know I dig into a jungle of plants in a garden left to go wild. Each tree choking the other out of the sunlight. I've found some nicely variegated trees that unfortunately had trunks that snaked along the ground for eight or ten feet before they could find the light. Mangled into sinister shapes, they're left more to rot and molder out of necessity so the plant could have just those few bits in the light to keep on growing. I'm still talking about English girls.

"For now I sit like a dark pool. What will rise up out of the murky mess? I don't know what I will do now. I recognize that I have done absolutely nothing for a very long time. I'm frightened beyond words, but that is the wrong course for dealing with it. I have been living on everyone else's laurels for a long time, mostly yours. False adventures, false words, poses with a lot of good intent. All the crimes, all the offences seem to be summing themselves up at this particular moment. I've got to concentrate exclusively upon my position in the world I had a foot in once. Perhaps I'll manage it again. I feel I should throw myself down a hazardous line and see if I survive. Nothing short of risking my life will do. How else am I to throw off everything, how else to stand alone in the world? Either I stand alone or I am absolutely worthless..."

Back in Paris, under the benevolent, merciless eye of the Bureau of Times & Tides, I continue to fly along beneath a lucky star. The vendors in the food market on Rue Poncelet greet me as I pass by, "*Salut le pirate*," joke with me, toss me an extra orange, avocado or leek. "*Ça va mon grand?*" The tall man brings laughter, the whole line for spinach is cracking up. Ten perfect strangers suddenly talking with each other. I don't fit in their world. The awnings hit me in the head, the neon lights burn my hair, I don't know the codes, don't know that you're not supposed to say certain things. So I say them. The barriers come tumbling down, everyone in the hostile city seems to be waiting behind the barricades to say something, this desperate need to touch and be touched, and it all clicks in, it seems, when I pass. "You must have eaten your soup, eh? How tall are you?"

"He must be almost as tall as General de Gaulle. How tall? *Deux metres?*"

"*Ni maître, ni dieu, Madame.*"

"My daughter's tall. Do you have a fiancée?"

"Of course. Such a question! She has breasts like full moons, and fertile hips, a delta of miracles. But it's tragic. I'm one eighth Cherokee, and her father is an *apache*, we're doomed, we're all doomed."

Thanks to a green belt earned in karate, thanks to my large frame and a fortuitous meeting on the soccer field with various Iranian exiles who seem to monopolize the concert-security services in Paris, I am hired as a goon for the Rod Stewart concert in Versailles. I stand by the backstage VIP entrance, checking to see that people have the proper sticker to get through. Hardly anyone has the proper stickers. Arms crossed, trying to look fierce but stupid, I'm besieged by young Lolitas in see-through blouses begging me to let them through for just two minutes with Rod. An eyeful, a tan, a little music and 400 francs in wages, not a bad day, not a bad day at all. And an added bonus from here on in: virtually unlimited access to any concert I might choose at the various venues around town, the *Casino de Paris, Olympia, le Zenith*, which means I no longer have to sneak in on my own…

The summer turns hot, beastly hot, and Room 18, right under the roof, is like a furnace, not a breath of air. Impossible to get to sleep before four in the morning. In a move long overdue, I finally shave off my beard on Bastille Day. Nothing cataclysmic happens as a result. Madame Lacombe's TV reports people dying of the heat all across Europe, but this is not because of my beard. Wilting, hoping to get a cross-breeze through the tiny window in the Turkish toilet, I prop open the doors to my room and to the toilet. The feeble breeze, virtually imperceptible, seems to affect Madame Lacombe down the hall more than me. "You have the bathroom door open don't you?" she says angrily, as if I'm trying to kill her, "And the window too!"

Baking in the heat, with her own windows sealed shut, she is too frazzled to retain her usual sense of oblique diplomacy. Turns out she is terrified of the flocks of pigeons she imagines roost in the narrow courtyard. Their acid droppings have destroyed her eyesight, she says. She can't see them, but she can visualize them: hordes of diseased carrier pigeons on her very threshold. The thrumming of their phantom wing-beats haunts her dreams.

"Come, come," I try to reason with her. "There's only one bird, a fat one who comes in to the courtyard when it rains. He sits on the ventilation pipe, and when the rain stops he goes away. Besides it doesn't exactly look like rain."

"No Josef. You must close it immediately!"

More and more, the *plateau* at Beaubourg becomes a regular part of my rounds. I hang out on the fringes of the circle coming up with gags and hunting for Amazons, the waves of impossibly graceful Scandinavian lasses flooding back tanned and charged from their *InterRail* tours to Greece. From *plateau* to café, to meals in someone's maid's room, it's a tiny world where the players have little in common other than the fact that we have come to Paris to learn, to chase the myth, and that we are exiles, which gives us everything in common. Not to mention the steady money which creates a climate of laughter, generosity and community and attracts an astounding variety of human types, tourists, artists, drug addicts, English neo-Nazis, thespians, libertines, *bon-vivants*, travelers, madmen, drones.

Some of the performers pull in 1500 francs a day, some of them only 60. Some, like Strahler, are like the ant in the tale, working hard and socking it all away, getting ready for winter. Most are grasshoppers, earn fifty, spend fifty, earn 500, spend 500: endless summer. And if winter does come, 40 days of rain, and it's not possible to work, the other artists are there to fall back on. Somebody always has money, that's their only bank, their only social security. "Man I heard you got twenty socks full of ten franc pieces."

"And..."

"Come on man, don't make me beg. I'm hungover, not in the mood to do a show. What do you say? How 'bout 200 francs to get me through to Monday..."

What makes a good show, what makes a bad one? "Don't I wish I knew," says Akro, shaking his head, sipping his beer. The weather, the political climate, the end of the month, which tourists are in town, Swiss, Italians, Germans, Americans: everything affects how much the street artists take in. Is it too hot? Is it raining? Is it neither? Did Walter[1] have a fight with his wife? Did *France Soir* splash on the headline about impending financial doom? When the mood in Paris is good, the spectators respond to the contact with the performers and the hats are full. When the time is bleak, the street artists are the first to know.

Blackie and Sleet discuss plans to go down to the theater festival in Avignon. After that they're going to play in Florence, and then Sleet plans to move up to Stockholm with his Swedish girlfriend. Back from Israel, Strahler has a contract to go to Japan. Apparently they have to import their laughter there too. Akro holds his head after last night's party: 12 people crammed into his four square meter room, around a marble slab piled high with fried eggplant, fried zucchini, spaghetti with clams, a liter of olive oil to grease the colon and a ten-liter jug of four franc red wine to coax forth a

---

[1] President Francois Mitterrand, aka Walter Mittyrand.

torrent of Spanish, Swedish, English and French from the guests. Lucien, Blackie's Guadeloupian bottler, will probably join Blackie in Avignon, but not before his Finnish girl leaves town. Last night he went to visit her at her maid's room in the 16th, but he didn't have the code for the front door. He started to climb the *pierre de taille* building, and got to the fourth floor before he realized what he was doing, before he looked down. Nothing to do now but keep climbing up to the roof and then slip in through the skylight.

"Was she surprised?"

"You bet!"

"Did you hear about Bob? You know he's been playing music three times a week at the Guinness Tavern? Well last night they asked him if he wouldn't mind playing a little worse. The customers are staying too long. They want to get other people in there..."

"Anyone seen Romi?"

"Yeah, the cops picked him up for selling yoyos, and they confiscated every yoyo he had on him. Even the one with the secret compartments. He had five grams of hash in there. They'll never figure out how to open it, but if one of the cops' kids plays with it and bangs it on the ground..."

"So he's dropped out of sight."

"His days at Beaubourg are over."

"Anyone know where City-Rat is?"

"I heard he's in Germany."

"He's smarter than we are," Sleet's lady says. Their street show, his straitjacket escape and a dramatic trick in which he pulls linked razor blades out of his mouth, and her esoteric, Decroux-style mime piece is just not working this summer. Just today the cops warned them about playing their ghetto-blaster and the crowds still aren't responding at the right time.

"Paris is so boooring," she says.

"Shut up," Sleet says, exasperated, "For Swedes everything is boring."

She storms off, and as soon as she's gone, he tells me himself, "Paris is dead. Finished. Look at this place. It's a mess. You should have seen it before, '79, '80, '81. City-Rat used to make them scream with laughter. And Strahler... Man we ran this city!" And what would Paris need to become alive again? "200 artists..." 200 artists!

Great Dungeham, Kent, August 17: "Still gardening, still 3.50 pounds an hour, after I put in ten hours against the room. But that's easy enough, I prefer to be in the garden than anywhere else. I'll have only 200 pounds by August 26. The first three weeks here were ideal. Now, eight weeks to the T (in eight) I have once again drifted into uncharted and useless space. I feel not at all productive, though profound spells visit me. I seem to have no presence in myself, in my doings, in my wakings and goings-to-sleep. All this time away from Paris, I feel like I'm letting opportunities fade away. I've got a gaping hole in me, and time passes through without looking back. There is no eternal recurrence in me. What paths I have left have been eaten by the birds as soon as they were laid. I build a world in sand. My empire is the littorals.

"I sent my passport away by registered mail to the Home Office in London, asking for an extension to my tourist permit and sure enough they extended it---to 14 September. Such extravagance. Last night, while finishing up two massive bonfires, I was trying to uproot a 200 lb stump. I used a tall scythe to cut away the nettles and ivy that had grown in, on, through and around the old thing. Placing the scythe well behind me, I proceeded to tug at the inert stump, first at a prominent branch that broke away and fell into dust. Then I reached to a cluster of dry, hard-wood branches and succeeded in rocking the stump before they snapped off. Well I needn't have to say that I went flying no less than six feet backwards, sprawling across the scythe, which spun the blade up quickly till it was piercing the twilight and eventually my right calf, seven inches below the knee. Lying on the ground, I had watched the event with shock; it happened quickly enough. I saw the thick, dark red begin to spurt out. With glove pressed against the wound and a dull ache already beginning to spread down my ankle I sprang to my left foot and went off for some aid. An hour later at the casualty department of the Deal Hospital, I was making jokes with the fat nurse while watching the scene from a rather impersonal and unconcerned point of view. The pain was all I felt, and not too bad, though my leg had begun to twitch. They thought old Bill the caretaker was my grand dad, assumed my Mongeham address was my true home and took care of me without charge. Two stitches were put in instead of six, because the Doc didn't want to be bothered. I told him that if he only put in one, we could bargain on a price. No local anesthetic---and I loved every pierce in the skin, including the false start. Right. It's hard to walk just now, but I figure that by Friday I'll be right as rain, running, cycling, *knullaring*. My view of the accident is hard to describe. I'm beyond chastising myself for such acts."

The unbearable, unsleepably hot summer of 1983 finally surrenders, autumn turns cold, the Beaujolais Nouveau appears on November 15, leaving mass destruction in its wake and a consensus: "It's not a big wine, it's a good little wine. *Un bon petit vin.*" Back from Japan, back on the street, Dorian Strahler has turned into a nervous wreck. He is pale, his hands shake, there are bags under his eyes. At night he can barely sleep; he has to run around to purge the poisons, to purge his anger. Beaubourg is strewn with broken green glass, choked by the smell of stale urine, cluttered with flying hamburger wrappers and mangy dogs leading drunken German hippies in purple cotton clothes. Four days a week, Thursday through Sunday, suitcase in hand, Strahler trudges down to the *plateau*, getting angrier and angrier. The other days he feels sick.

One day, an Arab lunatic, weaving drunk, completely out of his mind, steps into the circle, picks up the toy gun that Strahler uses for a prop, and starts threatening the crowd. "I'm going to kill you. *W'allah je vais vous tuer.*" No joke: he waves the gun under their noses, grabs their shirts, his eyes widen, his teeth clench. Strahler is horrified, immobilized. There's not a thing he can do. He stops the show, packs up, breaks through the circle and flees trembling to the café. He orders a beer even before he washes off the white-face. His hands shake as he sits on the broken-spring red velvet benches. "Got to get off the street." The matter is settled for good the next day during a show, when Strahler hears a loud splat above, on the other side of the balcony, a desperate soul who has thrown himself off the fifth floor of the Pompidou Center. That's it, there's no going back.

Winter. Rock, the Welsh fiddler snaps, but he was a bit unbalanced anyway, too much LSD. At the age of 19, he decided to walk from Wales to India, barefoot. He made it across the Channel and all the way to Avignon before stopping. Now at 27, he sits across from me in a café at Beaubourg, muttering to himself, asking questions that want no answers. "Well, and a fine day in'it? I played with Van Morrison, din't I? Van the man. Welly welly well well, and what have we here? Right, in'it?" and so on, a monologue I cut short by getting up thirty minutes later. Rock has smashed his fiddle once again. Smashed all the furniture in his apartment. Swan, his

Chinese girlfriend, ran away a week ago. Rock finishes his beer and asks me to pay for it. "I played with Van, din't I, Van the man," he adds before getting up and walking over to harangue a tree.

Winter. Salvation Army vans pulling up to the Gare de Lyon. The *clochards* come out of nowhere, a dozen or so, for a bowl of weak soup, an ergotic pretzel and a song or two to the Lord on an out-of-tune guitar. *Pour la digestion.*

Winter. After a last few valiant attempts at "sub-zero clowning" Akro is the last street artist to concede that winter is actually here. Even though it is no longer possible to draw a crowd, the actors continue to congregate around Beaubourg. The *Pinte* café is closed and demolished, and the scene shifts to a tea-parlor just off Boulevard Sebastopol. A fine, warm place, with huge windows facing Rue Berger.

Safe, behind the glass, waiting for the others to show up, I watch the parade and fill my notebooks with lightning bolts and calumnies. There are better days -- days walking on harmonious clouds after re-reading *Tropic of Cancer*, days when the humors are boiling inside, when it is just me feeling like a spark, a spark that will not be extinguished. Daydreams of hunters and saviors. And there are worse days, when focus is lacking and so am I, days when I tally the pitiful results of my passage on this planet and can't help but wonder if I will ever really have what it takes to write something approaching my standard, wonder why it is that the minute I sit down to begin a chapter I seem to lose all levity. Days when I am merely somewhat perplexed that life should require so much coffee to stay awake.

Back at Rue Gustave Flaubert, with a great banging of hammers, a trampoline-like net is installed on the roof, covering the courtyard. After all these years, a sort of Christmas present for Madame Lacombe. Her eyesight won't get any better, but I'm going to miss seeing the pigeon in 1984, like I miss all things that pass out of my life without giving me any trouble.

1983 ends, there is unusual excitement about 1984, Orwell's baby. A morbid young druid at Beaubourg, half-hidden by the small sign he has penned: "When the world starts going to shit, first thing next year, I am the only one who will know what to advise as a cure. You will find me here, right where I'm standing now, to give you the answers you will need."

I spend the first part of New Year's Eve on the Champs Elysees, hoping to find the same magic as the year before. Young girls run in fright from packs of youths trying to kiss them, firecrackers are thrown with malicious intent, it is more brutal than last year, but still the city's heart is beating, and this is so different from the rest of the year that all I want is to be swept away. Somehow a dour Romanian exile latches on to me, a melancholic black hole who insists I should write his life story until the anarchy on the avenue overwhelms his poor East Bloc soul. These dark-skinned people throwing firecrackers and yelling, there is no sense of order. "If they were at home in Palestine," he says, "They would be throwing grenades and shooting people."

I try to lighten his mood, he seemed lonely, a lot of refugees from the East Bloc seem out of synch, lost, it's not their fault, the consequences of oppression are in the blood. But by 11:30 pm, the marrow has drained from my spine. I plead with him to go off on his own, to leave me alone, I walk ahead of him a few steps hoping he will take the hint, but he doesn't. There is anosognosia, the state of not knowing that you don't know, but there is also anusognosia, the state of not knowing you're an asshole.

Finally, ten minutes to 1984, I just break into a sprint, and slalom across the avenue, leaving him far behind. There's a party with some of the street theater gang not far away at Alma Marceau, and the last thing I need is to have him there wrecking that for me too.

At the party I get to talking with an *avant garde* Swedish actress who holds her cigarette between her pinkie and third finger. By the end of the night, the fires are kindled. "I'd take you home, but my brother is there," she says. "Don't worry, we have a whole year ahead of us," I answer. There is so much time ahead that I vault over the rally cars setting off on the Paris-Dakar. There's enough time to discover whole new continents, even to invent the new emotion.

The next morning I come out of my room a bit later than usual. Through the window of the Turkish toilet, I can see the ventilation pipe across the courtyard exhaling its usual winter plume of steam. Madame Lacombe turns off the Sunday religious service on TV. "Don't ask me If I'm OK, I'll only be OK when I'm dead," she says, something is clearly bothering her. "Nowadays in the churches they call God '*Tu*,' I don't like that," she informs me. "When I had my communion we called God '*Vous*.' That's how it should be." The New Year has left her irate. On the TV they report hundreds of arrests, pick-pockets and drunkards. She blames the Arabs. "In the old days we used to get dressed up to go to the Champs

Elysées. Top hats and tails for the men. The very best dresses. And now..."

CHAPTER 5

The expiration of his visa in Great Britain affects Angel Desperado very little. In October, he visits his brother and sister-in-law in Wales, then in November, with 40 pounds in his pocket, he makes his way from Kent to London to try his luck there. "Quite an ordeal of acute suffering," he writes. "Two nights out sleeping in discarded mail bags with bums, other nights staying with friends of friends. Good moments and bad moments, nothing for those who perceive the passional rainbow.

"I have been reluctant to return to Paris without a small legacy in tow, yet in four months, I've not sown any seed that might bring me such a legacy. Still lowly and disbelieving, I recoil from everything. The world with its invisible arms and exiguous strength has me in the same corner. I can't trace my own reasoning which puts me here. I don't muster the will to escape solutions, and the search for solutions."

Six and a half months after leaving Paris, Angel, foundering in purposelessness, simply stops writing. I cut the stamps off of two years worth of letters, and hand them to the stamp-collecting Concierge as an offering to the mail gods, but even that does not a whit of good. Electricity bills? Reject slips? Sure, plenty of those, and even an occasional letter from home. But from Angel? Not so much as a peep. And he was only supposed to have been gone one month.

"Monsieur Josef. You had a girl up here last night." Madame Lacombe sticks her head outside the door as soon as she hears the key in my lock.

"A girl? Wasn't me..." It couldn't be anyone else, there's no one else on the floor.

"And she was smoking!" she adds triumphantly, the thin smile of victory on her lips. "Ever since my coma, you know I can't take the smoke." She nods her head with her eyes half-closed, the way she has when the rules have been broken. Of course, with an olfactory system as refined and evolutionary as Madame Lacombe's, three day-old bar smoke on a Levi's jacket is an infraction every bit as severe as chain-smoking a pack and a half right in front of her keyhole. It draws the same look: "Well you betrayed me again, but what else should I expect? You're just a man. *Et les êtres humains, vous savez..."*

As far as women are concerned, smokers and non-smokers alike, I'm afraid I've virtually surrendered. Sirens, beauties, students, and acrobats, German dancers, French artists, Dutch au pair girls, I've tried to connect my dream to the women of nearly every country in Europe so far. I haven't gone south to Spain yet, because what do you do when that goes sour too? Jump off? Some come close, some are jealous of the muse, can't imagine why I would prefer to write rather than idle the time away. Some of them have tapes that run two days, others run twice as long before repeating. The same stories, the same exact laughter, same exact timing. The woman I dream of has a script that never repeats, an endless tape that never loops. It's a mystery really, I'm willing to believe that I've just had an extended run of bad luck and bad choices. But I'm beginning to fear that the loving life is simply incompatible with the writing life, that writing is a mistress, a rival, no woman can really accept. That even the game of Pygmalion, which many men laud, is not a solution, can only turn into Pygmalion-in-a-poke.

Now, on the rare occasions that I feel the need for female companionship, I ride the escalators at the BHV department store. Escalator romance: she rides the down escalator, she's beautiful, her eyes blaze with desire. For a second the passion is white-hot, soaring. Then the up-escalator takes me up, and the down-escalator takes her down, out of sight. Perfect...

Desperate to get off the street, in fall of 1983, Dorian Strahler begins working in a tiny circus called "*Le Puits aux Images*" which sets up a tent in a park in the 16th *arrondissement*. By January, the job has qualified him to enter the "Circus of Tomorrow" competition at the Cirque Gruss. Fragile and angry, Strahler's clown is a distillation of this tenebrous period of bread-eaters and lunatics. His performance at the circus, partly his street act, and partly a new mime piece created for the occasion, is a response to the era, a necessary riposte. The two Russian judges are for throwing him out in the preliminaries: he's a mime, not a clown, or so they say. Two excellent Russian clowns take the gold medal, Strahler settles for the bronze medal. But he's the darling of the crowd and one of the other judges on the international panel happens to be the owner of a German circus. He signs a contract with Strahler on the spot.

"This is it!" Strahler exults after the show. "I'm off the street. I couldn't have hoped for anything better."

After two more tenants move in and fail to pay the rent, Room 19 on the sixth floor once again falls empty. I offer to take control of the room, guarantee that the 200 francs rent will be paid, and send off a letter to Angel in the UK.

At the bottom of the narrow, wooden service stairs, the Concierge puts up a small plastic bag so that she will no longer have to hand out the mail. Her anemic two-year-old son comes down with hepatitis, and then, while in the hospital it turns out he needs hip surgery. She shuttles back and forth between hospital and home, looking increasingly frazzled. Her hair turns peroxide blond. Absent-mindedly she uses the wrong color dye; there's no time to change it. She barely has time to take a breath, to deliver even the most exiguous calumnies about the building's residents. Except about Madame Tournier and her English Admiral who aren't going so well: she doesn't like sherry, and he behaves like an absolute beast on the claret she favors.

The bakery on the corner downstairs changes hands. Instead of the gummy *pain infecte* of the last regime, under the supervision of the meaty fists of Monsieur Bigot, the new owner, the ovens turn out quality bread of all shapes and tastes, garlic alligators, walnut roosters, crunchy rye lemmings, for which customers begin to flock from all over Paris.

The building *syndic* replaces the Concierge's rickety glass-paned door with bullet-proof glass. Nourished on *France Soir* headlines and the advertisements of security contractors, the stingy inhabitants of the building finally catch the fear and decide to install an elaborate security system with *interphones* in every apartment, and a special key, impossible to duplicate, to get inside the building. A gypsy had been discovered removing the brass bars that hold the stair carpet in place. "And four years ago there was Mme. Tournier, robbed right outside her door. And there was the young boy who had a calculator stolen out of his room on the sixth floor..." Monsieur Corsano, the *syndic*, explains half-guiltily as he issues me a key. The sixth floor is not to get any *interphones* at all, too expensive.

"What if my doctor has to come in the middle of the night?" Madame Lacombe is furious. "How will they be able to deliver the coal, Josef? How do they expect *La Bouchère* to come up with my meat when Mme. Jeunet isn't here? No one cares about an old lady."

I shrug my shoulders. I understand her position, but I'm actually delighted. Without Angel along to joke with, to bounce off of, the foraging for food has become tiresome, the cost of paying for dinner with stories has begun to seem excessive, I'd rather go hungry. No money for a phone, no way for anyone to come in off the street, sealed off from the world, I'm in heaven. The permanent exile, permanently exiled by my dream of something more absolute, something beyond cultural being with all its shouting and patterns, ephemeral elation and parades of changing whims. Too little patience, too little money to drink anymore, but inebriated anyway with my lust for something more basic, some place where the rules can't change. The sixth floor.

After much effort, and to my great disappointment, Madame Lacombe finally manages to convince her doctor to write a letter demanding that the sixth floor be equipped with *interphones* as well; the workmen installing the phones have a good laugh when I ask them to show me how to disconnect the buzzer.

With somewhat questionable taste, the Bureau of Times & Tides provides me with a part-time job at the Shiva Press photo agency just before the Winter Olympics in Sarajevo, February 1984. At least temporarily, no more kitchen painting, no more moving furniture and the rest of the under-the-table, barely-scrape-by, bread-to-fill-the-gut existence. Life devoted now to Shiva the creator, Shiva the destroyer. I am to show up a day and half a week, Tuesdays and Thursdays, 50 francs an hour. Somehow they figure there's a loophole in the employment laws allowing foreigners like me to work, the category of translators and people with special skills that cannot be provided by French people.

A package comes in from Beirut. Six rolls of explosions, vendettas and battles. Is it in West Beirut, East Beirut, are these Christians in mufti, Shi'ites loyal to Berri, or Jumblatt leftists? What kind of guns do they have, Belgian G3, old or new Kalash, Chicom, Israeli, RPG-7's? Is that the blue of Amal or the insignia of the Lebanese Army? The captions say, Roll 1: bomb. Roll 2: GE Birut. Roll 3: forces layol to milita investigate. Roll 4: the Mercedes after. Roll 5: soldiers sweeping night. Roll 6: checkpoint for teror. Impossible to figure out. Have to invent.

Inside the walls of Shiva Press, life and death don't have the same significance as outside. Three in the afternoon, the word comes over the

AFP wire: two Iranians assassinated in the streets of Paris. The agency buzzes, "Are there pictures?"

Glynnis, my boss, a tall, red-headed American woman who came to Paris to write twenty-five years ago, knows all the gossip, and shares it in her nasal voice every chance she gets. She's a walking encyclopedia of international celebrity sodomy, a cocktail party catalogue of famous tongues, fists and orifices and their globe-trotting adventures in nightclubs, planes and limousines, when, why and how. She can recite the genealogical trees of the royal families of Sweden, Norway, Denmark, Belgium, Holland and even Luxembourg. Fridays, nearly every time she gets her hair done, or so the joke goes, some world figure dies. Around the agency they beg her to get her hair done in the morning so that the death and the black and white captions can be processed before midnight. So they don't have to stay until four in the morning.

The decibel level at the agency is simply deafening. The myth business, or so it seems, can only be conducted by shouting, hysteria, and tears in French, German, Italian, Russian, Turkish and Farsi. Apparently the noise keeps everyone focused.

I've never been fond of newspapers, don't believe in allowing the subjective and flawed perceptions of a "perfect" stranger to alter my view of the world. I would rather trust my own eyes, my own intuition to understand what's really going on. But boiling under the lights, legs crammed under a too-low typing table, I have no time to philosophize about the ramifications of what I'm doing. The photos rain down on my desk and all I can do is struggle to keep up. My fingers feel like stiff sausages, I put the caption paper in backwards, knock over the paper clips, get whiteout over everything, leave large black eraser-swaths in the middle of my texts.

"Josef, Daniel used to do four pages an hour, and you're only doing one," Glynnis throws out.

The odyssey of the traveling Pope. Stars and black holes, the advance of civilization. The war in Iran: maimed bodies, foxholes, ragheads, hypnotized youths with roses in the barrels of their M-1s, marching proudly past the fountains of blood on their way to heaven. Frothing collectivists and wailing women, a dab of mustard to taste. *"Iraq-Iran War Enters 41st Month With Slaughter Of Attacking Iranians."* "The Iranian attack consisted of some 60,000 men who were mowed down by Iraqi forces commanded by

Iraqi General Abn El Rashid who described the unfortunate enemy as 'Illiterate vagabonds, bothersome insects,' They counted 13,000 dead and wounded..."

"Josef! You're doing less than two pages an hour. Maybe we should lower your salary until you speed up?"

US Marines leave Beirut, and the US battleship New Jersey shells Druze and Syrian positions in the Shuf with their 16" guns, firing shells as big as Volkswagens... Yannick Noah marries Cecilia Rohde, in Yaounde... Police raid the *Ilôt Chalon*, rounding up 620 people, the majority Malian, Senegalese and Mauritian, most without papers. 20 drug dealers picked up in the raid, as well as one kilo of heroin and 20 kilos of hash, quantities which police claimed were not larger because the dealers were tipped off to the raid. Only a stone's throw away from Paris's Gare de Lyon, home base of the TGV train, the pride of French technology, the squalid *Ilôt Chalon* is the center of the Paris heroin trade...

"Josef, you *cannot* call Frank Sinatra a dinosaur!"

Stefano Casiraghi, better known as the husband of Princess Caroline of Monaco, goes skiing without his wife... A boy with three hands photographed in Peshawar, Pakistan, his third arm extending from the back, three fingers and a claw-like hand... Princess Di attends a Genesis concert. She has kept a busy schedule as her second pregnancy continues to go quite well... Sant Jarnal Bindranwale, a mad-eyed Sikh in Amritsar, Punjab has taken over the Golden Temple. Barefoot, beturbaned, carrying a golden spear in his hand, he walks beside the pool at the Golden Temple, followed by forty Sikhs armed with rifles...

"You need to focus, Josef! The bloodiest pictures, the real gore, maimings, spurting amputations, that sort of thing, go to Japan and Spain. Please keep that in mind when you write your texts! Horror, blood, sex and drugs are what bring in the money. That and the royal families of England and Monaco..."

"Which fall under all four categories?" I ask innocently, sticking my feet back under the desk as Glynnis glares.

Great Spongeham, March 20, 1984: "Bob has offered me a tremendous amount of work and under very handsome conditions. Handsome? Not only does he want me to continue with the garden, (which has seen a dramatic improvement over the three months I've been at it), but he's offered me the work of painting the outside of his home. All at my leisure. 'Take as long as you want. For instance, if you don't feel like any of that, you could spend the day in Canterbury. Yes. And pick up some art supplies so you can do some more watercolors of the house. It's on me. I'll pick up the tab for the supplies.' Generosity out of the blue. A flat fifty pounds a week for which I am to do 12 hours a week plus another eight for my room. I don't see why I can't arrange to spend my time between here, Paris and Wales. Coffee at St. Loto's around mid-April?"

By Easter it is once again warm enough for even the least-adventurous, most thin-blooded to hit the *plateau* at Beaubourg. Rebelotte, the organ grinder, tweed at a rakish angle, "*Parce qu'ils aiment ça,*" sets up in his usual spot right at the top and sings as he turns the handle of his machine, trying to drown out Néné the fakir and Néné's woman.

"*Plus que vingt cinq francs,*" Néné screams hoarsely, "*C'est fini Beaubourg,*" Henriette chimes in with her usual lament.

The tea parlor closes, to be turned in to a by-the-slice pizza counter, and the scene shifts to the second floor of the *Café Beaubourg*, a creperie just above the *plateau*.

"Did you hear? City-Rat is back."

"Imagine that!"

"Who's in line?"

"Akro then Blackie."

"Did you hear Samson punched out Kenny the hypnotist yesterday? Left him with a nice black eye."

"Anyone got any hash?"

"Fucking Italians! Twenty 100 lira coins. Man next time I see Italian down jackets in the crowd, I'm going to stop the show. The way they drop, swaggering up, throwing in a handful of coins. Like we don't know the sound of worthless money hitting."

"Check this coin out. Anyone know where it's from? Saudi Arabia? Libya?"

Hair dyed orange, having moved on to Shakespeare, Gurdjieff and Iggy Pop, Robert Sleet appears after the winter in Sweden. "What's going on in Sweden? Nothing. The artists? They've got money. Rich. But man if they ran out of money, they'd panic. Art? Forget it. First thing they'd do is try and get some money again. That's how important their art is. What is it in this world? It's not any better here. Last night I was walking along Faubourg du Temple and a man began to beat up a woman. How could anyone walk by without saying anything. I didn't. We got to have some responsibility in this world."

I continue to take advantage of the karate lessons at the American Church, and the free showers afterward, diligence rewarded by a blue belt, I'm starting to be a serious customer. One day we practice fighting two opponents, a skill, with my long legs and long arms, that I seem to manage quite well.

"Yes, but what if there are more than two opponents?" One of the students asks.

"Demonstration! Josef?" The master bows to me, inviting me to come forward, gulp. "You make sure that they only come at you two at a time," the master says. "And when they do come, you hit them so hard that the rest begin to think twice about moving on you."

I straighten my *gi*, listen to the instructions, take a deep breath and pray I won't let the master down. He bows to the rest of the class. Fight's on! "*Ajime!*"

The first two students in line bow and come at me. I hit the first with a roundhouse kick to the head, the second with a punch to the sternum. Two more come racing up. A back kick to the chest sends one staggering back. Front kick to lower gut puts the other out. After five minutes, much to my astonishment, I have bested the fourteen other students. The master bows to me. "Thank you, you may sit down."

An innocuous anecdote, except that a few days later, four in the morning, Place des Ternes, feeling limber and powerful as I walk a Dutch lass to a taxi, I see a fight break out right in front of us. A solidly built 30ish black man in a tuxedo, probably on his way home from a dance at the *Salle Wagram*, and two thinner whites in jeans and cowboy boots, who look like they just stepped out of their souped-up Citroen DS 21. Impossible to tell what the skirmish is about, but I can see how it's going. The white boys come at the black man with awkward, film-inspired versions of karate kicks which the black man blocks easily with his forearms, backing away. The sound of leather against jacket and muscle. A third white boy runs up and pulls a can of mace out of his letter jacket. The jet of mace sprays towards the black man, into the wind and back into the sprayer's face, causing enough confusion so that the black man is able, quite calmly, to stroll away through the Place des Ternes. At this point a fourth white boy appears. Taller, hair greased back, wearing Weston loafers and a long green raincoat: the caricature of a student attending the *Assas* or *Dauphine* law schools, bastions of the right, he is clearly the leader. The one you want to punch first, in other words. With a few words his boys' eyes get the fight back in them. Full speed they run to catch up with the black man. As they surround him, he looks calm, weary with disgust: so you haven't given up yet?

"Stay here," I tell the Dutch girl, then dash over to step inside the square the white boys have formed around the poor guy. "Stop this right now!" I bellow, stunning them momentarily. I stand shoulder to shoulder with the black man.

"Un conseil: pars!" Raincoat snarls at me, his hand in his pocket.

"What?" The words don't quite register.

"A piece of advice: beat it!" he snarls even louder. Cars cruise by, the few pedestrians out at this hour scurry along as if the event is not happening. The reality of the situation suddenly hits me. This is Paris, which isn't yet a violent city really, but what if Raincoat's got a gun in his pocket? Wouldn't it be wise to slip outside the square? Once outside, if he happens only to have a knife, it's possible to dart back in. The fear reaches down to my testicles, the adrenalin pumps, but I don't move. I feel weary, immeasurably weary, even wearier than the black man, my own life doesn't seem very important, this is too ugly. What happens next time, when I'm the black guy? I think. I can't leave him here alone, my ancestors would never forgive me.

I look at Raincoat's weasel face, and brace myself to call his bluff, see what he's holding. "Come on pull it out of your pocket, let's get on with it." The four savages slump, disperse, begin to walk away. I can't believe it: a triumph of resistance! I think, until, out of the corner of my eye I see the explanation roll in: a police black-and-white. Saved by the Times & Tides! The lackeys empty their pockets, scattering toy switchblades and the can of mace in the gutter as the cops step out of the car. The police check their papers and begin to frisk them, but I don't stick around to see what they find. My own papers aren't in order, my visa expired a month ago. The Dutch girl quakes with fear as I kiss her goodnight and stick her into a taxi. She is shaking even more than I am.

When the taxi pulls away, I catch up to the black man on Avenue

Wagram, ask him if he's OK.

"Thank you for that. If I see you around the neighborhood, I'll buy you a drink," the black man says.

"They're a disgrace. Savages. It's nothing," I reply. We shake hands and part ways. I fly up the 121 steps to the sixth floor, three by three. For an hour I pummel the air with karate punches, full power, to purge the adrenalin from the almost-fight. At six in the morning I finally fall asleep.

I spend an indecent amount of time at Shiva Press in the service of blood, horror, sex and the Holy Trinity, Princess Caroline of Monaco, Lady Di, and Mr. T. All of a sudden, Glynnis can't do without me. My half day on Tuesday ends up running eight hours rather than four, and my full day on Thursday lasts 12 hours. I'm writing 25 pages a day, minimum, a prodigious amount of trivia which leaves me completely drained, depleted, and desperate for a beer at day's end. My head is an encyclopedia bursting with useless information, the birthdays of Princess Caroline's children, the names of Queen Elizabeth's dogs, the number of chains around Mr. T's neck. At the end of the month, I bill them for the translation of so many pages, putting my old address in the United States on the bill. In exchange they hand me an envelope of cash, minus 7% contribution to the AGESSA, the social security service for translators, the subterfuge the Shiva accountant comes up with, since I'm still not *really* legal to work. It's more money than I've had in years, 3500 francs, $450, which I sock away, no telling how long the job at Shiva will last. A pittance in anyone else's terms, but another step up the ladder, most timely and welcome for someone grown weary of singing for his dinner.

Madame Lacombe turns 81 and nobody notices except me. I bring her flowers. Not the greatest flowers, true, 15 francs is all I can spare for the bouquet,[1] but at least relatively fresh. She smells the flowers, fills her nostrils with a perfume other than the musty one of the unventilated corridor. At first embarrassed, Madame Lacombe finally accepts: you can't refuse a gift of flowers. Her eyes go moist, her frown softens and a tear runs down her cheek.

"You know Madame Lacombe. I was thinking of writing a book about

---

[1] Despite the influx of money, I'm still in the old mindset, I can't help it. 15 francs is a day's food, which seems like an enormous amount to spend on flowers.

the sixth floor. I would very much like if you could tell me some more about your life."

"Yes. I would be delighted."

The next day I come home to try to write after taking a much-needed shower at the pool. There's a smell of gas in the air, overwhelming the usual smell of death. I snoop around a bit, then decide that if Madame Lacombe has gassed herself, I shouldn't do anything to bring her back. If she felt happy to be needed, then she might as well die that way.

The gas smell turns out to be a false alarm. Madame peeks out her door the next morning, as grey as ever, nothing changed, but it's a harbinger of things to come. A month later, I'm dashed out of my dreams by a tremendous commotion in the hall.

Madame Jeunet bangs on my door. "She's locked herself in her room, and we can't get her out. Maybe you can talk some sense into her. She listens to you."

Outside the door of Number 15, the normally sunny Spanish Concierge is irate. "She's doing it on purpose, why doesn't she just die and get it over with, *une fois pour toute*? If she wants to die, let her. Only I've got better things to do than waste my time on an old bag." With those thick glasses magnifying her perennially black eyes, Madame Jeunet, quite concerned, leans into the door and pleads, "*Antoinette, allez, soyez raisonnable.*" Be reasonable!!! "Antoinette, *Josef est là, il veut vous parler.*" It's my cue.

"What's wrong?" I yell through the door.

"I can't get up," comes a feeble answer.

"At least she's talking now," Mme. Jeunet is relieved enough to regain some of her peevishness.

"She's doing it on purpose," the Concierge repeats and throws her mop rag down in disgust, spreading a generous puddle of Ajax on the floor and having at the indelible streak of coal that blackens the red hexagonal tiles.

By the sound of it, Madame Lacombe struggles to get up off the cold tile floor. Soon it is clear there is no other option. "*On va appeler les pompiers,*" Madame Jeunet yells through the door. She's going to call for help.

"*Non!*" comes the feeble reply.

"Either you get up or we call the fire department."

"Leave me in peace. Just leave an old woman alone."

The pumpers arrive quickly, unusual for them, going through the room next door and out the window. They break a pane in Madame Lacombe's room, tear away the felt and dusty blankets and open the door. Madame lies on the floor, struggling like some sort of exhausted insect to right herself. Reflexively she berates them for breaking her window in the dead of winter, how is she supposed to keep warm now? It is going to cost her a fortune to replace the pane of glass. Madame Jeunet wrings her hands, "*Vous nous avez fait très peur,*" but Antoinette is already lapsing into unconsciousness. The firemen put her on oxygen and fetch their stretcher. Awkwardly they maneuver her down the narrow wooden stairs, through Madame Tournier's apartment and into the elevator.

I doubt that she needs to worry about the cold in winter, or the heat in summer. Her 35 year sentence is over. The pigeon net falls down, not all the way, but enough to show that the idea was a bad one to begin with. Mice scurry out from under her door, and scatter through the hall, into my room and into Room 19. I think of Madame Lacombe in intensive care, unaware that the fragile balance of her sixth-floor world has vanished. We waste so much time, and then it's too late. I hunt the mice with my copy of *Journey To the End of the Night.* Here Mickey, here *Me-Kay.* But my legs shake, I'm terrified of the little beasts, and they're too quick anyway.

Celine's words are a kind of eulogy. "The greatest defeat in anything is to forget, and above all to forget what has smashed you, and to let yourself be smashed without ever realizing how thoroughly devilish men can be. When our time is up, we people mustn't bear malice, but neither must we forget: we must tell the whole thing without altering one word, -everything that we have seen of man's viciousness, and then it will be over and time to go. That is enough of a job for a whole lifetime."

CHAPTER 6

City-Rat walks down Rue Saint-André-des-Arts and across the river to Beaubourg. After a year away in Italy and Germany, Paris looks like heaven. The buildings, people in the streets, the green of the trees, the old ladies with their impossibly deformed, ass-dragging little dogs, the Seine: City-Rat quivers with pleasure and anticipation. It's true what Dupont says about the street, that it forces the actor to prove things that he shouldn't have to prove. "You didn't like that one folks? Well don't go away, I've got a thousand better gags. Check this one out." In the theater, they've paid their money and they're seated, they're not going to walk out after thirty seconds. In the theater you don't always have to have the idea of money in the back of your mind. But: ever since his coffee this morning, he's been feeling like doing a show. Just go out there and have fun, make 'em laugh, make 'em cry, make 'em fall in love again, let 'em know that City-Rat is back.

In the left corner of the *plateau*, six people are already in line waiting to perform as Akro finishes. "No, it's O.K., you go ahead, City-Rat."

"You sure?" Black shoes, black pants, black arm warmers, black T-shirt, black suspenders, no white-face any more, short hair that is beginning to go grey, City-Rat puts his bag down in the middle of the circle, moves forward a few steps, looking over the crowd left by Akro. He raises his hands to the sky then jumps into a handstand. He bends his legs into a full lotus, then lowers himself down to kiss the cobblestones, rolls into a fish dive and then into a sitting lotus. Applause. He spins to his feet. *"Mesdames, Messieurs, je vais vous faire un peu de pantomime. Un peu de silence s'il vous plaît, la salle est très grande, et le plafond très haut."*[1] Get ready for miracles, there are miracles all around, and don't forget.

Dupont taught that a clown should always have one trick he can rely on, one funny little mannerism or tic that gets an automatic laugh. And if it doesn't get a laugh? With all due respect to your audience, you just have to accept it: *"Il y a des Belges dans la salle."* You're playing for Belgians.

---

[1] Ladies and Gentlemen, I will now do a bit of pantomime for you. Quiet please, the room is large, and the ceiling quite high.

City-Rat pulls his handkerchief out of his right back pocket. He cracks it open, wipes the sweat off his forehead and then wrings it out with a squeaking sound. They laugh, gets them every time. "Hot isn't it?"

He motions to the audience to come closer now, "A little intimate mime." The first sketch is called *The Crow*. A crow flies high overhead as a desert wind blows and a coyote runs through the desert, tongue dragging, looking for water. City-Rat turns from crow into coyote; the story begins to flow automatically, move after move. The sun is broiling, but still the coyote runs and runs. He smells water and begins to dig with all his might. Deeper and deeper he goes, and still no water. Finally he just collapses and dies. The crow flying overhead circles and lands next to the carcass. Flapping his wings and cawing, he tears into the feast. Mouthful after mouthful the gluttonous crow fills himself with coyote meat, until he is sated and almost too heavy to fly. He flaps his wings and finally makes it off the ground. At this point a cowboy comes riding by on his horse, pulls out his rifle and shoots the leaden crow out of the sky. He makes a fire and cooks the crow on a spit. Ravenous, he bites into a crow wing. He rips off the meat, gnaws at the wing then begins to crunch the bone. The bone gets stuck in his throat. He begins to choke; he falls to the ground, gasping for air. Then he grabs his rifle, sticks it in his mouth and pulls the trigger. The bone is dislodged. He gets on his horse and rides away.

Coyote to crow to cowboy: the metamorphosis is smooth, the body feels loose and free. City-Rat bows when he finishes. Almost as an afterthought, might as well pull in some coin, he throws down a hat.

At *Café Beaubourg* on the corner, the chairs are out, the sun is shining and the whole gang is sitting right by the door. Akro screams at the hunchback waiter, and the waiter comes over and smacks him in the back of the head. Robert Sleet runs his magician's hands over the knots and bumps of his newly-shaven skull and pontificates about the virtue of a brown rice diet, every mouthful chewed 35 times before swallowing. Paula the Eccentric laughs loudly as she tells about going back to *Père Lachaise* cemetery yesterday with two friends to celebrate Isadora Duncan's birthday. They filmed Paula naked under a diaphanous dress, drinking champagne and reading poetry in Isadora's honor. Until the cops came and they had to run away. She laughs again, an ingenuous, ear-splitting cackle which makes Lucien, Blackie's bottler, cringe, pound the table, beg for mercy. "*Seigneur...*"

"Party at my place tonight," City-Rat announces. Sharing the dream of a return to a mythic era. With ten good clowns they could take over this old grey city.

Back at Rue Gustave Flaubert, the assistant at the bakery downstairs moves into Room 3, a four-square meter cheese box without window, or ventilation of any kind. A 30 year-old Portuguese man in standard issue wife-beater T-shirt, blue-and-white checkered baker pants and heavy Lusitanian five o'clock shadow, he's not a poet, but when I inquire about the possibility of getting a tour of the bakery, (partly in the spirit of my personal Open Door Policy, and partly a sort of unofficial visit by the Ergotism Squad), he is instantly amenable, suggesting only that it would be best to wait for a time when the boss is away. Unfortunately, before the visit can actually be arranged, the flour creates havoc. Insults and threats are exchanged, knives are pulled, and the assistant ends up running off with the bakery cashbox.

Monsieur Bigot, the baker, a huge man with a large gut and barrel chest, puffs up the steps, and, dizzy from apoxia, convinced that *le portugais* is hiding inside, beats down the door to Number 2 with his meaty fists. Number 2: Madame Lacombe's TV-and-day-room next to the stairs, instead of Number 3, the baker's room. "Come out you Portuguese son of a whore, I know you're in there!" he bellows, while his man cowers safely in Number 3.

Three days later, the weather has turned hot. Madame Lacombe's door hangs on its hinges, rent asunder up the middle. A new assistant, a young Tamil from Sri Lanka, moves into Number 3. Madame Lacombe's niece takes the train in from Normandy to arrange for the door to be fixed: there's a television inside, a radio, and a refrigerator. The next day, as soon as two heavy padlocks are snapped shut on the door, she returns to Caen.

"*L'hindou,*" as the Spanish Concierge insists on calling the newest resident of the building, despite the golden cross he wears around his neck, and the sticker of the Virgin Mary cradling the Baby Jesus that he slaps on his door. "The Hindu leaves his sandals outside his door," she tells me, wringing her hands. It was well known that he, like all the other Hindus, would soon have fifteen relatives staying with him in the tiny room.

A week after he moves in, terrible heat. Worse than ever. With all possible windows open, Room 18, Room 19, the Turkish toilet, the windows at the top of the stairs, there is still not a hint of air. A smell of something rotten begins to seep out from somewhere. Five days later the odor turns into a pestilential effluence that permeates the whole sixth floor, burning the eyes, dissolving the grout on the windows.

On his fourteenth day on the sixth floor, "*l'Hindou,*" as meek and apologetic as could be, finally decides to bring this matter to the Concierge's attention. "A smell like a rotting corpse coming from the room next door." Madame Lacombe's niece comes in from Normandy again with the keys. It turns out that the culprit is a piece of meat left accidentally in Mme. Lacoma's disconnected refrigerator. The offending filet is evacuated, but the smell doesn't go away.

At City-Rat's apartment the party is just beginning when I get there, magicians, mimes, jugglers talking trade.

"I made a great hat at Saint Michel, behind the bookstore."

"Did you see the latest wave of summer jugglers? That fat American with the torches: 'You think this looks dangerous,' he says, the flattest, least excited voice ever. 'Well you should see it from where I'm standing.' I think he made five francs in three shows. Not even enough to pay for the apples he eats during the show."

Across the narrow street, in the window of their third-floor room at the Hotel Saint-André-des-Arts, four Italian girls, one of them quite beautiful, the other three so-so, finally accept Sleet's invitation to come to the party. Blackie and City-Rat beat each other up in slow motion. Lucien shows off his washboard stomach to an American mime and his wife. The wine flows, joints pass around, Willie the Dadaist pulls City-Rat's Japanese woman mask off the wall, plays with it then disappears into the bedroom, jabbering Geisha.

A few minutes later he returns, dancing out of the bedroom, a Japanese devil mask on his face, completely naked except for a sock over his cock. Behind him, Lucca, an Italian magician in boxer shorts, dances along in the same shamanistic rhythm, an African mask on his face, a bull's head on a broomstick in his right hand. City-Rat pulls a policeman's hat off the wall next to the door and directs traffic as they file into the living room, shocking the Italian girls, then file out again, to see what other mischief they can get into with City-Rat's props.

After a month, after a year, there always seems to be more work for Angel at the Manor House in Kent: the windows need painting, the wild grounds have to be cleared of ivy, hedges and trees run amok, there are lawns to put in, Rhadamanthus the goat needs to be trained to beg. After promising to return in April, Angel promises to come in May. But the work goes on and on, delays, interruptions, acts of God and he never manages to save enough money anyway.

Why hasn't Angel saved anything? He's sent a large sum to his brother and sister-in-law in Wales, because they were having a hard time. He has paid back debts, he has gone to London for a little company, he has simply been under a black cloud. He plays the soccer pools, picking eleven score draws out of thirteen. But instead of filling out four columns as he had intended, he only fills out three. The Monday paper gives him the news, his slip of mind cost him 39,890 pounds. The wench good fortune is sleeping elsewhere. Angel collapses into darkest depression.

In West Berlin, Dorian Strahler rehearses like a madman, getting ready for the opening of the Roncalli circus. The director of the circus takes videos of him so he can see for himself the damage left by the years on the street. "You've got to slow down. They're not going anywhere, don't worry. Slow down. Slow!"

Coincidentally, thanks to the Times & Tides and Shiva Press, just in time for the opening of Roncalli, I find myself heading north by train to Berlin, to meet up with Igor Morosov, Shiva photographer, on the set of the film *Forbidden*, starring Jackie Bisset.

Roncalli, it turns out, is a gem of a circus, music, color, light, costumes: a fantastic world. Creativity, poetry, imagination in every detail, it's total immersion, a voyage to a different world. For twenty minutes, wearing whiteface, a pointy felt hat with a small brim, a bow-tie a striped shirt and a too large blue jacket, Dorian Strahler, calmer, slower, more powerful, shows them clowning like they have never seen before. He does the gag with the camera like he used to do at Beaubourg, he takes unimaginable liberties with the spectators, the Germans have never seen anything like it. He pulls off his hat and hits them on the shoulders, on the head. Embarrassment, tension, bring 'em to the edge, and then release 'em. 1600 spectators bent double, laughing fit to blow the blue tent roof off. Gasping for air, begging for mercy, crying for joy, and then stomping their feet and clapping their hands for more. At the end of two hours the King of Beaubourg has become the King of Berlin. Tears of joy and pride roll down my cheeks, my heart swells. Quality!

By the third day of the show, perhaps the word has already gotten around, Strahler only has to make his entrance, show his face, to set them howling. Pic, the clown he replaced, the star of last year's show, is all but forgotten. But the purity is gone, the electric connection of astonishment, the pure response at the sight of novelty. It's the cult of personality, the funny man walking in a world where humor has died.

"This must be a dream," Strahler says. No lunatics, no broken glass, no need to beg people to watch. "Living in a little circus wagon, right across from the lion cages. Who could ever have imagined it? I'll never go back to the street!" Within weeks, Strahler is everywhere in the German press, Spiegel, etc. What's going to happen in six months? I have a sense of foreboding, but I keep it to myself, don't want to rain on Strahler's parade, nor set tragedy in motion with idle words.

Going down: with Strahler in Germany and Sleet back in Sweden again, City-Rat attempts to remain on an even keel. He still hasn't gotten any work, and after a month in the grind, Paris is no longer looking so good. To be a successful artist it is necessary to be open, completely open. But on the street it's not that easy, because being open for the audience also means opening yourself up to the poisons in the air, the drunks, the madmen.

When he was in Italy he had money. So what did he do? He bought himself a Borsalino hat, ate out in restaurants and fell asleep. Why is there always such pain in his life? Is it impossible for him to live without pain? To create without pain? "There is nothing we can defend in ourselves," Dupont used to say. "We are not Canadian, or American, or tall or ugly, or good lovers or writers or mimes. Are we going to defend the experiences that have made us who we are? No!" That's all fine, but what does that leave you with? Purged of absolutes, still unable to rebuild, City-Rat founders.

He breaks up with his Italian girlfriend, his third straight two-year term. Why is love always such a war? Why do women always try to hurt him so? Why doesn't he ever have the guts to pick a woman he really desires? Is every woman going to remind him of his mother, that fat German cow?

"No use crying over spilt yogurt," I say, trying to cheer him up, but

City-Rat doesn't even hear.

The party is still on at his apartment nearly every night, but he sits numbly in the corner, the actor pretending that he is having a good time, smiling weakly, drinking wine until he's plastered. Forgetting. He waits until everyone leaves, sets up in front of the mirror and pulls faces until he falls asleep.

In between headaches, he hits the street solo, Beaubourg during the day, or the *Deux Magots* after nine at night. *The Crow, The Cowboy, The Chewing Gum*: he's been doing the same skits for years now, pulling in just enough to pay for one day's food and wine.

Mme. Lacombe returns from the hospital after her third coma. This time she was clinically dead before they managed to revive her. At the gates of death she saw a long tunnel with lights, and she could see the doctors discussing her case, before she decided to come back. "I guess *le Bon Dieu* wants to prolong my suffering," she says.

"You still believe in God?" I ask.

"*Bien sur!*" Of course.

In a high wind, a pair of jockey shorts, irretrievably soiled, blows off the drying line outside my window, gone for good. Three days later, I discover a plastic bag hung on my door containing one pair of boiled, perfumed, ironed and starched shorts, immaculate, along with a note from Madame Tournier. "*I found that on my balconnet I washed it and dryed it Sincèrement votre voisine du dessous Madame Tournier.*"

Back from the hospital, Madame Lacombe's eyesight has not improved. She can see just well enough to tell that, "*l'hindou,*" the newest addition to her sixth floor, isn't exactly white. "Do you think he'll leave diseases on the toilet seat?"

During the day she is now forced to remain camped in room Number 2, behind the fractured door, unable to leave her oxygen machine, doctor's orders. She sits blindly in front of her television set, clear plastic tubes in each nostril, dark glasses on, the colors dancing over her face.

I get out my long-sleeping copy of *The Journey* off the shelf, intending to resume the reading of Celine. "There were mice coming out of your room, while you were gone."

"Yes, I used to have a cat, but after I couldn't use my legs anymore, I had to give it away," she is barely audible over the hum of the oxygen machine. Why I think I will manage reading to her any better than last time, how I think I can find the energy, I don't know. But the odor of decay and putrefaction in Room Number 2 is so intense that I hide the book, hand over the mail from the plastic pouch downstairs and step out.

The work at Shiva Press continues to have its pros and cons. Balancing between two worlds: the real world of newspapers, "*French Widow Wants Dead Husband's Baby*," and the more real world of the Paris streets. Too bad that for now, what with recuperation time before work and after, the sheer quantity of words spit out, (30 pages a day now), and the demands of this strange style of writing, ("Past tense clichés, no idioms please, think of our Arab clients!") the hours at Shiva all but prevent me from working on my own stuff.

Glynnis, the boss, runs hot and cold. One day she hands me a hundred francs worth of meal tickets, because she thinks I look too thin. The next day, rabid hellion, she stomps over to my desk, rips my text out of the typewriter and slashes it with her blue Bic ballpoint pen, punching holes in it, until there is no choice but to start over. "You can't say this, Josef. Madonna is *not* the latest peroxide retread."

The job is not *all* bad, occasionally there are interesting stories and inspiring encounters with some of the more intrepid photographers. Gifted, sensitive, daring, living on the edge, their hands shake, their brows furrow, their eyes dart from side to side as they light the next cigarette with the previous one. But they are alive, no excuses, a hundred times alive and eager to tell their stories. I write one about the Trans-Gabon Railway, shot by a tiny, French woman who, already in Vietnam, had a reputation for fearlessness under fire. I do another about the condition of women in Khomeini's Iran, brought in by a courageous Iranian woman who had slipped clandestinely over the border, who assures me she would have been killed if they had found her.

But then there are the paparazzi, men whose bad taste, ability to load the proper film, check the ASA, read a light meter, frame a picture, focus and push down their index finger has turned into strutting roosters. Like Dullard, who brings in photos of Brigitte Bardot naked on her beach at La Madrague, "Look at these! How could she let herself go like that. She's unfuckable. *Inbaisable!*" Dullard who is famous for the picture of Romi Schneider's son, who died after trying to climb over a fence and impaling himself on the spikes. A picture Dullard got, the hall of fame of bad taste, by bribing an orderly at the morgue, pulling back the sheet and snapping the photo.

I do what I can to stay sane, adding a touch of subversion in my texts, polyglot puns, obscure references, humor so dry that virtually no one, Glynnis especially, even notices. But sometimes after work I actually feel physically sick from promoting and spreading this pollution, this madness, from collaborating in such mediocrity. How would the Saint of Tuvrig have handled such a job? I wonder. Is this really the mission I have been put onto the planet to accomplish?

With the money scheduled to come from Shiva at the end of the month, I'm able to breathe a bit, but I'm still pretty much broke. Which may not be dignified, but still isn't a problem. A Dutch lady I met when I first arrived in Paris is now the manager at The Studio, a Tex-Mex restaurant next to Beaubourg, and she lets me sneak into the July 4th party. A second kind soul offers to buy me dinner. Dressed in my usual unlaundered wolf-skin, I circle the party eavesdropping on conversations, looking for opportunities, hunting for Scheherazade, keeping my eye on the entrance.

Finally, a gorgeous, slim, dark-haired woman wanders in. A Beatrice[2], clearly. I sidle up next to her, wracking my mind for something to say and coming up with nothing. The usual problem when I see a woman I desire. But instead of walking away, as would be normal, which is what the other members of the Sisterhood would do, she turns to me, "Are you American?" It turns out she is a model.

"I don't like fashion," I say. I could be absolutely any nationality she wants.

"I don't either," Beatrice answers. "It's such a game. Stupid. The

---

[2] "Turn, Beatrice, o turn your holy eyes upon your faithful one,' their song beseeched, 'who, that he might see you, has come so far. Out of your grace, do us this grace; unveil your lips to him, so that he may discern the second beauty you have kept concealed.' O splendor of eternal living light, who's ever grown so pale beneath Parnassus' shade or has drunk so deeply from its fountain, that he'd not seem to have his mind confounded, trying to render you as you appeared where heaven's harmony was your pale likeness-your face, seen through the air, unveiled completely?" *Dante's Inferno. Canto XXXI, Purgatorio*

photographers are so superficial. They don't like me very much. And the models. Always talking about fashion and constipation. Did you know that when girl models go away on shoots, they always get constipated. 90% of them. As for the boys, they always have diarrhea..." she laughs, a genuine, unforced laugh that begins to tickle the very bottom of my soul.

"Were you pretty as a young girl?"

"Oh no," she laughs. "I was tall and skinny, everyone laughed at me. They called me the spider..."

"And what about love? You know anything about love?"

"Hah! Love, I don't believe in love."

"I see, hang on just a second." I whip out my notebook and pretend to write, as if taking a survey. "Doesn't believe in love. Very good. Age?"

She laughs. "Twenty-six."

"Hmm, same age as me." She has a tragic look that says she doesn't quite believe in her beauty, a mysterious look that says this beauty has wounded her. I gaze deep into her eyes. A thought goes through my mind. We could have lovely children.

I tell her about living in a maid's room without money, and she doesn't vomit, run away or break out in a rash. I tell her about the Open-Door Policy and Shiva, about heart-break and traveling. She tells me about working as a model in New York, about earning $2000 a day, about being on the cover of *Belladonna* magazine five times in a row, and *Elle*, six times in all. She's just gotten back from Brazil, where she spent three months on a sailboat. They were supposed to sail across the Atlantic, but she decided she'd had enough, and took a plane back instead. The stories flow, and each time that remarkable laugh. "Look, I've got to work tomorrow," I say before either of us turns into a pumpkin. A good fisherman lets the fish take the hook. "But I would like to see you again."

"Here's my number," she says, taking the notebook and pen from my hands and writing it down. "Call me."

The Rodin Museum, dinner, a Garden Party out in the country: the courtship is quick and brutal, as such things must be. Rapture, we fall asleep in each other's arms, animals made for each other. I feel like I am home at last, like there is someone to live for. The graceful curve of her hip, the way her upper lip curls back in the throes of passion...

"How would you like to go down to the Ile d'Oleron for a week," she says. My family is renting a house down there."

"Summer vacation? Why not?" I burn with passion, I'm dancing through the streets. Her face hides a thousand and one mysteries, I could gaze forever into those eyes.

We take the night train south down to the city of Saintes, chugging through the night then watching the golden dawn through the big old train window, a tapestry of sun-worshipping sunflowers followed by the vineyards of Cognac. From Saintes it's a bus to the island just off the Atlantic coast, opposite La Rochelle. Lunch is waiting on the patio outside, and M. and Mme. Chevrier too. Hands are shaken, small is talked, information is traded about the dimensions of the perfect intestine, not too long, not too short, anecdotes shared about digestion, heraldic digestion, past, present and future, the food is evaluated against that of previous meals. "A little *Pineau*?" "A little cheese?" "A little wine?" "I think I like carrots." "As for me, I never say no to a few more greens." "A little coffee?"

I try to convince myself that it's just the nervous conversation of first meeting, wracking my brain unsuccessfully for ways to contribute, food stories of my own important enough to share. But deep down, I fear the problem is more serious, over the years you develop a radar. They don't seem the least bit interested in me. I'm a fish out of water, a visitor from a parallel universe, an outsized interloper, a poisoned Marshall Plan gift, a transparent Yankee fornicator, sentence passed before I even open my mouth. "I'm interested in ergotism, myself," I blurt out regardless, in time for the *fromage blanc*.

"Ergotism? It come from *ergoter*? Quibbling, splitting hairs?" says André Chevrier. "Well I imagine as a writer you must have to be quite an ergotist."

"No, no. Ergot: *claviceps purpurea*. Did you know that when the Gauls attempted to besiege Rome, the Romans threw bread over the walls and onto the Gauls' heads so that they would know the siege was pointless. This ergot is very powerful stuff."

As soon as the table is cleared, Beatrice announces that she and her brand-new boyfriend are tired from the train trip and will take a short nap. So, as the second round of post-prandial coffee appears with the Scrabble board, and M. Chevrier settles in on his *transat* behind his copy of *Le Monde*, Beatrice and I retreat to our room, ground floor, *right next* to the patio. She closes the shutters, rips my clothes off and throws me down on the bed. The springs squeak wildly as we nap once, then nap again shortly thereafter for good measure. "No Beatrice, I can't nap three times in the same afternoon," I beg for mercy. "Especially not with your parents right outside the shutters." I'm just not that tired.

"*Venit, manducat, venit,*" André Chevrier huffs as he folds his paper, and places it on the table. He comes, he eats, he comes.

During the day Beatrice and I go for bike rides and long walks. At low tide we pry wild oysters off the rocks, squeeze lemons into them and knock them back, dozens of them, at high tide Beatrice tries to teach me how to windsurf, a hopeless task even if the boards were designed to support the weight of a man my size, which they aren't. Shopping for food in the morning, cooking, washing dishes, preparing *tartines* for the children, drinking tea, cooking dinner: the day revolves around food. The conversation at lunch the first day which I mistook for awkward politeness, is actually the norm. Not a meal passes in which food is not discussed, in which Beatrice's mother does not embark on an interminable discussion of the latest France Soir drama, or the cat's diseases, the scabs forming over its eyes. It's like they're terrified of silence, terrified of connecting, so they fill the air with whatever comes to mind, anything to prevent them from confronting the emptiness.

Beatrice's parents like me better than Beatrice's last stiff, she assures me, even though they interpret my continuing inability to contribute to the conversation as haughtiness, as if "the artist" is too good to share his thoughts with them. But clearly, I need training, I lack even a child's level of common-sense. I use the bread knife to cut the cheese, sacrilege, I refuse to drink my breakfast coffee from a bowl, as the Bible intended, I don't have a single story about string beans, I fail to grasp the heresy in eating "salty" after "sugary. "

"Artists are necessary, no doubt," says Monsieur Chevrier, "But where are the artists when it comes time to build a bridge?"

Already by the fourth day, I'm more than ready to flee back to Paris. I know I don't really belong in France, not more than anywhere else I've lived, but that doesn't mean I like to be reminded of it. I need to get back to my own rhythm, to purge, to get away from the kingdom of small cheeses. This isn't adventure, and new horizons, at the very best it's anthropological research, survival. Down the road, at the end of the beach, is a trailer park where the slaves of the industrial machine enjoy their month off, wandering around completely lost, a month to kill before plugging themselves back in. The place haunts me. *Ricard* in hand, wearing thin, ribbed T-shirts and Bermuda shorts, the men play *pétanque* next to the highway or on the gravel between the rows of caravans parked together as far as the eye can see. Seated on aluminum lawn chairs, the women fan themselves, bored, swatting flies while listening to the gossip on *Europe 1* radio, and dreaming of next year's vacation.

"Terrifying," I say.

"It takes all kinds," Beatrice reminds me, sweetly.

"Does it?"

"Come on, let me show you," she says with a sexy giggle, taking my hand and leading me away. Invigorated by the fresh air, and by my laughably pathetic attempts to learn how to windsurf in the *little* breeze blowing over the *little* bay, Beatrice remains insatiable, demanding Intra-venus therapy so often that, that at the end of the week, when she puts me back on the bus so I can make it back to Paris in time for work at Shiva, I've napped so much I can hardly walk.

"I you, mackeroh," the Hindu greets me as I haul myself slowly, willfully, gratefully, up the last steps to the sixth floor. By now the bakery is so successful that the baker is driving a brand new Volvo, which *l'hindou* has to wash, in addition to his duties walking the baker's dogs, an old stupid Weimaraner, and a brand new Gordon Setter puppy as well. "I Wimbledon. I, you, Rendo? Yes! Uh, uuh, Mackeroh?"

"I'm afraid I don't know the exact answer to that question. What do you think, Madame Lacombe?"

"You were gone."

"That I was. *Ça va?*"

"*Oh, tout doucement.*"

The Olympics start in Los Angeles on July 28, an opening ceremony featuring 84 grand pianos, a rocket man with a jet pack, and card and flashlight tricks performed by the spectators that astound the entire staff at Shiva Press. "In France you could never get people to do that." I virtually move in to Shiva Press, sixteen hours a day for two weeks. I have no time to go down to Beaubourg, barely time to see Beatrice when I collapse into bed at six in the morning. Stephanie of Monaco, studying fashion design at

Christian Dior, left her house on 17 July, wearing a pink sweater, white blouse, blue jeans, and bangs that match her dog's. At a McDonald's in San Diego, James Oliver Huberty, 41, a Vietnam Vet, opened fire with a .45 caliber pistol and 9 mm semi-automatic, slaughtering twenty-one people. With the money I should end up with, 6000 francs or so, I could fly to India, stop working at Shiva for four months. Do some real writing, at last, and take a long, long rest.

I make the mistake of sharing my good news with Marie-France, my landlady. She hands me a 2x4 meter scrap of tan carpet, arranges her Hermes scarf and announces that come September my rent will rise 50 francs a month. The cost of living's going up, she says.

"Fifty francs, come on! What is fifty francs to you? You want some Portuguese family in there cooking sardines?" I bluff, going straight for her weak-spot. But I'm no match for her, there are generations of perfidy in her bloodline, she can see right through me. India? You must be joking. She knows I won't move out.

CHAPTER 7

The knives pierce City-Rat's stomach as he makes his way down the *plateau* and drops his bags. Beaubourg is a rat hole, but he is City-Rat, and if he can keep coming out here to do shows, he figures he can do anything. He raises his hands to the sky and jumps into a handstand. He steadies himself: the balance feels good, he's in control, it could be a good show. His legs split and cross until both feet rest on the opposite thighs. Slowly he lowers himself and kisses the ground, and then rolls onto his chest. They stop to watch, amazed at the strength in his slight body.

If they help him out, he knows he can make magic. He can fly, and they can too. If they help he can forget himself and just *be*: the power, the moment of grace, of invulnerability, of wholeness. He rolls back on his knees, settles into a lotus position, his forehead on the ground, and remains still. They applaud. He sits up, smiles, spins out of the lotus position, gets up, pulls the red bandanna out from his back pocket, wipes his forehead and pretends to squeeze out the water. They laugh at the sound he makes. He looks them over, pulls on his suspenders. Something is already missing. The way they talk to each other, the way they watch him, without energy, without life, waiting for something to happen, waiting to be entertained, to be given emotions. Don't they understand that there is something more?

He closes his eyes to chase away the dizziness, then starts his Chewing Gum skit. Out of thin air he conjures a piece of gum and begins to chew. The gum tastes great, today's a holiday. He takes it out of his mouth, stretches it, ties it in a bow around his neck, and snaps it. He stretches it again, until it's long enough to be a jump-rope. Skip, skip, skip, ha ha, he's having the time of his life. He wads the gum up again, chews, and blows an enormous bubble. See that? Not bad, eh? He seals the bubble off and circles it, bounces off it, a brand new toy. Why don't I stick my finger in? Hey that was easy. Why don't I stick my arm in? Hey, no gravity. Stick the other arm in. Then the head, the torso, the whole body. He floats in the bubble, complete oneiric ecstasy. Look at me, I'm flying!

OK, time to get out again. But he is a clown, and in a clown's universe things must always go wrong. He sticks his finger in. Wait, what's this? He pushes harder. Help. He tears at it, *rien à faire*, the bubble is solid, impermeable, he is trapped. Help! What do I do? Help! He jams his hands into his pocket, ah hah: a needle, of course. You see, a needle, no need to panic folks. Pop! His rubber face is flattened, his arms pinned awkwardly to his sides. He flaps around like some kind of stricken bird, exaggerating the grimaces, pushing, pushing because they're not laughing as much as they should be.

When he finally gets loose, he wads the gum back up again, and sticks it in his mouth. This time it tastes terrible, awful, he sticks his coffee-stained tongue out in disgust. He takes it out of his mouth, tries to throw it away. But it sticks to his fingers. He shakes his hand, tries to pull the gum off with the other hand. The other hand gets stuck. Shit. He sticks his knee between his hands to pull them apart. They come apart, ah, but with such force that the hands stick to his hair. Shit! He pulls at his hair until the hands come loose, then rubs the chewing gum off of his hand and on to his foot. Ah, he tries to walk away. Shit, his foot is stuck to the ground. No, that's expected, completely normal, he smiles, trying to free his foot. A few arabesques, the foot is free, ah; shit, the gum is back on his hand. Only one solution: swallow it. It goes down in a lump, like a rabbit in a python. Uh oh, he grabs his gut, he's going to explode.

He opens the door to an imaginary bathroom; they follow him in. He closes the door and locks it, pulls down his pants and sits on a make-believe toilet. His cheeks inflate, his face turns red as he strains to shit. Now they're really with him, this is it: popular theater, vulgar, crass. Unnnnnh, ah, unnnnh, ah, ah, ah: it comes out. Ooof! He pulls out his handkerchief and wipes his brow.

Now that they're eating out of his hand, he draws it out. He takes forever to wipe himself. He stands up, pulls up his imaginary pants and looks back: the turd is huge, shoulder-wide. Proud, delighted, he pulls the chain. Uh oh. Uhh ohh! The toilet's *not* flushing. He jumps around, water rising, what shall I do, pulls on the chain again. The waters overflow. Soon his ankles are covered. Yech! He grimaces and rises onto his tiptoes, pulls at the toilet door handle. It won't open. The waters rise to his knees, to his waist. Frantic, he pulls again, bangs on the door, cups his hands and yells voicelessly for help. The waters rise to his neck, then over his head. He bangs on the door again, his fist moving in slow-motion through the water. Holding his breath, inflating his cheeks, he breast strokes through the turd-cluttered water. The crowd groans as it laughs, holds its breath with him, completely taken in by the nightmare.

His lungs give out, he sinks down to the ground. He prays to God, crosses himself. Winged angels fly down, then vanish, replaced by the horned devil who pulls out a chess board to determine the clown's fate. Four moves: Fool's mate! The devil begins to fill in the grave, when it finally occurs to City-Rat: the door was locked. He turns the key, the door opens, and City-Rat rolls out with the wave of shit-water, gasping for air like a beached fish. The sketch is over, he lies motionless until they begin to applaud. He gets up and takes a bow. They whistle and clap. He is exhausted. He goes back to his bag, pulls out a hat. In the back rows the spectators have already begun to drift off, to slink away, afraid he might catch their eye.

How little he must have touched them. He has taken them on a voyage, does it really hurt them that much just to pull out a coin from their pocket? The knives saw at his guts. City-Rat slams the hat down without a word, and retires backstage, wiping the drops of sweat off his forehead. Not a bad crowd, but not a good one either. They didn't really follow the rhythm of the story, they didn't applaud-laugh-react with the proper timing, they made him work too hard, the story didn't flow. Their energy was all wrong, they took all his juice, nothing left. Why is he still on the street, why can't he get any jobs inside?

A three year-old hitches forward clutching a ten franc coin in his fist. He drops it in the hat then runs back to his mother as everyone laughs. "*Merci*." The rest finally get the idea, walk up to the hat, toss in a franc and stick their chests out, virtuous, equal exchange, right? "Thank you, you made us laugh," they clap him on the back and shake his hand before heading off to the museum. The scrawny little comic with the rubber features and the yellow skin has gone deaf. At night he dreams about killing them, taking the knives from his stomach and sticking them in theirs, motherfuckers. Such anger inside, a dragon which he knows could jump out any minute. City-Rat struggles to control himself, breathes deeply, tells himself once again it is his fault if he did not make the love happen, his fault if he was not able to open up for them.

He tries to put his sweater on, but there is hardly room to move. The last of the crowd has closed in, surrounded him. They look in the hat to see how much he has earned, wait for an opening. They stare, touch him, try to possess him, get his attention. "Eh, you do this for a living?" "Where ya from? Canada? Really? Wherbouts?" The same old questions. He really can't take it anymore, not a second longer. Don't they understand their role? Don't they know the show is over?

He's seen this too many times. Yesterday, the day before, last week, last month, the year before last. Too many shows begging apathetic crowds to join him, too many shows pleading with them to collaborate just for a few minutes so that he can show what he can do, so that he can lose himself in their attention. He could give them magic, he could envelop them in the power he radiates when he is creating. When he is creating he becomes invulnerable, his body buzzes with harmony. Through him, if they would only believe, if they would only follow him, they could attain the same state. But when was the last time that happened? It did happen, didn't it?

Dressed in a black tank top and loose black pants, Blackie, the apostle of mime, incubus of ten thousand dreams, the King Of Beaubourg by default now that Strahler has run away to the circus, begins to gather a crowd. The shape of the circle has to be just right, flat and long across the top, front rows seated, thick on the sides so that no one can get through, can use his stage as a sidewalk. He sneaks in behind an old woman and hobbles along with her as she moves over the cobblestones to the entrance of Beaubourg. Arms, gait, posture, the imitation is right on. A few people stop to watch. A young tough carrying a skateboard comes strolling by the other way, and Blackie falls in beside him, chewing gum and tossing his hair. An old man shuffles by, Blackie opens a door to let him through, and then plays out an imaginary rope. A group of blacks, obeying the cool sartorial dictates of the Be-Bop culture, (American basketball shoes, Major League baseball hats, sweatpants) swaggers and rolls near. Does he dare mess with them? No problem, of course he does, this is *his* stage, he owns it. He steps in front of them, adopts their walk, checks their reflections, their mannerisms, on the tinted windows all around the stage. When it works, he makes it seem like the puppet is actually the puppeteer. He hitches his shoulder, exaggerates the motion, tries to find their limits, pushing for a reaction. 300 people, so far so good, have stopped to observe this demonstration of power.

"OK. Now I'm going to do a show," Blackie runs back to the center. "OK. Now you come forward to here. Good, no a little further back. And you come here, along this line," not a hint in his voice that they might have the option to do anything else. "OK. Now you in front, sit down. Sit down so that the people who are going to come can see. Sit down. *Sit down!*"

"Are you ready?"

"Uh, um, yeah."

"Waiwaiwaiwai wait! ARE YOU READY!"

"Yeah!!"

"OK, OK, OK." He backs away, hands out to calm the crowd. "Now I'm going to a mime show. The first sketch is called: "*The Disco, Le Disco. Ça va?*"

Blackie has been here since the days when six acts could play at Beaubourg at the same time, smaller, more intimate circles, crowds of 200 spectators. He has been here since the right-hand corner of the cobblestoned slope, where everyone lines up to play now, was still regarded as haunted. While the evolution put more money in the pockets of the performers, it also produced an evolution of style. 1000 spectators demands five times as much anger, five times as much control, five times as much vulgarity: those are the things that work on the street.

The Disco: a vain young man prepares for a night on the town. He steps in the shower and begins to wash, taking particular care of his crotch and crack where a tiny piece of shit seems to have lodged and dried. The man shuts off the shower, gets out, dries off and begins to get dressed. He chooses a shirt out of a closet-full, picks out some pants. The pants are impossibly tight, the zipper gets stuck on his cock. He turns red with pain, until he manages to free himself. He grabs a glass of water, drinks some then sprinkles soothing drops on the head of his penis. He has an enormous penis and balls as big as watermelons, which finally, after a tremendous struggle, he manages to stuff inside his jeans.

600 people look on. Lucien picks up a hat and begins to snake through the crowd. *"Pour l'artiste s'il vous plaît."* Put the hat in front of one person, look him in the eye, leave the hat in place, travel with your eyes, then your body to the next person, then bring the hat: Blackie codified the choreography and Lucien, fearless Lucien, the insomniac scammer, does the talking.

By the time 45 minutes are up and Blackie has run through his other three sketches: *The Train, The Skier,* and *The Samurai,* Lucien has passed the hat around the circle three times. The first hats after winter are invariably good, generosity and giddiness of early spring.

Now that business is over, time for pleasure. Lucien moves over to a Dutch Amazon standing on the fringes as the circle disperses. He had already espied her on his second tour with the hat, happened to notice what kind of cigarettes she smokes. "Drum!" he says to her. His French-accented English is virtually incomprehensible but that doesn't slow him down, it's his best weapon.

"Oh, you want a cigarette…"

"Yes. That's what I said. Come on!" Pretending to be outraged, he rolls the cigarette in front of her, looking into her eyes as he licks the paper.

"Time to get serious now. Buy me a coffee?"

"Huh?" she still can't pierce his accent.

At a table outside the *Café Beaubourg*, drowning his pain in Côtes du Rhone, City-Rat is already three sheets to the wind by the time Blackie, shirt off, stomach rippling, completes his show. He comes up to the corner trailed by three young lovelies and drops his hat full of money on the table, bangs it down to show what six hundred francs sounds like. "Come on City-Rat, whaddayasay. Come on. Let's work together, come on, we'll do an improv. What do you say?"

"Leave me alone." This isn't the first time Blackie has asked.

"Just an improv, we go down there, five minutes, we come back." Still high from his show, and high on the romance he has just begun with Paula the Eccentric, Blackie persists. Sure he can make more money on his own, but he's tired of working the street alone, bored. He bangs the hat down on the table again.

Néné the fakir, red headband on his forehead, hands blackened from spitting fire, chest caved-in, comes up to the table with a German shepherd puppy on a string. "Not great today, is it?" he says. I lean down to pet the dog. "It's a dog, not a rag," Néné yanks the dog away. "Hands off."

"Yeah, yeah," I say. Néné pulls his Opinal knife off his belt, opens up the curved blade to settle this like a man. Néné's woman, Henriette stops him, fishes five francs out of her change purse and hands it to him to go play pinball. "*C'est fini Beaubourg*," she says to City-Rat. Beaubourg is finished. "Yeah, yeah," I say. She slaps me in the head, once, twice.

"OK. OK already!" This is too much. Even clouded by wine, City-Rat's anger refuses to rest. If he doesn't purge it somehow, soon, he's going to explode. He calls the hunchback waiter over, orders a *double express*, lights a cigarette, drains the coffee, orders another single coffee and lights another cigarette. "I'll do an improv with you Blackie." One condition: "We go down there and beat each other up. Slow motion."

Followed by Blackie's harem, they head back down into the corner and drop their bags. City-Rat swings his fist at Blackie, missing his chin by inches. Blackie reels with the blow, falls back. City-Rat kicks his leg up, again missing the chin by inches; Blackie falls back further. Blackie aims a punch at City-Rat's gut, City-Rat bends in half at the missed slow-motion punch, then falls over backward, tumbling once, twice. Blackie chases him and City-Rat, still on the ground, aims a kick to his balls. A crowd has gathered, but the actors are oblivious to it. Blackie kicks City-Rat in the head, once, twice, three times. City-Rat pulls out a mime pistol and holds it on Blackie. Hands up, Blackie backs away, backs away. A flurry: suddenly Blackie is holding a rifle. City-Rat backs away slowly, tosses away his pistol, looks around furtively. It feels so good to play. Just to play and forget everything else. The tension, the anger is draining from his body. Suddenly he whips out a bazooka. "Ha, ha!" Why not, why *shouldn't* he and Blackie try and play together?

The next day when they start, the word has already gotten out. Blackie starts as usual, by following people, mimicking them. When enough people have collected, he molds them into geometrical form, "Now I would like to introduce a Canadian mime: City-Rat."

City-Rat bows, jumps into his handstand, and lowers himself into the fish dive, feeling strong and steady. From the lotus position he jumps to his feet, crackling with energy. They're already clapping like mad, and they clap all through the Chewing Gum. When he is done, the applause is even louder, he runs around the circle, jumping into the air, flying, with Blackie right behind. They run to their props and put on baseball caps, black for Blackie, red for City-Rat.

"Now," Blackie says, "We are going to do a sketch called "*The Train, Le Train.*"

"*Il treno, der Zug,*" City-Rat throws out, slipping a set of rabbit teeth into his mouth. "How are we going to do *The Train*?" he says to Blackie *sotto voce*. "I don't know *The Train.*"

Blackie rears back and socks him in the face, mime style. City-Rat reels, stumbling to catch his balance, then reels some more. Gets the laugh.

"OK, we're doing *The Train.*"

The *plateau* has rung a thousand times with the skit, about a locomotive engineer who tries to stop his train in time to avoid running over a little bird, Blackie conducting the crowd through the sounds of the train: the whistle, the engine, the brakes. But now, with City-Rat trying to follow, just a fraction of a second off, learning to perform the moves he has seen so many times, looking completely lost and innocent with his rabbit teeth, the sketch takes off. With Blackie there by his side, City-Rat feels almost safe, more open to improvise than he has in years. He lies down on the ground as Blackie climbs up onto the locomotive; looking impossibly frail next to Blackie, he struggles to lift a shovel-full of coal to toss in the boiler; when Blackie can't get the crowd to make the sound of the train whistle, City-Rat takes over and as the train starts rolling, he looks out the side window and flips off an imaginary being on the side. Blackie's laughing so hard he has to stop playing. Transported, witnessing creation, imagination, two men discovering something new, the spectators roar.

When the train has stopped and the mimes have rescued the bird, only to have it fly away and shit down on them, City-Rat and Blackie don't even wait for the applause to die down. "Areyouready! OK. It's the Olympics now. We're going to do some improvisations. Any suggestions?"

"Volleyball."

"Oh Volleyball," City-Rat claps his hands together in effete delight. "Volleyball," he leaps gracefully, hugs himself like a prima donna.

"Volleyball, let's play volleyball. Poof!" Blackie serves the ball.

"Volleyball! Pif, hi hi," City-Rat hits the ball back. The audience is collapsing, and the mimes play it for all it's worth.

Tennis, boxing, the 100 meters in slow motion: improv follows improv. Capitalizing on the contrast in their physiques, Blackie bigger and healthier looking; City-Rat with his sallow look, the corpse-like features, only 30 but looking more like 55, like a fire eater whose soul has been eaten by forty years of kerosene, the act is innovative, funnier every day. Blackie dominates each contest, knocking City-Rat around the *plateau*, sending him flying to the cobblestones. But by some subterfuge, some unpredictable, illogical twist, City-Rat always comes out the victor. It wouldn't wash any other way.

The crowds are huge, 1000, 1200. Lucien passes with the hat, *"Pour les artistes, s'il vous plaît,"* Lucien says, energy electric, his head bouncing back and forth as he raps and sweet-talks the people out of their money. 1200,

1500 francs, the hat overflows with coin, at least more money than City-Rat has ever seen. For the first time since Strahler, the magic has returned to Beaubourg.

By the end of the first week, the whole city is in their hands. Not just the usual tourists, but Parisians who come down to Beaubourg day after day, and bring their friends to see the 4:00 o'clock show. There can't be anything better going on. Walking down Saint Germain those soft summer nights, every night, a half-dozen people point City-Rat out, all 5'6" of him. "That's the guy I was telling you about." Girls with that lustful look.

Leaving depression behind, City-Rat begins to wake up again. He's eager, he's got a little cushion of money, and he's grateful to Blackie for that. But he is a clown, and in a clown's universe things always have to go wrong.

For one, Blackie is beginning to hold him back, he's too stiff, not open enough, too proud. Where City-Rat is wide open, ready to respond like lightning to present the contrasts, the unexpected, all those twists which make the crowd laugh, make it live, Blackie protects himself, cuts himself off. And as much as Blackie radiates power and sexuality performing on his own, when he works with City-Rat, the contrast makes him seem overbearing, like someone trying too hard to be funny. He doesn't like the role of straight-man, of villain: he wants to receive as much adulation as he does in his solo show, he wants to be loved as much as City-Rat. He wants the crowd to pay more attention to him. They used to like him. The girls used to flock around after the show, he could take his pick. It's frustrating. He waves his hand in front of their eyes, lets his jaw hang out as if he is a slobbering fool, says in his fractured French, *"c'est pas télévision."* He unscrews the head of the offending member of the audience, looks inside, and puts his hand to his forehead as if it were some tragedy. He cries great sobs.

Safely back in his apartment that night, City-Rat opens his second bottle of wine. "You should have seen City-Rat, used to make 'em scream with laughter," he says as he pours the wine, his brow furrowing. "What's this insulting the crowd? *Il faut respecter le public.* You got to win them over with love. You hold 'em, you hold 'em, you hold 'em. And then bam. You give 'em the look: complete compassion. You can touch even the most dead person." What's missing, why doesn't Blackie's clown work, was what

Strahler did way back when really all that different?

"Blackie hasn't discovered, he hasn't touched his own anger," City-Rat tries to explain it again for himself. "He isn't even aware of it!" he yells. But he'd never tell him that to his face.

Soon after raising the rent, Marie-France suggests I give English lessons once a week to her nine year-old daughter, Marie, 50 francs a session. Why not? At nine o'clock on Wednesday morning, I'm ready to go. The first four sessions, she seems interested, English seems like an exotic new toy, and her playmates are even jealous. We go into her room and I ask her to point to the things for which she would like to know the names. "Doll, crucifix, book, pencil."

But after the first month, her enthusiasm seems to wane. Boy, girl, child, one, two, three. "Three, not free. Thirteen not dzerteen. Say it, come on." She has trouble concentrating. "Come on..." Marie looks at me, puts on the French pout, refuses to play along. "Maybe we could go to the park. Would you like that? The *parc*? We could go out to the park and see the ducks. Quack, quack, quack. Duck, you know what a duck is? Quack, quack, quack," I flap my wings. "*Un poulet?*" (A chicken?) "No, *duck*." She doesn't want to go out to the park. And what kind of teacher is this, she wonders, who thinks that chickens quack?

With the American College back in session, karate class starts up again at the American Church with a new master, a Nigerian fitness maniac, who runs us until our ears buzz. "Smash, kick, kiai! Smash, kick, kiai!" After two and a half hours, the class ends with a ritual called the Crocodile walk, which involves dropping down to the ground, and traversing the gym on your hands and feet, like a crocodile, chest a few inches above the ground. Aside from building physical strength, the object of the drill is to force the students to let their minds push them to feats that their body balks at. We crawl once across the gym, twice, and once we are softened up, he introduces the next exercise, the Crocodile *hop*. "Shore! Shore! The body is weak. Use your minds to work through the pain."

Two and a half months after our meeting, Beatrice celebrates her 29th birthday. It turns out she was not 26 after all when we met. "I tell people I'm 26 because it isn't good to be old."

"Sure, but at this rate you'll be a hundred before the end of the year," I laugh.

After two and a half months together, like all couples past the rush of initial infatuation, we begin to see cracks, flaws here and there. I worry that she's a bit too lethargic, she's never on time, and not just a few minutes late, but 40 minutes, an hour; she thinks I'm impatient. I want her to be more communicative, she wishes I would be more understanding. I'm spending twice as much money as I was before I met her: she's not willing to live on rice and pasta; she thinks I'm cheap. Too many easy years, too much easy money, she doesn't really understand about my financial restrictions, the delicate tightrope I walk to be able to keep writing, the desire to devote myself to my work. She wonders why it pains me so to go out to the country with her parents, and what on earth is so exciting about Beaubourg and all these so-called artists. I wonder about her sense of humor. She laughs at people slipping on dog shit or banana peels, she laughs when I bump my head on the low-lying objects that are everywhere in this world of midgets. And when *I* try to make her laugh, she refuses to let loose, to succumb. "Are you done yet?" she says. *"T'as fini?"*

"What do you expect?" Lucien says. "She's French. French, French, French."

"Thing is, all that doesn't even matter. I'm never going to be satisfied, it's just the way I'm made. Have I ever met a woman who really makes me laugh? But with Beatrice it doesn't matter. Trifles, all of it, because on a very basic, animal level, we have a harmony which I didn't think I'd ever find."

"An animal level, eh?" Lucien snickers.

"Yeah, well that too. But it's the little things. The way she walks without banging her heels, the way she doesn't try and put on a pretend face, the way she laughs, the look on her face when she comes. Anyway, we're just dogs. Either we get along with another dog, or we don't."

"Um hmm. Celle qui nous fait souffrir le moins." Lucien says. The one who makes us suffer least.

Still, every morning, when I wake up and look over at her... The sight of her head next to me, her brown hair fanned out on the white pillow, her face, her beautiful face! I could look at that face forever. My heart sings. I'm in heaven. Rapture. A pure moment!

At the end of the summer, Beatrice's ex-boyfriend, Loïc, shows up in Paris, back from Brazil by sailboat. "I don't blame you for taking another man in my absence," he tells her. "But I am back now and you love me, and you can't kick me out."

"Don't worry, *chéri*," Beatrice attempts to reassure me. "I don't like him, he was awful to me. He just doesn't have any place else to stay. He'll move out as soon as he finds one."

"OK, no problem," I go along. "I guess we'll just have to sleep at my place."

From my window, no matter how far I lean out, I can't see the street below, but like a little dog, I learn the sound of her car engine by heart. I dash downstairs, four steps at a time, to greet her even before she has finished parking her car. Full of passion, she walks with me through the beautiful mirrored entrance downstairs. There's a bounce in her step as we break off our kiss and move up the first flight. By the first floor her pulse is racing. By the second flight of steps she shudders; on the third floor, she asks "Is it much further?" By the fourth floor I offer to carry her. She doesn't like this maid's room, there's nothing romantic about it for her. The peeling grey oil cloth wallpaper, the dust balls on the yellow walls, the wooden steps worn away by countless indigent feet: by the fifth story she has lost all desire.

A week later she has a dinner to attend. She promises to come by at midnight. By four in the morning, heart beating miserably, I am still awake and listening for her car. "I would have called you if you had a phone," she says. One night, two nights: the same thing. I take the cigarette from her mouth, and begin to smoke, anything to touch those sweet lips that she no longer wants to share. Night after night it goes on, Josef Klein bewitching himself into love. I'll do anything for her, polish her stiletto, sharpen her dirk, even get a phone.

"She's driving me crazy," I tell Marie-France. "The phone company says I have to get permission from you."

"You wouldn't be happy if you didn't have problems with a woman," says Marie-France, handing him the note.

"Says you." The phone is installed within two days. Beatrice calls and invites me to dinner. Over rabbit in tomato sauce, I tell her I love her. I've never told any woman that before. She laughs in my face, lights another cigarette and glowers when I take it from her mouth and begin to smoke, so that she has to light another. "Sure you say you love me. But how long is it going to last?" She goes back to my room with me anyway, gets into bed fully dressed, and whines like a young virgin when I try to take her clothes off. A week, two weeks, I get a hard-on when the metro passes five blocks away but she won't give it up for love or mercy. "It doesn't excite me when you're excited," she says.

Caught in Maya's toe-hold, slammed in mid-stride, I write letters to help the time pass. Falling in evol. Did I really think that Beatrice was the one for me? Did I really accept that the mere fact of being exhilarated upon waking every morning, seeing her lying there, was enough? How superficial can you be? And what about her fatigue, her lack of enthusiasm? Temporary malaise, or genetic deformity?

"No one is worth suffering this much over," says Madame Lacombe. Through her weak eyes, even she can see I've been run over by the Times & Tides. "Pretty girls expect too much. *Il faut les choyer*. I don't like to see you unhappy, Josef."

"Can she cook? No?" says the Concierge. "Forget her. Find a girl who will treat you right."

Madame Jeunet puffs up the last steps to the sixth floor and pauses, holding the railing, to catch her breath. "The cigarettes," she says. In the light from the window she notices me looking at her eye. "Oh that? That's nothing. It was at somebody's birthday last night. A champagne cork bounced off the ceiling and right into my face…"

By mid-October I have almost given up completely when the phone rings and she invites me to a party on Avenue Foch. I step inside the door, she sees me and instantly turns away. A few minutes later she wanders over but turns her mouth to the side when I try to kiss her. "Loïc is here. You can't stay."

"What? You've got to be kidding."

"I didn't know he was going to be here, or I wouldn't have invited you."

"That's hardly the point, is it?"

"What do you mean?"

I turn on my heel, storm up the stairs to the front door, and turn around for one last look at her.

"Well aren't you going to kiss me goodbye?" she says.

"What for?"I slam the door and walk all the way home. An hour, pure volcanic rage, don't-anyone-get-in-my-way. A gang of toughs eight-strong sizes me up in the shadows of Avenue Wagram, but I take my hands out of my pockets, stare them down, walk right through the middle of them, just daring them to make their move.

I pace away the whole night. Unable to sleep, unable to calm my twisted guts. I've got to forget her. Nowhere to escape the small room, nothing to take my mind off the rage, the bitterness. I've got to forget her. On my way to American Express, there she is: her picture in the window of the hair salon, advertising a permanent. I turn my head away and yell. Got to forget her. In the metro, there she is again, right next to the PARA lice spray ad, demure, smiling Kelly Girl, luring the unwary to temporary employment. Like a bull with liniment on my balls, I don't know where to run, where to hide, how to get away. I go to karate class at the American Church: "Crocodile walk, up and back. Concentrate. You must get used to pain." But then in the shower doncha know, there she is again, cute as sin on the Babydop shampoo bottle. I scream. Got to forget her. Can't last much longer. What foul curse caused me to put my faith in this heartless gorgon, this merciless fury? I gave myself completely to her, and she trampled me. The city is hollow, forbidding. Once again, every street is a painful reminder of illusory joy, of a moment spent with her, back when those moments were going to last forever. The city laughs at me, mocks me. The buses close their doors in my face, the milk I buy turns sour as soon as I open it, couples stop to laugh and kiss in front of me, deliberately, just to make me miserable. "Forget it. You're going to hate each other. Stop!" I spit, but it doesn't help.

The buzzer of the interphone rings: "Hello, do you believe in world peace?" That voice: it's the Christians again, how did they find me here?

"No!"

"Do you believe in love and happiness?"

"You've got to be kidding! There are parasites in your wafers. The body of Christ is driving the people insane. You know that don't you!"

"Uh, Jesus loves you..." click.

After so long in the wilderness, after so much wasted time, so many women who left me cold after only one night, the fool thought he had found a soul-mate, someone to rely on.

Why are we cursed to put our faith in something so fragile? Please no more pain. I crawl back up the stairs and past Madame Lacombe who nods but doesn't say a word. I open the door to room 18, sit down on the bed and stare at the wall. My heart is crumbling, exploding. Got to find something to keep my mind off it. Got to find something more solid, something that won't betray me. Something that won't betray me. A book.

CHAPTER 8

Winter blasts in like a poodle in formaldehyde, like other winters before. So cold one night that five thousand pigeons and twenty *clochards* never woke up. Honest citizens on the bus, given something to talk about, joke that it was just as well: "You know how much of a nuisance those pigeons can be." France Soir barely has time to get out its "Record-Breaking Cold," headline. Amputee pigeons, the survivors, walk around next morning, their legs bleeding stumps, gnawed off after freezing to their perches while they slept. The Christmas season brings the usual suicides. A policeman dangling a syringe as bait talks a desperate junkie out of leaping off the fifth floor at Beaubourg, a man jumps in front of the metro at Wagram. An old woman looks at her watch and clears her throat in disgust. *"Il aurait pas pu attendre!"* Couldn't he have waited...

Winter. The Firebird fountain next to Beaubourg freezes. The red lips sport long icicles, the white skull is crowned with opaque thorns, the bird of fire is riveted to the ground with frozen wings, and the large red heart drips clear gelid blood.

Winter. An accident at the Union Carbide plant in Bhopal, India, kills 2,500 people and maims countless others. The cloud of toxic gas leaked out while the people slept.

Winter. I read through the six abortive versions of an anti-Utopian novel I have been dabbling with for the last five years now. Called *Fun City*, somewhat in reference to the seeming incapacity of Americans to use any adjective than "fun" any more, it's a story about an isolated metropolis where everything is perfect. Except, as the city approaches its 30th anniversary the citizens are collapsing of boredom in the streets.

The book isn't pretty, the characters don't quite work, the story is too thin, but there is enough material there, it feels prophetic enough, that I don't feel instantly compelled to jump out the window. Wherever I go on my rounds around the city, on the metro, in cafés, trying to get warm at the various familiar hot air vents, I take notes, write a passage or two, move along. To write exceptional books you need to live an exceptional life? This life doesn't feel exceptional, not anymore. But what am I going to do, blame my incapacity on others? In the end, you've either done it, or you

JEFF GROSS

haven't, no excuses. If the outer life is no longer exceptional, if it's no longer the adventure it was, perhaps it's just an opening to the inner life?

Winter. City-Rat and Blackie continue to perform long after everyone else has given up, grey-skinned City-Rat needs the money. Leaning into the howling wind, shirts off, somehow they manage to collect a crowd as they beat each other up in ten below centigrade, even sixteen below, before breaking off the partnership, coming to their senses.

In the off-season the only place warm enough to perform is the metro, and the metro is for musicians, not mimes. As for the musicians, some are talented, soulful, free spirits and travelers, proud enough to play their own tunes: welcome warmth and color in the grey. The rest, pale-skinned vultures squawking out Dylan, the Beatles, the Rolling Stones, Johnny B. Goode, or sappy versions of *Bolero*, guitars and keyboards distorting on crackly amps, hang out at Châtelet metro station, get on the train, play for three stops, brow-beat the passengers for two stops, commuters too embarrassed not to fork over a coin, whichever coin in their pocket first comes to hand, at least one franc, sometimes ten. Then they hop off and do the same thing back in the other direction. The signs in the metro say "Do not encourage the vultures," but in an hour or two a day they make enough to get by. It's a living: Le Maso bar underneath City-Rat's apartment, where they collect to drink expensive pints of beer, play pinball and prepare their souls for hell, is almost always full.

Winter. In Germany, Dorian Strahler's dream doesn't last even half-way through his two year contract. Strahler begins to crack under the strain: impossible to be funny on command two times a day, seven days a week. The circus director who was once Dorian's savior, who shot the videos to teach Dorian to refine, slow down and remove the habits of the street, turns merciless to get his star to perform, begins to ride him a little too hard. Strahler is angry at all the people who refuse to understand him, angry at the imperfections of the world at large. Alone, cooped up in a tiny circus wagon, and never a moment's rest from those fucking lions, Strahler begins to suspect that someone is putting poison in his white-face. He doesn't want the world to be right any more, he doesn't want to be angry, he doesn't want to cross swords with the ocean, he just wants a little peace. He runs away from the circus and checks into a clinic in Switzerland.

City-Rat, skin and bones, deep, dark eye-sockets, mired in yet another Strindbergian whirl, slaps his knee with delight at the image of Strahler throwing his clown away. "You should have seen Strahler," City-Rat says. "The man had his finger on the pulse of the city. No one made 'em laugh the way Strahler did. And City-Rat before he started on the bottle! *Hurler de rire...*" Feeling as low as he does, City-Rat knows exactly how it must have been for Strahler that night when, in tears and desperation, he took his clown suit and threw it in a trash barrel. They were trying to kill him. Who's next?

Winter. I wait outside the door of my building for Beatrice's grey Peugeot. She pulls up and I get in. "I'm just a selfish girl, in case you haven't already noticed."

"Selfish is OK, but you're stupid too," I say. She doesn't like that. "You're so selfish you're penalizing yourself. You could have everything from me. But instead you only get 70%."

"Well 70% isn't that bad..."

"Forget seventy! Ten, or twenty. Jesus you're driving me crazy! How long *is* this going to go on?"

"I didn't want to tell you. Nobody knows. When Loïc and I went to Brazil, I lent him 30,000 francs. He never had any money. He was going to buy emeralds, but he ended up buying cocaine. He brought the stuff back on the sailboat. Now he's selling it so he can pay me back. As soon as he does I kick him out."

"Is that so?"

"That's why I've been so nervous. He's using my apartment to deal in. They come over to the apartment. I keep thinking the cops are going to break down the door. I'm seeing cops everywhere."

"So, how much *does* he owe you?"

"20,000 francs."

"20,000 huh? It's nice to know how much love is worth." Another part of my heart shrivels up and drops off. A part I know will never grow back. "Tell me: if he pays you back 10,000, will you come back to me? 11,000, 12,000. How much *am* I worth to you? How about if I give you 20,000?"

"Come on. Don't say that. Just be patient." She knows I don't have such a sum in hand. What is it, about $3000? My life for $3000...

"I'm leaving, going to the States," I tell her, shaking my head.

"Why?" She's honestly surprised.

"If you want me, you can come get me. If not, thanks for a nice moment or two."

Loïc finally pays Beatrice back, all but 6,000 francs, leaving an ugly green painting, supposedly worth a lot of money, as collateral for the rest. She changes the locks, throws his stuff out on the landing, asks him for her keys back so he won't figure out that she changed the locks, escorts him to the train at Gare de Lyon, and buys herself a ticket to LA. We try to fix what is broken, but I'm not sure we really do.

Forced to move out of his tiny maid's room over by Saint Georges, Akro the clown asks about the possibility of taking over Room 19. He'll hardly be there, he says, he has various contracts around Europe, he just needs a place to stash his gear, two trunks full of props, clown shoes and costumes.

"Why not?" I say, Angel is still nowhere in sight, "As long as you understand that if he comes, the room is his."

Which is how, on the sixth floor, when Akro's trunks finally appear, the lingering smell of decomposing beef filet and Madame Lacombe's decay is supplemented by a further olfactory texture, the stench of Akro's rotting sweat socks, of which there appear to be an inexhaustible supply. A few months later, hair grown out, yellow stain on the insides of middle and index finger from the roll-your-owns he has begun to smoke, milk-fed innocence all but disappeared, replaced by the indigenous pallor that comes from drinking too much bad *robusta* espresso, he moves out again and into the cross-town apartment of a French lass he met while on tour in Sicily, so that by November, when I return to Paris, I have a new neighbor in Number 19, an American painter named Zoff. I'm not overly pleased. Zoff has a way of talking and slinking about, a slanted look in the eye, that says Akro mentioned Angel to him when he handed over the keys, but told him to pretend he didn't know. Angel still can't get his act together to make it back to Paris, perhaps he never will, so it isn't really an issue, but the sneakiness doesn't leave a good first impression.

It takes a couple of weeks for Zoff to get Akro's trunks out of Room 19, and with them the odor of rotting socks. He pulls down the bits of wrinkled wallpaper, splashes on a coat of white paint, tacks a few photos up on the walls, brings in a piece of lime green carpet, and a tape player, then invites me over for coffee to make peace. Pastels of terra-cotta-roofed houses, and pictures of dancing men, his sketch book is a little too heavy on the pinks, not heavy enough on the blues for my taste. Another one of many American artists I've met who flock to Paris in desperate need of a swift kick in the teeth to wake up and actually open their eyes. But he certainly is devoted, and serious about his work. From his wallet he pulls a small slip of paper, a quote from Hokusai that he's carried ever since the age of 14: "From the age of five I have had a mania for sketching the forms of things. From about the age of 50 I produced a number of designs, yet of all I drew prior to the age of 70 there was truly nothing of any great note. At the age of 73 I finally apprehended something of the true quality of birds, animals, insects, fishes, and of the vital natures of grasses and trees. Therefore at 80 I shall have made some progress, at 90 I shall have penetrated even further the deeper meaning of things, at 100 I shall have become truly marvelous and at 110, each dot, each line shall surely possess a life of its own. I only beg for gentlemen of sufficiently long life to care to note the truth of my words."

Marie-France, Mme. Tournier, Monsieur Corsano, the whole building is delighted to have a *bona fide* painter in residence above them. And so nice! If the smell of turpentine coming from Zoff's room bothers Madame Lacombe, she barely mentions it. The piano concertos that drift under his door as soon as he wakes up remind her of her youth. She tells him about her victory in the piano competition at the *Conservatoire* in 1935. Without going out of his way, he does little favors for her, fetching something for her at the street market, or picking her mail out of the plastic bag at the bottom of the stairs and handing it to her: bank statements, electricity and phone, the cancer society, the insurance company, or *Les Amis*, the charitable organization responsible for sending Madame Jeunet. Even the Concierge is pleased when she goes through Zoff's garbage and finds empty paint tubes and used brushes: proof beyond doubt that he is what he claims to be. "Tell him that my husband is a painter too," she tosses out to me in passing. "If he ever needs any money, there's always work to be had."

Spring isn't really supposed to rush in fully until April, but there is a glimmer of it in early March. The first flowers pop up in Parc Monceau and the optimists shed their heavy winter clothing. The sky is almost too blue, but instead of the deep cold of winter blue-skies, these pre-spring clearings let the sun warm the bones. I sit in *Le Weekend* café on Avenue Wagram, where I have gotten in the habit of going when a letter comes, or I'm feeling rich enough to pay for a sit-down coffee, and do a pastel drawing of a red and yellow primavera. Trying my hand at colors, a more peaceful, more harmonious state than writing, I shudder at the sun coming in the window, as the winter lets go, the blood races through my veins. The peroxide blonde is posted at her usual spot at the bar. Standing on the counter, her Yorkshire terrier trades sips of kir with her, eating the peanuts and sugar lumps she holds out to him in between cigarettes. At the table behind me, four old women with rouge on their cheeks, and one old man with a hearing aid, a cane, and a red *Legion d'honneur liseret* in his lapel, discuss *la grande guerre*, the way they do every day. The dour café *serveuse* sees me smiling like that, and she cannot help but smile too. I take the stairs back to the sixth floor three by three, and pat Madame Lacombe on the ass as I go by.

On the street, the police begin a vendetta. The policy: to snuff out the last breath of life in Gray Paree. It is only permitted to perform in certain areas, Beaubourg, the Forum des Halles, Saint Germain and sometimes Rue St. Denis or Saint Michel. But the restricted zones seem to change, or multiply, on a whim, and not just because the shows disturb the residential areas. Jugglers juggle with one eye on their clubs and torches, and one eye scanning the horizon for signs of blue police lights. Mimes build their walls without mortar.

One week, notices are posted to the effect that henceforth the Forum des Halles is to be closed to performers. The Forum des Halles: levels one, two and three of the inferno, canned music and neon lights, full of shops with new fashions, and everything you will never need, to keep you in limbo. Robert Sleet does a show there anyway. A spectator has just finished strapping him into his straitjacket when six cops burst into his circle and surround him. They grab him roughly by the arms and escort him, still wearing the straitjacket, to the police precinct at the top of the escalators, as passersby gawk, open-mouthed.

Willie the Dadaist, dressed-in-pink, a tattoo on his knee, his wild hair held in place by a rubber band, publishes a protest letter in *Libération* about the harassment of street artists by the police. He decides to chain himself to a tree in front of the *Deux Magots*. A gag in his mouth, and on his chest a sign: "Don't panic, the police have been called."

When the police actually *do* arrive, they tie into him with truncheons and fists, try to tear him away from the tree. As he slumps, the chain slips around his neck and begins to choke him: resisting arrest. They beat him until he is half-conscious, before it occurs to them to undo the chains, then throw him into the paddy wagon and hold him overnight.

City-Rat's apartment on Rue Saint-André-des-Arts remains the gathering point for the street artists and occasionally the reunions explode into the old joy, drunken dancing, guitar playing, naked processions that last into the wee hours. But there is a hint of pretending, of pushing the joviality to the limits, a frantic taste as if everyone knows that it is all over but for the dancing.

Most nights dwarfs bearing bottles of wine come over to the apartment to fill the air with clouds of marsh-gas and sulfur. Real cases, all of them. Memorized tripe, stuffed philosophers, adopted opinions, third-hand jokes from fourth-rate humor merchants. City-Rat smiles gamely, but his heart isn't in it. "I need a woman," he moans. The wine flows, he just wants to feel light for even the briefest moment, and so what if the alcohol leaves him flatter and flatter each morning-after?

"Look at that smile you're wearing. These motherfuckers are wearing you down. Why don't you just tell them to fuck off?" I ask.

"It's easy to see the negative things. If you're unable to see the enthusiasm in other people, it's your own fault," City-Rat answers.

"Yeah, but what if you lose your spirit looking for it?"

Prisoner of the mirror, far from the magic of an Amsterdam hospital, City-Rat has his *thumb* on the pulse of the city. Getting older, his blood now a sludge of coffee, cigarettes and bread, he barely has enough energy to cross the street. What is there worth seeing on the other side anyway?

The Chewing Gum, The Cowboy, The Crow, whenever he needs money he pulls out his old standards and shows them in front of the *Deux Magots*, or Beaubourg. From the outside it sounds magical, sounds free, but the newness has long worn off. "Nothing's happening in Paris anymore," City-Rat says, but he's been saying the same thing since last summer. Nourished by the dream of the last golden age, forgetting that the next golden age is just a snap of the fingers away.

"If nothing's happening it's because we're not making it happen," I say, which is more or less *my* line. The freedom we have seems so alluring, but it's a tremendous responsibility. The man who clocks in five times a week has his life planned for him, his tasks lined up beforehand. No imagination required to come up with something new, no rigor to make sure the brain stays active. And frankly it's a responsibility, a test, which most of us seem to be failing.

"You just don't understand!" City-Rat snaps, his left eyebrow arching into an inverted vee. "You can't just *do* it, you got to go through some heavy shit. You come around here saying that if I only start creating again, everything will be all right. Don't you get it yet? Comedy begins in tragedy. Your woman has just left you, your partner stole your whole act, someone snatched your bag, you got no money left, and you go down to Beaubourg to do a show. You feel weak with hunger, dizzy. Finally you get the circle going, and just then, it starts to rain. The crowd disperses, runs for cover under the overhang. 'You either commit suicide, or you laugh...'"

Maybe the tragedy just isn't serious enough these days, maybe he isn't desperate enough anymore. Who knows? The tragedy just seems to go on and on. The tragedy goes on and on, and no humor on the horizon. If he's right, the comedy can't be far behind.

City-Rat finally manages to get a few jobs to keep body, if not soul intact. He gets the part of a *voyou*, a suburbs punk, a *zonard*, in a play called *Macadam Quichotte*. It is an adaptation of *Don Quixote*, transposed to modern times. Instead of windmills, the modern Quixote jousts with the perennially malfunctioning Parisian telephone booths. The idea is plausible, the Plexiglas set interesting, but the script and execution by the leftist *Théâtre de la Jacquerie* lamentable. No matter how accurate the joke about the phones may be, the endlessly frustrating, forever out-of-order, coin-gobbling Parisian phones, the joke gets a bit thin after a while. During rehearsals, except for one old guy, the other actors seem to have no idea what they are doing, no professionalism. And every time they can't figure out what to do, they break for coffee. City-Rat doesn't want to say anything, after all, his is only a minor role, but the problem is so obvious that after three weeks of rehearsals he can't help but speak up. "Enough coffee!" he screams and slams his fist down on the stage. They are supposed to be pros, but they are exactly like the students at Le Coq: repressed impulses, instincts filtered through the rational mind. They won't get it in a thousand years of coffee. The actor has to feel with his body, his heart, his guts. They're French: it's not their fault, it's what their education has taught them. "Look, I think I know what you're trying to get at," City-Rat says. "Like this? Like this? That's it, isn't it? That's what you wanted, right?" The lack of sensitivity leaves a bad taste in his mouth. Finally he's made it inside, but he's almost embarrassed to have his friends see the show. Four months! Four months in this prison. Coming to work, going home.

"I just got to stop worrying about the others," he says. "Do my ten minutes the best I can..." The cobblestone grass at Beaubourg is beginning to look greener all the time. Beaubourg is a jungle, but at least he can do his show, then head home. His Italian ex-girlfriend has loaned him 10,000 francs to buy a wireless microphone. He wants to experiment with it, he has some ideas for a one-man show. At night, unable to sleep, City-Rat draws calligraphic pictures of geometric dragons. But the dragon he is really interested in now is the one inside him. And the Dragon wants to come out. By the end of four months, City-Rat is off-center, hollow and even greyer than before he started. They pressure him to sign on for the winter tour of the play through the provinces. They attack his lack of solidarity, promise him help to put on his one-man show after the winter tour, offer to raise his price, ask him to think about how nice it would be to be inside next winter, and money in the pocket. "No, I can't."

The money from *Quichotte* soon runs out, and City-Rat is suddenly in the hole 2000 francs, his monthly rent. He gets a call from an Italian mime: they need someone to perform in a skit for a government insurance program. Six days at 600 francs a day. I catch the show at Miromesnil metro station. The soundtrack blares while a "typical French family," runs through its daily life, skits which invariably end in calamity: a fire in the house, another child born, an intestine that refuses to digest, a camembert exploding.

"*Ayez le reflexe fleur bleu,*" the speakers belt out, City-Rat's cue to appear on stage. Very sweet, *papier maché* blue flower in hand, he casts loving *Pierrot* eyes at the flower and the commuters, hypnotizing them into missing a metro or two. Behind them, on my way home from Shiva, out of sight, I have to laugh, in sympathy and sorrow, the tragedy is too poignant. To laugh to keep from crying. The point where laughter and tragedy intersect, the matrix where eternity and evolution bisect the most unbearable banality. The greatest clown in the Western world reduced to this.

Because of his problems paying the rent, City-Rat's landlady reclaims her apartment on Rue Saint-André-des-Arts, but gives him another, less expensive, on the sixth floor of a building on Rue Monge, in the 5th *arrondissement*, high above the *Arènes de Lutece*. What is this, the tenth, the eleventh place he's lived in the last seven years? Here we go again.

The season of melancholy finally ends with a last job that falls in his lap: the part of a clown in a film called *Music Hall 42*, starring Simone Signoret. It's another small role, a bit of acrobatics and visual clowning, involving juggling a tray. For three weeks, day and night, he bounces that wooden tray off the floors and walls of his apartment until he can make it lie down and pee on command. Three weeks, the color comes back to his cheeks. "They'll see."

When filming starts, City-Rat takes over. Flying over the bar, swinging off of the pipes on the ceiling, tumbling over the tables, dancing with the tray, he can't be contained. When he sits down at the table with Simone Signoret, he points his finger at her, winks, rolls his eyes, points his finger again. In no time, she's laughing so hard that they need five, sometimes ten takes before she can say her lines properly. Signoret is overwhelmed. "You're very talented, young man," she says. Finally! It's City-Rat's big break.

CHAPTER 9

Beatrice's phone no longer rings half as often with offers of work modeling. She is obliged to sell herself at castings now, when before she was so hot, a "10," that she was hired sight unseen. "Pick your ticket up at the airport. When you get to Nairobi, you take a small plane out to the game reserve."

When the phone rings, more often than not, she has her answering machine on to find out who it is. And if she's forgotten to turn it on, she asks me to answer and say she's not in, which I simply refuse to do. For her it's incomprehensible, this lack of solidarity, this American moralism, this lack of life sense, this balking at telling just one tiny lie.

"It's not that at all," I try to explain, "You're hiding from the world..."

She clears her throat angrily. *"Qu'est ce que tu peux être chiant parfois."*

At the age of 29, she probably still looks more like 23, but it doesn't matter. "They're tired of my face." After six years in the business, she's tired of the game too. When she *does* get work, the days leave her empty, cold. "The photographer was so slow," she complains. "They expect the girls to be sixteen years old, to shut up. They won't hire me again."

In truth, we make a most strange pair. Me, the wandering son of Times & Tides, penniless, but still resolutely convinced that I was born under a lucky star. Beatrice, rich enough after eight years in modeling to have paid for an apartment, to have a comfortably padded bank account, and still convinced that she was born cursed, that if something bad is going to happen, it's going to happen to her. The traffic light will turn red as soon as her car appears, the last ticket will be sold for the movie just as she steps up to the booth, she will be in the running for a modeling job until it comes down to her and another girl, and the other girl will get the nod.

At night, before going to bed, she examines her ass in the mirror, tries to figure out poses, profiles, hip cocked, foot on tiptoes, so that she can get away, one more time, with doing bathing suit ads. There's a possibility of a job in Mauritius in August. But even if they take her, what will happen after that? What happens to a woman who made a fortune with her beauty, when she begins to grow old, when she loses that beauty? "I don't want to talk about it." Other models get married and have babies, other models work at the desk in the agency, other models die of drug overdoses or become kept women in fur coats, even porno actresses. What is she going to do after her career is over, what are her options? "I don't want to talk about it." She signs up for a theater school, maybe she can prolong her career a bit by acting in commercials. On the application form she writes her age: 25.

"You've got to trust me!" I try my best to reassure her. "I'm not Loïc. It's Josef. I'm here..." But it's no good, in her eyes I'm the male, the oppressor, the one who will chain her to the kitchen just like her father chained her mother, (even though I do all the cooking, because she can't even boil water or heat a croissant without burning it). I'm the very beast Simone de Beauvoir and her sisters warned her about. I'm Loïc, I'm her father, I'm every other man who has ever wronged her, from Adam to Yves.

Too many wounds, too many broken hearts, too much lost idealism, the whole generation is damaged goods: I understand why she might be reticent to open up. Still her silent mysteriousness has begun to weigh on me. I try everything: dinners, walks in the park, self-sacrificial little weekends at her parents' country house talking about nice little cheeses , but it's no use: the face that hides 1001 mysteries seems determined to continue hiding them. "God you bug me sometimes," she says.

Every morning at 6 a.m., the alley next to the bedroom reverberates with the sound of garbage trucks. Then the delivery trucks pull in to resupply the grocery. When they are done, it is time for the symphony, horns honk loud and long to bring down the owners of the double-parked vehicles blocking the way. Awakened by the commotion, a lonely German shepherd howls for company. Beatrice puts a blindfold over her eyes, and *boules quiès* ear plugs in her ears to shut out the world.

Somehow, some why, too tired to fight, too weak not to succumb, after a year together, Beatrice and I still manage moments of intimacy, total absorption. But the other seven days of the week, our maladaptation seems painfully apparent. Just living a regular domestic situation, not walking the streets, coming home to her every night has restricted my knowledge of the city, taken away my lightness. The TV is on too much, the blackout curtains are drawn so she can sleep late in the morning. Her silence weighs on me. I try my best to overcome it all, but it's a losing battle. Inertia, I discover, is infinitely more powerful than kinesis.

The further I get into *Fun City*, the more I wonder whether the writing way leaves any room for a woman, for a social life at all. How can she understand this need to be merciless, subjective as a way of attaining the universal? She hasn't walked the streets, she has never turned on herself, she's used to tickets to Kenya falling in her lap. How can "I don't want to talk about it," understand the artist's desire to create a world where the deprivations of the soul are erased? How can anyone comprehend my need to become a weapon with which to exact a certain revenge, with which to pour out a denunciation sufficiently loaded with anger and ridicule to make a point, to write an ode to life, an antidote to viciousness, thoughtlessness, lovelessness, collective insanity, and so what if the excesses, the lack of moderation, the lack of skill leave the impression of immaturity, of lack of compassion? How can I share with a woman in blindfolds and earplugs that I am sick to death of easy moderation, scared to death of the easy mean, of a future of mediocrity? How can I explain what it means never to belong?

Beatrice pays for us to go skiing in Val d'Isère, a long weekend with a few of her friends. Spring skiing, the last weekend of the season. "You're an American writer? Like Hemingway, *hein*." Who has the most references, who knows the most book titles? "You haven't read that? I'm surprised. A writer like Hemingway, and you haven't read *Babar and Father Christmas*!"

To my left is the expert on grammar, poised like a little dog, ready to correct the slightest deviation from linguistic canon. To his right, squinting behind his massively thick glasses, is the pretentious advertising executive who thinks the fascists aren't entirely wrong. The workers at the Renault factory, so many North Africans, pull out their prayer rugs at noon. It's a disgrace. Not only that: but a French acquaintance of his has been forced to move out of his building in the 9th because he was the only white person left, because the Arabs cook 400 kilos of garlic a day to make *harissa*. Before moving out he had gone upstairs one night to complain about the children roller skating on his ceiling. An Arab woman came to the door and called out to her husband, "*Il y a un blanc à la porte*." There's a White at the door...

"More wine? This is a good little wine, isn't it?" With a sigh of relief, the man across from me leads us to more neutral ground. "I'm quite fond of the little wines of Savoie." Argyle socks and Argyle sweaters, how is it that the same people seem to come to every dinner I attend?

"Eh Beatrice, your boyfriend doesn't talk much. Tell us Josef: what do the Anglo-Saxons think about French culture?"

"You really want to know? Speaking as a Ukrainian-Lithuanian Cherokee, they think it's moribund, necrophiliac, a corpse connected to a battery. They think it's because of the *Pari de Pascal*, what a bunch of cowards. You either believe that God exists, or you don't. What is this bullshit about 'Well I don't really know, so I better play it safe, just in case?' How do you expect culture to prosper when the artists won't step outside unless there is a net to catch them? That's what the 'Anglo Saxons' think about French culture, *cher ami*. Not only that, but they think Prowst is overrated."

"We say it Proost, not Prowst," says the expert on grammar. "And if you don't like it here, why don't you leave?"

"Hmm..." Did Henry Miller never encounter people like this? Were they not alive back then? Or in his self-mythologizing, did he simply neglect to mention them?

The largest laser in the world is unveiled at Lawrence Livermore Lab, in California in connection with US President Ronald Reagan's Star Wars defense program. The size of a football field, the $176 million device called Shiva is intended to help scientists simulate atomic explosions, and study nuclear fusion energy. Jean Bedel Bokassa, deposed dictator of the Central African Republic is photographed at Chateau d'Hardricourt with his 55th child, Jean Bedel. In Florida, a water-skiing parrot steals the show. In East Beirut, a car bomb kills 50, and injures 200. In Rome, 27 year-old Ali Agca, the Turk who shot Pope John Paul on May 13, 1981, is finally put on trial. "In the name of the omnipotent god," he fulminates, "I announce the end of the world. The world will be destroyed." In Brussels, May 29, 1985, drunken English hooligans stampede at the European Cup Finals at Heysel Stadium: 38 dead, crushed and suffocated. The match between Juventus and Liverpool goes on anyway, ending in a 1-0 victory for the Italian team. Palestinian residents of the Sabra and Chatila refugee camps are massacred by Amal Shi'ite forces. Arabs killing each other, that's the way it's supposed to be. The newspapers hardly let out a peep. Hard to dispute Ali Agca.

My old Smith-Corona portable gives up the ghost with a puff of smoke, and is replaced by a sleek *silent* Canon typewriter, which uses small cassettes in lieu of ribbons, and which is compact enough to carry back and forth from maid's room to Beatrice's apartment. A few days later, I find some filing cabinets abandoned on Avenue Wagram, and those too quickly end up on the sixth floor. Caught up in the spirit of office upgrade, Beatrice, bless her heart, contributes an office chair from IKEA, padded, adjustable, with wheels, then heads down to Milan for the summer fashion season, taking photos, or being taken by *Bellalugosi* magazine, and flying back every other weekend when she gets too tired of being surrounded by lecherous playboys: the rich, slicked-hair flies who swarm around the hotels where the models stay, invite them to dinner, lure them up to their villas at Lake Garda.

In Beatrice's absence, I walk the streets again with eyes wide open, indulge the most outrageous thoughts, turn into fiction again. Now that I have a phone, it seems strange that it doesn't ring, but after the first week or so I begin to get used to the solitude again. An invisible couple moves in to Room 17, M. Corsano's daughter and her seaman husband. They come home every night at about midnight, close the shades then jump into the sack. She moans wildly for a minute then feigns a climax. In the morning they are gone.

"It lasts a minute, I don't even have time to get excited," I say.

"*I'l y en a qui sont plus rapides*," Madame Lacombe smiles from the end of the hall. Some are just quicker than others.

Left to myself, I Xerox the first 175 pages of *Fun City* and take them down to City-Rat's for safekeeping. "If the right bank burns down, then we'll still have your copy," I say. "If the left bank burns, then we'll still have the original. And if the whole city burns, what better sign that I wasn't meant to be a writer?"

Back from Milan, Beatrice has picked up a strange laugh, a high, thin, hollow model's laugh that hasn't the slightest connection to humor. What is this now?

"Where on earth did you get that laugh?" I clap my hands over my ears.

"What do you mean?" She honestly isn't aware of it.

"Never mind, I'm sorry. I guess it's just hard for me to be with people after spending so much time writing." She turns over in bed and refuses to talk.

The next morning she calls up her sister, who says "It's not easy living with a writer, I imagine." At tea, a friend of hers shows her the jacket of a book which says: "It isn't possible to write a novel and love a woman at the same time." She feels better. She sets her face to weather the storm and arranges for me to get a bank account. She needs to launder some money from her work in Italy, or so she says. She invites me to join her on the yearly pilgrimage to the Ile d'Oleron, but I turn her down. "It's OK," she says, but when I come back from Gare d'Austerlitz after putting her on the train, I find a note on the Canon: "I love you and need you too much   so iI will not see you for a while because you are afraid of the wickness of anybody you are   too strong for me for the moment, too powerful adn I feel too low, too wick in front of the indestructible wall." I-don't-want-to-talk-about-it's first declaration of intimacy, or was she just practicing her typing on the new machine?

Around the city, everyone talks of summer and where they will be going on vacation. I dream of going any number of places, but am resigned to staying in Paris. With only some $500 to my name, money being what it is, I debate long and hard about accepting the offer of summer employ at Shiva Press. I finally decide, regardless of the position it will put me in come September, up to which point the $500, if watched carefully, may just last, the crucial thing is to gestate *Fun City*. I don't mind filling in from time to time, but I must write the book. Only then can life begin anew.

The weather turns hot briefly, but then turns nice and cool, rain at least once a day, around three o'clock, so that the fan I spend 350 francs on during the hot spell, 10% of my remaining money, looks quite out of place. Beatrice's money finally comes from Italy, and much to my amusement, suddenly the bank can't do enough for me. "Visa card? Car loan? Apartment?"

Going down: working alone again, City-Rat begins to die with increasing frequency. A hundred ways to die, a tragic age. Die drowning, die hanging, die run over by a car. With his hepatitis-tinged skin and the dark circles under the eyes, the way his ribs show on his skinny frame, he looks like he is on his last legs anyway, disbelief is easily suspended.

He's been working for 30 minutes on the *plateau* at Beaubourg, the show is about to end. He gets an idea. He asks for a cigarette *"une blonde,"* gets a light, then retreats to the middle of the circle and takes two, three large drags. He exhales a huge cloud as the nicotine rushes. His tongue sticks way out, he succumbs to the pleasure. "Ha, ha," the demonic sounds come from the depths of his gut. Surprised, they laugh at the bizarre sight. Another two drags: the smoke consumes him, it is no longer pleasure but compulsion. His back curves, his head lowers, and he takes two more puffs, his face now distorted into mad caricature which draws howls of mirth from the circle. Two more heavy hits and the cigarette is three quarters gone. He twists and falls to the ground, half-homunculus, half-fetus, trying to throw the cigarette away but unable. With one hand he tries to hold the cig away, but the other hand brings it back to his mouth. His eyes sink into his skull, his jaw locks down, and his hand trembles as he takes one last puff. Feeling quite dizzy, he reaches for his hat and places it in front of him. His hand goes limp on the cobblestones and he dies to wild applause. He pulls in nearly 400 francs, twice as much as before.

I continue to have the usual peripheral relationships, the Concierge, Madame Lacombe, Madame Jeunet, Pierrot the vegetable salesman on Rue Poncelet and Saint Loto at *le Brazza*, but City-Rat is about the only person I still go out of my way to see. I catch the end of his show and we walk back to his apartment. "Dupont used to tell us: *'Ne vous en faîtes pas, personne ne vous aime,'*" City-Rat says. Don't worry, nobody loves you. "I guess it was to help us keep from being destroyed if we got on stage and it didn't work. But he began to take this really far. *Bouffon*. I wasn't *d'accord*. Heavy stuff. Hea-vy. I just had to stop."

"*Bouffon?*"

Distorting his features, playing the parts, City-Rat tells me about *bouffon*, a style of theater from the Middle Ages in which all the actors were deformed: club-feet, hunchbacks, noseless, armless, midgets. Born to be the butt of jokes, to be scapegoats, to be humiliated, when they got old enough, when they could take no more, they would flee to the forest where they would meet up with others like them and would band together into theater troupes specializing in re-enacting historical montages. A nativity scene with a midget as the baby Jesus and a clubfoot giant as Mary, a hare-lip, a hunchback and a hydrocephalic as the three kings.

"'Imagine,' Dupont would set the scene, 'that you have been hunted from your village. Now you have returned to make your torturers laugh at your grotesqueness.'" City-Rat says. "I can't avoid it anymore. My deformity is the dragon, the violence in me. I go down to Beaubourg: freak out, make 'em laugh, whoopee! Make 'em love me. But Dupont's right: they don't love me. The dragon. I tried to ignore it, but I can't anymore."

Winter finally lets go for good mid-June. In a most amazing show, the collective mood seems to gladden overnight. Partly responsible for the turnabout is a free concert held on the Place de la Concorde, thanks to *SOS Racisme*, an organization set up by an articulate *Antillais* black with the magnificent name of Harlem Desir, to draw attention to the alarming rise of racism in France, to mobilize against the increasingly ugly National Front Party, Jean Marie Le Pen's outfit, which seems to be attracting the least intelligent, most emotionally crippled bunch of collectivist scoundrels since Tom Brownshirt's school days.

SOS Racisme first gains visibility thanks to the sales of hand-shaped pins on whose palms are written the slogan, "*Touche pas à mon pote*," ("Don't Touch My Pal") five francs apiece, you pick the color. Thousands of these "Stop!" buttons are snapped up in a few months. "*Touche pas mon pote*," becomes the punch line of hundreds of jokes before the winds of style change once again, and the buttons fall apart or are stuffed back into drawers, forgotten. The concert, a consciousness-raising event, is put on with the profits.

Behind Place de la Concorde, the *Grand Palais* glows red from the summer sun setting through its transparent roof. The bridge is jammed. On the classical background of the *Jeu de Paume* and Rue de Rivoli, huge inflatable "*Touche Pas à Mon Pote*" hands float, fingers to the sky, next to the two stages, a montage like the de Chirico painting, *Song of Love*, upside-down.

500,000 show at the concert, including Lucien and me, unexpectedly large attendance which the organizers attribute to the common concern for racism, and which I attribute rather to the common interest in the free offering of music. Of the bands who donate their talents, the only ones of international stature are Murray Head, or Téléphone, performing their hit, *Je rêvais d'un autre monde*, I dreamed of another world, accompanied by an enthusiastic audience of idealistic young girls, screaming the too-true lyrics as loud as they can.

For the most part the remaining groups are unfortunately both lousy *and* anonymous. The highlight: an Italian group with a Neapolitan Rap number which has me in stitches, much to the consternation of 499,999 of my closest *potes*, who are of the opinion that Neapolitans should be entitled to express their heritage any way they see fit.

"*Téléphone, téléphone,*" the crowd yells, thumbs and pinkies in the air, a very weird sight. I turn to Lucien and start miming and yelling out the names of other domestic appliances, refrigerators, televisions, microwave ovens, as if trying to blend in. "*Mon frère,* you must understand the cultural context," a Ramadan-weakened Arab very generously offers to elucidate. "*Téléphone* is the name of a group..."

Six days later, Bread and Circus, Part II, it's the *Fête de la Musique,* the summer solstice, and the streets are alive, vibrant, the grey city dressed up in its finest. An amazing moment, the old city finally opening up, a pandemic of joy. Exhilarating. Everyone is playing an instrument, Samba bands snake through the streets, the old dance with the young. *Carnaval* exists so that fools, who cannot be expected to remember the dates of holidays, can celebrate in one day, all the forgotten occasions of the year. "Yes," says Beatrice, "But if every day were like this, how would we know how to appreciate it?"

Chapter eight, chapter nine, chapter ten, I go down to Shiva to Xerox as soon as the work comes off the press. Some days I work so much that when I step outside, I'm in a trance, hallucinating. Stars dance in front of my eyes, pedestrians cross my field of vision like disembodied ghosts. Fractured, out of rhythm with the city, I am nonetheless in rhythm with myself, flying from the diet of writing.

A psychedelic-painted Rolls Royce that used to belong to the late John Lennon, is auctioned at Sotheby's in New York for $2.29 million. Stephanie is snapped wearing almost nothing at the Monte Carlo boat club. A TWA jet is hijacked and Robert Dean Stethem, a Navy Diver, is shot in the head and dumped on the tarmac in Algiers by men in blue hoods. The plane flies on to Beirut, where the rest of the passengers are removed to a secret location. An Air India jet explodes off the coast of Ireland: 329 dead.

Blackie signs a contract with Fuji Television in Japan to go over there and do street shows. They agree that he will give them six hours work a day for eleven days. They had seen him on the *plateau* at Beaubourg and they want to make him a star in Japan, bring street theater to the Land of the Rising Sun. But they haven't really thought it through. Unfortunately, when he arrives in Tokyo, it is July, the rainy season. Not only that but they don't understand what it takes to establish a circle for street theater. They take him to places where he is expected to perform in the middle of avenues, fighting off traffic. No matter how hard he coaxes, the spectators line up behind hedges on either side of the thoroughfare, not crazy enough to jump into rush hour traffic with the mime. "No interaction with spectators, no street show," Blackie tries to explain. "What do you think of Japan?" they answer. "You like Japan?"

Back at the studio, he is wide-eyed at the display of technology. 3-D video! They could make mime work on TV. Just be patient. But the comedy of errors continues. There's a different cameraman every day, and not one of them has caught the good moments of his show. He can't even try and explain it to them, his translator doesn't speak English. "What do you think of Japan? You like Japan?" He signed to give them six hours a day, but because of their clumsiness, and lack of foresight, the work day sometimes stretches out to twelve hours. Into the van, out of the van, set up equipment, pack equipment, into the van. The steam is rising; he may be just a street artist to them, but they don't know that he is the apostle of mime, and not a very patient apostle at that. To hell with the future and 3-D video, Blackie finally explodes. He rails against the organizers, calls the director incompetent, "You give me a translator who doesn't even speak English, your cameramen move the camera around arbitrarily, take shots of traffic while the crowd is laughing at the expression on my face, come in tight on my face while the humor is in the movement in my hands. You want to know what I think of your country? It's like Blade Runner."

City-Rat begins to take singing lessons from a Polish woman named Jolanta. After the first few lessons, she hardly lets him sing at all, she can hear in his voice that he is disturbed, unhealthy and that's the first thing they have to fix. She goads him, accuses him of running from himself, of actually desiring the condition into which he has fallen: poverty, strife, tempestuous relationships with women. He gets furious with her, sometimes he cries for the whole hour. But he comes back every week, and he has to go down to Beaubourg to make enough money to pay her, 150 francs an hour.

In Blackie's absence, Akro becomes the King of Beaubourg. He juggles a Diablo, throwing it up to the fifth floor of Beaubourg, he sweats, he drinks water from a Perrier bottle, steps on his red bucket assumes a pose like a fountain and spits it out, saying "*Perrier c'est fou.*" They laugh because they're supposed to, the Perrier commercial has been out for half a year already.

After a thousand, two thousand shows on the *plateau*, Akro has learned an important lesson: with the proper circle it almost doesn't matter what your act is as long as the timing looks sharp and you keep the speed up. Stolen gags, repetitive humor, reading the phone book, eviscerating a pigeon. Broken-hearted, City-Rat watches Akro pull the money out of his hat; Akro is now making more than he.

Zoff flies back to America for the summer and Madame Jeunet leaves for vacation, *dans son pays*. The young Guadeloupian woman who replaces her informs Madame Lacombe that she will not be able to come on Saturdays. She must take care of her child. Madame Lacombe accuses her of lying. "She has no child. They're all the same. She just doesn't want to work." What Madame Lacombe is really worried about is that she will have no one to buy her a piece of meat for Sunday. The weight of eighty-two years crashes down on her, her loneliness, her bitterness, her illnesses, all because of 150 grams of choice *filet de boeuf.*

"If that's all it is, let me do the shopping for you," I say.

The Concierge is hanging up her laundry in the courtyard as I pass on my way back up. "Sure, but she won't give you anything. She sent my little boy out, and didn't give him anything. She has bags of gold in her mattress," she spits as she stuffs three clothespins in her mouth and hangs up a shirt in record time. "You know she used to be the cashier at the Lido," she says, nodding and miming as if to say we both know you don't do a job like that without filling your pockets.

121 steps later, Madame Lacombe is waiting for me at the top of the stairs. I hand her the change, the receipts and the meat, she reaches into her little coin purse to give me something for my trouble. There may have been times in the last years when I could have used the help, but this is different, this is need. "No, no, I couldn't."

Chapter Eleven, Chapter Twelve, Chapter Thirteen. Stephanie of Monaco gets a new boyfriend, Patrice Rayot. They are photographed piloting a jet ski off the Monte Carlo Beach Club. A Shiva photographer disappears in Beirut while covering the TWA hostages. Scientists in Germany calculate that one million tons of unfiltered sulfur dioxide belch into the atmosphere every year. They figure that the ecological clock has been set back 25,000 years with lignite coal sulfur damage. The *Rainbow*

Warrior, the Greenpeace flagship preparing to lead a protest against French nuclear explosions in the South Pacific, is sunk in the harbor of Auckland, New Zealand, killing Fernando Pereira, a 35 year-old Dutch photographer of Portuguese parents, who drowned in his cabin when he couldn't get free of the sinking ship. In Geneva, three Israelis are exchanged for 1155 Palestinians. In Southern Lebanon, a 16 year-old Arab girl kills herself after driving a Peugeot 504 car bomb into an Israeli control post. She left behind a video suicide letter, in which she explained that she only hoped to kill as many Jews as possible. In London, following the success of the song *Do They Know It's Christmas?* 72,000 rock fans crowd into Wembley stadium for the "Live Aid" concert. The second part of the so-called "Global Jukebox" takes place in Philadelphia, where, following the success of the song *We Are The World*, rock musicians perform in front of 90,000. The two shows raise some $50 million for Ethiopian famine relief.

Back from Japan, raving about 3-D video and laserdiscs, Blackie begins to play once again with City-Rat. Beaubourg closes temporarily, there is to be a premiere of *Ran*, the Kurosawa movie. Four thousand guests, many VIPs. For a week already crews have been out removing the bits of glass from between the cobblestones, the hamburger wrappers from the corners, spraying ammonia to cut the smell of urine. A huge screen stretches across the facade, and folding chairs cover the *plateau*. The only place left for City-Rat and Blackie to play is in Saint Germain, in front of the *Deux Magots*.

They arrive early to scope it out. Sometimes it's good in the afternoon, but at night, the action never really starts before ten. Corpulent men with made-up blondes watch from the terrace, half-bored, as two French fakirs grind their faces and backs into a pile of broken glass, while a half-dozen German tourists (the heaviest ones in town at this time of year) stand on top of them. Another moth-eaten fakir with blotchy blue tattoos spurts flames from his mouth. It's a horrible show, pathetic, mutilation as entertainment. The fire spitter's girl passes the hat, and the people on the terrace pretend they haven't watched. "They're just gypsies," one man explains to his date as the hat moves on. Another man, more Christian, tosses in all his yellow coins, the five, ten and twenty centimes, you can tell by the sound. He thanks his stars that he can laugh lightly, that he doesn't have to do anything this degrading for a living, and orders another 40 franc brandy. The first man picks up the change from his table, debates and then realizes that he does not have the courage to get up without leaving a few extra coins for the *garçon*.

As the fakirs clean up, Blackie announces to the other performers that City-Rat and he plan to play, then moves off to stretch and warm up. It isn't "Would you mind if we play?" or "Is it OK if we play? Beaubourg is closed…" He just says, "We're playing." The news takes a half hour for the regulars to digest.

Greatest-Hits-Of-Mime, the Iranian performer that nobody has seen do an original gag yet, is up after the fakirs. One third Strahler, one third City-Rat, one third Blackie equals 500 francs, charms the crowd. He looks like he's having such a good time, and he's got them laughing at even intervals. Behind their Remy Martin and Courvoisier the folks are thinking that they might really want to give him some coin. He's really funny, he's got some real talent. He's better than TV.

He collects his money as the applause dies down and the pedestrians disperse. Greatest-Hits-Of-Mime's best friend stopped playing the street because Blackie muscled him out. He was copying everyone as well, but he didn't have the power to make it work. "If I see you doing any more of my act," Blackie threatened him, "I'm going to make you regret it." It's his street-actor tough guy, the performer who psyches himself up with anger, the egotist. Over the years, Blackie has just stepped on too many toes, given too much unwanted advice.

A muscle-brained dancer, French, sandy hair, heavy base makeup and tights, plants himself firmly in front of Blackie, his fists swelling and unclenching like a gunfighter's. He is their emissary. He glows with righteousness in defense of the *patrie*. "You can't play here."

"Says who?"

"Says me!" The dancer sticks his finger under Blackie's nose, then gives him a little shove.

"Get your hands off me."

"Who are you telling to get his hands off you?"

"I know *savate!*"

Blind men walk arm in arm, pedestrians crawl along the cobblestones, scabrous beggars catch the last clients coming out of Saint Germain church across the way. Faces float by, the night expands, the poisonous air withers the leaves on the chestnut trees, the city grinds on, oblivious to the adrenaline, to the thumping hearts, gritted teeth and snarling lips of a mime in black and a dancer in white. It starts like that: Mime Wars! You can imagine the rest, little boys battling in the sandbox. Haughtily, the dancer walks away, chest out like a rooster.

"Come on. Four of us?" Blackie says as soon as the dancer is out of earshot. "He's not that big. We could beat the shit out of him."

Holding his breath, City-Rat vaults over the walls of the sandbox and scurries away for oxygen. Once again Blackie is in the middle of a spat. City-Rat takes a deep lung-full, shuts his eyes and sighs. "He's got some very heavy negative energy, he's asking for trouble." Willie and some of the other artists gather around to talk it over.

After ten minutes of diplomacy, City-Rat returns to the sandbox with a compromise. It's OK if *he* does a show, but not Blackie. His last show was a week ago, City-Rat explains, he needs the money. Blackie sneers at him, frankly disgusted. A total rout. "You chickenshit City-Rat," he says under his breath, and storms off enraged across busy Saint Germain as cars screech to a halt to avoid hitting him. "The fucking Gandhi of mime!"

Mime Wars. City-Rat plays along for awhile. In the window of a novelty store, he sees two starter pistols on sale for 100 francs, and snaps them up. That night, with Blackie home trying to digest his disgust, City-Rat brings the guns down to the *Deux Magots*, and opens his knapsack to show me. They look like real snub-nose Saturday Night Specials: wooden handles, black barrels. City-Rat is not proud of his lack of solidarity; his physical side wishes the guns were real. But there's got to be some way to bring everyone to their senses. His intellectual side says: Pull these things out and go after them. Show them the consequences. Blam, blam, blam, scare the shit out of them. A moment of truth, a subtler retort than actual violence, a hint of where this sort of behavior can lead. Later that night, after two bottles of red, his metaphysical side finally struggles out, he comes close to tears. This whole thing is an outrage. He pounds his fist on the floor, shakes his head, gasps. "The street was special, we were spiritual, there was love. What is this now? 'You can't play!' What is that? This is our space, you can't play, I'll beat you up? Smash your face? What is that? Are we just like the rest? Are we just dogs like the rest of them? What is that..."

The last golden age: "You should have seen Strahler," I tell Madame Lacombe. "The man had his finger on the pulse of the city. No one made 'em laugh the way Strahler did." "And City-Rat before he started on the bottle! *Hurler de rire...*"

Madame Lacombe smiles, amused to see me waxing nostalgic.

"It's changed, you don't understand."

"Last night my heart was beating so strongly that I couldn't sleep," she says. She does understand: nothing changes, there are just men and their follies, and lack of imagination breeding cruelty and death. She can't really get excited by her Monsieur Josef telling her that where once there was quality, there soon enough was none.

"In the old days people used to get dressed up to go to the Champs Elysées. You didn't dare go out there dressed just any old way. Now you can go down there in shorts..."

Chapter Fourteen, Chapter Fifteen, Chapter Sixteen. After 250 million visitors, Disneyland celebrates its 30th anniversary. *"July 17, 1955, The Beginning Of The Decline Of American Culture."* It turns out that French commandos are responsible for the "Rainbow Warrior" incident. David McTaggart, head of Greenpeace, comes to Paris to sue the French government, which reels with embarrassment at the clumsiness of its cover-up attempt. In Brazil, overcrowded prisons lead to a death lottery in which straws are drawn and the unlucky winner is beaten and strangled by the others. *"Fortieth Anniversary of Hiroshima."* A Japanese Boeing 747 smashes to the ground near Tokyo, leaving 520 dead and incredibly enough, four survivors. The 8"x10" color photos sent to Shiva, severed arms, bits of heads, trees full of intestines, are about the most gruesome ever seen. Bomb blast in Beirut: at least 25 dead. Manchester, England: fire breaks out on a Boeing 737, asphyxiating 54 British tourists on their way to cheap holidays in Corfu. Count 'em up, count 'em up: 1,150 people dead in plane crashes in the last two months, 2200 since the beginning of the year.

Absinthe makes the heart grow fonder. With no reason to get up in the morning, in the vacuum of mime wars, City-Rat begins to miss his father again. It's part of his cycle. Never one for practical matters, he calls me to ask for advice. "How do you think I could locate him?" he wants to go about it seriously this time. He knows from his mother that the man was named Dege, that he worked in the cabaret, traveled from town to town, that he seduced and left many women. I consult the Times & Tides and suggest that City-Rat check the German Embassy, the Red Cross, the German Actor's Union.

All dressed up, the steps neatly outlined in his small red leather notebook, City-Rat gets nowhere with the first leads. Next step, check the phone books; in the main post office on Rue du Louvre, there are phone books for the whole world. There can't be that many Dege's in Germany. Painstakingly he jots down the numbers, makes about a dozen phone calls, from Aachen to Bonn, before conceding. The Dege's he reaches in Germany are sometimes sympathetic, more often outraged. They hang up as if he were a prank caller. "Looking for his father indeed. A cabaret actor in our family, indeed!" The long row of phone books stretches away to infinity, one man with one pencil will never be able to sift through so many thick tomes, so much gothic print. One man with two ears can't possibly endure so much raised hope, rejection from Aachen to Zweibrücken. He'll never find his father. His money will run out before the Dege's do. "Besides," he says, resigned, "My father had a reputation for changing his name to escape his creditors."

City-Rat buys a rat file, and, just the way they used to do when he was a kid in Germany, begins to file away the ridge in the barrel of one starter pistol. The ridge that prevents it from firing real .22 bullets.

CHAPTER 10

Two years and two months after Angel Desperado's departure from Paris, Beatrice, in another moment of generosity and thoughtfulness, decides that it would probably do me good to visit him in Wales to get his opinion on the first three hundred pages of *Fun City*. Knowing that I have no money to pay for the trip after devoting myself to the book, she even, most graciously, offers me a loan. The money comes wrapped in a note, "I hope you enjoy your trip. I would very much have liked to come with you, but you didn't ask me."

"Why didn't you just tell me you wanted to come?" I say. "Of course you can come! But I'm warning you, it's going to be high energy, *on* all the time. Wake up and go. Run, run, run."

The trip turns into an inspired five day rush on Times & Tides rhythm: train, hovercraft, Kent, London, Wales and return. Thanks to Angel, Beatrice discovers a side of me she has never seen. The writing hermit takes a rest, the traveler, the joker takes over. Mad dashes through fields full of rabbits and sheep and laughter. Catching trains on the fly.

Back in Paris, glowing, Beatrice starts the fantasy rolling. Over a dinner of mozzarella and tomatoes, she tells her friend Alexandra about a certain Angel Desperado: writer, *bon vivant* with a cute little ass and seemingly endless energy.

Dearest Desperado, I write to him the next day. "Was going to call but decided it was best not to anger up the phone bill. So here's the news, short and sweet. Beatrice was absolutely charmed by you, to the point where she was offering you a place to stay in her apartment as well as bits of work, here and there. Since then something potentially better has come up. She talked to a friend of hers named Alexandra, 35 or 36, two children, two and four, Vassili and Igor, a British nanny (not *au pair* girl, mind you!) a huge apartment and a recently repainted *chambre de bonne*. Apparently she has a fondness for free spirits as well, so that she proposed I tell you that the room is yours if you want it. She says she doesn't want to make a profit off of you, and that she would like to see if she gets along with you, but that basically the room is yours for the price of electricity, and showers which you are to take downstairs. She seems intelligent, occasionally masterful in that French way. She is already calling the room 'Angel's room.'"

La rentrée. New films, newer fashions, back to the old 10 to 12. Paris weather turns as nice as it gets, the perfect opportunity for the rats to show off their healthy-carrot good looks, acquired at enormous expense over the summer. They walk down the street looking at themselves in the mirrors outside every shop to make sure they haven't changed in the last ten meters. Alexandra's impatience to make the fantasy come true demands that she and I have lunch. She had been a bit impulsive, hadn't she? What *is* she getting into?

Wedged in between clouds of smoke and shark-breath, I sit in the booth and listen to her story over camembert sandwiches. After a youth of travel and adventure she fell in love with a Russian man much older than she. They got married and had a child, then learned that he had cancer. As his condition worsened and it appeared that he would not survive, she knew what she wanted: to conceive a second child with him. Four months after he succumbed to his pain, the child was born, a boy she named Vassili. Since then, she and her two boys, memories of passion, had been pretty much alone. The insurance money took care of her needs, paid for the apartment. She decided to take a job at a modeling agency to put a challenge back in her life. Once, twice, three times she had tried to bring a man into the circle, a father for her boys, but it had never quite worked out.

We order coffee. She asks me if I have written to Angel. "And what did you say about me?" Her hands are twisting under the table: she's very nervous. Occasionally masterful? "Ma-stair-fool." She tastes the word, her shoulders loosen up, she smiles, her pencil-line thin eyebrows rising half-way on her forehead. "Ma-stair-fool," she blushes, and then reddens even more when I laugh warmly at her reaction. She pays for the sandwich and coffee, "Someday you can take *me* out," she reassures me. "Ma-stair-fool."

Angel's answer comes soon enough. "The machinery is working - the massive cog wheels are translating their tinty power to the great booted lever which is aimed right at my arse, to send me akimbo back to the white city of Lutecea. There to submit my innocent pudenda to the gluttonous labia of my future benefactress. Gladly. For a day."

On the sixth floor Madame Lacombe remains in character. I carry her mail upstairs one day. Among the bills and requests from the cancer society, is a postcard from Zoff in Massachusetts. Her face lights up. She is thrilled. Until Mme. Jeunet reads the PS to her. "...And give a kiss to Mme. Jeunet." Madame Lacombe's first piece of personal mail in the last two or three eternities, and she has to share it! She stops me in the hall, shows me the card, asks me if I can explain what Monsieur Dean might have intended by such vulgar language, what sort of nuances should be read into the postcard. She shakes her head, refuses to believe my explanation that neither Zoff's French, nor his understanding of French culture are sufficiently refined to deal in nuance like that.

When he returns from the United States a month later, Zoff knows instantly that he has fallen into Madame Lacombe's doghouse. She still hasn't gotten over the postcard. Not only that, but she doesn't like Dominique, the French woman Zoff is now sharing his tiny room with. Dominique never comes to talk to her like that nice Dutch girl Zoff made the mistake of bringing home at the start of summer. Dominique is too loud when she and Zoff make love, the sound of her moaning resonates through the hall. Dominique, it's virtually certain, smokes in the hallway.

"That Madame Lacombe, I tell you..." Zoff says. His walls are now covered with oils of pregnant women, still lives of mackerel and vegetables, whatever is for dinner that night. "So how's Beatrice?"

"I don't know what it is. Maybe Paris is just bad for her. In Wales she was full of spunk. Now that she's back she's got no energy."

"Well maybe she's just tired."

"No it's beyond that."

"Well she sure is beautiful. I would love to have her pose for me. You think she'd be too expensive?"

After almost a year together, and with Angel on his way, I've grown to respect Zoff despite our rocky beginning. But there couldn't be two more different people. Zoff lives on the south side of the building, the sunny side, and I live on the north, the cold, the dark side. Zoff thinks I'm a cynic. I just believe that in times like these, you either have to have your eyes closed, or be a simpleton to retain a positive outlook and that if the artist doesn't look at it clearly, it's only going to get worse. Zoff seeks the harmonies, in nature, in relationships. My eye is drawn to where the seams will rip, the weld come apart, the compromise explode. "He who would perfume a scorpion will not thereby escape his sting..." The city is strewn with wrecks, exiles who came here in the 50s, the 60s, chasing Henry Miller, determined to take on the world, and now living on regrets and crossword puzzles, Time, Newsweek and the Herald Tribune. They had their bars: *Le Tournon*, the Top Banana, and now they just have their past. They had vowed never to be trapped, but their imaginations leaked away, flushed out with liters of four franc red wine.

And what about the street artists who push it to the limit, forget to protect themselves and then snap? Duvillard, Koji, Strahler and Rock the Welshman. It's fine to think of nature and harmony, like Zoff, but what about all those people who are nourished, who perish because of the nuances on postcards? Sometimes it is tragic, sometimes heroic: the trick is to capture the parade.

"It doesn't look like me," the woman protested in front of the portrait that Oskar Kokoschka had just painted of her. "It will," he assured her, "It will."

Robert Sleet writes City-Rat from Sweden. At first things are going well: he escapes from a straitjacket while hanging above Stockholm from a crane and the picture makes the front page of *Expressen*, the Stockholm daily. Then they're not going so well after all: Sweden is too clean, the stakes aren't high enough, they're just playing at life.

A Swiss clinic, psychiatric help in the United States, and time away from Circus Roncalli, Dorian Strahler begins to learn how to use and control his anger. He arrives in Paris in fine shape, and City-Rat jealously keeps him to himself. After three days of laughter and stories and understanding, Strahler returns to Germany. In his absence City-Rat's sense of isolation intensifies, becomes overwhelming.

He finally unveils *The Dragon* to a few select spectators at the Le Coq mime school. A two hour show which begins to bore City-Rat himself before it is even half-done. In front of the audience he realizes that it doesn't come from the heart, it's not new, it's a collage of subliminal images: Charlie Chaplin and Tex Avery. How can he expect to play it for six whole months? He is depleted. In the empty city he doesn't have the courage to face himself, face the Dragon.

Misery never comes alone, Simone Signoret dies of cancer. City-Rat is destroyed. "She was a great lady." He had made her laugh. He doesn't mention the effect her death will have on his career, but he's certainly thinking about that too, feeling cursed. He sits at *Café Beaubourg* drinking, beer after beer. The bags under his eyes get deeper and deeper, and his skin turns even more yellow. He has no one to turn to but the bottle. A brief moment of lightness, before the shutters close again, the familiar spiral.

After 355 pages of close-personal tragedy, I write THE END in bigger than big capital letters, experience an hour of intense exhilaration during which I take an other-worldly, mad-eyes Photomaton photo of myself as a record of the occasion, then promptly sink into kick-in-the-balls depression. Before *Fun City*, I was like Angel: too tempted by all there was to see, the shows at Beaubourg, the parade, so much to do, so much coffee to drink. But one morning a year ago, after the drama with Beatrice, after another disappointing outing with City-Rat, I woke up and decided that more than anything I needed to put my trust in something, that if I didn't set to work in earnest, I would lose my foundation. I imagined that I could write a book and that when it was done, it wouldn't betray me. I was possessed, assembling years of notes, attempting to learn what does and doesn't work. A quick dash to the bakery for a baguette, and across the street to the butcher for a slice of *pâté* was all I had time for. My finger tips burned as they flew over the keys. Six months later, the bread began to take over. And after a year, when the first draft finally came to a close, I discovered, to my dismay, that a book too can betray you, can be a gem one moment and pure horror the next.

It's the vacuum of suddenly having nothing to do, the fear that it might not be good enough, that *you* might not be good enough, that you lack what it takes, desire, devotion, intelligence, vision, lucidity. It's the paradox that you started to write in order to bridge the gap in communication between you and the human race, only to discover, in this age of distraction, the era of Fun City, that the incredible concentration needed to summon something out of thin air, to pull rabbits out of hats, to make magic, makes you even more distant, more unable to connect. It's the negative reflex, essential to the artistic process, to doubt your assumptions, to tear yourself apart mercilessly, to face the void unblinkingly and challenge yourself to fly higher. Or maybe it's none of that, and Nietzsche had it pegged, "It is too bad! Always the old story! When a man has finished building his house, he finds that he has learnt unawares something which he ought absolutely to have known before he began to build. The eternal, fatal 'Too late!' The melancholia of everything completed!"[1]

---

[1] Nietzsche, *Beyond Good and Evil*

I check the prices of flights: 5100 to Rio, Athens as low as 1300, Monastir: 1380, L.A.: 1800 one way. If I came to Paris to be Henry Miller, to prove, somehow, to myself, to the world, that it is still possible to live a life of meaning, unique, free, inspired, then so far I have failed. But I have not just failed myself. There is a death wish in the air, an entire culture of death, ICBMs pointed east and west, and the sense that someday, someone, out of boredom more than anything, might just push the button and start the fireworks rolling, and nobody would even really care. There's a cult of destruction, a reveling in mediocrity and ephemeral fashion, a visceral rage masked by disposable moments, changing hair and skirt lengths, trendy dances and sports: it's the legacy of the Industrial Revolution. What is really worth saving?

That is where the artist comes in, that is his relevance in these dark times, this is where I have failed. You can't blow up a world in which Beethoven is possible, Mozart is possible, Cezanne is possible, Dostoyevsky is possible, Nietzsche is possible, the city of Paris is possible, Muhammad Ali is possible. You can't destroy a world which is capable of such beauty, such glory. You cannot destroy a world that demonstrates, despite all the suffering and injustice, all the cruelty and stupidity, that there is light, there is generosity, there is ecstasy *ecce homo,* there is hope. The failure to write a proper book, (if failure it is, which, from minute to minute, I'm not even sure of), is not just a personal failure. It is a failure to rise to the heights, failure to approach the stature of those who have demonstrated that life is the miracle it is, those enlightened, luminous beings who are the antidote to death culture, to a vision of humanity with its feet mired in the mud of Hades, to industrial slaves toiling in eternal servitude, to meaninglessness, heartlessness, absurdity.

The guy who sells coffee in Beatrice's neighborhood begins to glow with excitement. At 11 p.m. on October 25, there are going to be big changes. In a matter of ten seconds the phone company is going to change 23 million phone numbers from seven to eight digits. First there were phone cards for the public phones, phone cards with microchips embedded in them, a French invention, and now this! It's a wonderful world, he says.

For weeks now I've been trying to get him to concoct a blend of coffee that tastes like Milanese rocket fuel. The man's given me inspired, enthusiastic lectures about roasting techniques, how an Italian coffee consists of one roasted bean to one unroasted, (I'm skeptical) about the laxative properties of this roast or that. But when it comes right down to it, he still hasn't managed to mix the taste I want, the body, the bitterness. He's enthusiastic but he lacks a sense of nuance. Another *nice* guy.

There are other markets elsewhere. On Rue Poncelet, Saint Loto, the robotic barman, puts a coffee on the counter for me without even asking. "*Alors Roger*," I greet him. "It's not Roger today, it's Robert," he says. "And you mustn't talk to me." Out in the market, dwarfed by mounds of leeks and beets, little Pierrot is more receptive. He stands only 5'2", but he understands what it means when someone's faith in the Almighty is restored because it only takes the phone company ten seconds to add an extra digit to your phone number. "*Quel con!*"

New white paint on the wall. I'm at Shiva, trying to forget the book, putting my heart and soul into an article about reindeer herding in Alaska. Right at the part about how the average Korean family consumes thirty grams of reindeer antler a week, a yearly expenditure of $1,500. The phone rings: City-Rat, sobbing. "I'm gonna end it man. I can't take this anymore. I don't know why I'm here, I want to jump. I went out on the balcony and I looked down at the pavement." Behind me in the agency, business as usual. It's five o'clock, time for the mail to go out, and those reindeer slides have got to get off the table. Tonight. Salesmen rush in and out, the black and white photos for the day slap down on my typewriter. I go through them as I listen, clucking sympathetically into the phone at proper intervals. The Pope again, even more vital than reindeer antlers, the packages can't be sent until the captions are done.

This sort of drama doesn't sit at all well with me, but I can hear City-Rat has been drinking, and it seems wise to keep him talking. He needs no prompting. "I don't know who my father is. I don't even know why I am in Paris anymore, except for the architecture."

"Except for the architecture? That's a good line!"

"I've got these guns man, I'm going to use them. You don't get it, do you? Simone Signoret is dead, she was a great lady." He sobs, sputters, it's time to change victims. "You just don't get it. You got no feeling. You it's always push, push, push. What's that? Is that creativity? And Beatrice. She's closed, man, she doesn't want to open up. Who are you kidding? I love you, that's why I'm telling you this... I can't stand it any more. Too much pain. Too much fucking pain, man..."

"Josef, really, *tu exagères*," Glynnis clucks as she passes by, her grating American socialite accent, that mixture of French and English, *Franglais*, that everyone succumbs to sooner or later. But I give her the sign of the suicide gun-to-the-head, and that seems to calm her down a bit. She warns someone not to scratch the leather top on her recently refurbished Louis XV desk.

Twenty more minutes reprieve it gets me, twenty more minutes of hearing from City-Rat how inadequate is *my* approach to life, how I will never be a writer, until Glynnis finally can't stand it any more. I'm tying up the line, the Pope is in limbo. "We need those captions."

By the time City-Rat has settled down enough to get off the phone, someone else has done the captions. Once I'm back to inventing the news, I'm shaking so hard that the price of reindeer horns goes up from $1000 to $11,009 a kilo. No time to change it. It might cause a revolution in Korea, can't be helped: a deadline's a deadline.

When I return home that night, I drag myself heavily up the stairs one by one. At the end of the corridor, light spills from under Dean Zoff's door. He's working late, a series of canvases of pregnant women, but as usual is more than ready to listen to the story. "I had a friend who killed himself," he says. "If someone wants to commit suicide, there's nothing you can do. You just got to let them."

"You're just dripping with sympathy, aren't you Zoff? And you say *I'm* the cynic? Just let your friend die? I'm a bit tired, Zoff, I'll catch you later…"

"What if you called Dupont?" Zoff says as I step out.

"Now there's a good idea. Maybe I will." If anyone can snap City-Rat back to reality it's Jean Dupont. City-Rat is maybe the only student who ever really understood about the clown. "You either commit suicide or you laugh."

Dupont answers the phone gruffly, none too pleased to be interrupted at dinner, but he *is* concerned. "Is he using drugs? Drinking?"

The next morning I don't want to tell City-Rat what I've done behind his back. But I am curious. "So, feeling any better today?"

"Yeah, Dupont called me."

"Really? Wow. What did he say?"

"'Monsieur City-Rat?' City-Rat takes on Dupont's voice. "This is

Monsieur City-Rat isn't it? City-Rat *le Canadien?*' he cracks me up, that way he has. I was laughing so hard."

"I warned you that you were going to need patience," Madame Lacombe says.

"Sometimes I can't help but fear that I'm going to end up like Celine, a bitter old man, deserted by any friends he ever had, trying to accept his loneliness but finally giving up, a caustic shield and a cat his only companions... My only hope is that I don't like cats..."

"*Allons Josef!*" This perennial striving, this talk of madness seems futile, ludicrous. She understands what it's like not to have anyone to talk to, but why whine about acts of God, *force majeure?* That's just the way life is. From her perspective my burdens seem laughable, light as a feather.

City-Rat calls after a week, asks where I've been. "The other day I bought a stuffed ape for 400 francs, brought it home and propped it up on a chair. I took out my pistol, put it to its forehead and pulled the trigger. A hole right through its head. I felt much better after that," he laughs.

"That's great news, City-Rat. Really great." My heart has gone grey.

Even City-Rat can't help but hear that I'm flat. "We only hurt the ones we love," he explains why he chose me as a victim. Love! As we talk, I flip through the newest edition of the Dictionary of Times & Tides. "Love, n. 1. carnage, slaughter, blood bath, trucidation, registering to vote..."

Oriah, a Romanian astrologer, calls out of the blue with an alternate solution. "I told you this before. You are a Libra. Compromise. You must find a reality whose ground is high enough for you to sink your roots into, so that your ideals may grow ever higher to the sky." Lovely imagery that, I tell him, but no longer valid. "Draw up a new chart, my sign has changed to Yield! Uranus on my ascendant."

There is a man living in India who is hundreds of years old, who can materialize objects at will, castles, gold, Oriah persists. "Think how far we have to go."

"OK," I answer. "Come over if you want to, but I'm not coming out. The "Hindu" was out in the hall, washing up in the sink, looking pale and exhausted. In cold weather like this, the demand for bread increases 30%, he has hardly had any rest in weeks. What bread-induced folly, what tremendous insanity lurks around the corner waiting for me to set foot on the sidewalk? Best stay put: there's a ten day supply of rice, books to read.

Madame Lacombe, glued to her TV, frets about the guy running around murdering old ladies in the very next *arrondissement*. I worry about old ladies wearing weasel-fur coats and riding the buses carrying naugahyde bags full of poodles worth more than I am. No, outside there are ergotism and cold-maddened pigeons attacking garbage trucks, I'm not going out.

"You're short Oriah, you don't realize it, but there are mad shoppers out there carrying umbrellas with knitting-needle-sharp ribs lunging for my neck; there are bus mirrors that'll take a man's head off; there are butcher hooks on the RER C train that will skewer a tall man's third eye; there are bantam-sized doorways and seats with Procrustean intentions. Come over if you want to, we can talk about the time you went back to Romania and cried for a whole week because the spirit of the people was shattered, and everyone was worried about being denounced by everyone else. Come over and we'll talk about all these young idealists who see communism as a solution. You can pound the walls if it's not too late. We can talk about the Kurds in eastern Turkey who place their babies on roads to stop and rob the trucks going through to the Middle East, and the truck drivers who know they cannot stop, who run the children over, because the men in the bushes have knives between their teeth. Come over and we'll talk about spiritualism and Allan Kardec and his tomb covered with carnations by all those who have had a wish come true thanks to him. We'll talk about all the others buried at *Père Lachaise*, Oscar Wilde, Victor Noir with his erect bronze penis rubbed shiny by women with barren wombs, Jim Morrison resting in the middle of graffiti, 'Fuck me raw, Jim.' Come and we'll discuss sprites, and pixies and Edith Piaf. I saw a crazy woman last summer, walking up the street under the influence of baguette, doing her cracked soprano Edith Piaf imitation. *'Non, rien de rien, je ne regrette rien, Ni le mal qu'on m'a fait... Non rien de rien.'* The good citizens in the *arrondissement* of pharmacies and octogenarians hung out their windows and tittered. She shook her fist up at them, braced herself against the wall for another song, *'Allons enfants de la patrie... bande d'enculés.'* Raise the bloody standards. We'll talk about materializing castles, we'll talk about aligning the planets, manipulating the tides, concentrating our desire until Scheherazade herself rings the buzzer downstairs. We'll drink tea, if we have to."

"I don't think I can come today, I'm not feeling so good," his voice drops, "I can't walk."

"Yeah?"

"Yeah, I spent the afternoon yesterday healing a junkie. This morning I woke up paralyzed. My legs won't move. He had a lot of poison inside him, and it all came to me."

"I know the feeling..."

CHAPTER 11

The first proof comes from Italy. In Florence, a clinic is opened by the Italo-American Chamber of Something or Other, especially for treating Stendhal's Syndrome. Americans come to Europe on their "Gems of Italy," nine day tour, and when they get to Florence, with its colors and paintings and intricate designs they come down with it: Stendhal's Syndrome. They see one more painting, they clutch their heads. "I don't feel so good, Mabel..." The eyes roll back, they keel over: sensory overload. The symptoms are amnesia and disorientation. The treatment at the clinic consists of gradually introducing the patient to familiar images, images with fewer dimensions, less intricate, old videos of Johnny Carson. That old "dada, dadada" picks 'em right up.

A month and a half after my letter to Wales, by which time Alexandra has truly, incredibly, almost forgotten her offer of sanctuary, Angel Desperado himself finally materializes in Paris. Too much steamed fish, too many overcooked vegetables, too much boiled lamb and too many pints of warm lager, the only thing he really has to show for his two years in Albion are the scars.

"Stendhal's syndrome? Yes!" Back in Paris, back with an audience at last, the last two years drop away with a snap of the fingers. Disgust? Passionlessness? No desire in his cheap heart? Unwanted? In Limbo? Out of place? Not he, not anymore. He is instantly ready, full of purpose, electrified. "Stendhal's syndrome? Shit Klein, we knew about that before Stendhal himself." What else has our humor always been but an instinctive crusade to expand the perimeter, to draw the eye to the side with something unexpected, a response to where we have come from? TV and movies, disneyness and vomiting, technological man is closing down, his eyesight is less and less drawn to what is not directly in front of him, not immediately capted.

On the Champs Elysées, Angel sees a couple linked together by a Walkman. It drives him mad, he jumps up and down in front of them, a crazed ape running circles around them. The proper thing would be for the Walkboy to punch him out, but he can't figure out how to get out of the earphones, hand over the cassette player and shift to violence without looking ridiculous for his Walkmate.

A beautiful lass, long black hair, black vinyl model book under her arm, walks by with a scowl. "Carry that cross for you ma'am?" Angel says. "Straighten your scowl? Grind your teeth for you? Ma'am?" Angel fishes into his pocket, and tosses his brass key at her feet with a clang. She walks over it. He picks it up and throws it again. She tosses her hair in the wind. He picks it up, races in front of her, holds the key right in front of her nose and drops it. She smiles. "Gotcha!" Angel shouts, but there's no time to follow her.

Right on her heels, a group of Italian kids ten-strong, down jackets and Timberland shoes, comes waltzing down the avenue. It is the year when otherwise harmless people have taken to demonstrating their individuality by wearing headbands with Martian antennae sticking out. Angel dashes in front of them and lies down on the pavement, succumbs to a religious-epileptic fit. The Italians jump right over him, but some of them are looking back.

In centuries past, on coronation day, it was the custom for the new King and Queen to ride through Porte Saint-Denis and down Rue Saint Denis to get to Notre Dame. All the streets on their passage were carpeted, the building walls covered with silk. The air was thick with rose water, and fountains flowed with milk, hippocras and wine. Now, no kings left to crown, the street roils, overflows with Turks and their sandwich shops, Pakistanis toting huge bales of fabric to the garment sweatshops all around, peep shows, 10 francs, 20 francs, whores dressed in hot pants and fishnet shirts, letting a nipple, a strand of pubic hair show to entice the seedy customers. You can smell the sperm in the gutter, the urine, the rotting meat hanging in the Arab butchers, the globules of French fry and gyros meat oil floating through the air from the sandwich joints. Rue Saint Denis, a chancrous cock laid end to end, as Henry Miller described it.

How to explain that in this cloaca, this cesspool, the air also bears a scent of possibility for Angel, an elixir completely absent in the last two years of bucolic settings? The walls, the shadows: the city recites to him just like it did before. He can still see sidewalk-to-sidewalk carpets, gurgling fountains of milk and mulled wine. "See that place?" Angel points to a sandwich stand displaying a windowful of greenish chicken and purple *merguez.* "Coming here from Greece, before going back to Stockholm, I ran out of money completely. I got a ten franc piece from someone at ACP. I bought a sandwich. The guy gave me forty francs change back. *Allahuma, allahuma!* I used the money to get a hotel room, back in the days when they were still dirt cheap. I washed my clothes and myself in the sink and lay down naked on the bed, in the radiator-warm room. By morning my clothes were all dry, and my shoes, and I walked out the door forever."

Phantom king without a crown, Angel dances through phantom streets, the streets Haussmann razed over a century ago to make way for the last new Paris. *There was a street called The Kneeling Steer. A young man had gone into a church in 1523 and torn the host out of the Priest's hands, saying "Quoi! Toujours cette folie!" Right then, two cows being led to slaughter kneeled down in front of the Sainte Chapelle.* Drunk with his sudden good health, Angel fantasizes about someplace, some chimerical continent where he would really be put to the test. Where he would need every bit of his wits to survive. Here, Europe, Paris, there's always a way around the rules, always a way to survive. *On another street, a passageway to Saint Severin Cemetery, was a door with the inscription: "Tous ces morts ont vecu, toi qui vis, tu mourras. L'instant fatal approche et tu n'y penses même pas."* All these dead ones were once living, you who live will also die. The fatal moment approaches and you don't even think about it...

"Do you think Miller ever had any doubts?" I say as the oil refinery, comes into view.

"What do you mean?" Angel stops.

"I don't know, about his point of view, his desire for ecstasy? Do you think he ever worried about whether he might be wrong, be mad?"

Down on the *plateau* at Beaubourg, dressed head to toe in black, City-Rat swings his legs, limbers up, while Blackie gathers a crowd. A plastic shopping bag floats down onto the *plateau*, and he screams, pulls out a mime walkie talkie, shielding the people from the bag, pushing them back. "City-Rat, City-Rat, we got trouble here, trouble!"

"Trouble, roger. Where is he? Where is he? OK, roger, I think I see him, chh." He pulls out a rifle. In slow motion, on tiptoes, he stalks the bag.

"I go left, you go right," Blackie whispers into the mike.

"Trouble, roger. I got him, I think I got him." City-Rat dives on to his belly and snakes forward across the cobblestones.

"He's coming this way, got him, got him." A gust of wind catches the bag and blows it towards City-Rat. "NO!" Blackie screams. "Look out! Comin' right for you!"

City-Rat scrambles to his feet and runs for protection. He turns right, turns left, finally chooses to cower behind the crowd. His rifle trembles. "I got him. Don't panic. Everything in control."

The air is cool and calm, maybe the last nice day before winter, the *plateau* is quiet, no construction noise, no Peruvians blowing their awful pan flutes. An in-crowd today, twenty other jugglers, actors and artists gathered to watch the show. Aware, hip to the gags, they know, without being prompted, when to respond, when to laugh, and their enthusiasm transports the rest of the crowd. *This* is street theater: a dialogue, a conversation. *The Chewing Gum, the Train, the Cigarette...* City-Rat lets go, Seety-Raht flies again.

Boxing, The Hundred Meters, gag after gag, the show goes on and on, the first new stuff in months. Finally City-Rat does *The Cigarette,* and they put down their hats without a word. The audience swarms forward to pay, then goes back to its place, ready for more.

"You want more?" Blackie says. "Get lost! You're crazy. The show is over." He turns to City-Rat. "They want more," he says, loud enough for everyone to hear.

"Well what do you expect me to do about it? If they want more, give 'em more."

"Why don't *you* give 'em more?" Blackie whips out a mime rifle.

City-Rat puts his hands up and backs up. He lowers one hand carefully, pulls out his handkerchief, slowly wipes his brow and squeezes out the handkerchief. He puts it back in his pocket and raises his hands again. "OK, I'll give 'em more. More, ha ha." He begins to tap-dance. It takes forty-five minutes more of improvisations before night falls, it turns cold, and it is clear that the conversation is finished. "Thank you," says City-Rat. "Now get the fuck out of here. We're tired. All right? Go!"

"Poof! Disappear!" Blackie says. He could just as well say "Thermonuclear holocaust," and they would understand. In the last hour and a half, they have laughed harder and longer than they thought possible. A few of them bring a second coin up to the hats, the rest file away, completely satisfied. The street artists, all twenty of them, walk through the twilight and file into the *Dame Tartine,* the cheap sandwich café by the

Stravinsky fountain which has become the new secret retreat. Down the stairs to the basement. The packed cellar is almost instantly filled with cigarette smoke.

"So you're the guy he's been telling us about," Blackie says to Angel, but with so much testosterone, that it sounds less like a warm welcome, than a gunslinger's challenge. "Josef said you two would write us something as soon as you got here. You sure took your fucking time."

"Yup, and I may be gone again tomorrow. But if I do leave, don't worry Blackie. We'll meet again in hell."

Leaves turn yellow, and summer clothes go back into mothballs before the stories run out, the miracles go into hibernation, the past has been put to rest, before, in the city at large, the blues and browns are brought out once again smelling of camphor and naphthalene.

Angel feels it coming on: there's a book to write. For that, no more of this sharing rooms with Josef Klein, a man needs quiet and a room to call his own. He needs a chance to dream uninterrupted, solitude to help him tune in the Times & Tides. This time, for sure, Paris! Another fresh start. The task dances before his eyes: "A book that will make it impossible for my family to be the way it is, the quiet indifference. Home Sweet Home Inc."

Angel screws up his courage, washes his jeans and two of his three shirts. He picks out the green one and puts on his sweater to cover up the ripped armpits, the holes in front, bleached and eaten away by specks of cement and mortar. We make our way over to Rue de Moscou. Alexandra lives on the second floor, behind a massive oak door.

"Hello Ma-stair-fool," she greets him with a smile, warm but neutral. Her children cower behind her legs, curious about mummy's new fantasy. Angel, no less terrified than the kids, smiles nervously.

"Hello…" Uneasy, Angel squeaks like a parakeet. Hello Ma-stair-full? What the hell does that mean? It's definitely not love at first sight for him. The red, calf-high ostrich cowboy boots, the pencil-line thin eyebrows, the slightly crooked, bunny-ish front teeth, the impeccable jeans, the billowing work-shirt descending below the ass, disguising the evidence of indulgence, of city life, of childbirth, of bulges in the wrong places. Her appearance is like an elaborate act designed unsuccessfully to disguise desperation, but he can see right through her. The armored front door bangs closed, bolts click, the parakeet squeaks again, "Delighted to be taking advantage of you."

The TV plays in the background. Clumsy Sergeant Garcia is scratching his head and whining in dopey French as Zorro once again gets the best of him, but the kids, little Igor and littler Vassili, remain in the hallway behind their mother's legs. She pretends not to hear what Angel has said. "Don't-you-think-Vassili-looks-exactly-like-Josef, yesterday-I-removed-the-boxes-from-*your*-room, I-just-had-it-painted-too, how-`bout-some-tea?" Masterful Alexandra, concealing her doubts, marches down the hardwood hallway, casting a smile behind. The kids snap out of their trance and scurry to catch up, then crab-walk behind her, their hands clutching at her reassuring form, their eyes on the impressively tall and golden-haired new addition to their lives. "You coming?"

With the faded Polaroid landmarks of his life tacked on the wall for inspiration, the first month in Alexandra's *chambre de bonne*, Angel cavorts with the muse every night on his manual typewriter, working out the details of the life story of Avery Gast, aka A. Gast, man without a will. Stuck between Paris and London, permitted to walk the earth to become the repository for other people's fantasies... The working title: "Eros Hung."

"Sure I was born, the evidence was everywhere..." he writes the first line of the novel, and promptly bogs down, back to the drawing board. It takes him a month of notes and false starts to decide that the tone isn't right, that it's like kindergarten Salman Rushdie or John Barth on dialysis. A month to discover once again that sitting at a desk is just not his style, that his soul belongs to the street, to movement, to experience and the spark of life. The peripatetic trickster, born two and half millennia too late.

As funds dwindle once again, the life he leads begins to look familiar. Saint Loto for coffee, American Express for mail, the American College for loose opportunities and toilet paper. At the end of the street, across from the Liège metro station, a Greek named Kostas runs a crepe stand. Karate on Thursday and Saturday, crocodile walks and long, hot showers afterwards.

"How much does this look like?" Angel shakes a handful of change in front of my nose.

"Like 14 francs and 2p." The ten franc coin and the British two pence coin actually *do* look pretty similar in size, weight and color.

"Yeah but if it were dark, and I did it quickly, do you think you'd see the difference?"

He continues to keep his distance from Alexandra, the more he gets to know her, the more he's subconsciously certain that it would be a mistake to let this go any further than living arrangements. As long as he can keep her at arm's length, he has his freedom, but one little slip-up, one moment of self-forgetting (and it *has* been a while since he's been with a woman), she'll slap a collar around his neck, chain him to a doghouse and call him John the Baptist.

Increasingly possessed by her fantasy, Ma-stair-fool Alexandra shakes her head, can't imagine how he's managed to resist her, how he's managed not to succumb to her charms. She tries everything she can think of, seducing him the only way she knows how, with money, with material, when the only thing that would work is imagination. She takes him to movies, she buys him hot chocolate in Saint Germain des Près, *La Palette*, *Les Deux Magots*, feeds him steamed salmon once or twice a week, takes him out for Vietnamese food, or for Chinese, and reminds him incessantly that she was once a Bohemian too.

"I don't know why you keep saying that," he says, calm, matter-of-fact. "I don't see myself as a Bohemian."

"Come on Angel you fucker. Come on." It's driving her nuts to have his warm body sleeping a mere four floors above her. She spends a lot of time wistfully fondling his blond curls. Her hands smell of lemons, she uses lemons instead of soap, it cuts the smell of the salmon. "I think it's good that your name is Angel, your hair is exactly like a Botticelli angel's."

She takes him window shopping, she wants to upgrade his wardrobe. She wants to buy him Weston shoes, plaid pants and argyle socks, cardigans and boxer shorts with imaginative prints. "I hate that watch you have," she says on an impulse, and darts into a store. He waits outside, refusing to be a party to her whimsy. She comes back out and hands him a black Swatch. Which doesn't seem to sway him either. It begins to rain. She buys him a red beret, to refine his image, "You look like a Guardian Angel," she smiles, quietly proud of her joke, the subtle brilliance of her trans-cultural reference. And still he refuses to step into her bed.

Instead, and she knows it, he stays up till all hours typing and reading Joseph Campbell's "Hero With A Thousand Faces." "...And we recall the trickster-god Edshu, described in a tale from the other coast of Africa:

spreading strife was his greatest joy...In him are contained and from him proceed the contradictions, good and evil, death and life, pain and pleasure, boons and deprivation. As the person of the sun door, he is the fountainhead of all the pairs of opposites. 'With Him are the keys of the Unseen... In the end, unto Him will be your return; then He will show you the truth of all that ye did."

One month, two months. Increasingly unhappy with her job at the modeling agency, Alexandra returns home at night, where her noisy boys, transformed into sword-slashing, masked Zorro and ray-gun specialist Luke Skywalker, compete vociferously to skewer or vaporize Mummy's angel-curled incubus. When they get too noisy, or when they won't stop attacking, she loses it, backhands them, kicks them with the toe of her red ostrich cowboy boot, then puts them to bed to cry themselves to sleep. Which doesn't really impress the Trickster either. To cool her ardor he suggests that she introduce him to a Canadian girl in her agency, a young lass whose naked form, artfully concealed and posed in a hammock has been in the metro ads for weeks now, driving him wild.

One evening, rubbing her hands on a lemon after yet another dinner of steamed salmon, she breaks it to him, "I'm an Aries, you're an Aries, my boys are both Aries." The implication is clear, even if the logic and mathematics isn't, in three weeks he is expected to inseminate her. When that deadline passes she decides that she will have her breasts lifted, as if by becoming younger-looking she will regain her powers of seduction over the spare-parts-Angel.

"Your spring renewal I presume?"

More than anything Alexandra needs to prove that she still has those powers of seduction. She shares with him her vitamin cocktails: D, C, Magnesium, B-6, B-12. Among the pills, vials and nostrums she keeps on the top of her refrigerator, he picks the one he would like *her* to take: B-36, at the very least. Before he can even *consider* playing friction rituals with her, he needs to see her mature, move beyond whims and fantasies, present herself to him as a woman, not as some caricature of femininity. He pays her back for each steamed salmon, for every tomato, basil and mozzarella salad, with anecdotes from his down and out experiences, axioms from the Bureau of Times & Tides. "Stretch the limits. Never repeat a joke. This life is hard enough, don't make it any harder. Secrecy is pointless, there is no such thing as privacy." She finds his dedication charmingly naive, it reminds her of her own youthful fugue to San Francisco. So what if her boss is a thief, so what if the kids are getting out of hand? She goes to sleep thinking that it was good after all, this impulse she had to put this man in her sixth floor maid's room.

In the morning she wakes up resolved to try yet another tactic: jealousy. For a few weeks she plays it coy, aloof. She makes a big show of going out on dates, with "The Baron," or a second mysterious white knight, who turns out to be her psychiatrist.

"How's the writing going?" the shrink wants to know, but there's an edge to his voice, as if he and Angel are rivals.

"Fine," Angel answers. "I've just finished a story, the second in a series, trying to ascertain the role of pornography in discovering how to tap the well-spring of will power that resides in all of us. And you?"

Angel's money runs out soon thereafter. His brother, his sister-in-law, various other people in England owe him money, but they can't imagine that his situation might be as desperate as their need to fatten their saving accounts. No matter, life remains rich, it's like old times, the Open Door Policy is back in full swing: sneaking into the ends of plays, sneaking into concerts, using all the old contacts, the Iranian bouncers at the door of the Olympia, the Casino de Paris, Le Zenith, Bercy.

Tom Waits passes through the Casino de Paris on his "Tom Waits For No One" tour. No one we know working the front, we are forced to squeeze through the back door. Same old trusty door, four years now it hasn't closed properly. A uniformed woman stops us but Desperado tells her, in very bad American-tinted French, that we are just looking for the *Toylettes*. Once inside, the adventure over, the adrenaline settled, the concert hardly seems worth the effort. The music industry and its idols. Tom baby runs through his simian poses. The kiddies go wild when he does something that was mentioned in the *Libération* account of his London concert the previous night. They go wild with what they imagine must be the real thing: the boozy voice and posturing of the true American artist.

Something a little more classical, we surprise Beatrice at the second half of a very dark production of *Lucrezia Borgia* at the *Théâtre de Chaillot*. The dark causing even greater confusion than necessary for Mr. Final-Acts-Only Angel Desperado. Why did they all die? he asks Beatrice, but even she cannot say.

City-Rat gets a contract for Japan, a department store wanting to promote its French days with some real French street performers. Beatrice and I go off together to the United States, and Beatrice leaves Angel her keys and a 500 franc advance to paint her hallway and build some shelves. At karate one Thursday night, after four sparring partners, Angel finally connects a roundhouse kick to his opponent's knee, sending a bolt of pain into the base of his skull and a shriek of agony echoing off the ceiling of the gym. By Saturday his foot is an ugly clotted mess from heel to toe, and he can hardly walk, but he's writing and reading and flying under the influence of Henry Miller's *Wisdom of the Heart*, and Bukowski's *Factotum*, which he reads in French, learning all the worst words. He's elated.

Alexandra calls. "Are you coming over? No? Don't call me five minutes before and tell me you're going to come. You're not going to come? Really? You fucker. You know I was thinking it over. I want you to pay rent. You can paint my living room for me," she says. "Yes Al, no Al," he says, putting the receiver on his forehead, his stomach. "Yes Al, no Al." He picks up *Factotum* and begins to turn the pages, reading various passages while she rambles on, ten minutes, twenty minutes, thirty minutes. "I don't think you're taking me seriously," she says.

Back from Tokyo, City-Rat rings Angel to ask him to call back and test his new answering machine.

"So how was your trip?" Angel wants to know.

"I'm so tired. I slept most of the time." City-Rat sounds half-dead.

"You what?" Angel is incredulous. It will be three incarnations before he has enough money to get to Japan. How could a man possibly travel that far, to someplace so exotic, and then just sleep?

"There was a typhoon, we saw it on TV: dozens killed," City-Rat finally rises to the occasion. "We had to drive down to Osaka through the storm, a mad, weaving van ride. I was terrified, the whole time I thought I was going to die. We got to the *ryokan* in Osaka, I was shaking. I took a bath, got into my robe and just stretched out, eyes closed. Then the door opened and a beautiful woman in a silk kimono came gliding in. Porcelain skin, silence, rustling silk, every movement graceful, studied, flowing. She lowered herself to the side of the bed and poured my tea. Pure beauty. I was breathless. 'OK God, I'm ready. You can take me now. As good a time to die as any.'"

The next day, Angel hobbles down to Beaubourg to watch City-Rat perform. "That was great," Angel comes up after the show. "You got 'em, they're feeling good. Why don't you do another one?"

"No man, I'm too tired." City-Rat packs his rabbit teeth into his wallet and walks up the *plateau*, off to the *Dame Tartine*, with Angel hobbling next to him.

"You go ahead," Angel says, stopping to rest. "I'm a bit slow today."

"OK." Nobody asks him what's wrong, nobody offers to give him a hand, nobody seems to care. Not It-Was-All-About-Love-City-Rat, not Blackie, not nice Dean Zoff. Where's the generosity of spirit, the sympathy, the compassion? What's this confederacy of narcissists, this cluster of the self-absorbed and hypocritical? Inside the café, City-Rat orders a beer and is well into his account of a visit to the dentist by the time Angel finally arrives. City-Rat imitates the sound of the drill. He imitates the dentist forcing his mouth open, wider, wider, pushing him off the chair until he has him pinned to the floor with the drill. Zoff gets up, on his way to sketch dance class again, at the dance school by *Café de La Gare*, where Beatrice and I met. "You should see those girls!" He and Dominique plan to move to a small apartment on Avenue de Saint Ouen before the end of the year. He needs to be alone to finish a painting. Living with a woman in six square meters has made it very difficult to get anything done. City-Rat drains his beer, his eyes have sunk into the sockets, and the sockets have turned black.

"I'm a Taurus. I'm meant to keep banging my head into walls," he says. "I was reading Ouspensky, and he made many things clear for me," he says. "Jolanta says I have to get a woman, just go out and get one, so I can prove to myself that it is possible." Angry, abandoned, alone, City-Rat longs for absolutes, explanations; he longs for the world to make sense. Dupont's structures, Jolanta, Ouspensky, astrology, full moons, tea leaves. A world that leaves him alone doesn't make sense; a world that gave him a fugitive cabaret performer for a father, and a mother who would bring drunken men home at four in the morning doesn't make sense. In a world that makes sense, he would be offered jobs in theaters with actors and directors who burned with desire, who were professionals, as devoted as he was, not pretenders who go out to drink coffee when a problem pops up. In a world that makes sense, he wouldn't have to beg for lousy parts. "I need a woman..." he says.

His lament is finally answered by Swan, the ethereal, mystical Taiwanese woman, a student at the Marcel Marceau mime school, with whom Rock, the Welsh fiddler had been living before he smashed up their apartment and ended in the mental asylum. Healer, sorceress, when Swan moves in, City-Rat's life changes dramatically. The apartment begins to smell like tiger balm and incense, she makes him tea, fills him with Chinese medicines, forbids him to turn on the heat, asks him to take the devil masks down off the walls, because they scare her, she can feel their evil vibrations. In the morning she goes down to the *Arènes de Lutèce* below and does Tai Chi exercises. Between classes at Marceau she paints tiny, delicate watercolors which she sells on the street, even though the police have picked her up and taken away her paintings a half-dozen times already. She smiles. She has no fear of authority. She climbs over the barrier in the metro, the new barriers that the RATP, the transit authority, has put in to prevent people from riding for free. The space is too narrow and she gets stuck. There's a line behind her, and there are *contrôleurs* waiting to give her a ticket, to fine her, but she can't stop laughing. Soon everyone is laughing with her. City-Rat and she get on the metro and when it gets to their station, he picks her up and carries her. "You're going to drop me on the tracks," she says.

"No I'm not." Next thing he knows he has stepped off the *quai*, and they have fallen on to the tracks. City-Rat is completely bewitched. "She's not as passionate in bed as I'd like, but I really love her."

Swan is less sure about her feelings. Rock may be in the asylum in Wales, but she can't forget him. She can't really go back to Taiwan, her family has repudiated her. But Paris, so much negative energy, so many people dressed in black. One day she wakes up and she can't talk. Why? No, I just can't talk. From his window, six floors above, heart breaking, City-Rat watches her do her Tai Chi exercises in the snow of the *Arènes de Lutèce* below. What can he do? He gives her massages, cooks for her, writes poetry for her, tries to make her laugh, takes her to see *Les Enfants du Paradis*: *"Je ne suis pas fort. J'ai eu une enfance difficile. Il a bien fallu que j'apprenne a me defendre. Quand j'etais malheureux, je dormais, je rêvais. Mais les gens n'aiment pas qu'on rêve. Alors ils vous cognent dessus, histoire de vous reveiller un peu. Heureusement j'avais le sommeil dur, et je leur échappais en dormant. Je rêvais, j'espérais, j'attendais. C'est peut-être vous que j'attendais."*[1]

Last resort. City-Rat pays for her to go see Jolanta. "You *can* talk, can't you?" Jolanta cuts right to the chase, no beating around the bush. "If you want to?" The Polish woman can sense her pain, her loss of harmony. Yes, Swan nods. It's just that sometimes words have no purpose.

In his north-facing room with its dark orange walls, it doesn't get light enough to wake Angel up before eleven thirty. He's sleeping long and having disturbed dreams. He pastes a little paper sign on the door that says "Hell." It's meant partly to terrify the insipid young Swedish *au pair* who lives down the hall, to keep her away.

He manages to score some lunch tickets from a young girl at the American College who buys his writer's story, so he heads off there as soon as he wakes up. Just as it was when he lived in Paris the first time, the students' pockets are still full of meal tickets and 200 franc notes, which still occasionally fall on the floor while they drink beer at the bar. But their minds are increasingly empty, and for Angel, enduring their presence alone, first thing in the morning is like sitting on knives. They talk dresses and cars and vacations and rock music and movies and favorite cocktails: "What's a Long Island Ice Tea?" "Umm. Two parts amnesia, three shots it's-a-small-world, and lemon to taste." The Challenger Space Shuttle explodes, and they come to lunch teary-eyed. Angel is horrified. "I'm not exactly pleased, but why are you crying? Why these six people? Did you cry when Arthur Koestler died? Or the victims in Cambodia? Or is it because the rocket went boom that you're really sad?" They look down their noses at the disagreeable fellow, move to another table, shun him. Alone in the cafeteria, surrounded by devolution, Angel has trouble choking down the chicken. He doesn't ask if anyone has any spare meal tickets. Call it a luxury: their babbling becomes more intolerable than his own inanition.

He finds fifty francs on the *quai* at the Gare de Lyon, but fifty francs is only five kilos of rice and a half-dozen baguettes. There are a few jobs, moving furniture, putting up shelves, once-a-week English lessons for an Italian woman who sees him as the perfect opportunity. "I've always

---

[1] I am not strong. I had a difficult childhood. Naturally I had to learn to defend myself. When I was unhappy, I slept, I dreamed. But people don't like it when you dream. So they knock you around so as to wake you up a bit. Thankfully, I was a heavy sleeper, and I escaped them by sleeping. I dreamed, I hoped, I waited. Perhaps it was you I was waiting for.

wanted to learn English," Mrs. Buggerelli says, that's what they always say. He prepares the lesson the night before, comes on with full energy to teach her all the nuances of the present imperfect, the past imperfect, the future imperfect, but after the second week, familiar story, it already becomes clear that she cannot force herself to study when the professor isn't there. By the fifth week, her whim has dimmed enough so that she decides she wants her Thursday mornings free. One week she is sick, the next she is called away. "I'm not making any progress," she finally confesses, leaving no doubt as to whose fault it is. She thinks: "If I only had a good teacher," but doesn't say it to his face.

Angel paints a bathroom, a hallway, a few kitchens, a network of people who hear that he has no money, and come forward to help him out. But the painting almost invariably turns out to be just as frustrating as the language lessons. When he first looks the job over they say, "Well we don't have much money," but by that they mean they're having cash flow problems, they don't want to dip into their Swiss accounts, their stocks are down two points in the last three days. After living without money for so long, Angel has no idea what to charge, the sums he should demand seem enormous to him. 1500 francs! A fortune greater than anyone could possibly afford to pay. "1500 francs?" they evaluate the sum, divide it in half, add the cost of a good dinner. "OK, you got a deal, but *you* buy the materials."

The following Monday, fortified by coffee and bread, Angel, cheerful and good-natured, sets to work. Before even half the walls have been sanded and washed, the clients interrupt. "You're big and strong, could you help me move the couch?" Every day it's the same. They ask him to help them do this and that, set up a light fixture, put a dab of paint here, some mortar work there. By lunch time, Angel, already dizzy from the paint fumes, only the usual baguette on his stomach to mix with the noxious odor of the white spirit paint thinner, tries to act nonchalant when they dangle a ham sandwich at him. He could empty the whole refrigerator, eat all the chocolate peanuts, the marzipan, and the Austrian fruit cake too, but, thinking like a poor man, he is too proud, doesn't want them to know that he hasn't been eating a thing recently, that he will only be able to eat for real once they pay him the money for the job.

By the end of the day he is pale, flecks of paint on his hair. He sweats white spirit from his eyeballs, oozes white spirit from his brain: the evolution of the hired man. And when the job is finally over, when because of the thin paint they insisted on buying for the job, it has taken three coats to do the job instead of two, when, thanks to all the little "Would you lend me a hands," and "Do me a favor Angels," the job has taken twice, three times as long as it should, 15 francs an hour, ten days out of his life, No-Beginnings-Angel always hopes that they will reward him for the effort he has put in. They're paying a tenth of what it would cost them to have a real professional do it, an official French outfit, with social benefits and retirement factored in, it would be 165 francs an hour, minimum.

"*You're* the professional, *you* should have known how long it was going to take." Friends suddenly turn miserly, charity becomes business. They know how much they want to pay, "We don't have much money," nothing else matters. "Hey, you don't have papers, you should be happy for the money. If you're tired of living like this, why don't you just go back to the States?"

One Saturday morning when the kids are at her mother's, Alexandra sneaks up on Angel while the effervescent Vitamin C tab fizzes loudly in the water glass on the kitchen table in front of him. "Exactly like an angel," she strokes the long blond locks. Suddenly scissors materialize out of nowhere. She grabs a fistful of hair, hacks and saws until the trophy comes loose: six inches long, and thick enough to leave Desperado storming out the armored front door with a bald-spot the size of a gold Napoleon.

That very night, Angel, on an impulse, asks me to shave his head. "What an ugly fellow I am," he wrinkles his nose at the results, shorn of his Botticelli halo for the first time since he can remember. He rubs his hand over the smooth surface, the knotty scars that now stand out red and angry, and shakes his head. But better to look like a weasel than tolerate the scissor-wielding tyrannies of a certain talisman-collecting fury.

Rather than cool her ardor, Angel's change to chrome-dome proves to be an elixir for Alexandra's fantasy, gives her all new momentum. A chance to envision whole new wardrobes for him, concoct all new schemes. If anything, her hands are drawn to him even more now, stroking the downy skull, tracing the tributaries of the scars. She has understood. "You're no longer my guardian Angel," she tries to look sad. "You're my Gordian Angel!" If there is still no solution to the mystery of how he could resist her for so long, all the way through Christmas, she has at last gotten a reaction out of him, an honest, impulsive reaction. The kind of reaction that lovers in books have. In her frustration, her impatience, she has discovered how to unravel the knot. It's that simple: cut him! She goes on a diet, the same steamed salmon, but no chocolate between meals now.

Unfortunately, the breast surgery does not turn out as she had hoped. Briefly forgetting doctor's orders, she lifts her arms above her head too soon after the operation. The stitches rip, and she begins to bleed. Once the cotton wadding comes off two weeks later, she spends long hours at the mirror looking at her new self, fingering these scars of her own, wondering if it was worth it. Little five year-old Igor takes time off from beating up his younger brother to watch with her. "I like Mummy's new breasts," he says in his five-year-old voice. It changes everything, that darling little Igoracle. She rewards him generously for telling the truth: new Laura Ashley wallpaper for his bedroom.

Bit by bit, her confidence blossoms, she begins to feel young again, masterful. One night, when nothing else is on, she huffs and puffs her way up to the sixth floor, to the dark, orange-painted maid's room upon whose door her Gordian Angel has pasted the word "HELL." The Polaroids stare down accusingly from the wall as he tries once again to patch up his past. His birth, his first haircut, the Pony League triumphs. He continues to type but bangs his glabrous head on the keys when she finally informs him how it's going to be. "When my scars heal I'm going to put you in the pot. *Tu vas passer à la casserole.*" To sweeten the pot, she has a plan. Her living room needs painting, she says, as if it is the first time she has ever mentioned it. And she thinks she knows the bald, rent-owing man for the job.

Angel can't help but dream. "If I just had a little money. Just a little..."

A possible solution appears at the Front Page bar, in the person of a thin Brit named Martin, a middle class kid from Bristol playing at being a hooligan, as proved by the fights he and his mate Danny provoke on a daily basis with some random French pussy or another. In fact, he'll probably go back and run his Dad's accounting business when he's done sowing his wild oats, but for the moment he's done a bit of everything to get by, some pimping and any number of schemes for conning tourists out of their money.

In between the fat English girls and Foreign Legionnaires on leave from Djibouti, Calvi and Beirut, the usual clients at the bar, Martin gives

Angel the once-over before deciding he can trust him and telling him of his latest scam, selling art at the Louvre. Somewhere in the 19th *arrondissement* is a warehouse which offloads cheap paintings made in Calcutta and Taiwan. One guy does all the skies, one guy does all the rivers, a third brushes in the trees. Idyllic scenes of Paris, the City of Light transformed by the distorted perspectives of sweat shop, assembly-line painters. Children diving happily into the Seine below Notre Dame, the Eiffel tower looming gracefully over Sacré Coeur, Ganesh strolling along the *quai* looking for used books, cows lowing contentedly in front of Saint Laurent and Dior. They're not real oils, or real canvas, but most of the tourists don't know the difference.

"Some of the people are going to be skeptical: 'Those aren't oils!' like that. 'Not oils?! Look!' you tell them. The Japanese are the hardest to convince. The guides in the tour buses warn them about the paintings. It's worth a bit of effort: if you get one Japanese to buy, the whole bus wants a painting. The cops come, you run. It's a bit hard because of the construction now, they've cut off the escape routes. But don't lose the paintings."

By twelve the next day, they are at the Louvre, with Angel observing as Martin sets down his portfolio, leaning it up against a column, lights a cigarette and gets to work. "Yeah, I'm on my lunch break from the University of the Louvre, and I just wanted to sell a few of my paintings so that I can have enough money to eat lunch. I don't want to part with them, but..." he says to a husband and wife. The woman is enthusiastic, the man cold: "How come all the other paintings here look the same?"

"Oh, well, I have a lot of people selling my stuff," he says but they don't buy it. Martin lights another cigarette and motions Angel over:: "Next time, you walk the husband around the block, OK?" Martin says. An American woman, absolutely charmed, buys two pictures for a $100 bill. "Can I have your autograph?"

"Well it's on the painting," he glances out of the corner of his eye: what name did they sign in Calcutta? El Dreco.

"So what do you say? You want to work?" Martin asks at the end of the day. "I'll give you fifty percent of anything you move." The small, forty franc paintings can go for as much as 400 francs, it's a lucrative proposition. But Angel-shorn is not feeling much like a Desperado. Deceiving the poor people, eluding the cops: it's not a job for a philosopher, not a profession for the higher man. He's not that desperate.

Not yet.

Spring rolls back in, and the whole city seems to succumb. It's that blissful state that Henry Miller described so well, "the green carpeted earth and men and women moving like panthers, soft music welling up from the sappy roots of the earth." The fullness that flows through even the poorest, the least man, when the first blast of spring warms and impregnates the winter air. A long-lost sensation: to feel abandoned, alone but free; that moment when, hungry and friendless, you rediscover that you are your own sun. Warming, feeding, lighting, regenerating yourself, adrift almost in another dimension

When it is spring, when you are alive, there is no way not to become intoxicated by your own voice, your strength, to bounce along on the currents of your joy, your anger. Women walk by casting lustful glances, flirting shamelessly, a promise of passion, renewal, deliverance. No way, with such fullness, not to overflow, to paint this infinity in words that express the impossible optimism you feel or to stake your life against all in the city that grinds away the absolutes, instant harmony, redemption.

At Shiva Press, I do a light one-pager on Sylvester Stallone and the differences in the posters for his latest film[2] then follow it up with a story about how the city of Paris is keeping the pigeon population down by feeding them with special seed. There's one seed from America called Ornithose, that works as a contraceptive. There's another one called Ornisteril, made by the Swiss. It's like saltpeter, it cuts their desire. 100,000 pigeons in Paris at the end of the 60s, only 45,000 now. I can't wait to share this with Madame Lacombe.

The next morning, when I return to my room I find Mme. Jeunet wringing her hands. "She won't open the door again," she says, nodding at Madame Lacombe's door. "She fell off her bed during the night and spent the whole night on the tiles. She says she can't get up. Do something Josef." Rather than call the fire department, I fetch a screw driver from my room and manage to force the latch.

"*Bonjour, Josef,*" a plaintive murmur from the ground, a dog wagging its

[2] In the English ads Stallone looks a tad pale, fierce but hops-deranged. In France, *si tu veux,* he's not quite so muscular, and the disdainful curl to Rambo's sneer is a bit deeper. In Rome, he wears a neat pair of tiny horns, so as to conform more nearly to the Italian image of a real man.

tail gamely, understanding that this is the end of the road. I try to reassure her. "Let's just get you off the floor." It's the heaviest forty kilos I've ever tried to lift, a hundred bags of cement, as if her whole being were just seeking to go down, down, down.

The heater had run out of coal during the night, we can see our breath. Madame Lacombe sits in a daze, perched on the side of her bed while Mme. Jeunet mops up the puddle of urine on the cold red tiles. "She must have been sitting in this all night long. Oh Antoinette..." she shakes her head and finishes the chore. We have to get her out of this freezer and into her other room.

Step by step, we squeeze out of Number 15, squeeze by the coal bin. One of us on each arm, we can advance no more than three inches with each footfall. "She'll never make it," I say, "Can you hold her up?" Leaving Mme. Jeunet to prop her charge up against the wall as best as she can, I race back to my room, and return rolling my office chair before me.

Oblivious to it all, Madame Lacombe is rigid. Her fist, white knuckled, grips her ebony cane. She tilts and almost falls, sending the chair rolling back. The cane gets tangled in the wheels, stuck at an odd angle, almost snapping her wrist before it is finally wrenched free to fall clattering to the ground. Somehow, working together, Madame Jeunet and I manage to slide Madame Lacombe into place. It's not such a long ride down the hall, right and right again, to Number 2, but with Mme. Jeunet steering, Benedictine-bottle glasses and all, it turns into a nightmare. She rams Madame Lacombe's frozen, thin, wood-colored and wood-stiff leg into every wall, every corner. The chair careens out of control, I push against Mme. Jeunet, trying to counter her clumsiness, *"Doucement. Doucement, j'ai dit!"* What is she doing? I straighten to look at her and am horrified to catch a glint of revenge in her eye, growing with each of Madame Lacombe's feeble squeaks and moans of pain. Inside Number 2, we struggle again to hoist her on to her bed. Her skin is blotchy and red, and her pulse weak as Mme. Jeunet slips the oxygen tubes into each nostril.

Later that morning, I step out to buy some food and look in on the butcher. "Madame Lacombe's in bad shape," I say. "She's not going to make it this time.

"Ha," he scoffs, giving a disdainful toss to the *escalope*. "You don't know Madame Lacombe. She'll be back. Last time she was even dead before she came back." He pulls his mallet off the wall and pounds the meat. "A nice thin piece, *hein*? You know she lives up there in those rooms, but *il faut pas croire*. When she was younger she used to have a taxi come here and fetch her every morning, same time. Don't believe she doesn't have any money, either. She never eats anything but the choicest filet of beef. *Attention*! If there's too much fat, she sends it back. Last winter, dead of winter, she made Mme. Jeunet go out and get her peaches. Peaches. You know how much that costs? No, you can bet she has money. She's just a stubborn old woman, she'll be back..."

As Angel's hair grows back, Alexandra, increasingly imbalanced, goes on the war path, accusing him of carnal cavorting with the English nanny, and then with the new Swedish *au pair* girl who tends the de Villier kids on the fifth floor. A brief storm which blows over when Alexandra discovers that Madame de Villier suspects her husband of coveting the Swedish girl as well, but is quickly followed by other accusations.

Beatrice and I go to the US for a month, but the minute I get back I go over to Angel's, stand on the street below and whistle up to the orange-tinted six floor window. Angel rushes downstairs in the usual lightning time, with the usual enthusiasm. But at the café on the corner, standing at the bar, as he drops the sugar in his mud, Desperado has that look in his eye, like he's feeling guilty, like he made a decision and wants to be proud of it but cannot quite manage, like he senses he has sealed his fate. "I committed rent," he says. After a six month stand, twenty kilos of salmon, five liters of hot chocolate, hundreds of vitamin pills, a beret and a watch finally pay off, he tested the waters with his toe and finally stepped in to the casserole.

Feeling young again, masterful, Alexandra buys the paints for him before she goes to the mountains, three different types for the walls, the doors and the ceiling of the living room. It's a five thousand franc job, *minimum*, but when she gets back from her ski vacation, all tan and bouncy, she looks over the job and offers to pay him 1000 francs. The job isn't perfect, Angel points out the spots where the spackle didn't dry properly, the difference in the three paints' shades of white, but that's not the reason for the low price. It's a matter of principle: he really should do the job for free to show how much he appreciates the use of her maid's room all this time, how much he appreciates her generosity, how much he appreciates her. He can look at the job as future rent, if he wants. He manages to talk some sense into her, thirty minutes of Nietzsche and Plato, nickel-making ethics, so that she finally agrees that it is only right to pay him. The thousand francs she will give him as soon as he puts a coat of paint on the radiator, will be further demonstration of her goodwill.

Attracted originally to Angel by the liberty he represented, she begins to think that he is flaunting it over her. She begins to see the relationship differently: now that genitals have finally come into play, her responsibility is to give him a lesson or two in reality principles, to show that the life he is living, this life of ideals and striving towards blurry absolutes, is not really possible. She wants to defeat him, crush him, put the power back where it belongs. She buys a 30,000 franc Le Corbusier sofa, designer chairs, an enormous color television and video recorder. Angel Desperado doesn't have enough money to buy the right kind of brush for the radiator, a long-handled, angled one.

"I can't believe he didn't know this would happen to him," Beatrice shrugs her shoulders when I give her the low-down. As a French woman, as a human being, it is impossible for her to imagine someone as uncalculating as Angel. She just shakes her head when I try to explain.

How are you supposed to get a sense of beginnings when your past only exists in faded photographs? How is an Angel supposed to be anything but innocent, when his exposure to culture has come by sneaking in to concerts or plays after the start or at intermission? How is a man who lives mainly on a diet of bread and final acts, supposed to note the nuances that announce the onslaught of hysteria, the first hints of I'm-in-the-mood-for-love viciousness, supposed to understand the basic rules of hydro-dynamics where sleeping waters turn into merciless maelstroms?

Angel Desperado can, for example, tell you that there are such things as Capulets and Montagues, and that something in the names seems to call for blood, but it all seems so petty, and he can't imagine why. He can tell you that men are prone to turn into rhinoceri, but there doesn't really seem to be any reason for that either. He can't understand how fate can trap the most noble of the Greeks, can cause them to foam at the mouth and gnaw dried corn husks until they finally take revenge. He can't imagine, short of stupidity, how people come to feel threatened, how they grow stingy, lose their energy, lose their smiles. Or how they end up in sand pits sinking lower and lower as the hands on the clock turn and turn and turn.

Squeezed in the vice, Angel puts the pieces together and commences to understand that this is exactly what he had coming to him. The drama, appropriately enough, seems to have no real beginning, and now he is in the thick of it. He wanders the streets in a funk, soup-faced, peeking into every crevice for something to help him get out of this situation. On his LOTO tickets, no matter how hard he tries to visualize those balls falling out of the tumbler, no matter how he manipulates the algorithm, he's been getting two numbers per *grille*. In front of American Express he stops to rub the lamppost, right where he's rubbed it since the first time five years ago. It was a big joke back then, a jest about leaving his mark on the city from the man who refused to take himself seriously. The spot is shiny by now, the brown paint worn through. He wonders if this is the only mark he will ever leave on the heartless city. He goes downstairs to check the mail, but the basement is deserted, no money there either.

As the buildings empty for lunch, and the workers walk by, Angel wallows in the different, slower rhythm of impecuniousness, feeling naked, vulnerable, completely open. By the side of the Opera he notices a German fellow with a backpack stop a pedestrian, show him a piece of paper and a little money. The pedestrian reaches into his pockets, retrieves a fist-full of coins and hands it over. Melting into the masonry, crouching from statue to statue, Angel spies on him, watches him pull the stunt five, six times, collecting more coins, and even bills, before the German with the backpack finally notices him.

He is from Munich, but has been living in Paris for the last year. He looks clean and dresses middle class, like some mother's son. In the four or five languages he speaks, he tells them the same story. "I've run out of money, and I'm trying to get home to Munich. The train leaves in an hour and a half..." He makes them look at the train schedule on which he has underlined the 13:15 train. "I have a hundred and twenty francs (he shows them the money) and I only need another 80 to pay for my ticket (he shows them a price list on which he has circled the price of the train). Can you help me get home?"

He claims he makes a thousand francs a day. When he hears that Angel hasn't even eaten in the last two days, the German reaches into his pocket, pulls two shiny ten franc pieces from his collection of fifty, solidarity of outsiders, and sends Angel on his way, gets back to work. The con seems like a dream to Desperado, the answer to his prayers. Things are looking up.

Back at Gus Flaubert, Marie-France, my landlady, informs me that they will be moving to Lyon, and that I will probably have to move out. I write a letter to the banker who owns the place, pleading for my renter's life. "Writer, inspiration, a roof over the head, moving in the middle of a project, etc..."

A week later Marie-France calls. "I talked to the owner today, and he said he was very impressed by your letter. He wanted you to know that he had nothing against you..."

"But?"

"But he says that if you are not out in a week, he will continue to charge us rent." Marie-France, bless her heart, does the rounds of her friends and finally convinces her brother to let the American take up residence in his maid's room on the other side of the 17th. Filing cabinets, plastic gooses, books, papers, a fan, a piece of carpet: what an accumulation since the days I used to live out of a backpack. It takes Beatrice three carloads to lug my stuff across the 17th. How will I fit everything in?

Room number 9, after room 18, half the number and half the size. Six square meters and no sink either, just a sink in the hall. "I'll give it to you for 500 francs a month, and the first two months free if you fix it up."

Angel helps me scrape off the old wallpaper, fill in the holes in the thin walls, put up shelves and paint the walls white, helps me lug an IKEA fold-out couch up the stairs, which fits perfectly even though you can't open the door when the couch is unfolded. No more lingering smell from Madame Lacombe, no more Madame Tournier, no more dizziness from the bakery fumes. On the other hand, no more freezing room: the new place has a big window facing south and a heater built in, central heating running off the building boiler, no extra charge. It's on the seventh floor, not the sixth any more: moving up in the world. There is a view of Montparnasse and the Eiffel Tower. At night you can see a tiny slice of the red neon sail from the Moulin Rouge. From the roof is an uninterrupted view of Sacré Coeur. The trains pass all day and all night, hooting, clacking as they go under the bridge on Rue Legendre. On the stone buildings on the other side of the tracks there are faded blue ads for Vichy water and Dubonnet. I've got horizons again. On the fence above the tracks there is a sign which says "*Danger de Mort.*" I finally muster the courage to dive back into *Fun City* and discover to my surprise that it's not nearly as bad as I had feared. I keep the keys to the old room, just in case.

It takes a week of starvation and one last coupling with Alexandra to get Angel moving. After a brief Raphaelite detour, Alexandra is back to her Gordian Angel phase, solving the mystery by cutting. Greedily she rubs the scars on his hands, skull, back and calf. Impersonal, a mere observer, every woman is an experience, Angel watches and notes as she scratches his back to ribbons. He feels her lead him to the bathroom and scrub down his rough skin with abrasive bristle wash-cloths until his shoulders bleed. She discards the wash-cloths as they become smooth. Coldly he examines and catalogues the bruises and bite marks she has left, her sounds of pleasure, the escalation, the futility of it all.

"Ooh I could just eat you all up," she says in the afterglow, shuddering. "Do you know what a praying mantis is?" If every woman is an experience, Angel, realizing that she is about to devour him completely, recognizes that it is time to bring this particular experience to a close. Time to get out of this maelstrom, this Bureau of Ties and Binds, before one of them gets hurt, time to hit the streets. With a thousand francs a day, he can build his own fortress, with money he can protect himself.

Angel borrows my backpack, but with all his clothes inside, his entire wardrobe, it isn't even a quarter full, so that he is obliged to add crumpled-up newspaper to produce the proper bulges, to enhance the image for his clients, to make it seem like he really is traveling, like he really does need to get home. He refines and practices his story, collects the proper train schedules and price lists then combs his hair, puts on his sweater and heads for the Opera, backpack on his back. With all the languages he speaks a smattering of, Swedish, Greek, German and French he should be able to bluff in any of them, explain his problem. But he doesn't really feel at ease in anything but English. Thanks to all the time in England, he can muster a suitable English accent and pass himself off as English. With the story he has, it might be difficult to bluff his way into enough money for a trans-Atlantic flight. "Hello, my flight leaves at three and all I need is another $350..."

He paces nervously, waiting for an American or English tourist to walk by. He waits and waits. Don't seem to be many tourists around. Or not the right kind. Or their faces look too thin, their noses too long, their chins non-existent. Angel espies the quarry, steps forward, and then turns back in a graceful 360. A problem of courage.

At last, a very chic couple wanders into his sights; obviously American, dressed in matching suede coats and boots. Angel hitches over to them. "Hi, speak English? I'm trying to get back home and..."

"No!" snaps the woman, quite curtly, nose upturned. Just like that she grabs her husband's arm and leads him away. Angel takes it like a punch to the solar plexus. He stumbles away gasping for air, completely deflated, the "no" flown into his very core. *Feierabend.* No more work today.

Alexandra's job bores her even more, the boys never stop fighting, and Vassilis, the younger and weaker one, the loser, is beginning to turn into a spineless jelly fish. The pink toe of her ostrich cowboy boot no longer helps control them. After losing all that weight she has once again become self-indulgent, eating whole boxes of Belgian chocolate at a sitting. "Oh come on you fucker. You don't really think that about me, do you?" she says, but Angel has once again retreated behind the barricades, climbed out of the casserole, and even managed to talk her out of the 1000 francs she planned to pay him for the painting, despite the fact that he has yet to complete the radiator. Gobbling chocolate, she gives Angel until June to get out, ultimatum #1. The last thing she needs is more frustration. He's confident that he can talk her out of this too, but he is tiring of interruptions, of being in this uncertain position, where the roof over his head can disappear on a whim.

Six weeks reprieve he gets with the 1000 francs, six weeks before he decides that he'll need to take a serious look at the German scam once again. We set to work in earnest on his act, hardening his skin, pumping up his prosperity consciousness. I buy a couple of greasy ten franc *merguez-frites* sandwiches, for strength, and we sit on a bus bench at Place Clichy. "You got to look at it this way," I tell him, an echo from what feels like a past life. "That money is actually yours, it's your advance, and they're just the temporary custodians. Your experience is going to make them feel rich, make them dream, make them feel free. If they say no when you ask, you don't take it as an insult, you just figure that they've forgotten that the money is yours, that they will remember next time." The logic of Times & Tides, but I'm not sure either of us really believes fully any more. "What you have to remember is never to ask a question which can be answered yes or no, unless you're sure the answer is yes. You speak English?" "Yes."

Angel borrows 200 francs to flash, gotta have some to get some. Even though time presses, it is a week before he manages to work up his courage, before he is willing to head back out, before he thinks he has mustered the irresistible aura without which a positive outcome is impossible.

This time he tells them there is a plane ticket waiting for him in England... if only he can get over there. The ticket will get him home in time for his mother's 60th birthday. He handles about twenty customers, even a few French. Some brush him off immediately, "Yes we speak English, but not to you." Others are kind enough to listen to his whole story before suggesting that if he is really in dire straits he can go to the embassy for help. A French woman, *Poison* perfume smelling sweetly, has no pity at all for someone suffering and garbling his way through improper verb conjugations. "*Non merci, merci, non!* No mercy..." He tries with his hands in his pockets, his hands out. He starts talking two meters away, three meters away, four meters away from the client; he tries it with stooped shoulders, classic style, and ramrod straight, Annapolis-grad-down-on-his-luck.

Towards the end of the day, the shadows lengthening, the light back-pack digging into his shoulders, he improvises a new tactic. He explains that the notion of England, the plane ticket and the 60th birthday should be understood figuratively, metaphorically, as symbols for France, for a Carte Orange metro pass, and enough time to write. "They look right through me, it's like I don't even exist," he says despondently when he calls to report the day's failures. To find out how horrible people can be, you only have to be in need, on the streets.

"It's still a good idea, it can work." I try to cheer him up. "Maybe you're in the wrong place. Maybe you should try Gare du Nord..."

Madame Lacombe dies in March, never returns from the hospital, never really comes back to consciousness, doesn't make it through another miserable winter. I hear about it from the Concierge a week after the funeral, when I come into the bakery on Rue Gustave Flaubert. The way she says it, the tone, she might as well be telling me she had just finished cleaning the stairway. "Well what do you expect? She was old," she shrugs as she collects her change. The Concierge was the only one at the funeral.

CHAPTER 12

Beatrice waits till I step out the front door before she lets the tears roll down her cheeks and onto the pillow. "He doesn't love me anymore. He doesn't even stay for breakfast," she tells her sister over the phone. She sobs. They know what kind of man doesn't stay for breakfast.

She gets out of bed and fixes herself tea instead of the coffee she would have drunk if I had stayed. She reviews the lines for the scene from the Fassbinder movie she is presenting that night in front of her acting class. "Very good," says her teacher. "Very impressive. But how come you never do anything but tragic roles? Why don't you try something humorous, something light?"

"I can't," she says, this is what life with the writer has turned her into. The day before yesterday she went to a casting for a Peugeot commercial. "Can you cry for us?" asks the woman behind the camera. Beatrice nodded, took a breath and imagined what it would be like if her Josef left her. The tears came flooding out. "Amazing!" said the woman behind the camera. "Let me get my boss. She must see this."

When I awaken in the morning, twenty ideas are lined up in my brain, gifts from Morpheus. I barely dare breathe as I slip into my clothes, kiss Beatrice on the forehead and tiptoe out the door. If I even blink, the ideas will fly away and never come back. "What do you think the biggest problem with the world is?" says the guy outside the Scientology center on Rue Legendre as I pass by. I look at him, the eyes of a zombie, then look away. Over the railroad tracks by Rue de Rome, up the seven flights taking the stairs three by three, coffee on the stove, coat off, typewriter on, and to work. One coffee, two coffees, three. The ideas fall into place, until fifteen are out of the way, and the last five can no longer be forgotten. The desk is piled high with papers, the filing cabinets are open, the beige carpet is strewn with coffee grounds and reject slips. The phone rings, Angel checking in. He can't muster the courage to go back out with the backpack. "I want to give you back your 200 francs."

"What time is it?" I ask. My knees are sore, my ankles ache, fearsome vermin scatter in and out of my periphery. It is dark outside, I've just realized how hungry I am, haven't eaten yet today.

"Nine."

"Nine?" I've been chained to the typewriter for fifteen hours, no wonder I'm seeing stars. "Listen maybe we can do it tomorrow." I write down the last five ideas, stumble back down the stairs and outside as the church of Scientology is closing. Back from acting class, Beatrice lies on the bed, television on. She doesn't bother to get up, or even to say hello. I shrug my shoulders, cook a dish of pasta, and fill two bowls. I put hers on a tray and settle down next to her on the bed to eat. "How did it go today?" she asks. "I'm exhausted," I say. She hides her head under the covers and rehearses her lines from Chekov's Uncle Vanya: "When he plants a sapling he wonders what will become of it in a thousand years. He dreams already of the happiness of mankind. Such men are rare, they must be loved." It sounds like she's praying.

Released from the mental asylum in Wales, Rock the fiddler makes his way to Paris and waits outside the Marceau school until Swan appears and falls into his arms. Worried sick, City-Rat waits for her to come home. He calls me, "You haven't seen Swan, have you?" He goes to the school but no one has seen her there either. He walks the streets, waits around Beaubourg, in case she shows up there to sell some paintings. When anyone sits down at his table, he just gets up and walks away. Maybe she fell in the street? Lost her memory? Forgot her name? He talks with the plainclothes cops, but they haven't noticed her either.

Three days later she calls to tell him she won't be returning, but at the end of the week, when Rock returns to Wales, she comes back to City-Rat after all. She has no place else to go.

"Don't worry, I understand, it's OK," City-Rat says. "What's done is done. The important thing is that you're back." Swan doesn't answer; once again she is unable to talk. Two weeks later, she disappears again, and this time City-Rat knows it's over. The world folds in on him, he is crushed, flattened.

Desperado and I come over to try and cheer him up. We tell our own stories of loves that grew and suddenly vanished. Angel reveals Alexandra's latest folly. "She wants to get a dog now."

"She already has one."

"Yeah, but she wants one that will be a fashion statement. She's narrowed it down to the dogs in the Black and White scotch ad, and the one in the Coppertone commercial." I laugh, City-Rat lights a cigarette and sighs. Sight gags, little diversions, we sweat to take the weight off City-Rat, but he just keeps lighting cigarettes and losing oxygen.

"I bought a bag of rice today," City-Rat says. "Five kilos for 35 francs. Got home, and I found out the rice has bugs in it. Every grain." He slumps down in the corner, listless, shrugging his shoulders, slowly turning the lever on a tiny music box he brought back from Japan, Stephen Sondheim, *Send in the clowns*. "Isn't it rich? Are we a pair? Me here at last on the ground, you in mid air. Where are the clowns..."

In the real world, the Shiva world, voting French malcontents bring the Right back in to power, so that President Mitterrand is forced to name Jacques Chirac Prime Minister. "This text is all wrong," Glynnis screams. I just shrug my shoulders and start over. I've always had trouble telling my right from my left. While the Socialists were in power, they changed certain traffic laws. In selected intersections, the right-of-way was dropped in favor of *priorité à gauche*. Now that the Right has regained control, the experiment will probably be curtailed. "What's the difference Glynnis?" When the structures disappear, when there's a general strike, the electricity is cut and the traffic lights go out: total madness. Horns honking uselessly, stubborn drivers battling for every bit of open pavement, and so what if it blocks the intersection, so what if the whole city is locked up, so what if it takes ten times as long to get home? "If I don't take the space, someone else will."

Monaco, bombs exploding in the streets of Paris, nuclear power plants exploding on the plains of Ukraine, bombs exploding over Tripoli, "*Khaddafi Ducks*." the real world marches on. The racist National Front, in an unusual burst of originality, comes out with a yellow hand-shaped badge of its own, saying "*Touche Pas à Mon Peuple*," don't touch my people, wow! A fifth television channel planning to run American adventure series around the clock is inaugurated after a furious debate. "Cultural mediocrity," says one side. "Liberty of expression, we are French, we will never be affected," says the other side, with winsome naiveté. Sex, blood, guns, at Shiva Press, after four, death is not so welcome, it impedes with plans for dinner. The bad tidings come over the AFP wire: "The Duchess of Windsor just died." "Shit!"

For City-Rat, of course, the tragedy continues. At the start of spring he and Blackie had begun to think about their street show again. 15,000 francs in debt and out of money once again, City-Rat hasn't paid his 2000 franc rent for four months, and his landlady, who has always been incredibly understanding, very gracious, begins to call him regularly, she has debts of her own. He has a 1000 franc gas bill to pay on top of that. Even the Canadian government has begun to send him menacing letters concerning the loan he took out six years before to come to Paris. He doesn't want to go back out on the street, but he has no option.

Blackie wants to try some new skits. He writes them down, invites City-Rat over for dinner and rehearsals. City-Rat shows me the new story, something about a treasure hunt involving a trip in a canoe, parachuting over a waterfall, sword fights, and the like. It's all technique, no psychology to the piece: a poor imitation of *Raiders of the Lost Ark*. The way their characters mesh, City-Rat submissive and fragile, Blackie gung-ho, enthusiastic, aggressive, City-Rat is quite unable to tell Blackie that he doesn't respond to the new material, but is also unable to come up with a story of his own. City-Rat still wants the scenes to come out naturally, the magic to spring again from improvisation, but it is such a long time since he has had the magic, since he has felt really whole, that the gags won't come.

"You should get yourself some new shoes," Blackie says. "Here I'll give you 200 francs." "You should make sure to warm-up before we start, that way you won't be so sore."

"You should, you should, you should," City-Rat finally rebels. "You're always pushing. Leave me alone!" They end up taking their old show to Beaubourg.

A well-known French singer who plans to tour France lets it be known that he might want to sign Blackie and City-Rat on as an opening act. The opportunity is tremendous: they would split 120,000 francs, they would get off the street and onto a stage, they might even get residence papers out of it. Wednesday, Thursday, Friday, Saturday, Sunday, Monday they perform. Each day the singer's agent is supposed to come watch, and each day he fails to appear. The shows are good, the timing hot, and the large audiences, 600 to 1,000, respond enthusiastically.

Finally the agent schedules the audition for Tuesday. Tuesday when Beaubourg is closed, when no one is around. Oh well. Gamely they go out there. Blackie sweats bullets to get a crowd, giving it his all. The circle is almost closed, 250 spectators materializing out of nowhere, an honest-to-god miracle, when a CRS cop breaks into the middle of it and informs them that they must leave, that some VIP is on his way, and the *plateau* must be cleared. The crowd disperses. After conferring, City-Rat and Blackie decide to try and put on another show in front of St. Eustache church.

They drop their bags next to the huge sandstone head sculpture in front of the church, and try to start up again. After a week of shows, plus this abortive effort, Blackie, normally the strong one, has run out of gas. There is hardly any foot traffic, after five minutes they have assembled three drunks and two dogs. Desperate for the job, City-Rat gives it his all, but without a crowd around, he is in a cave, the routines don't seem funny. His spirit leaks away. Killing himself for nothing. The agent crosses his arms, nods his head, clears his throat, shifts from foot to foot, begins to think about dinner. The huge head, the *clochards* and the dogs, the pigeons, even Saint Eustache, are completely indifferent. *Le bide*. No need to say anything.

Shaking, City-Rat and Blackie stumble to the Front Page for a beer. With the first sip, City-Rat's eyes head west. Angel, who happens to be passing by, tries to talk to him, but City-Rat can't hear a word. His skin turns yellow, his chin quavers, he is completely unhinged. "I'm finished with acting. Finished! Not just the street. I'm finished with everything!" He sublets his apartment and disappears. City-Rat could make 'em scream with laughter. *Hurler de rire*.

Beatrice checks the bulletin board at her acting school and notices an announcement for a casting of a television pilot, a series to be called *Deauville, Normandie*, an unabashed French rip-off of *Dallas*, complete with arrival in Deauville by helicopter and limousines that take an eternity to arrive at the spot of "drama." After a short screen test, Beatrice is chosen for the role of Jane, the bitch, *la garce*, the frigid wife of "the international art expert." The script, which has the orthodox stench of the French Screenplay Academy, is clumsy, artless, terrible. Forty-five minutes of helicopters, limos, and typical Norman settings, before the first hint of drama: "Me, an international art expert, having put 100 paintings in escrow, and now to find that ten of these are fakes! I'll be prosecuted and exposed as incompetent. I will be ruined." In the meantime, the disreputable Jane spends all her time dressing, undressing, taking pills and taking baths. In ennui and emptiness, moribundity and cleanliness she finally succumbs to temptation, betraying her homosexual husband with the handsome, young con-man. They kiss, she pouts, she throws atrocious lines at him out of nowhere and finally, losing her head completely, drags him into the bath, tuxedo and all. *Quelle folie!*

"It's not great," Beatrice says, "But you have to start somewhere..."

When they actually start filming in Deauville, I move into my tiny room, dreaming, eating, sleeping my book, no time for anything else. Full speed, total focus, total intensity, a state close to madness. When I walk down the street, I'm in another world, snapping my fingers unconsciously, so that old ladies cross to the opposite sidewalk. When I sit down at the *Père Tranquille* café in Les Halles to take notes, the whole terrace fills up, except for the semi-circle of seats around me. I imagine I'm speaking perfectly clearly, "Coffee please," but the waiter answers: "Right, coke and a cheese sandwich." "No, just a coffee please." "Got it. Two quiches and a *citron pressé. Tout de suite.*" I feel like I'm going crazy, like I need to finish the book before it finishes me. And then, as soon as it's done, I need to get out of town. Anything to avoid the melancholic spiral I suffered last time, the withdrawal.

"Greece?" Angel says.

"Yeah, maybe."

"What do you think Beatrice is going to say?"

"She's just going to have to get used to it. I've got to be alone for a while. Different horizons, different wine, different air."

"And you say I'm the one who doesn't know how tragedy starts..."

On May 16th, the black day honoring Saint-Honoré, patron saint of bakers, I write the last words: "It was another fun day in Fun City, there would be many more..." On wings of elation I run over to Angel's. We make the last copies together and send them off to publishers in New York. In the Latin Quarter I check the prices for flights to Greece. They have gone up to 1250 francs, except for one flight leaving the next afternoon which is approximately a third the price, a Times & Tides sign if ever there was. "There are only two seats left, but it's too late to book them. If you show up with cash at the airport, there's a slight chance you might get on."

That night I try three times to reach Beatrice in Deauville, but cannot get through. It is only when she returns the next morning that she learns I might leave that very afternoon. "I need two weeks alone, and after that you come down. OK? I just have to get out of here. Come on girl," I laugh. "I'm not abandoning you. You're not even going to be in Paris for the next two weeks."

"Could you give me your keys?"

"My keys? Sure..."

She turns away first, and doesn't turn back. She doesn't want me to see her tears. "I'm not abandoning you, I'm not abandoning you," the words echo in her ears. Josef even asked her to give him a ride to the airport! "Abandoning you, abandoning you, I'm abandoning you..."

Back in Greece, in Camp Sparta, where I lived just before coming to Paris, the effect of the last four years is shockingly obvious. The change of venue provides instant contrast. "You look awful." "You're thin!" "Your hair, it's gone white!" The women gather around, wring their hands and dab their aprons at their eyes. "Quick, get him something to eat!"

Mourners by profession, Greek peasant women are not the most objective of judges. At 6'6" I would have to weigh 300 pounds to begin to look healthy to them. But walking down those familiar deserted dirt roads, shirt off, caressed by that soft, warm breeze, I feel how much my heart has wrinkled. Fishing, emptying the nets, swearing my head off in Greek, under those familiar stars I realize that it has been an age since euphoria has washed through me, since I have been seized by laughter. The man of standards hardened against the world, immune to magic. The man of the streets who no longer sees variety? The man of letters who searches for what surely must be granted him, another person in whom the echoes of his words are not instantly muffled, in which his light finds its accurate reflection as well as its source. How much is my fault, how much is the demands of writing?

On the other hand, the change of scenery, the soft embrace of the breeze, eating fresh calamari on the port, I'm not nearly as imbalanced as I was after finishing the first draft of the book. I write to Angel, "The decision to come to Greece was the right one, no doubt in my mind. I'm fatalistic, calm, serene. Is *Fun City* good, is it bad? I don't know, it is what it is, and the next book will be what it is, and if I finish a book on the day that I die, that will be the sum of my experience, and I won't apologize for that either, only realize that I have offered everything I know, that it was presumptuous to be a writer in the first place, but that it's too late: what's done is done. And that of human beings who have passed through this life on earth I have managed better than some and worse than others, but that I have tried my level best to strive towards the perfection I could perceive. What else is there?"

A week after I arrive, I call Beatrice to tell her when the ferries leave from Athens, so that she can coordinate a flight. International code, country code, 00 33. 00 33. 00... It takes a whole morning to get through, and when I finally do, all I get is her answering machine. *"Bonjour, nous ne sommes pas là pour l'instant..."*

00 33, 00 33, I try again the next morning, and then the next afternoon. Sometimes I can't get through at all, sometimes I get through, but it's just the answering machine again. Where could she be? 00. Dizzy with zeroes, I begin to have premonitions, begin to wonder if somehow the bad *Deauville* script might not be inspiring worse life. "On the first ring," I joke over ouzo in the *kafeneion*, "I imagine him running his hand down her thigh. *'Bonjour je ne suis pas la...'"* he has slipped inside her. 'Hi Beatrice, I'm just calling to tell you that the boats leave Athens on Monday mornings at nine and Thursday at midday.' I say. And by the time I've finished talking, they come with a roar."

After nearly a week, we finally connect. "What happened?" she says disdainfully. "Isn't there any TV on the island? Did you get lonesome? No one to talk to there? No of course I can't come down, I have my theater test..."

"I see."

She promises to pick me up at they airport when I come back, I'm flying into Orly. An hour I wait after the plane lands, but she doesn't show. She's never really been known for her punctuality, but this is too much. I take the bus into the city, then the metro, and climb up the seven flights to my room. The answering machine blinks with a gut-full of messages, and when I raise the hood to rewind, a herd of cockroaches pours out. I play back the last few messages, including one from Angel announcing a trip to England, he's got another painting job at Manor Mouse estates, but promises to be back by July, and one from Beatrice: "I went to the wrong airport," says her tender taped voice.

Soon thereafter she calls, sweet as honey, and invites me to dinner, outdoors at the *Closerie des Lilas*, a real treat. I watch her park her car, watch her bounce out smiling in high heels and green satin skirt, absolutely ravishing. She laughs happily at my stories of Greece, she says I seem renewed, at peace. After dinner, under the trees, she pulls me to her and kisses me for nearly an hour, kisses me like she has never done before. Ever. We drive back to her apartment, climb into bed, my tan red-brown body against her white skin. Small bodies lusting to connect back to passion, tear each other to pieces. But there is a hitch, something is not quite right.

With Angel and City-Rat out of town, the Bureau of Times & Tides reviews Josef Klein's case and decides it is time to turn the screws, take off the gloves. "He doesn't understand, does he?" "Still a bit too confident, but that'll change." "Character and psychology, that's what he lacks as a writer." "We hit him slow, but we hit him hard."

Very conveniently, while I am in Greece, Beatrice's answering machine comes down with a blocked intestine, so that it stops erasing the recorded messages. When I return, there are something like twenty minutes worth of messages, all the ones I left from Greece, ("I don't know where you are, but the boat leaves on Wednesday at 12:45...") and, sandwiched between them, dozens of messages, entire conversations with another man. "Who is this guy?" I ask.

"Oh, he's just some guy who was in Deauville," she says. But her voice sounds a little too insouciant, and her eyes have that look.

"You're not a very good liar." I laugh, taking her in my arms, beginning to caress her. She turns her back to me, whining like a little girl, a familiar, chilling sound.

"What is it? What's wrong?"

"I don't know. I guess I'm just having a hard time forgiving you for going to Greece." She goes off to Milan to work for three days, but doesn't give me back my keys. Two days late she returns, cold and stony as before, without even so much as a kiss hello. "You're the writer. Don't be so conventional," she says. "Listen, by the way, I'm going out to the theater with Isabelle tonight, then dinner afterwards. I'd rather you not be here when I get back. I need some time to myself." Why? She doesn't want to say. I throw my hands up. She gives me a little mouse fart of a kiss on the cheek goodbye. I walk out shaking my head, slam the door and drag myself back to my little room, but at midnight I make the seven minute walk back over to her place, examine the shades, the curtains, to try and discover whether she has come home, whether she is alone... Yellow shades in the kitchen, one down, the other up. Bedroom shade down, but curtains not drawn. She isn't there yet. I head back home. Impossible to sleep, I take a slug of ouzo and at two o'clock do the rounds once again. The curtains are drawn, impossible to tell whether she is alone or not.

The next night, before bed, while she brushes her teeth, I listen to her answering machine, a week of messages, always that same male voice. "Are you back from Milan? Call me. I got the theater tickets. Meet you at nine. I love you *so* much!"

"Hmm," she walks in with the toothbrush still in her mouth. "I thought so."

"So who *is* this guy?" I ask.

She goes back into the bathroom, spits and rinses her mouth extra carefully. "Well?" I say, my heart sinking to that place in the Inferno, where all the other cuckolded hearts go.

"I was miserable after you left. It was obvious. I couldn't smile for the happy scenes, I spent all my time alone, crying. I thought you had left me..."

"All I said was 'I'm not abandoning you." She shrugs her shoulders, and I have to urge her on. "Yeah, so then what happened?"

"Well I was in the bar, having a drink and he saw me there and he tried to console me. He made me laugh. And we went up to my room and we began to kiss."

"Well how did that happen, tell me. I want to know the details. I have to know." She kissed him! I feel like I'm going to die!

"No, I don't want to tell you..."

She kissed him! She settles into bed next to me and quickly falls asleep. I listen to her heartless rhythmic breathing for almost two hours, hands locked behind my head, staring at the ceiling, before sleep, merciful sleep carries me away.

Perhaps I deserved this, perhaps I didn't treat her right. Or perhaps this was all fated, perhaps there were lessons to learn and no other way to learn them, perhaps the desire to follow in Henry Miller's footsteps had condemned me, to lack of money and heartbreak. Henry Miller had June, I have Beatrice. At the Bureau of Times & Tides, the technicians light cigars to celebrate, everything is going just as planned.

"How did it happen? I have to know!" I cannot leave well enough alone. "Tell me!"

Beatrice goes into her living room and lights a cigarette. "Well we went up to my room, and we began to kiss and then he laid me down on the bed... Oh this is stupid."

"You fucked him? You said you just kissed him." The sobs tear from my chest, I kick the phone.

"I thought you had understood. The whole time I couldn't stop thinking about you..."

"All the men I know always say women are whores. I've never said that."

"Well are you going to say it now?"

"So how long did you wait after I left before fucking him? Three days?"

"No I waited until the end of the week."

"Oh five days, great, great, that changes everything. This is the woman I loved?"

I stumble into Shiva Press the next morning, slump into my seat and start to work. Not a joke, not a word to anyone. The Pope in Colombia, preparations for the 100th anniversary of the Statue of Liberty, Stephanie at the Monte Carlo Beach club. "Fresh from a year of accomplishments, including a hit single record and her own line of designer swimwear, Princess Stephanie was overdue for a meeting with old friends..." Beatrice calls at noon, she wants to have lunch. In silence she watches me order, then announces the news. "I'm going off to the country this afternoon. To try and figure out my feelings for you. I'm going to abandon you like you abandoned me."

Princess Caroline soon to give birth to her second child, the World Cup in Mexico, Don Johnson returns to "Miami Vice," after threatening to leave the show, because he thought he was worth more than the $35,000 per episode he received last year. No human waves, no car bombs, nothing in Beirut at all. The big headline of the day: "Julian Lennon Gets a New Haircut."

I wander out into the night and down Rue St. Denis. There is a peep show called Hara-Kiri, ten francs only. I step inside, put my coin into the slot and wait for the shade to lift so I can commit hara-kiri. On the turntable a blonde in high heels only, rises on to her knees and thrusts her pussy at the mirrored windows around her, bowing her back like a caricature from Rutting Male comics. She slides down to the carpet, rolls onto her back and fingers herself, spreads her labia, licks her lips, thrusts her hips. The song ends, the door opens. She gets to her feet, collects her frilly undergarments, and closes the door behind her. Two other girls step onto the turntable, strip each other down to the garter belts, and quickly form into a passionless pretzel as the shade in my cabin closes slowly. I put another coin in, then another, until the song comes on, "R.E.S.P.E.C.T.", and I have to pull out.

In Les Halles, I look into various bars, but there are too many people laughing too easily, and alcohol would only make things worse. The city is full of Pakistanis selling windup plastic shoes or bouncing Schtroumpf balloons between their legs, full of women with teddy-bear knapsacks slung over their shoulders, on every corner there seem to be mechanical chickens full of plastic eggs cackling "Ba-ruc, buc-buc-buc-buc-buc-buc," d, c-sharp. I head home, take off my shirt, the room is a furnace. The small fan rotates lopsidedly on the floor, squeaking from side to side. The white paint on the wall cracks a little more as the concrete cools.

Seven floors below, the shadows from the 53 bus stop race back towards the city in the summer light. Beneath the chain-link fence with its skull and crossbones and *Danger de mort* sign, the last trains clatter through the void from Saint Lazare towards the suburbs, ferrying the tired last commuters back to their problems. They don't want to go there either, another evening at home, but they're too whacked to keep working. Levallois, Rosny, La Défense: the hideous high rise buildings circle the city, modern French design getting ready for the kill. Cergy-Pontoise, Evry, Marne-la-Vallée: "The new suburbs will not really find their souls until their cemeteries are full," the ex-Prefect of Paris is proud to say. Necropolis Now.

With the door open, a weak cross-wind blows in but doesn't quite dry the sweat that runs from my gut down into my shorts. I reach for the beige towel next to the window, right behind my head and some twenty cockroaches come scurrying out. "Not too smart, are you." By the time I'm done, the white wall is smeared with tobacco-spit, why should they be spared? "We are all equal, but in times like these there is just not enough space for the both of us," I type lazily, karma wrecked for all time, trying to get going, there's got to be somewhere to put the pain. Typing in stereo. Two paces up, two paces back.

In the morning life resumes. Heavy-eyed, I wake up to the 8:15 commuter train from Cergy Pontoise. I fold up the couch, turn on the fan and put on the coffee before going out to take a piss. The little cockroach cadavers have all disappeared, carried off or devoured by their compatriots. Not a symbol of anything...

The work at Shiva still gives me a sore throat and a will to homicide. But for the first time in my life, I'm grateful for the chance to go on automatic. Wake up, go to work, eat lunch, come home, kill the cockroaches, sleep. Stephanie of Monaco, Pope John Paul, Mr. T... Sarah Ferguson is going to marry Prince Andrew in a little over a month. France beats Brazil in the quarter-finals of the World Cup in Mexico, and the city explodes with joy, National Front thugs driving their DS 21s down the Champs Elysées, waving flags, honking horns, looking for Arabs to beat up. "*On a gagné, on a gagné, on a. On a gagné, on a gagné, on a...*" It must make sense to someone that they are beating up Arabs when half the team isn't even really French.

Beatrice returns from the country, but in her heart nothing seems to have settled, and the very next night, I sit on the edge of her bed, watching her get ready for dinner with Jean-Philippe. After dinner she returns, hard and distant. I hang my head, can't smile to save myself. "What is it?" she says.

"Nothing." I can't wipe away the sour mood.

"With your face like that, it must be something."

"Never mind. Give me a cigarette." I don't know half the truth, but she is incapable of telling me. "What are you worried about?" she snaps. "It's not as if I don't come home to sleep every night."

A few days later we head down south to Ile d'Oleron. A week out of the city! A week away from the answering machine! This time I jump at the chance. But as the train heads south, races through those once-promising canvases, those rows of cognac grapes and fields of sunflowers turned towards the rising sun, leaving Paris and problems behind, she still refuses to talk. "Please Beatrice. This is a very important week..."

The very morning we arrive on the island, she disappears for fifteen minutes. Upon her return, her face is so twisted that I know she has called him. "Great way to start an important week."

Doodling on my napkin, lips pursed, I sit through breakfastlunchdinner, listening to the conversation. Little wines, little melons, Ludwig Van Baytuv. Mme. Chevrier leads the assault. Bernard Pivot, the host of the Friday night TV show, *Apostrophes,* without which no book in France can get off the ground floor, came up with the idea of giving a dictation to the French nation. Hardly anyone got the whole thing right. Even celebrated writers and intellectuals were reported to have made as many as eighteen mistakes. A national disgrace, that's what Beatrice's mother thinks. *Une honte.*

"Crise de foi," I scribble on my napkin. Crisis of faith.

"Foi is written with an 'e,'" says Mme. Chevrier. *"Crise de foie."* Crisis of the liver.

"Yes, I suppose for some people it is," I say.

No, the news has not been good recently. The French government has just agreed to pay damages to the family of Fernando Pereira, the Dutch photographer of Portuguese blood killed in the sabotage of the *Rainbow Warrior.* 2.25 million francs ($300,000) to his wife, young children and parents, a figure taking into account his age, potential earnings and whatnot. Mme. Chevrier thinks the figure is outrageously high. *"Après tout ce n'est qu'un portuguais,"* she says. After all he's just Portuguese...

After lunch, I follow Beatrice down to the beach, follow her to the market, beg for alms, a drop of tenderness, a hint of warmth. She ignores me, goes off bike riding with her sisters, reappears just before dinner in time to ask me to stop looking so long-faced: "Make an effort." Beatrice's mother begins to speak about *Le Petit Gregory,* the poor little boy who died drowned last October and who has been in the news ever since. Accusations and counter-accusations, blackmailers, the affair has kept France Soir in headlines for nearly eight months.

"I have it on good authority that France Soir killed him to sell the newspapers." I try to joke.

"No, I don't think so," Mme. Chevrier says. Beatrice scowls at me, apparently the *effort* is not adequate. A wave of children hangs around the table, clamoring for *tartines* and deserts, squealing when I threaten to give them Indian burns. As soon as they are dispatched, and it is silent enough to talk again, Mme. Chevrier shifts from *Le Petit Gregory* to us without missing a beat. "Tell me, so when are you and Beatrice going to have children?"

I snort.

"Yes why not. Three children. They would be beautiful."

"In any case, if we do have children they'll be American and Moslem, not Christian and French..."

Does Beatrice have no affection left at all? Does she really not know what I'm going through, or is it that she just doesn't care? All night long I have horrible black dreams: Jean-Philippe comes into the room, takes off his pants, lies down in the bed and hip checks me onto the floor. "You can watch, if you want," he says as he takes her not once, but thirteen times. This too will pass.

Three days, four days, the meal never ends, and Beatrice never stops running. I check the times for the bus off the island and come back to the house. Beatrice is getting into her bike shorts.

"Either you talk to me, or I'm leaving," I say. She puts on her socks without a word and stands up, ready to go downstairs. "If you put your foot on that step, I'm gone." She glares at me, poor male half-wit, shrugs her shoulders, and steps onto the stairway. "That's it!" I throw my stuff into my bag and am out the door before she is two minutes down the road. I catch the 12:30 bus and am back in Paris that very night.

Her answering machine is ready and waiting, constipated with evidence, "Yes this is Jean-Philippe," says the slimy orangutan. "Two times I see you in two weeks. The first time you are forty-five minutes late for dinner, the second time you forget to call. I think we made a mistake, I mean as far as I'm concerned I didn't. But I think you hid much of the truth from me. I think you like this guy very much. *Enfin*, I don't want to talk about this guy. It makes me furious. I want to talk about you. I want to find, yes I want to find someone because I really want to fuck, to have emotions and everything. I wait impatiently for the next phone call from Ile d'Oleron. It would please me enormously. I hope I'm worth a little more than ten francs in your spirit."

"I looked all over for you," Beatrice calls from Ile d'Oleron that very night. "We didn't know where you were." I don't say a thing. I can't. Love is the word they use when it is time to get the knives out. The price of Hara-Kiri goes up to 20 francs.

Around the *Fontaine des Innocents*, a little tank-like vehicle explodes an abandoned briefcase. Radio controlled. The bombs have been exploding for years now, but never in such numbers as the last six months. The crowd of innocents watches the little tank maneuver from a safe distance, and then swarms closer to inspect the two-foot tracked miracle once the empty briefcase blows to bits with a loud bang and the police cordon relaxes. The fountain flows with its usual flotsam of aluminum cans and detritus, the hash and smack dealers clear out for a while, and then everyone back to work. The cops, more courageous in their new storm-trooper outfits, the punks with their protest purple hair and black lips, the West Indies and Guyanese Rastas with their usual stoned eyes and poker faces.

At the *Pédé Tranquille* café it's the parade as usual: the first waves of tanned Scandinavians, back from InterRail tours to Greece, sprinkled between the young, bored and beautiful, pretty boy clones, greased back hair, a snatch of French-accented English, conversations full of the latest hits, "Some of them want to use me, some of them want to be used by me." Wearing a Popeye sailor cap and shirt, and smoking a Popeye pipe, the little guy who can swallow half his face passes by and does a few tricks with a cigarette. The idol-rich nearly knock their beers over with laughter as he mimics them: how can anyone be so ugly?

A pale junkie with watery eyes and still-bleeding cuts all over his chin, shaving with steel wool, wanders up the street with those shoulders bent forward. He stops at every table outside. "*Un franc pour manger.*" One franc to buy something to eat…

"As opposed to one franc for furthering your education," I say in English. Two Swedes open their pocketbooks wide. "We cannot go forward," the script wells up before they can control it, "until the lowest of us is raised up." A fine sentiment; everyone else can tell he's a junkie.

On Rue de Verneuil, where Serge Gainsbourg lived before he died, the white walls are covered with all sorts of graffiti. Racist threats, idolatrous mutterings. I don't get Gainsbourg, it all seems like a big act, he's not a great songwriter or singer, and his role as a provocateur seems like the sort of thing one should grow out of by age 18, but somebody thinks enough of him to have painted a quatrain by Baudelaire: 'Dear God, my Lord, give me the strength at least to write a few verses which prove to me that I am not inferior to these people I despise.'"

Angel returns from England, only a couple of weeks late this time. Someone to talk to, to share the story, share the pain, share the city. The railing on the Pont Notre Dame worn shiny by all the hands that have run along it, Abelard, who loved Heloïse so much that his corpse reached out from the coffin to embrace her when she was placed in the casket with him, the fountain where Saint Denis washed his neck after the Romans cut his head off. The fountain whose waters were alleged to guarantee fidelity.

At Beaubourg, at the *Deux Magots*, the scene is the same: fakirs, summer jugglers, an occasional glimmer of talent from a performer who has not yet learned compromise, King for a day. "Where's City-Rat?" the street artists all want to know. The Prince is gone, the summer is empty. Rumors drift through: he is in Spain, he is in Switzerland.

In Switzerland, City-Rat is given a house in the mountains. Exercise, diet, meditation, in the quiet, all alone, his head finally begins to clear and he sets to work writing the story of his life. When he runs out of money, he comes out of the mountains and, very relaxed, follows people in front of the cafés. There is so much less pressure on the streets in Switzerland, and the people are generous enough so that he doesn't have to kill himself.

From time to time City-Rat meets up with Dorian Strahler, now feeling healthy again and touring through Switzerland with *Zirkus Knie*, the Swiss national circus. Akro the clown catches the circus in Bern, and reports that Strahler is a bigger hit than ever, but "He's lost his anger." Be that as it may, Strahler is holding it together. After the shows, he returns to his hotel and puts his energy into building a large wooden model airplane. "I don't want to become my clown anymore," he tells City-Rat. "The angry guy beating people because they have missed the point. When I was at Roncalli, I wanted to be the best clown ever. But how far could I take it? Clown Prince of the universe... I had to get sick to realize the clown is just a movie. The big clown looked down, turned the lights off and said, hey, joke's on you."

"Uh huh, uh huh."

Beatrice rings me up the night she returns from Ile d'Oleron. "I suppose you never want to see me again," she says. I can't answer, I don't know how. "Well?" The silence lasts forever. "OK, I'll call you again." That first night I stay away, but the second night I walk by her apartment, check the shades, the curtains, look in her car for signs. There's nothing noble about it at all, but I long for revenge: I want to slash her tires, pour sugar into her gas tank, take out the Italian money she keeps in my savings account and run away to Afghanistan. "You're still too weak," Madame Lacombe's ghost points an accusing cane. And it's true: the desire for revenge is just sad proof that I still can't live without her.

While I spy on her from one side of the apartment building, Jean-Philippe waits for her on the other side. "I must see you," says his voice on the answering machine. "I'm going to wait outside your door until you show up."

Beatrice doesn't tell me, but every time she's seen Jean-Philippe it has ended in a fight. They scream at each other, she tells him to get lost, tells him that she has made her choice. The day I came back from Greece, she didn't really go to the wrong airport, she was telling Jean-Philippe it was over. But he didn't listen then, he doesn't listen now, he's still convinced they are meant for each other.

She leaves a message on my answering machine, her voice is almost crying. "I need you Josef," she says. "I need you."

"Not so soon, not so soon, regrets," say the boys at Times & Tides. "The lamb isn't roasted yet."

On the occasion of the 200th birthday of the first ascension of Mont Blanc, they remeasure it with modern instruments. The height, 4807 meters, is like Babe Ruth's home runs to Americans, a number engraved on the national psyche. With the new measurement it comes out four meters shorter. Panic. Mass hysteria, the year won't end without significant turmoil.

Beatrice's doorbell rings and I get up to answer. Levi jacket, jeans, cowboy boots, elbow against the wall, hair falling into his eyes: no question who it is. I'm surprised: after all the slow deaths I have plotted for Jean-Philippe, seeing him in front of the door like this, I almost feel sympathy for him. Now that the other guy is on the outside, I can feel his anguish. "You caused me a lot of pain, you know."

"Come and have a coffee. Man to man. I want to talk."

"OK." I close the door and go back to inform Beatrice. "It's Jean-Philippe. We're going to have a coffee."

"Nooo!" Beatrice whines. "I don't want you to. No!" I go back to the front door and tell him I can't come out after all.

"I don't understand. How could he fall in love with you after fucking you only once?" I ask Beatrice when I return.

"I don't know."

In her presence again, I know the answer to my own question. I remember, the first time I slept with her, dazzled by her beauty, how drunk I was with the hopes she had raised in me. How I felt like everything was possible.

Beatrice takes me to watch the tape of *Deauville, Normandie*, more torture. I try my best to ignore the kisses, try to push away the sight of him standing in the doorway, the exact pose he had assumed when he came to Beatrice's door. I try to concentrate on the lighting, the costumes, the script, the way Jean-Philippe has of adjusting his sunglasses, flinging his hair out of his eyes. I wonder if either of them would have thought to get together if the script, bad art, had not given inspiration to even worse life. I wonder how I can possibly remain with a woman I can think such things about?

Before the end of the week, only one night of grace, then the cycle starts again. She may need me, but she doesn't want me. She asks me to drive her out to the country the following morning, so that she can go bike-riding. I feel like a convenience, a tool, but I go over to the apartment anyway. I ring the bell to the front door, even though I have the keys, because it makes her mad to get the door. As expected, when the door opens she is scowling. I take my clothes off, step into the shower, hands shaking with rage. When she comes in to the bathroom, I step out of the shower and towel off. "Why is it that you have no desire for me?"

She smiles unwittingly, trying unsuccessfully to conceal it.

"What is it?"

"I can't tell you. You wouldn't understand. No one would."

"You've been fucking him again?" I venture a guess.

"That's an obsession of yours, isn't it?" *Mais c'est une obsession!*

"Well what can it be? I'm your man... You can tell me."

"That's precisely why I can't tell you, because you're my man. I've said more than I should have already."

"What is it that you can't tell me, if you love me? It's worse to have a secret."

"I'm not so sure. I want a future with you. But if I tell you, you may not want one with me." She moves off to the living room, pulls out a bottle of whiskey and pours two stiff ones, then lights a cigarette. I light one too.

"So what is it?"

"Well," she says, "You know how they say the soul is unfathomable? Well I think my body is too. I don't know why, but my body is just drawn to him. I've tried to feel good about you since I got back. I've tried. But I'm blocked. I've never told him this, but I don't care about his soul. I just want to fuck him and leave. When you told me about going to the peep show, I thought to myself, well he's like my peep show, like a drug. And I thought maybe if I went off with him for a week, I would begin to hate him. And then I would be ready for you again."

"Good, good, good," say the boys at Times & Tides. Now that I'm softened up, time for act three.

In the morning Beatrice takes pity on me, rolls me from the other side of the bed, on top and inside of her. I have to restrain myself, no contraception; she tells me she comes hard and fast. There is something impure, vile about this. We drive out to her parents' country house in Normandy. I walk in the door and say hello. Her father sneers. "Well at least we have a right to your hello this time."

"*Et alors?*" So...

"A strange way you have of behaving, you Americans. Truly a strange way."

"What do you know about what happened?" I snap, so much torture and now this!

"All I know is that you could have at least left a note. We made lunch and looked all over for you."

"So?"

M. Chevrier gets up and goes outside to the small barn. I follow and let him have it: "Listen I didn't really appreciate the way you greeted me. You really don't know the story."

"What is this sort of behavior?"

"You don't know how much I have agonized over Beatrice in the last month and half."

"No, and I don't want to know! We made lunch and we looked all over for you." The parasite, the fat fuck, the worthless son of a whore!

"I don't give *a fuck* about your lunch."

"Well in that case you can just get back into the car right now." He motions to the door with his finger.

I'm furious, enraged, I could smash my fist down his freckled throat, exterminate this insect on the spot. But such behavior would not be likely to heal Beatrice's wounds. "Were you never young?" I take a deep breath and try diplomacy. "Did you never feel any passion?"

"There *is* such a thing as the quill."

"You really don't understand."

"No and I don't want to understand. You have a strange way of acting, you and your generation. I don't say anything to Beatrice, because she will never come see us anymore." He finds the bottle he had come for. "Well listen, we better forget all this, OK?"

"Sure, just forget it. Sure." You son-of-a-bitch, you worthless piece of shit.

After lunch, Beatrice is stretched out on a *chaise longue*, reading, hostile territory. I drag my unattractive soul over to her, desperate for words of solace. "*Tu m'ennerves,*" she says. You bug me.

"You know, many people have been advising me to leave you. This situation is impossible."

"*Who* has been telling you that?" she demands.

I shake my head. If I told her I had met a woman who had irrefutable proof of the existence of God, she would probably demand to know who the woman was. "Listen, if I bug you so much, why don't you just take me back to Paris, and we don't have to see each other ever again."

"With every argument are you going to keep putting our entire relationship in doubt?" And on and on.

I awaken in the morning after dreams of how I don't excite her, how my body repels her. How Jean-Philippe's hand must have caressed her pussy the way she likes, how she must have placed him inside her and bent her back, curled her lip in pleasure right before orgasm. I kick her, a sharp jab with the heel, so she will sleep a little worse.

"I think I'm pregnant," she says.

"That's all we need."

"You don't want the child..."

"Not much chance that it's mine, is there?"

"Forget it. I'll just get rid of it."

"Is it mine or not?"

"I don't want to talk about it..."

"OK wrap it up boys," says the head of Times & Tides. "I think he's had enough. Now, maybe, he's ready to write."

CHAPTER 13

In February, the first bomb on the Champs Elysées misses Angel Desperado by about 30 yards. The second one in the first wave, at the Saint Michel branch of the *Gibert Jeune* bookstore, misses him by about 20 yards. The third one, at FNAC Sport and the fourth one, thirteen loaves of pentrite which fail to detonate in the RER subway, presumed to be just a warning, miss him by about five minutes.

In July, just after Angel gets back from England, a bomb blows out the fourth story of the *Préfecture,* the central police station, 22 wounded. In September, a bomb goes off at the Hotel de Ville post office, one killed. Another one at La Défense, 51 injured, two seriously. A previously unknown Arab organization claims responsibility for the explosions. Two days later, yet another on the same axis, the Champs Elysées this time, right when Prime Minister Jacques Chirac is to go on the radio to denounce the cowards, to announce the new laws he will put in effect. Angry shouts ring out as the maimed, charred bodies are loaded into the red fire department ambulance vans in front of the snarling crowd. "We'll hang an Arab from every lamp post!" It turns out that one of the victims was a policeman who saw the bomb behind a booth in the crowded Pub Renault restaurant, picked it up, and carried it down to the basement where it blew him up.

It is then that Desperado decides he will carry a camera around. If by his mere presence he is going to be setting off the explosions, he figures he might as well take pictures, perhaps make some money that way. One big picture could pay for a year's living, he thinks, but Desperado is only one of many prowling the city with cameras, trying to cash in. Shiva Press is on crisis footing. The photographers crowd into the agency, mill around the newly purchased police-band radio, while the motorcycle messengers keep their big BMWs hot by the curb. It's not like Beirut, or Iran, or some plane crash far away: everyone is grim. The deaths, the blood are right around the corner. The texts I write are full of plastic explosives, two kilos, one kilo, six kilos, and cadavers. The light tables groan with the weight of the gore, hundreds of slides to choose from to find the most impressive photos. The news kiosks race to plaster the latest bloody and blackened bodies all over their fronts to sell magazines: the little child carried out of the *Hôtel de Ville* by a fireman, the policeman who rushed the bomb to the basement at the Pub Renault, lying on a stretcher, still breathing through an oxygen mask, his skin blackened, his arms below the elbows reduced to bleeding stumps.

The *Préfecture de Police* blows: a two kilogram loaf of plastic explosives said to belong to *Action Directe* demolishes the car registration section. Of the fifty-one injured, thirty were police officers or civil servants. The days are filled with sirens and alerts. The Parisians walk around with their heads up, everyone is suspect. The cops answer hundreds of bomb scare calls a day. Hamburger boxes, abandoned shopping bags, parked cars, anything out of place is immediately cordoned off and the bomb squads come screaming in. On the Champs Elysées, trees in planters, just recently installed, are hastily removed. Overnight, for maybe the first time since before 1968, the police become heroes, protectors once again, respected citizens. *"Bonjour Monsieur l'agent. Merci Monsieur l'agent."* Posters recruiting new policemen spring up all around town, and somehow they don't seem out of place.

On the 17th of September, a bomb thrown from a black BMW explodes outside the Tati clothing store on Rue de Rennes, leaving six dead and fifty wounded. Of all the targets that the terrorists could have chosen, Tati, with its dirt-cheap clothing, is perhaps the most powerfully symbolic. Nobody, not even the poor will be spared. Newsweek pays Shiva $100,000 for the cover photo showing the carnage, the shattered glass on the sidewalk, the bodies ripped to shreds, the stream of blood trickling down the street. War.

Jean Tweedledee, Minister of Fat Stomachs, announces a law to appease the masses. From now on there will be stringent requirements to live in France. And to hell with the country's reputation as a land of asylum. Tightening immigration is something the Right has been wanting to do for years, and smug though Tweedledee might be, the move seems very popular. "If this law had only been in place when Khomeini was here..."

The cops are everywhere, their presence overwhelming. They're stopping everybody, even the most unlikely suspects. Businessmen with brush cuts, grey suits and briefcases. Does anyone seriously believe the change in laws will have an impact on terrorism? Like the terrorists are just going to stick their hands up and say, "Now that I have to register with the police, I guess I either leave the country or renounce violence." Plato said: "This and no other is the root from which a tyrant springs; when he first appears he is a protector..."

At Beaubourg life goes on as usual, it's still its own little world, no one is really concerned yet.

"How's Beatrice?"

"Beatrice is fine."

"When *are* you going to leave that girl?"

"When are *you* going to leave Paris?"

"Did you hear about Romi? He locked himself into his apartment, hasn't been out in a week. If they send him back to the Philippines he's a dead man."

"It's not great out there today, too much brown skin."

"A friend of mine's in a play. Playing the role of Jesus. He has to stand over the orchestra pit for 45 minutes straight with his arms out, nothing holding them up."

"You hear about Bob? He played the banjo in a video with Jean-Jacques Goldman. They made him sit down, because when he was standing next to Goldman, he would tower over him."

"Fucking midgets!"

In the aftermath of the Tweedledee Law, and in spite of screams of protest from the press, a plane-load of Malians, 100 in all, is sent back to Mali. A friend of Zoff's, an Austrian woman who sings in the metro, gets picked up: she has ten days to leave. Zoff is the first to get anxious about registering with the police. He's determined to go legal.

First he inquires at the Mairie of the 18th *arrondissement*. They send him to the police station of the 18th: it's a police matter. The police send him on to a building on the city outskirts. He waits in line for six hours, only to learn that the building is for handling political asylum cases. They give him a slip of paper: the place he's looking for is the *Préfecture de Police* on *Ile de la Cité*. He hops the metro, takes his place in line, and waits for an hour before they tell him to come back the next day.

At eight the next morning, he's back at it. But so is virtually the entire Indian sub-continent. Balloon hawkers, wind-up shoe sellers, chestnut vendors, newspaper salesmen: every Pakistani and his cousin has also decided to go legal. After three hours in line, Zoff finally slips inside. From office to office he drifts, every category has a category, and the uncivil servants can't be bothered. Keep 'em moving. With his idiosyncratic French, with their explanations, he lurches through the labyrinth, getting nowhere. Finally after another two hours, exasperated, he stops a detective and tells him the problem. He's getting married in two months, and all he needs is a visa to get him through to the wedding. The detective leads him to the temporary visa department on the ground floor. By the end of the day, he is finally set: a stamp that will get him through to the wedding. It takes him a week to purge the bureaucracy from his blood, to feel like an artist and start painting again.

I have tremendous reservations about going through the official wringer myself. Partly because I have an aversion to bureaucrats, and they to me, like dogs who hate each other on sight, and partly because, ostensibly, the only way to pull it off is to go back to the States, apply for a visa at a French consulate, proving that you have a job and resources sufficient to support yourself, which makes me a less-than-ideal candidate for official sanction, even if I had the money to get to the States, which I don't. Not to mention, wandering son of the double diaspora, I actually prefer the freedom of living below the radar, living without a net and nobody knows your business.

Until now, the game has always been relatively simple. Take a trip every three months to get a new stamp in the passport, or if you can't, and the visa expires, just play dumb American, dumb Canuck. In the days of the almighty dollar, with all the examples around, and with the genetic prejudice most French seem to have about Americans it is an eminently believable role, you don't even have to be a good actor. "Visa? Me? *Le* passport? I'm sorry, no parlay vous..."

Visa or not, for four years, wearing the proper choice of poor man's camouflage gear, three stripes on my windbreaker, notebook in hand, running shoes on my feet, I have been virtually invisible. Only once have I been stopped by the police, for taking advantage of a free phone. They stop the Arabs and kids with leather jackets, earrings, rebellious hair, tight jeans and pointy cowboy boots, anyone who looks like they might have drugs on them. Invisible, yes, but even after all these years, my heart still races every time I pass the law, every time I cross a border, every time I see a uniform, police, meter maid, Salvation Army. With the bombs going off, my heart has been racing overtime, there must be ten times as many uniforms around the city as before, gendarmes, CRS, regular cops, and army commandos too, in cammy gear, black boots and blue berets, machine guns ready to roll.

An epidemic of constabulary unpleasantness which the Bureau of Times & Tides, for some mysterious reason, becomes convinced I need a closer look at, as if life weren't difficult enough. The event is scheduled in the morning, outside the BHV department store, where I used to go for escalator romance, and where Beatrice has a quick errand to run. As usual, she parks on the crosswalk. "You stay here, won't be two minutes," she says. Two minutes go by, then three. In the rear-view mirror: at the end of the street, a four man patrol of CRS, the riot police, all walkie-talkies, bullet-proof vests and machine guns, fans out, checking for bombs under cars, heading my way. Four minutes, and still no Beatrice. My heart starts to race, the vein in my neck pulses the way it does. This could be serious, the stamp on my passport expired two days ago, and with the city on war-footing, the dumb American act is not nearly so likely to succeed. Five minutes on the crosswalk could turn in to five years exile. Knuckles tap against the window. "Hah, what a pleasant surprise, *Monsieur le Gendarme*, fancy seeing you here..." The man in blue salutes smartly, and I'm so charmed that I can't help but roll down the window. "*Bonsoir*," I croak, inadvertently, "Good evening!" even though it's ten o'clock in the a.m. Very suspicious: the foreigner plays with time. May I see your papers? Why of course, hah, good evening! Ha, ha, ha. My papers...

I reach into my pockets as the barrels of the machine guns stiffen, but the passport is hiding. It's always in the back pocket, but I can't feel it there now. I pull out wallets, orange cards, chewing gum, rabbit's feet, three-day-old baguettes, a not-unimpressive collection of charred feet and hands, last wills and testaments, tossing the lot on the dashboard. Everyone is waiting, waiting, but the passport still refuses to materialize. "Unpublished writer was a terrorist!" I imagine the headlines in *France Soir*. "Josef Klein: Red Army Fraction Linked To Tamil Tigers." "Terrorist writer killed *Le Petit Gregory!*" The machine guns go off safety. At long last the recalcitrant document appears: an American passport, worn but apparently authentic. Phew. The cop leafs through the pages and, what with all the other stamps collected through the years, goes right by the proper page. He snaps the wrinkled book shut and salutes. "Enjoy your vacation!" Thank you, yes-of-course, my vocation, thank you. *Bonsoir*, ha ha.

A possible solution comes via Dean Zoff, impressively assiduous point-man in the exploration of French bureaucratic absurdity, who discovers that somewhere on Rue Saint-Dominique is a place called the *Syndicat des Travailleurs Intellectuels*, the Intellectuals' Union. The word is that if they approve you, certify you as a *bona fide* intellectual, you can slide through the visa service like a king. I've learned to be wary of Zoff's tips, in the last year he has given me more expert advice about trains that don't exist, events that never happen, cheap deals that end up twice as expensive, more untruths than I write in a day at Shiva Press, still it seems like this Intellectuals' Union is worth checking out. If that's what it takes, I'm more than willing to be an intellectual for a couple of days.

For a week on the seventh floor I practice intellectual poses, every day from nine to five. With a borrowed *Gauloise* cigarette dangling from my lip, index finger punctuating the air, I practice in the mirror until I can truly impress myself by saying nothing, and then saying it again for good measure. "*Tu vois? Tu vois ce que je veux dire?*"

On the big morning I pack up my manuscripts, two versions of a novel, three screenplays which no one will probably ever see, ("Parasites," "Will it Play in Peoria," "Vampire Poodles From Outer Space," etc...) two tear sheets from magazines and any number of reject slips and negative travel articles. I practice one last aphorism from Nietzsche: the true artist has a bit of the rogue in him. In German, it sounds even better. I twist my tongue around some of the philosophical bromides and lancets I have heard thrown around at intellectual dinner parties, when the discussion of vegetables and cheeses bogs down. Lacan: "*La femme n'existe pas.*" Then I slip into my ratty, flea-market trench coat; the scotch tape holding the hem is losing its glue. I scrape it off and put on a new strip of tape. Finally I put on an English tweed cap which came back from the cleaners a size too small, so that now it makes my head look bigger. I'm as ready as I'll ever be.

I meet up with Blackie for the metro ride across town, and all the usual good omens are in place: lovely women, friendly café owners, timely transit connections. We locate the plaque on Rue Saint-Dominique. I.I.I.I.I., it says. Inside, we are greeted by a 25 year-old blonde woman, very attractive. We're the first customers of the morning. Hold the phone. I take the hat off, throw Nietzsche into the umbrella rack: this is no time for aphorisms, it's time for charm. No matter what Blackie's reputation with the other street artists, when it comes to women, dressed in black the way he is, long thin braid running down his muscular back, charm is his middle pseudonym.

She warms to us almost immediately. "Yes I see..." she excuses herself to fetch some information. Blackie and I exchange glances: all systems go, it looks like it's going to work. Except that when the door opens again, the blonde is nowhere in sight. She has been supplanted by another woman, obviously her superior, more like 40, most likely a divorcee by the look of her, not quite as attractive as the blonde, not responding half as well. "Frankly I'm not sanguine," she says, "But I'm not the one who decides. You have to wait for the department head. Should be in any minute now."

The waiting room walls are covered with faded cloth, more brown than pink. The shelves hold a few fat dossiers, and some envelopes to be mailed. On the table next to me is a metal carousel holding a half-dozen rubber stamps. *Par Avion, Recommandé, Port Payé*: no luck. Nothing like "This man is an intellectual, give him whatever he wants."

"Looks kind of like a coffin," Blackie says. The optimism is infectious. The room, long and narrow, walls slanted up to the ceilings, gives that effect. My sartorial intellectuality weighs on me like cerements. It's beginning to feel very hot, I'm down to my last T-shirt. Finally, twenty minutes later, the front door opens.

In comes a woman, 60, with a cane, looking very pale as she wipes her nose with a handkerchief. She marches through the waiting room without a pause and into the main office: the boss. I look at Blackie, Blackie looks at me: trouble. She takes her time as the air gets heavier and heavier. The room begins to shrink.

She comes back in, blows her nose again and tucks the handkerchief into the sleeve of her green cardigan. "Sorry I'm late. But I've had the flu. So what can I do for you?" She seems nice enough, very sweet, but already absolutely immune.

"*Ben voilà...* I am a writer, and I wanted to try to get a paper to prove it so that I can get a residence permit. I heard that it was possible?"

"Yes, it's possible... Can you prove to me that you're a writer?"

No problem. I've got five kilos of manuscripts in a bag at my feet. I open the bag and show her, offer to sell her a couple of kilos at a good price, cut-rate, a show of good faith.

"Yes, but have you published anything?"

No problem either. I pull out the articles with my name on them.

Articles? Only articles?" She's afraid that just doesn't qualify me as an intellectual. "Have you published a book? Translated a book? Have any credits on a screenplay?"

"Go fish. But the novel, you see, I've been working on it for five years. It hasn't sold yet..."

"*Desolée, mais je ne puis rien pour vous.*" Sorry, there's nothing I can do.

"Excuse me very much please, *Madame.* So what am I, if not a writer?"

"Well," she huffs. "Nothing prevents me from saying that I am a writer too. Except that I don't earn any money from it. If you're an amateur, you are not a writer. It is not I who decide." Then she softens up again: "I would like to help you. I am only here to establish a dossier. Then we send it on to a commission which decides your case, based on qualifications established by the Ministry. They're the ones who determine if you qualify." The old bad-grandmother good-grandmother routine, I'm not fooled.

As she drones on I imagine the poor sots in the commissionary position, fat cats, smoking mile-long Cuban cigars from the Cuban Embassy commissary, and drinking Cristal in long-stemmed goblets. "Uh, uh. *Non!* He's not an intellectual." "You call this a book?"

"... it is pointless to send them an incomplete dossier. Now if you can come back with some proof that you have published a book, a note from your publisher, I'll be happy to help you. Until then, I'm sorry..."

She turns to Blackie, "And what can I do for *you?*" Blackie is much better prepared. Hunched over, she leafs through his contracts, notes the letterheads. When she has made it through the last Japanese, Italian, Hebrew, German, Dutch contract, he hits her with his press book. She wipes her nose and points her eyebrows, clearly impressed, under the plastic sheets, article upon article in Japanese, Italian, Hebrew, German, Dutch, some with his pictures, some not. She doesn't make it half way through before she decides that he is the real thing: a mime, an intellectual. She closes the book and smiles. She wants to keep the books to show the committee. It will make a very good dossier.

A temporary solution: I bite the bullet, and go down to the *Préfecture de Police.* By now, nine days have passed since the explosion in the car registration offices. Long plastic sheets cover the damage to the building. A state of siege. Today, for no apparent reason, the doors are to open at ten. The visa applicants, mostly Arabs and Pakistanis, and, a sprinkling of blond heads between the black, Swedes and Austrians, are kept at bay by metal barriers and unsmiling policeman in flak jackets. Next to the *Préfecture*, a deafening roar from trucks, cranes and jackhammers repairing the *Cité* metro station, a gaping, mud-filled crater, half a dozen epochs laid bare.

When ten o'clock rolls around, it's a mad dash. Frantic for their papers, the foreigners crush together against the wall of the *Préfecture*, hemmed in by more metal barriers on the right, and policemen in front. I tower over everybody, at least I can breathe. As the line moves forward and the cattle elbow and trample each other to conquer each cubic inch, a uniformed shrew walks up and down screeching for everyone to hold out their *convocations*. Bad news: you need a piece of paper to get inside to get a piece of paper.

I pretend I can't get my hand down to the pocket where the paper is, but she doesn't fall for it, and orders me out of line. "Where do you live?" she asks, then scribbles furiously on her pad, giving me the address of the 17th *arrondissement* police station. It's a trick. Zoff has already done the leg-work on that route, and that's not the right way to the center of the maze. She moves on, forgets me, I've turned invisible, the old urban hunter skills coming in handy, but anyway we're packed in so tight, it's impossible to move. At the front of the line a policeman checks the *convocations*, and lets a trickle of people through. The crowd behind me surges, pushing me forward. A policeman slams his fist into my chest to push me back, but fails to notice that I'm not bearing the proper pink slip.

Before the law stands a second guard, twice as large and twice as terrible as the first one. A fat motherfucker, red braid of honor on his shoulder, mustache on his wine-burned face, and wearing clear plastic gloves, one of which happens to slip off and fall to the ground. He stoops to pick it up, slips it back on and punches me in the chest for crowding him. His right is only marginally better than the first doorkeeper's, even Beatrice's mother hits harder than that. Before I know it, I've managed to slip by.

Inside the hallway, foreigners channel through a row of metal detectors and plucking machines run by more men with more gloves, but a little bit of variety here, *un peu de fantaisie*: some orange dishwashing gloves to complement the clear plastic ones. Unruffled, I continue into the courtyard where a third doorkeeper waits, this one so terrible that the first doorkeeper cannot bear to look at her. "I just want to be regularized," I tell her with the proper measure of subservient whine. She smiles and directs me to the visa extension department.

Thinking quickly, I come up with what I hope will be a credible lie: that I came in on the train from Germany, that they forgot to stamp my passport, and that therefore I am entitled to three more months. Before the new laws they almost never used to stamp US passports unless specifically requested to, so the lie could work.

Finally they call my name. "So you came in from Germany? And through what town was that?" I think hard, but try as I may, no preparation, I can only recall the name of the town on the German side of the border, Saarbrücken. This is possibly the stupidest Yank she has ever seen. "I know the way the train goes, Metz, Nancy etc..." I stall, wrack my brain, but still nothing.

"Strasbourg?" she suggests, trying to trip me up, to expose me for the louse I am. But I stick to my story through a half-dozen other suggestions of northern French towns, Montpellier, Nice, Cannes, Madrid, Marrakech, until she comes up with Forbach, the right town. Now she wants to see my train ticket. Now she wants to know the exact date I crossed that border. I don't have a ticket. And the day? "Why that would be before they put in the new laws, about three weeks ago, uh uh, 18 Brumaire." By now, we both know I'm lying. She goes off and consults with her superior for an unnecessarily long time. My goose feels cooked. What should I do in my last ten days, before I am forced to leave the country?

At long last she returns, a disdainful look on her kisser. She could smell this lying Yankee rat in her dreams last night, that's how strongly I smell. "You came in on 18 Brumaire? Very well, you get three months from that day." A little breathing room: two and a half months-worth, to be precise.

Relieved, safe, light again, I go out that night to celebrate. In the Montparnasse metro station, I stroll down the 300 meter-long rolling rubber sidewalk. Half way through I see the police blockade at the end of the tunnel. Uniforms and plainclothesmen with orange-cardboard "Police" armbands filling the hallway more completely than it is filled at rush hour. Checking papers and searching everyone. Black cops checking blacks, women cops checking women. Forgetting the fresh stamp in my passport, I panic, my heart speeds up, I think of hopping the rail and sprinting the other way, and then I remember. Protected by paper, I smile at them as the sidewalk deposits me right in front of them, "Come on, come on. Frisk me, I dare you." Once again, I'm invisible, they don't even notice me.

That night at dinner, the adventure through the labyrinth makes an excellent story. The host, a French publisher, can hardly believe his ears when I inform him that in France there actually is such a thing as an Intellectual's Union. He finds the very notion so funny that his judgment is temporarily clouded. "No problem, we'll get this fixed for you," he nods, quietly convinced, lips together, chin down hinting of access to channels, puppets on strings, crumbling treasure maps where X marks the spot of the dusty, cobwebbed cellar office of the legendary Bureaucrat-Who-Knows-How-To-Say-Yes. "How long do we have?"

CHAPTER 14

At the start of autumn, Alexandra's ultimatums begin to rain down on Angel with increasing frequency. "You have to be out in two weeks, you have three days, if you're not out by tomorrow..." A little talk, a merciless fuck always seems to banish the latest fantasy, and bring her out of the hallucination. But the constant drama is wearisome; and for Angel, weariness is now turning to disgust. "I can't imagine how I managed to sustain the illusion," Angel hangs his head. "I've never met anyone so self-obsessed. She calls herself the black widow. She's been eating more and more chocolate, over a kilo a day for the last month. If she ever runs out, I'm finished."

"He's become passive," Alexandra calls me to justify her tactics. "Someone has to give him a kick in the ass." There's a hint of victory in her voice. "Maybe when he goes back to the States, he'll appreciate what he had here."

"Say what?"

"Yes, didn't he tell you? He wired his brother for money yesterday."

"No! He would have told me..."

Heavy-hearted, I hang up the phone and run over to Angel's. Through the open window the orange ceiling of Angel's hell is visible from the street. I stick my fingers in my mouth and whistle. Angel pops into the window, smiles, and appears on the street in no time flat.

"Alexandra called..." My face tells the rest of the story.

"Oh, the wiring for money?" Desperado laughs. "That shut her up good. She even gave me 300 francs until the money gets here. All in the interest of the higher man," he says. But he's hardly convincing. Beaten, limp, scarred, so used by now to being a plaything, a victim of the wind, that he is unable to even begin to manipulate his own destiny, Angel has lost his resilience, and he knows it. Either you have money or you wait for the boot to wind up again. "I'm ready Josef, ready to say yes to everything, yes, yes, yes, I'm open to miracles. I believe in miracles," he says, but these words too sound like something he has memorized.

"It looks like you're going to need one."

On Sundays I start going to tea at Igor Morosov's near the Invalides.[1] If it were up to Igor, there wouldn't be any Sunday teas. But his wife, who is also Russian, used to hold a salon when they lived in Moscow, and it's one of the conditions of their relationship that she continue the custom here.

The walls of the apartment are covered with icons and paintings done by Russian émigré painters, an inch, at most, of wall between the frames. Dogs and children run around as the samovar empties, the vodka comes out, bowls of thick borscht materialize out of thin air. The conversation switches back and forth between Russian, English and French.

"They think I'm KGB. They think every Russian is KGB."

"The DGT taps my phone. But it's a joke. You can hear them come on the line. I tell them things to make them suspicious. In Russia, you see..."

"I went to *La Samaritaine* yesterday, Zhusev," says Morosov's wife. "They wanted to search my bag. 'Everyone has to be searched *Madame*, for the bombs,' they said. I told them I was Russian, and I had left Russia behind. If they insisted on searching me, I would just shop elsewhere..."

The tea is supposed to end at seven, but more and more people arrive, writers, painters, sculptors, heroes and what have you, most of them dissidents, all of them longing nostalgically, noisily, for mother Russia. Such laxity in the West, and no authority to resist. They eat spoons full of jam straight from the jar, sip their tea, knock back their vodka. A muscular fellow in a tight T-shirt, even louder than the rest, tells about escaping from the Soviet Union by rowing a boat across the Baltic.

The woman next to me laughs delightfully at his boorishness, raises her eyes. I ask her for a cigarette. "Yuri and his rowboat story. A legend," she says as she offers me the pack and my thick, inexpert fingers try suavely to extract a nail. Yuri pauses briefly, swallows a spoonful of jam from the jar, then another. "You bet I rowed," he says, using a full spoon as an oar to illustrate. The jam drops on his pants, on the head of Morosov's little girl, Dunia, who bursts into tears. Yuri takes a napkin off the table, pats her on the head, a half-interested attempt to remedy his clumsiness which only succeeds in spreading the jam further. Eager to tell even more, he forgets about the little girl, who stands there looking up at him, a ferocious pout on her tear-streaked face. "You got to have muscles to row that far. Muscles!"

---

[1] Morosov, the Shiva Press photographer for whom I set up the Jackie Bisset story in Berlin.

he flexes his impressive biceps, knocking his half-empty cup onto Dunia's flowery dress. She bursts into even louder tears and runs off, squealing, to her room. Morosov follows her, everyone laughs, without a hitch another bottle of vodka appears. They begin to sing.

"My name's Aglaia. So what do you do?" the woman next to me asks over the din. She smiles. "Shall I light it?" She's got a lovely laugh, she's attractive, she manipulates the lighter with sure confidence and grace.

"Writer. Sure. Other questions?" I answer rat-tat-tat, coughing as the smoke pours into my lungs, nearly falling over from the nicotine rush.

"Can I get you some more borscht? How about some tea?"

For two hours we talk. Problems with papers, how long have you been here, why do you stay? "Because some day, Aglaia, the tragedy is going to end, and then the humor will come back again..." Charmed by my goat-and-brimstone dialectic she fishes into her purse and pulls out a card, black with silver lettering, "Why don't you come over for tea tomorrow?"

The apartment turns out to be in the Marais, right above the Swiss Cultural Center, an oxymoron if ever there was. Pots and pans stacked high in the sink, layers of grease on the water heater, the tops of cabinets, right at eye level for me, a grand piano in the living room and snapshots tucked into the frame of the mirror. "My children," she says sadly, bringing in the tea. She pulls out a cigarette and I light it for her. She takes a long drag. "I was married to a French man. He kidnapped my children..." she exhales and walks over to the window, looks at the piano and plays a note or two. "He kidnapped them once before, but this time I haven't been able to find them. He's a writer, and in one of his books he accused me of being a KGB agent. He told that to the judge too..." She pours the tea, stubs out her cigarette and smiles sadly. That's life. She sips her tea and smiles again, this time seductively. "I talked to a friend of mine. Maybe there's another way for you to get papers. Are you hungry? I have some herring, and I can boil some potatoes."

"I've been hungry for four years."

She laughs. "OK. I'll get it ready. I'll boil some potatoes, would you like that? Good, listen, you wouldn't mind going down to the *tabac* and getting me some cigarettes?"

"So do you have a girlfriend?" she says when I return. "Tell me about her." Aglaia's pretty, but not quite as pretty as she thinks, not quite as pretty as the way she bats her eyes, and throws her head back to laugh. Unwilling to walk down that road with her, I entertain her instead with the story of Angel and Alexandra. She fixes sandwiches, laughs beautifully, says *"Oh non, oh non!"* as the atrocities mount. "I don't believe you," she says, and then, almost in the same breath, "Yes I do believe you. It's too much."

A few days later my phone rings well past midnight. It's Aglaia: "Sorry to call you this late, but I had an idea. You see, I want to change careers, I'm tired of working for the woman I work for. I don't want to play the game. I want to be my own boss. What I really need to get ahead is some command of English." We both know what she is saying, but, like a good Russian, she knows that you have to be diplomatic, slightly oblique. "You wouldn't by any chance know an American who might be willing to give me English lessons in exchange for a place to stay? Of course he or she would have to forget that he or she knows French."

Yes, I say, I just might know someone who could possibly be interested in such an exchange.

"It's a strange offer, don't you think?" she asks as we're about to hang up. "Are you surprised?"

"No, I'm not surprised. But I'm pleased. I expect good things to happen, I'm only surprised when they don't happen more often."

"So, any more decisions about what you plan to do?" I ask Angel the next day.

"Well the worst solution would be to go back to England, find work there..."

"And convince someone else that they hate you? Better to trust in miracles..." I tell him about Aglaia.

The next Sunday, Angel arrives at tea, scrubbed and glowing, Mr. No-Beginnings ready to prove that he is the ideal, the compleat, English teacher. It's a perfect escape. A difficult situation, but Aglaia handles it like a queen. She explains about her children and her husband, the reason for the spare room. "In exchange for the room I will expect two evenings of lessons a week. And we will talk in English." She doesn't want him to feel pressured: "We'll see how it goes. If after a month it doesn't work out, well then fine." He can move in when he wants.

Just the hint of an option and Angel is back on Fortuna's good side. He gets a job painting an Italian girl's apartment, five days work for 2000 francs. "I'll show you generosity Alexandra," he laughs, teeth gnashing, as he packs his papers, the notes and abortive starts on the novel, pulls the photos off the walls. "Every bit of drama, Alexandra. All the hours of my life you wasted. You'll pay. Every steamed salmon bone I've had to pick out of my throat, every painting you asked me to hang, every drain you asked me to clear, every bit of babysitting for your sons and yourself. You'll pay." He drops the keys off at her Concierge's, and leaves without a word.

That night the phone rings again, waking me from a dead sleep. This time, predictably, it's Alexandra. *"Ça vole pas très haut cette histoire."*[2] Half-asleep, I listen dully as she begins to insult *me*. What kind of man has friends like this? You Americans! You think you can... You expect everyone to...

This isn't the first time Angel has flown away leaving me to face the music, they always have to purge themselves on someone. After ten minutes of insults, I try to appease her. "Yes. True enough..." At this, she shifts her focus to Desperado. "He left the room a mess, he's not even a man, he's worse than a pig, you call him a writer, he'll never be a writer, he took 300 francs, is this what I get for my generosity?" Dazed, my head falling over the bed, the receiver to my ear, I let her talk. Her words flow together, I tap the earpiece. It sounds to me like she is actually telling me to pass on quite a different message: "He has one week to come back."

A new beginning! A yellow room, a *light* yellow room. Angel has his days to himself while Aglaia is off at work. He has time to play the piano, to study a bit of Russian, to take notes and read as much as he wants, to walk around and explore the Marais. He stares into the windows full of food on Rue des Rosiers, and the owner invites him in to sample everything for free.

On Yom Kippur the police seal off the Jewish quarter. Angel, the trickster rejuvenated, sees this stoppery and searchery as an intrusion; a free man walks where he wants, even if he doesn't have papers. He buys a few bananas at a local Arab's, peels one and walks straight through them, munching tranquilly. When Aglaia comes home from work, the food he has bought is waiting on the table. He opens a bottle of wine. The hours fly by as they talk, it is 3 a.m. before he retires to his room to read some more before sleeping. *Crime And Punishment.*

Aglaia continues to see other men, but when she comes home from her

---

[2] This story does not fly very high.

various dinners, she and Angel resume the previous night's conversation till all hours. She is getting closer and closer to him, so close that she begins to be embarrassed by the poor level of her English. No matter: Angel carries on in his French, only slightly handicapped, frustrated by his inability to articulate precisely the notions he wants to express. He tells her about his run of bad luck, about the English girl who came to live with him in Colorado when he was a drummer in a rock and roll band. He tells her how he fed and kept that English girl laughing for six straight months while they toured America, how he watched her transform from girl to woman. He tells her how she brought him back to her family in Kent, set them up in separate bedrooms and didn't sleep with him for four months, because it would offend her parents. He tells Aglaia how she drained him of his money, drained him of his humor. When he had no money left, it didn't seem natural for her to take up the financial burden. Now that he was down, now that he no longer made her laugh, she could begin to kick him.

In Angel Desperado's blue eyes, Aglaia begins to see a world of hope. A man to deliver her from her nostalgia for Moscow, to guide her to live with him in exotic, exciting locations. When she finally invites him into her bed, the transition seems unforced, natural, and he does not resist her. He feels as if he is on solid enough footing, as if she is so grateful to him for terminating her loneliness, that he will be able to weather any storm hatched by the shift into intimacy.

"If I were pregnant, what would you do?" she asks him the next day, needing confirmation for her feelings.

"If you were pregnant?" What does she mean? "Well *are you* pregnant?" He is still too fresh, dizzy from the merry-go-round with Alexandra to abide such unsubtle play.

"I mean if I were," she insists. "Would you want to keep the child?"

"Tell me if you are. Then I'll tell you."

"Never mind."

I get a number of reject slips for *Fun City*, polite, positive overall, but hard to digest nonetheless. Probably the best thing would be to just throw them out, to forget them and move on. But I don't, I can't, I tuck them in my back pocket, and walk the streets reviewing them again and again. For days on end. The way I figure it, there are only three possibilities. One, I'm not in the right place, and if I want to get published I should be in New York, on the cocktail party circuit, not in Paris, literary Siberia. Two: the book is just not that good; it was important to write it, to get it out of the system, to put the first one behind me, but now the embarrassing evidence should be buried or cremated. Or three: I'm mentally ill, deluded, talentless, and this fantasy of being a writer, this Henry Miller infection, must be treated before anyone else gets hurt.

As a sort of a joke, a bit of black humor, I start a reject slip competition with an American writer named Dwight, who has a novel going around called *Midland*, a story about the crucifixion of a young writer by his high-strung Italian wife. The writer and his wife share a 12 square meter room in a rundown building in Milan. To wake up in the morning it takes her three hours, four cups of coffee and a fistful of special pills washed down by Coca-Cola, "Ahh, I feel human again." To get back to sleep at night, it takes her another fistful of pills. Plus she must have the black and white TV screen on, a giant night light to scare away the spiders. A combination whose soporific effect is only fully unleashed when catalyzed by a few pages of Marcel Proust's *Remembrance of Things Past*, which she reads *sotto voce* to her stuffed animals.

I receive a reject slip from 20th Century Fox that opens: "The only thing worse than a comedy that isn't funny is one that doesn't even make sense." But the critique is so confused and so off the mark, sign of TV and cocaine-addled brain, that despite an excellent finishing line, "You finally decide that this is just inept," Dwight refuses to allow it into the reject slip competition. A real reject slip is more subtle, full of devastating half-truths, clichés and carrots. Dwight has one from The New Yorker which says: "You have some real ability. I encourage you to try again." He has one, three lines, from an agent recommended to him: "Thank you for sending me your novel and short stories. There is good material in them but I did not feel that I could find a publisher for them in today's difficult market. I hope another agent will feel differently." He has a third one from a New York publisher: "I have come back to your novel a number of times and have been impressed by the writing. You create interesting dialogue, and on a line by line basis I am interested in what is happening to these characters. But after about one hundred pages I begin to wonder what was going to happen. I detected no main thread. Which character matters most? Who am I supposed to care about so much that I'll follow them to the end?

What is the PLOT of this book? What I see here is a nicely done collection of *scenes*, but scenes tacked end to end don't automatically add up to a novel. One needs some dramatic tension, development of goals or conflicts for the characters and all that good stuff that makes the reader want to follow your lead. I'm sorry I can't make an offer for this work. You write well. I'd be glad to read your work in the future, and will promise to respond more quickly." The answer comes July 23; the manuscript was sent Feb 10. He has a fourth one from an Italian publisher. "We liked it and would like to buy it but our printing schedule is full for the next millennium." Where in the job description did they ever mention so much rejection? Where is the woman of the fourth dimension?

After facing south for seven months, I get a call out of the blue from Warner Bros., asking me if I might be interested in working on a screenplay with a noted director. Turns out the director in question is Roman Polanski, that he's doing a film with Harrison Ford, (eager, at this point in his career, post-*Star Wars* and *Indiana Jones*, to do something a little more serious), and that he needs an advisor on American idiom to make sure the script sounds realistic. When I go to Polanski's apartment to meet him, Canon typewriter in hand, just in case, it seems like a formality, not a job interview at all. He tells me the story he has come up with so far, asks me what I think. I say "Is that all?" An honest answer that I guess surprises him, as if he's not used to people telling him what they really think. "Good," he says, "The more skeptical you are, the better the screenplay will be. It doesn't matter who's right or wrong, what matters is that the script be good. So let's get to work…"

The first two weeks of work with Polanski are ecstatic. I feel like I've stepped out of the wilderness, like my ideas finally have an audience. I arrive at his apartment every day at 11 and leave at 7. We sit on either side of the dining room table, a tape recorder between us. When we need to come up with a character, I pick one from the thousands I have met over the years at crepe stands, at gangster bars, at night walking the streets. Jokes fly back and forth, whole scenes are improvised that go directly into the script, the debate is focused, passionate, challenging, and in the spirit he promised, it doesn't matter who is right or wrong, the only thing that matters is the script. Sometimes disagreements are settled by debate, sometimes they aren't settled at all, but I restate my case just before quitting time, and the next morning, after sleeping on it, Polanski has come up with an alternative, a winning solution which we both recognize the quality of. Sometimes he'll put a video on the television, a scene from "Chinatown," and say, "You see it works." For the first time, someone besides Angel is there to appreciate the fruits of my odyssey.

It's a different world, commuting from my *chambre de bonne* above the railroad tracks to Avenue Montaigne. There is always a big black wooden bowl of Granny Smith apples on the table, and when they run out, which they do every day, I'm voracious, more appear. Thanks to Polanski's almost daily invitations to lunch, at *Chez André*, on Rue Marbeuf, usually, my stomach is full for the first time in four years. On the street, in restaurants, everyone wants a piece of Polanski, it's ugly, it's obscene, starlets, young directors, women of every age and shape, card-carrying cretins. It pains him, but you'd never know it. He handles it gracefully, like a pro, putting on a charming public persona, telling jokes, recounting anecdotes so that nobody sees the pain. Mother killed in Auschwitz, the horrors of the Krakow ghetto and World War II, the murder of Sharon Tate, eight months pregnant with his child, he's closed the gates, no one gets in or out any more. There are Russian tanks parked all along the borders of Eastern Europe, just waiting to invade, the end is near...

It's a different world, I learn to work on a computer for the first time, I'm privy to telephone calls with Dustin Hoffman, and Harrison Ford, some of which I transcribe, there are encounters with Polanski's friends, meetings with the various Warner Bros. producers, nauseating scenes with his young girlfriend, who has tasted every fruit, and pouts about their dinner plans in the various three star restaurants he suggests, "Oh no Roman, not the *Tour d'Argent* again! We went there last week..." "Oh no Roman, not Maxim's, it's sooo square."

What starts out as a job as an idiom advisor, translating pages written by Gerard Brach, Polanski's longtime writing partner, a notorious agoraphobe who hasn't left his apartment in the 6th *arrondissement* since 1971, quickly transforms into a full collaboration. Brach the agoraphobe has simply been in cold storage too long, the Paris he writes about no longer exists, and he is emotionally frozen, there is nothing we can use, translating is a waste of time.

We spend three weeks working out the story, then start on the script, writing one version for us, and one for the cowboys, which is what we call the Warner's producers. A version with more place names, and local color, "Because they love that stuff," as Polanski says. At the end of the week, there's a check from Warner Bros., 5000 francs, not a fortune in movie terms, but a goldmine for me. I'm tall, he's short, we make a strange couple, clearly different perspectives, but that's not a problem. "You've got your foot in the door now," Polanski says. But I don't really care about the movie business, deep down I still feel that cinema is a minor art, that writing novels is infinitely more difficult and rewarding, a leap into the unknown, a mountain to climb, an obligation to *become* that demands a level of concentration and engagement a hundred times greater than script-writing. There you have it: I'm a novelist, all I'm thinking about is how much money I will have once the job is over, money to give me the time to write the next novel. The novel about the sixth floor.

The weather turns winter overnight, a bad sign, cold hands, cold feet. But right now, maybe just today, Christmas lights glowing in the trees along Avenue Montaigne, the smell of chestnuts in the air, I've got the step in, the magic step, I'm feeling alive, funny, alert, aware, appreciated. Money in the pocket, and more where that came from.

After four weeks at Aglaia's, Angel has already spent his entire nest egg, 2000 francs, trying to demonstrate his good faith. "If you have no money," Aglaia says, "Why don't you get a job?"

Surprised, offended, good cheer instantly dampened, he tries to set her straight. "When I was at Alexandra's nobody ever told me to get a job." Not to mention that getting a job without working papers is virtually impossible.

"Yes you're right, I'm sorry," she says, contrite.

A few days later Aglaia sends him out for cigarettes, and when he returns, asks him if he will take her to a desert island. "No," he answers truthfully. Not that there's any question of him going to desert islands. This staying up till all hours talking is beginning to tire her out. She's dropping the masks, showing her colors more and more: the kind of woman who likes a man to do things for her, to demonstrate his affection with small chivalric tasks. Buying her cigarettes, putting sugar in her tea, finding her lighter for her. She's not nearly strong enough to move out of a big city, he thinks. She'd never survive.

"You're not very gallant," she attacks him. "A real man would be more gallant. I know that we're never going to go to a desert island, but you could have told me that you'd take me at least."

Going to sleep that night Angel understands that he must redress the balance of power. If he came here to teach her English, then it is time to begin, otherwise she will just trample him. But the first night she goes out; then, a sudden engagement, the second night as well. Echoes of Buggerelli. The third night she balks, humiliated, when she finds herself unable to pronounce the word "self-sufficiency."

She turns on him, chides him, "You're heinous, uncouth, you have no sense of cultural differences. How dare you presume to understand the high bearing of Russian people?" She laughs mockingly at his improper French until he too is too insecure to speak or even hear.

"Would you pour me some more coffee?"

"Huh?

"Do you know Madame de Paris?"

"Huh?" From the Swiss Cultural Center below a medley of music floats up to add poignancy to the situation. Fusion alpenhorn duets, rap yodeling, Swiss jazz singers belting out *Schwitzerdutz* blues from William Tell to Heidi, heavy tick-tock backbeat, goats and cuckoos in the chorus.

Diving deeper and deeper into *Crime and Punishment*, Angel walks the streets now imagining himself as Raskolnikov, window-shopping, comparing prices for axes and cleavers. Aglaia has shown him a type of character he has never before encountered. A Russian character with codes of behavior and fragilities he could not have imagined in a thousand and one years.

How can you live, after believing with all your heart, even for a week, for a day, that a certain woman is *the one*, then discover that she isn't and still delude yourself that you have some grasp on the truth, some ability to discern reality? You can content yourself with rationalizations: people change, a love that once existed cannot now be invalidated simply because it is no longer. But you know that a part of your body has withered that will never regain force.

He understands, (how could he not have understood before?), that when they say "I don't want to play the game," they only mean that the game they are willing to play must be much more subtle and well-engineered than the ones they have seen so far. He reads through his notebooks, his thoughts, which once seemed poignant, begin to seem horribly simplistic and naive, terribly incomplete. His words lack the grandeur of Dostoyevsky's. He has not lived enough, what matters of consequence does he really have to offer? Disgusted, once again he stops writing altogether.

"I always thought I was a writer until someone put a pen in my hand," he says, trying to be cute, but I've heard the song and dance too many times. In that moment I have a flash of Angel saying those very same words the rest of his life. I see Angel surrendering, assuming his place in line with the rest. Perhaps Angel has never progressed far enough in the book of Times & Tides to grasp that the highest work of art is to be a man, to give the complete expression of what you have been given, what you are capable of. To this end, writing is only a ladder, a scale to judge how far you have come, a merciless arbiter.

Easy for Mr. Foot-In-Door to say, thinks Angel Desperado, Angel-the-Aries, once again at the mercy of some half-mad woman. He hasn't been home in six years, he has traveled, accumulated a wealth of experience, but he still lacks the discipline to complete something worthwhile. Now, once again, he walks the streets with eyes down, looking for coin in the gutters, hearing Aglaia's insults echo through his brain, "Heinous, uncouth..." He checks the corridor off the Champs Elysées where Karim, the Moroccan gangster, used to hide wads of counterfeit 200 franc notes four years ago. The hiding place behind the pipe is empty. The idea of returning home to the United States is becoming more and more attractive. After six years away, America has a rosy tinge to it, a nostalgic quality which is making it difficult for him to function in his accustomed way. America: the place where you don't need papers to get work. He passes up a painting job, he refuses to discuss his situation with other people, to drum up sympathy, he doesn't even try to find new quarters.

We used to joke about what we would do if we got really desperate. There are still plenty of options. He could hook a patron at the tea dances at the *Coupole*; or he could sell his passport at Stalingrad; he could peddle newspapers, he could bottle for the street acts; he could try and do an act of his own; he could sneak into the movie houses and pretend that the fifty franc bill they have laid on the side, a customer who went off before collecting his change, is actually his. He could feed himself from the slightly rotten food thrown out at the street market. But he is defeated, he doesn't have the drive. He waits like the horse at the slaughterhouse in the postcard on my wall. A gunny-sack blindfold over his eyes, a sledge hammer held over his white forehead.

We go to dinner at the apartment of a Chilean film director, who, it turns out, was Henry Miller's cook during his last years in Pacific Palisades. The Chilean shows us some of Miller's water colors, beautiful oranges and blues with words all over them, *elation, deliverance, eros, echolalia, love.* The Chilean tells how Miller used to joke about the myth of his hardships in Paris, "What I called my days of suffering." He says that the night before Miller died, he fell out of bed. "I just had the most horrible dream," Miller said. "I dreamed we were all on a merry-go-round. Are we really on a merry-go-round? And if we are, why don't we stop it?"

On the way home, past Parc Monceau, Desperado can't shake the image of Miller waltzing through Paris. "It figures." Miller writes about his suffering, and hundreds of people chase after him, prepared to endure any misery to write. *Ci-gît* Angel Desperado: crucified by the Times & Tides, impaled on the quick and the dead.

The job with Polanski continues to be pure joy, exhilarating. The process of writing, Polanski confesses, is what he likes least about film making, but he doesn't really seem to be suffering. Constant improvisation, constant laughter. Some days we watch movies, videos on the TV, or private screenings not far away. Sometimes we're just flat, and we know it, so after an hour we call it a day. We talk about the evolution of film, and the evolution of the audience's visual vocabulary, the story-telling shortcuts you can take, the shortcuts you *need* to take to keep the audience's attention. Which is something French filmmakers just don't seem to get. An ideal French film, he says: ten people sit around a table, there's a problem, they discuss it for 15 minutes, while the audience nods knowingly, arms crossed, saying "Yes, how interesting…" Then, when the 15 minutes are over, and the problem has been solved, uneasy silence, and… another problem, sigh of relief. No, a proper story leaves a mystery at the end of each scene. If, at the end of each scene, you can get the audience asking "What happens next?" you've got them in your pocket. That's the only rule of screenwriting you need to know. What happens next?

Somehow a gypsy in the metro, Line 2, manages to snatch Polanski's tape recorder out of my bag, but I replace it before telling him, no harm no foul, just hand him the new one, with the receipt for the guarantee.

"A gypsy stole the tape recorder? How did that happen?"

"I don't know."

"You didn't have to replace it."

But I did have to replace it, there's an ethic. It was my mistake, my lack of attention. You make a mistake, you fix it, right?

A week later he invites Beatrice and me to join him for dinner at Goldenberg's Deli, on Avenue Wagram, just off Place des Ternes, my old stomping grounds. I always used to pet the nice Boxer dog belonging to the restaurant when I passed on my way home after the crepe stand in the early days; and the dog is still there, delighted to see me.

It's the first time Polanski and Beatrice meet, he puts on his usual public persona, slips into his charmer routine, telling jokes, playing little tricks with the dish and silverware, and she laughs, amused. He waits until she goes to the bathroom to drop the masks, "Does she hate me? I really get the feeling she hates me…"

"No no, she doesn't hate you. Why would she hate you? She's just shy, a bit insecure, worried about what people think of her, sometimes that comes off a little haughty."

"No, because I really get the feeling she doesn't like me. It's weird…"

What happens next? Lord have mercy! Is life not hard enough? As much as novel-writing remains my priority, my dream, the time with Roman has been euphoric, ecstatic. I can't think of a better job, wouldn't mind doing it again when the time comes. Beatrice, Beatrice, Beatrice. That foot I supposedly have in the door? I've got a sinking feeling I've just shot it.

Only seven weeks after Angel's arrival at Aglaia's, she asks him if he wouldn't mind finding someplace else to sleep for a couple of days. It has something to do with her children, she explains. Very mysterious. She wants the lawyers to see that she is a respectable woman, that she should be given custody after all.

Angel has quite simply had enough. He packs his meager belongings into two tiny bags, his papers and a few items of clothing which smell to high heaven; he has not even had the fifteen francs it costs to put them in the wash. Dwight, the American writer, is off to Milan for a few weeks, to pick up his residence papers from the French consulate, so Angel moves over to Dwight's room without a word to Aglaia.

With 200 francs that Dwight lends him, Angel Desperado tries to start anew. The room has a skylight, no window. When the rainy season begins, the walls run with humidity. He buys some food. He crosses town to wash his clothes, because the Laundromat downstairs costs a franc more than the one across town. Then the money runs out, and he spends a week without eating. He doesn't want to go to me for help. Josef Klein is going to be a success, and Angel "The Sponge" Desperado is going nowhere. His ribs stick out through his T-shirt, his skin is almost translucently white, stretched taut, in six years he's lost twenty pounds, tremendous migraines floor him almost every day. He goes by ACP and by American Express to check his mail: a runaway car knocked over the lamppost he always used to rub to leave his mark. A new one is being put up in its place.

One night it all just overwhelms him. He goes for a long walk and ends up on the Champs Elysées, by the legless macrocephalic dwarf selling candies and combs from his wheel chair. Angel sees a soul-mate, he wanders over.

"What is it you want?" the cripple asks. "You want to talk? You don't want candy. You have no money?" He waves his club hand up the street, tells him to fuck off *vite fait*. It's the final blow, even the most unfortunate man in Paris will have nothing to do with him. "Leave me alone, why are you torturing me?" the dwarf screams at him. "My life is so horrible, my life is so horrible." Here Angel thought he was at the bottom of the abyss; how much further the abyss of suffering extends. He stumbles away, climbs back up the stairs to Dwight's room, picks up the phone and dials 19, 1, 415...

Angel has neither written to, nor spoken with his sister in five years, but when he explains his situation she has an immediate solution. "Why don't you come home for Thanksgiving? How much will it cost you to fly home?" As soon as he hangs up he feels better. Already he doesn't want to go back to the States, already he's beginning to fear that it might just be his death sentence. He reviews the conversation, the way his sister, surprised at his accent after so long abroad said, "We'll get you back here and teach you how to speak American again." After six years of hard times and little food, he is to come back for Thanksgiving: football on TV, twice as much food as anyone can eat, the celebration of excess. Angel can almost visualize the airplane crashing into the Lethe. But the money, $500 that his family pools together, enough to pay off his debts in Paris and buy a one-way ticket, has been wired to American Express. And he knows, the way his family history has gone, that if he doesn't return this time to Home Sweet Home Inc., he'll probably never be welcomed back.

November 11th, a cold clear day, *Sacré Coeur* glistening whitely. One last *café-calva* for luck, and Angel Desperado climbs on to the bus, off to England and America. A smile on his lips, a sinking feeling in his heart, he waves as the bus pulls out. I run alongside, exchanging a last few signed messages, little jokes attempted to make the moment go over more easily. A shift of gears, a cloud of diesel exhaust, and the bus finally leaves me behind. At 11:11 a.m. the church bells ring for Armistice Day. A tear rolls down my cheek. Why not a city full of bells to signal the departure of the unknown soldier from the scene of his greatest battles, his most brutal defeats?

CHAPTER 15

After 56 days straight, Sundays, holidays, never a day off, my job with Polanski comes to a close, but the final days are considerably less euphoric. Polanski is tired, more distant, much less faithful to the original "the more skeptical you are, the better the script will be" ground rules. I'm tall, he's short, we'll be standing in the living room, talking, when all of a sudden he will lower his voice, become virtually inaudible, so that I am forced to lean down, way down, to hear him. But that is only one of dozens of unconscious small-man tricks he pulls from his sleeve to assert dominance, it's really quite a show. We go over the script, proof-reading, fine-tuning. He absolutely agonizes over a comma, or a period, crossing it out with his sharp pencil, then erasing the correction, rereading the sentence, then changing his mind and crossing the comma out again. "Comma or no comma? What do you think?" he asks.

"Either way," I say. What he seems to think is rigor and precision seems like blindman obsession to me, incomprehensible, pointless, futile. Creative exhaustion, loss of instinct. I have no idea how to contribute.

"Comma or no comma?" He's not expecting an answer. I am there as a physical presence in the room more than anything, an excuse so that he won't feel crazy when he talks to himself. Very strange. I try to keep my feelings to myself, but I'm no good at pretending. I pay off some debts, take a trip with Beatrice, buy myself a computer and reclaim my life. It's time to start writing a novel again.

With Angel gone, it doesn't even occur to me to check out the December riots. The rightist papers say the riots are a protest against a government plan to weed out the free-loaders in French universities by charging a minimal yearly tuition fee. The rightist papers say that the universities are a mess, the worst kind of anarchy, where adolescent ideologues interrupt their professors, threatening them when the lectures defy the dogma of the day. The leftist papers disagree. Rightleft, leftright, it's just more of the same. As for me, one-time janitor, I'm on the side of the guys who have to remove the stickers from the walls and bus stops, the spray paint from the granite, the confetti from the gutters.

At Shiva Press, where I start working again temporarily, filling in for the regulars when they go on vacation, I describe the student leaders distributing ergotism stuffed *pains au chocolat* before the rallies. I am convinced that the protest is a result of the tremendous mental imbalance left by the changing of the height of Mont Blanc. "The highest mountain in Europe is four meters shorter, and there is violence in the air..." is how the article goes out to Finland, Sweden and Saudi Arabia.

The *voltigeurs*, a hooligan squadron of kevlar-jock-strapped cops mounted on trial bikes, rule the night, roar through the empty streets. One driver, and one guy behind with a sawed off broom stick, who swings at anything that moves. All but a few street lights have been knocked out by rocks and slingshots so that the infernal flying wedge roars and skids through the night lit only by its own headlights and the carcasses of flaming cars.

An unfortunate student named Malik Oussekine is cornered in a building entrance, and beaten into unconsciousness. A short while later he dies, officially of a heart attack. The papers reveal that Malik had a plastic anus, and quote Minister Tweedledee, who claims that the responsibility for this tragedy should fall to Malik's family. "If I had a son with a plastic anus, I wouldn't have allowed him to go out and protest..." he says, or something similar. Some of the students cry, leave flowers and poetry outside the building on Rue Monsieur le Prince where Malik breathed his last. Others, their hands and feet burning, have cooler heads: the important thing is that they now have a new target for their anger, Jean Tweedledee, that they now have a martyr, and reason to continue the protests despite the increasingly cold weather.

More of the same, more of the same. Trying my best to shift back into novel mode, to find my focus and at least get a few words down on paper that look like real writing, I practice sketching the figures from a poster on the wall, a copy of a George Grosz painting I picked up in Milan: *Down With Liebknecht*, 1919. Germany going mad, a frenzy of distorted heads, porcine futures, veterans of lost wars past and present, of free-floating body parts leering at and joining in with shark-toothed damsels dancing their way to apocalypse.

From 1919 to 1986: how many seconds? One? Two? The resurgence of French racist nationalism, the yearly taking-it-to-the-streets, *petit vins, petit* *fromage*s: there's your France. Psychological imbalances, a populace crying to rediscover something basic, howling to purge itself, to live something essential. About time for another war, *n'est-ce pas?* France cries for a George Grosz, but where is he?

At a café near Bastille a woman who works at Ungaro explains to her sharply-dressed man: she had to design a dress for a hideously ugly and unimaginably rich woman who was holding a *Traviata*-themed ball in Fontainebleau. The woman wanted a discount on the dress. "*Vous me faîtes un prix?* After all I look ridiculous."

"*J'aime bien les trucs bien. Tu vois? Tu sais ce que je veux dire par bien?*" the sharply-dressed man responds.

The Ungaro designer can hardly hear him she's shaking so hard. It's January, it's July, the sales are on. The tan you get in Spain doesn't last as long as the tan you get on the Côte d'Azur. She wants to get a new Mini, black of course. Her feet are so hot the nail-polish is blistering; her hands are so hot the gold is melting into her *Vittel Menthe*. She wants to move, she wants to explode. He knows exactly what she means, *si tu veux*. He can't for the life of him figure out why no one will talk to him at the office. German shepherds bark, children whine for an extra square of chocolate for their *gouter*, sirens rattle his Eustachian tubes. He's starting to feel a little hot in his extremity as well.

I hop the 29 bus from Bastille to Saint Lazare, riding in the back, outside, on the platform. I'd like to make this winter my last. In November, when the cold comes, they hunch their shoulders and close their hearts. You have to be superhuman to resist the poison, to keep your energy, to stay above it. The faces of the people, their posture, each day I shrink a little more. Three little old ladies in imitation squirrel furs, and imitation weasel faces push through me, elbow to kidney. They finished off their husbands, now they only have their health and the Arabs to take care of. "You know, my rheumatism really doesn't take well to the cold."

"Well at least it's not raining. What really does it is the humidity."

"Before the Arabs came, it wasn't this way."

"You know they all have syphilis. It makes them sleep with their daughters. Filthy bastards."

These are real words that real people say, I am just the witness, the recorder. Sometimes I wish my hearing wasn't so keen.

There is something in the air, everyone agrees, something left over from the riots, from the last rotation of Venus, something turning everyone batty, especially the sensitive-as-sin artist types. An actress that City-Rat is courting, a lady who makes a point of dressing all in white, says that there has been a run on sedatives in the city. Her doctor gave her a prescription, but the pharmacies have run out. Blame the riots, blame the strike, blame winter, blame Jack Chirac.

City-Rat continues to wrestle with his Drag-on, calling me when he needs money, when there is no-one else. Riding the roller coaster of his sensitivity, he spends his nights collapsed on the floor, weeping, his head smashed into a pillow so that the neighbors will not hear the sobs over their own racket. Weeping in self-pity, weeping at yet another rout at the hands of love, weeping in guilt and disgrace for the sins of humanity, the death camps, the atom bomb, weeping for his cousin André in Germany, who was run over by a truck at the age of nine. At the funeral everyone had nice things to say about André. "He was such a good boy, when he peeled the potatoes, he was very careful. He peeled only the skin..."

"I don't know what keeps me from jumping out the window," City-Rat says.

"Why don't you move to the cellar so I won't have to worry about you?" I say, provoking the usual look from City-Rat, don't you know that there's nothing funny...

Tear ducts emptied, City-Rat fades back into reminiscences about the Golden Age, the time before all the smart people left. Sometimes the street was just a picture story book. And the city itself, a series of fast-forward images: the buildings, the impressions, parties, the wine, street artists, magicians, wow, just a picture book. Music, dancing. Laughter, intensity. Sleet getting out of a straitjacket. Epic. Almost too close to home. There were times when he was getting out of the straitjacket, when he was really *in* that straitjacket. Sleet built up his public, it was not for everyone. He had a certain communication. Very class, Sleet had class, like Strahler. Taking care of their costumes, the little details, taking care of the props. Natural class. In the street. A responsibility. A code. Strahler was one of the few people who started "ace" and stayed "ace" on the street.

The further away, the more remote it seems, the greater its dimension, the brighter its luster in his memory. "It was about love then." Sleet and Strahler used to throw hats full of money back.

And what about that time at Saint Germain, after they'd been tripping on mushrooms? Sleet disappearing the cigarette, waving his hand over the jacket, the sound of the wind, freaking out, right? Then snapping his fingers, crack. Right then the car backfired. Man, they were freaking out. Free-king out!

A day in the life of Mr. Late. In the morning I wake up convinced that I am a saint. I get ready to go out for a coffee, sure that I'm going to meet someone who will change my view of things: not only sure but feeling it with every pore. In the street I walk with my heart out to invite it. Five minutes from the café, a bus mirror clips me on the back of the head. I can't remember a thing.

I get on the next bus and the doors close on my arm. I don't say a thing, just move calmly to the back. A woman, old, but not feeble-old, slams into me trying to get to the choice seat by the exit, then runs into me again a stop later when she gets out.

"What are you doing?" I stare her down. She begins to panic, jabs at me with her umbrella, two, three, four times, whines like some sort of trapped gerbil. I refuse to move until she talks to me. She will have to admit I'm there if she wants to get out this door. She's almost crying now, what did she do to deserve this? Then she looks up at my face, and she almost jumps back in fright. The wall has a head too.

In the metro an hour later, a second old woman crushes my foot with her high heel. By now the word is out, I'm a marked man. Old women from all over Paris mobilize with bags, dogs, squirrel furs, umbrellas and blinders. They rendezvous at the next stop and crowd in to the car the instant the doors open. I only manage to swim out three stops later at *Filles du Calvaire*. Right there, one last grizzled veteran is waiting for me. She blocks the whole *quai* with her form, the swinging bag. "Move it, move it. Wake up!" I yell, but she's oblivious, there's no way to get around her. I fail to notice her second bag which carries a special weapon: a champagne bottle which she quite unconsciously slams into my knee. I snap, my fist pulls back, and then starts forward to pulverize her. I stop the punch within inches, so that she never notices. "Dogs. You're all dogs!" The scream echoes through the station as I foam at the mouth. Somehow I find my way back home.

The streets are littered with moths come to light the next golden age. Exiles chasing ghosts, thirsting for freedom, dreaming of good times and immortality. Artists, con men, hedonists, shipwrecked adventurers, *bouffons*, castaways. Survivors. They probably don't belong here either: the condition is permanent. But where else is there?

Framed in the window of my cubicle, I watch the commuters go north once again, watch the sun dance across the Eiffel Tower, Montparnasse. I can't stop shaking my head; I wish Madame Lacombe were still alive. I too am heavy with the memory of how it was. How, because of a few people, the city came to life. Not just my city, but Paris entire. At Beaubourg, at Saint Germain, in the midst of the grey was a splotch of color, there was spirit, there were people with stories to tell and miracles in the tips of their fingers. Not the same old things, but wild notions filtered out of the air, sudden inspirations distilled from suffering and joy, a demonstration that despite the weight of the city there were still men and women walking around. City rats maybe, city rats sniffing blindly for the cheese at the end of the labyrinth, but rats who believed in something more than cheese and futility, rats who had direct contact with a current of joy, the current of eternity.

And some went away, and some latched onto absolutes, any explanation to keep from getting crushed. The street was raw, it made them go crazy, they had to be too speedy to stop all the people walking by, to keep their attention, they had to deal with lunatics and drunken Germans and Arabs trying to prove a point.

Beatrice begins to sleep more than ever, eleven, twelve, thirteen hours a night. She goes to the doctor, and discovers that she is anemic. "Maybe so," I say, but to me the lassitude seems more a matter of habit, mental anemia, no reason to live. I'm frustrated. In this period before the next project, I excoriate myself, tear myself apart, fill myself with self-loathing, nothing is good enough, the only thing that looms in front of me is the prospect of sliding invisibly into mediocrity. The situation is intolerable.

Beatrice asks me to marry her.

"Is that a joke?" I answer without thinking, because things have been so bad recently.

"OK I won't ask you again," she says and closes back down.

In the middle of the night she wakes me up. "Josef? I really don't have what it takes to satisfy you. Do I?"

"No I guess you don't," I say wearily. The next morning I move back into my room, this time for good. Hang Polanski, hang Beatrice, I've been compromising for too long.

Back on the seventh floor, the cockroaches come in through the cracks, under the door, or march in right through the open window to fornicate on the photograph of my smiling mother. "The shoe, the shoe!" they roach-squeak as I stalk them, asking for it. But it's not what you think. They're the size of quail eggs now, and they don't run off anymore like regular cockroaches. They wait for the shoe. Filthy, nasty beasts, they can't even get their rocks off any more unless I spank them.

Air fare from Paris to India is 5200F. From London: 335 pounds. New Year's in New Delhi? Not so fast: my temporary visa has expired, I'm living illegally once again. The editor who promised to help me with my papers informs me that the Ministry of Culture is on the case. But while waiting for those rusty wheels to turn, for the residence permit to come through, the editor suggests that it would be best not to leave the country, for fear of not being let back in. Joy to the world, Christmas is around the corner. Busloads of riot cops in place to make sure that the celebration of peace on earth and goodwill to all men not get out of hand.

Long, reassuring talks with Jolanta, a little luck, City-Rat finally comes out of his slide when he gets a small part in a film, playing the role of a Brazilian transvestite. Not a great part, but better than nothing.

At the beginning of January, City-Rat is offered a part in the play *Kean*, to star Jean-Paul Belmondo. The director of the play, Robert Hossein, the biggest name in French popular theater asks Jacques Le Coq, City-Rat's former teacher, to recommend a mime for a *Pierrot*-style piece, and Le Coq steers him to the best. Winter off the streets, work six nights a week, a steady income for six months. But City-Rat, once again feeling strong enough to begin working seriously on his Dragon, decides to turn down the opportunity, much to Le Coq's dismay. "I've got to do my own show," City-Rat just shrugs his shoulders. It is Blackie who ends up getting the part, who steps into the gilded cage.

At the end of January, City-Rat is hired to do a commercial for Scotch-guard. But because he has no papers, he signs a contract which deprives him of residuals. The money will be paid to him in May, when the commercial screens for the first time. The work on *The Dragon* is progressing, but in late January he's wondering once again just how he is going to get by.

Polanski is supposed to start filming in February, then in March, then in April. Among the roles in the movie is one for a *clochard*, a bum, which, three months earlier, solidarity, I had done my best to tailor so that City-Rat could fit the part. A bit of split allegiance, but who could do the role better than City-Rat? At the beginning of February, I meet him at a café on Rue Marbeuf, where we lie in wait for the bum who was the loose inspiration for the character. A fellow whose path we would cross frequently when Polanski would take me to lunch at *Chez André*. When he limps into sight with his backpack and green army jacket, we follow him, stand across from him on the opposite corner. City-Rat lights a cigarette and notes his characteristics: the way he shifts his load, the carriage of his head, the way he hunches his shoulders slightly forward when he is about to ask for some coin. He practices the lines: "*Il y a eu de l'embrouille.*" The only problem is the accent, the argot has too much City-Rat German in it, the "r" is not quite right, the "ll" either. "*Il y a eu de l'embrouille.*" We cross the street and City-Rat pulls out his change-purse, fishes out a ten franc piece and gives it to the bum. "I got to get that part!" he says.

I call Polanski, but his secretary, his keeper, cold, arrogant, *suffisante* due to her privileged access to the master, refuses to put me through. In the two months I worked on the computer next to her, I had heard the way she spoke on the phone to those who wanted something from her Roman. She's got that voice, just like she's using now, like I'm being meddlesome, like I've served my purpose, fulfilled my duty, and don't I understand that? She informs me only that the casting is scheduled two weeks hence.

"Remember the name City-Rat," I tell her.

"You know, Roman decides for himself. He doesn't really like suggestions like that," she says.

"The guy's good, I wouldn't tell you about him otherwise, would I?" I say, solidarity and hang the consequences.

City-Rat assembles a *clochard* costume from the Theâtre de la Jacquerie, the company with whom he did *Macadam Quichotte*, and hits the streets, research. He walks around with a limp, stops in the middle of intersections and yells at the traffic: "*Bande d'enculés. Fils de ta mère. Espèce de pédé! Pédé va!*" He is transparent, they look right through him, he has complete license. In the metro, they move away from him to find seats elsewhere. He just doesn't care. In Etienne Marcel station he pulls out his harmonica and lets it howl to the moon. A hand drops a couple of francs at his feet, another hand slips him a piece of hash. He goes into a bar and spends the money on a glass of cheap red wine. "Do you maybe have some bread as well? Some bread? Just a little piece, *du pain quoi? Il y a eu de l'embrouille...*" She looks him over, glances around, disappears into the kitchen, and comes back with a ham sandwich instead. With a full stomach now, he smokes the bit of hash and walks around. Couples kissing in cafés, window-shoppers, heroin addicts and glue sniffers with porcupine hair, transvestites. He stretches out on a hot air grate by *Pont Neuf* and looks up at the sky. He hasn't felt this whole, this free, in years.

Angel writes from California, he has already begun to discover the back side of paradise, his personal version of the air-conditioned nightmare. "I'm mechanically plugging into this machine to dispel the ugly instincts that are gripping my bowels. It's a damn sight easier than writing my resume.

"I don't know how to log all that has happened to me since I've been back. So many impressions, so many realizations... ignorance seems to be shed like a skin, just to reveal the next thick hide underneath. Can a man discover his soul in a merry ca? Or merely recognize the magnitude of his ugliness.

"The storms of thought and feeling come and go only to leave those clear, indifferent skies overhead that speak forever of twilight and the fragile shadow we cast. I was first staying with Dolores in her new town house (down and out house). Poor girl had to witness the strain of my senses, the arrogance of a proud prisoner of war and my weakness in the face of this inexhaustible supply of Americans and their mousterpiece behavior. Have I ever seen America like this before? The wretchedness along Market Street, the humanity that retains not a vestige of gentleness nor grace, nor care. Did I accuse the Brits of being blood-thirsty and vicious? And all the while I bore the passport of the great abyss of humanity. The stark horror! A man stripped of everything, wandering in a climate where the sun beats down relentlessly in the winter months and lets nothing hide. We are washed out with sunlight.

"As ever when I returned I was operating under another illusion, another vague goal. I wanted to plug myself right into the financial district of S.F. and accumulate enough money to purchase a home in Wales or somewhere in Normandy or Burgundy. I kept this delirium before me as I donned jacket and tie and visited various firms. I stared ahead through the traffic and concentrated on the illusion, afraid to look at the brown hills, the barrenness, the ugly appearance of so many homes, so many perfect streets and curbs and driveways and lawns. These pop-up homes made of plywood and plasterboard, trembling for fear of a match. These offices and businesses all shuddering with a breeze, waiting to be snapped in two over someone's knee. But things haven't worked out as easily as that. No job, no qualifications. My illusion begins to fade, because time is passing, and I'm beginning to get the fear in me, the fear of being lost and forgotten, the fear of being swallowed up and 'that being that.' The inexorable forces in life seem to be goading me, weighing upon me more heavily with each indulgence, each forgetting.

"I could go on forever, and perhaps I will, but it all seems very unimportant now. Haven't we got other goals now? Enough money again to travel and off I go. Not as a bum from place to place. I'll find my place. I see how handicapped I am. Here the employers haven't got the imagination to deal with me, telling me that I'm either over-qualified (that is, they don't want me) or that I'm a non-functioning element of society (they don't want me). 60 wpm? No. Computer? No. College degree? No. Hotel experience? No. Two years office experience? NO! Snakes and ladders, back to the beginning. Content yourself with full time at two hundred dollars a week.

"I can't tell how many application forms I've filled out. Soooo many. In each case I find my little history dramatic and overwhelming in a different way. Each time I write the story differently, embellish the facts a bit. To the scaffolding firms I'm a scaffold/king. To the hotels I'm a perfectly refined continental. To the disposal company of Walnut Creek I'm a hard-working laborer. And so on.

"In the meantime, isn't it great to be back? No one bothers too much with me. It's all an intangible that I went abroad. Seven years takes only one second to say and has only one second's value. Europe, England, Scandinavia. Where biscuits come from."

With no one around who speaks his language, Angel hits the books again. Joseph Campbell on mythology: "A hero ventures forth from the world of common day into a region of supernatural wonder: fabulous forces are there encountered and a decisive victory is won: the hero comes back from this mysterious adventure with the power to bestow boons on his fellow man." Despite the setbacks, despite the bleak times, Angel Desperado knows that the time in Europe was a victory; he holds on to that with all his might. He has so much to offer, so many important tales to tell. "...if the hero makes his safe and willing return, he may meet with such a blank misunderstanding and disregard from those he has come to help that his career will collapse."

Listening from under Dupont's shadow, City-Rat doesn't buy it, but he never really had much sympathy for Angel anyway. "It's just *bouffon*," he says. "You have been hunted from your village. Now you have returned to make your torturers laugh at your grotesqueness..."

After months of rehearsals, *Kean*, the play, finally opens, with Belmondo playing the role of the 19th century English actor Edmund Kean, from his glory to his fall. Between the acts, in front of the grey curtain, Blackie and another mime perform four three-minute-long Pierrot sketches to the tune of Vivaldi's *Four Seasons*, while the elaborate set is changed behind them. The King of Beaubourg in the mainstream at last. Thanks to Belmondo's name as a draw, the first four-month-run of the play is sold out before it opens. If Blackie plays his cards right...

He practically moves in to *Théâtre Marigny*, the large theater in the park opposite Champs Elysées Clémenceau metro stop, works out four hours a day, refines every little move, doesn't eat until after the show, at midnight, because he performs better on an empty stomach: the perfectionist, the pro. He is the one who suggested the use of *The Four Seasons*, he's the one who created the pieces.

Except after six years on the street, the King of Beaubourg, the cobblestone expert, isn't content to be passive, without tension, to do what he is told. He expects the conditions on the inside, the theater, to be ten times better than outside. Twenty times better, to accord with the image he has had of it all these years at Beaubourg. He expects everyone to be talented, driven, quality, he expects them to bow at his feet, to scoop up his brilliant ideas with gratitude. Soon enough he discovers the reality. Of the four pieces, he only manages to keep *Autumn*, the last one, intact, the way he imagines it. It's twice as good as the other pieces, the ones Hossein, the director, comes up with. He wants simple mime, nothing too artistic.

Caught up in the rest of the play, Hossein doesn't have the time to notice how much better the last piece is; Hossein wants "*le mime Canadien*" to leave him alone so he can concentrate on more important matters. Blackie thinks he ought to be paid more than he is getting; Blackie doesn't like the idea that they won't let the late-comers in during the whole first act, but that they do allow them in during the first break when *he* is performing; Blackie can't believe that Hossein is oblivious to the response the mimes are getting. "Next to Belmondo, we get the most applause," he says. Some days he threatens to quit, most days he resigns himself to the gilded cage, thinks of the video equipment, the artistic freedom it will enable him to buy.

Angel writes to apologize for not writing sooner, but life in Pleasant Hill is time-consuming. He has taken a word processing course and now holds two jobs, one as a legal secretary, and one as a waiter in a Lafayette French restaurant. He works, goes home, sleeps, and commutes back to work. "No time to stop and trample the flowers.

"It seems the day begins Monday mornings and ends Saturday at midnight. One long day. Faithfully I have not fallen into the trap of longing for the day to end. At any rate, I know that that is tantamount for wishing for life to end. In this realm of double shift I see how fragile life is for the slave, how being involved in the arbitrary and meaningless work without also having the time to pursue the cause and follow the path leaves me with less than a plank between life and death.

"On the other hand, since I am not a slave within, since I have enough resilience to overcome the negative effects of all this work and all these basic people I have to deal with, I have a first-rate chance of viewing this beast from the inside. I am experiencing the commuter and the office totem-worshiper first-hand. I am also experiencing the mediocre health of this type of lifestyle and its effects upon my spirit. I have participated in the bloodlust of the freeway, where the hasty lane-change is a sign of moral depravity and punishable by subtlety death penalty. The senior partner at the law firm gets a kick out of me for some reason. He loves the way I take care of everything. I have fixed the sprinkler systems, the lights, the fountains, I have handled difficult clients with ease, handled pressured situations with ease (what pressures these people is nothing to us), have gone on missions posing as an attorney to take pictures. He thinks I'm infallible.

"It is a bizarre life. Lacking in any continuity, like my sentences. Lacking in any reason except earning enough scratch to keep the mill trod and to move inanimate objects around."

A month of 70 hour weeks later and Angel Desperado is beginning to despair truly. "I just can't imagine lasting any more than ten years longer in all this."

CHAPTER 16

During the big snow storms, virtual silence, the city comes to a halt, buses skidding, cars up to their axles in white snow, Range Rover owners with 92 plates looking even more supercilious than usual, snow sneaking inside my rotten running shoes. The gates of Parc Monceau remain shut, the Martiniquais guard explains that it is to spare the impeccably dressed hellions, the *"fils à papa"*, from the embarrassment that comes from the inability to land a snowball. Concerned newscasters ask Chirac if he doesn't think that the breakdowns of nuclear power plants and the snow left piled in the streets of Paris for three days are maybe a sign that France is actually a third world country. First, second, third world, count 'em up. And good old Jacques Chirac saying in his best ENA nano-speak, "A government is not at fault in such situations, etc., etc., the American should buy himself some boots."

Three months after he gets the ball rolling, JMB, the kind editor who promised me help with my papers, sends me a copy of the letter that the Minister of Small Wines (aka the Minister of Culture) has written to the Minister of Fat Stomachs.

DLL/340   081898-   Paris le 15 JAN. 87

--*Monsieur le Ministre et Cher Collègue,*
     Some editor friends draw my attention to the case of *M. Josef Klein*, writer of American nationality.
     M. Josef Klein who voluntarily chose our country for its climate of liberty and creation, and who does not desire to return to the United States for the time being.
     Living in France for the last several years, he is presently finishing his second novel, and finds in Paris an environment particularly propitious to literary creation.
     This being the case, I would be grateful if you could examine the case of *M. Josef Klein* with the most positive spirit possible.

Thanking you in advance for what you may do for the young American writer, I beg you to believe, *Monsieur le Ministre et Cher Collègue*, in the expression of my most cordial sentiments.

Hercule DWARFKIN

Monsieur Jean TWEEDLEDEE
Ministre des Gros Bides

By the new year, the bombs of autumn seem like a bad memory. The pedestrians no longer look up any more when they walk down the street, life as usual. The police relax their strangle-hold on the city, fewer patrols roaming around nabbing the innocent. Increasingly I feel like this desire for papers is a symptom of decline, my descent from elation to morbidity, but by now it's too late to get out. Dwarfkin's letter goes to the Ministry of Fat Stomachs, from where Tweedledee sends a letter of his own to Tweedledum, Minister of Horns. I'm scheduled to go down to the main police station in a week. The whole affair is so hush-hush that I have to make my way across town to the publisher's office, to find out what I'll need to show at the *Préfecture*. It can't be said over the phone: four photos, proof of address, proof of resources.

On the day of reckoning, I slip back into uniform - a writer, but more important than that: a close-personal-intimate friend of three ministers. At the *Préfecture* I go in through the side door, don't even have to wrestle my way in with my Pakistani friends. First class, I'm feeling fine. The belt of my trench coat hooks on the brass door handle, almost flipping me on my back. The doorkeeper cranks the metal detection machine up to full power. I pass through once, twice, three times, setting it off each time. "Huh? I wonder what that could be," I chuckle nervously each time, once again losing my power. I empty my pockets, shed another piece of clothing and walk back through. Ten minutes later my fillings are on the table, I'm in my stocking feet on the freezing cobblestones before I break down and tell them what it must be: the metal heart. After a short conference with another doorkeeper and one last frisk, the first doorkeeper grudgingly lets me through. Bent over to tie my shoes, I try to make light of the ordeal. "I don't how it turned to metal. It wasn't like that when I first moved here."

Left, right, they lead me. Through bullet-proof sliding doors, up elevators and down hallways, phone calls to check my identity at every stage. But at least they are cordial. Winded, I finally stumble into the proper office.

"Sit down, please. You realize that this is highly unorthodox. *Normalement*, we don't have the right to give you a residence visa unless you leave the country," the woman says. "These are special circumstances." I pull out the papers I have brought with me, such an avalanche of papers and confusion, duplicates and foreign languages that she begins to beg for mercy. "Is this the right one? No that's the right one, this one or that one, this one..."

When the proper figures have been highlighted and the dossier is complete, she wipes her brow and rings for the guard. He ties a blindfold over my eyes, spins me around three times and steers me off for the next episode of pin the papers on the donkey. We end up two floors lower, another office, Room 1509, where, for 100 francs, a second woman puts me through my paces again. "What's your trade?" she asks. "Mythsmith, ma'am, a writer," I say, I can't believe it's going to work. "Well I can't very well put that on your card, *vous comprenez*, until you can prove it to me." "Fine," I say, "Put anything you want, doesn't matter to me..."

"This is going to be good for four months." She hands me the heavy pink paper with my doleful photo riveted and sealed on: Request for a *Carte de Séjour*. "In four months you come back. You need a medical exam, you need to sign up with the tax office, you need to bring four photos, & you need to get a social security number..." Four months grace!

Social security? Sounds easy enough, but isn't. More days wasted, more encounters with unpleasant yellow-tooth dogs guarding gates, more barriers at every turn, more confirmation that even what I am entitled to, I am not entitled to, and that of all the possible categories of human existence there is not a single one into which I fit. Yes, Monsieur Klein, it's true we do say '*l'impossible n'est pas français,*' but that doesn't apply in your case. Can't you understand? No! Impossible." Cleaning out the terrorists, cleaning out the artists. *La France terre d'asile.*

At the end of January, next to the Pompidou Center, President Walter Mittyrand inaugurates an atomic clock counting down the nano-seconds to the year 2000. "The future! European scientific know-how! Eureka..." he says. The Genitron, as the monster is named, stands five meters high and five meters long; the digits flip over on orders from a blinking green neon curlicue. "Ta-pocketa, ta-pocketa, ta-pocketa." German and Italian tourists collect at the base, waiting to deposit their ten francs and receive a postcard of the clock with the exact second on it. What second is it? Exactly? Panic! 396,217,871. That many seconds till the apocalypse. Blackie vows that he will get the postcard with the number, 333333333. "Bet you a hundred francs," he says. "Come on, bet?" Tick, tick, tick. 396,217,815. When the Genitron hits zero it will remain there. Newspaper intellectuals have a field day: Does this mean the beginning, or the end?

Néné the fakir dies, and Henriette, his wife, comes around to collect money from the other street artists to pay for the funeral. Ludo, a huge pony-tailed Ukrainian shaped like Humpty-Dumpty, an ex-*Legionnaire*, takes Néné's place. For thirty minutes he beats the audience over the head with a plastic caveman's club. When he has finished terrorizing the circle, he climbs up the flagpole to the balcony, and beats the people looking down from above. "*Deutschland! Bezahlen. Italia! Pagare. Sweden! Betala.* I want 25 ten franc coins. One, two, three, two..." When the hat is full, he spits fire, and lays down on a nail-board with four people on top of him. For the finale, The Human Dartboard, he picks four women out of the audience. They stand six feet away, aim and let the darts fly so that they stick, into his huge chest, his enormous stomach. Three days on, three days off to let the dart wounds heal, to let his partner take his share of darts. Tick, tick, tick...

All around Beaubourg, it's a forest of men with greased-back hair, women with large round earrings and teddy-bear knapsacks. Of mechanical chickens squawking to sell five-franc plastic eggs, and Pakistanis bouncing huge phallic balloons between their legs. Of windup plastic shoes and checkerboard haircuts, of junkies and skinhead glue-sniffers. "*Un don du sang?*" the blood donation truck is empty, and the prettiest of the nurses, white coat, red lipstick dripping from her fangs, has been sent out to request a pint from the passersby.

"Got none left," I say. She scowls.

"*C'est fini Beaubourg,*" says Henriette. It turns out that Néné isn't dead after all, that Henriette had just come up with the funeral scam to help them get through winter.

A few months shy of his 87th birthday, Etienne Decroux is rushed to the hospital, the perfectionist has finally flipped. A few weeks later, when he returns to his old home in Boulogne, Blackie and I decide to head out there to see him. On the metro to Boulogne, Blackie is more ill-at-ease than I have ever seen him, gone is the abrasive arrogance, the pugnaciousness, the chip on the shoulder. Nervously, he leafs through Decroux's book, the bible of mime, a red paperback called *Paroles sur le mime*. "Mime unclothes the actor so that we can see what remains. Mime takes away everything that is not he, props, costumes, texts." "...Expressing yourself in lines of scrupulous geometry. The face reveals who we are, but when the face is covered in the interest of modesty we are left with the body, which can trace lines in space. We can become who we want."

We hop out of the metro and cross the busy avenue. "This is where we all used to meet for coffee before class," Blackie leads me inside the café. Stalling. The old woman at the bar greets him like an old friend. "You know, he's not very well. He was too angry, it ate him up. *Qu'est ce que tu veux?*" The coffee tastes like last week's socks, but we knock it back anyway, and Blackie orders a mineral water on top of it, before he finally works up the courage to open the door to the school and step inside the courtyard. "The dressing rooms were up the stairs there. Wow! Common dressing rooms, gorgeous women stripping before class. A strange tension in the old building, Decroux filling every cranny with his presence. He used to ring a bell, dong, and all the students would head down towards the basement. Then he would ring the bell again, and the student who was first in line would ring a series of smaller bells. Decroux would answer with his bell, trying to get a syncopated rhythm going. Some days he would be in a good mood just because he had managed to communicate non-verbally with someone. Then one by one the students would shake his hand. *Bonjour Monsieur Decroux.* '*Comment? Comment?* He always used to pretend he couldn't understand my French. He used to test me, he had a phrase from a poem by Mallarmé: '*Tel qu'en lui-meme enfin, l'éternité le change.*'"

"Which means?"

"Transformed at last into his true self by death..."

The courtyard used to ring with the talk of the students, used to buzz. Now no one is around, it's completely quiet. Decroux, apparently, barely has enough money to live, he's had to sell off the apartments that were part of his school. We come upon him in his office, strapped to a desk chair by a dirty *Bande Velpeau*, a sort of Ace bandage wrapped around his chest to hold him up, to keep him from tipping over.

A termagant of a maid stomps in: "You must leave in five minutes. Monsieur Decroux needs to eat."

Decroux's wild white hair sprouts in every direction, a hoopoe's crown. There's that smell in the air of death, like Madame Lacombe used to generate but Decroux, the master, looks up and smiles, delighted to have visitors. He reaches out to shake, his hand is enormous, muscular beyond belief, almost independent, all out of proportion to his wasted body. "What do you want?" he says, "I'll do anything you ask."

Blackie tries to explain that he was a student.

"*Comment?*" What?

His usually proud chest sunken, a timid little boy, terrified of his master, Blackie is silenced. He holds the book forward for Decroux to autograph, and searches desperately through his pockets before finally coming up with a pen.

"You want me to do a drawing?" Decroux asks him. He holds the pen and the book like they are objects from a foreign dimension. Blackie doesn't register the words. "I was a student of yours," he says, taking the book back.

"*Je suis pas très clair,*" I'm not very clear. Decroux shakes his head and turns to me. "Do you know what he wants? Can you understand what he's saying?" I laugh. Decroux is definitely gone, but not so far that there isn't a trace of the rogue in him still, a hint of that old flame giving Blackie shit for his bad French accent.

"*Bon on doit parti,*" Blackie gets ready to go. More fractured French.

"You know what he wants?" Decroux asks me again. Blackie, the apostle of mime, says goodbye just the way the master taught them: turn away, the eyes, then the head, then the *centre spirituel*, the torso, then the hips, then leave the foot open, look back at the person and turn your foot away.

La Marche Parisienne, Blackie hobbles back into the café and orders a double Calvados. He's destroyed. "I guess we see how not to end up, huh?"

I don't know. Maybe you live that way, angry, thirsty for perfection, and you have no choice but to end up that way. Nothing is free, you have to pay for seeing the fires of eternity.

With *Kean* coming to the end of its first run, and scheduled to start up again in September, Blackie begins to do street shows again, just for the pleasure of performing, for the drug. Beaubourg has not really changed, there is still glass lying all over the ground, still the stale odor of piss in the corners, the straight line walkers are still there, tourists with sore feet who walk down the granite slabs, turning at right angles, because the cobblestones hurt their feet. The various Parisian mime schools are out for the summer and the usual students with no talent, The Get Lost Generation, are imposing themselves on the public.

Blackie, with Lucien's smooth-talking assistance, is pulling in 1000 francs a show, or so he boasts. With the money in the bank from *Kean*, he's so relaxed that he can afford to play around, to try different shapes of circles for example. Why? What for? "Man started with the stick, which is basically what? Two points with points in between. Then he added another point and he got the triangle, which is really a circle, right? And what is the wheel, but moving away, a way to run? So you want to write something about that?"

"What is it with you, Blackie?" I say. "Did your mother abandon you when you were young?" The sheer volume of bad ideas Blackie has thrown out for me to write over the years is nothing short of amazing, and still he keeps trying. Always the same mix of inspiration, dubious philosophy and total conviction. And why *should* he doubt? Josef Klein, unpublished cynic, has never earned a 1000 franc hat in his life. Look at how stiff Josef Klein is, how inflexible, look how his nose is out of alignment, how his shoulder says "I'm impatient, I've got to go now, come on don't waste my time." How many women has Josef Klein fucked this summer? So who's right, eh?

At least as far as the women are concerned Blackie's got me. No contest. So far this summer, the parade of women through his bedroom has been nothing short of phenomenal. Wild Italians, Americans who wrinkle their noses when they laugh and let it be known that they're ready to be taken, but would never make the first move, a Canadian Indian, two British schoolgirls, a French etymologist, various mime groupies. Blackie the stud, Blackie *le mime de Kean*, Uncle Blackie, he plays a different role for each one, and they respond in kind, with theater sketches, paintings, poetry or just little messages, contracts which they leave for him to sign. "I the undersigned, Uncle Blackie, do hereby undertake to feed, clothe, entertain and generally take care of the entire expenses of Josephine B. until 1991, on the express condition that she give up smoking. In the event that she proves unable to quit smoking, then he will pay for her cigarettes as well."

In fact the only thing that seems to diminish Blackie's effectiveness is his libido. When the tank's topped up, the pheromones flow from his pores, his washboard stomach glistens lightly: he's irresistible. *Un certain style*. But then he goes off, vanishes from sight for a week. After the binge, the first show is invariably horrible, the second one better. By the third one the butterflies are back to hanging all over him. When it's time to pluck volunteers from the audience for his gunfight skit, he looks them over, snaps his fingers and picks the one he wants.

"Everyone wants to fuck a mime," he gloats.

"I don't," say I.

"Me neither," says Lucien.

"Man what kind of person even thinks shit like that?" I shake my head, laughing.

"Ah, you're just jealous!"

393897600 nano-seconds before the 21st century, more or less, Blackie turns 34. "I'd rather be 50 than 34." The woman he has been seeing most regularly, a 22 year-old Danish mime student at Marceau, suggests that they rendezvous at midnight on the Pont des Arts. By 12:30, musicians, street artists, and other Danish students of Marceau have arrived, full of energy, alive. "Come on it's your birthday, and you don't look happy," one of the Danish girls says to him.

"I'd like to see you when you're 34. How old are you?"

"20."

"20? Oh Jesus."

The party moves down to the *quai*. Singing, improvising, gliding, falling into incredibly erotic dances. It's like the early days, when the energy was always there, when everything was adventure and opportunity. The next set of moths. It's wonderful that the moths keep coming. But how will they nourish themselves after their ability to run purely on energy leaks away? Do they understand that they have to build themselves a foundation? How will they handle the defeats, how will they get to the knowledge of the heart, how will they manage something more intricate when they turn 34?

"I've got another idea for you to write," Blackie says.

"I still don't want to fuck a mime…" I say, rolling my eyes.

He takes a swig of wine and passes me the bottle. "Imagine a prison for artists," he says. "The inmates are put behind bars by the government because their senses are too acute. The idea for them is to escape from the prison. To do this they must overcome the prison defenses, loud noises which incapacitate the prisoners, brilliant lights which blind them. To get out of this prison, the inmates must learn to dull their senses."

City-Rat goes to the casting for *Frantic*, (the title Polanski has come up with for our film). He does a screen test for the roll of coke dealer in a club, a Rastafarian-type, mainly because the French casting director, an ancient women who has been around forever, has no clue what a Rasta actually is. Doesn't know that Rastas, as a rule, tend not be to Caucasian. In addition to Harrison Ford, the film stars Emmanuelle Seigner, Polanski's girlfriend, and Betty Buckley, as Harrison Ford's kidnapped wife, a woman so matronly that you don't really want to see her again, you don't want Harrison Ford to find her. Polanski tried to get Mia Farrow, but Warner Bros. apparently balked at paying her the extra $100,000 her agent requested. I go to the set one day, at the Grand Hotel, watch the scene with Harrison Ford and the bum, who ends up being played by a French actor named Dominique Pinon, the spitting image of the *clochard* we used to pass on Rue Marbeuf. Polanski, delighted with his choice, is like a kid. "Isn't he great?" he says.

When the film finally opens, I buy my ticket and, neophyte to the business that I am, sit down fully expecting that my name will be on the credits. But when credits roll, they read: screenplay by Gerard Brach and Roman Polanski, my name is nowhere to be seen. I hear later that Warner Bros. brought in 18 other writers behind me, including Robert Towne, the writer of *Chinatown*, but the script is not all that different from the first draft, my draft. I was naïve, I guess that's just how it works. I try to make light of the injustice, who cares about a few lines on a screen? Is that what I'm on the planet for? No! I still want to write novels, I'm grateful for the financial cushion. Two years of freedom ahead...

City-Rat inherits an apartment near Stalingrad for the summer. It's one of the poorer parts of town, many of the people are small, twisted, deformed, less lucky, a *Ricard* and a *café-calva* for breakfast. But the large apartment and the solitude bring him back to himself. His skin almost begins to look pink. He still gets those circles under his eyes if he drinks, but he is almost not drinking at all, devoting himself to meditation, yoga, reading and tap dancing.

Having still failed to get social security, I'm starting to be resigned to my fate, to the idea that the Parisian chapter of my life will soon come to a close, but I'd like to see some fireworks at Beaubourg one last time before getting kicked out. I ask City-Rat what it might take to get him back on the street performing with Blackie, hoping I might be able to arbitrate.

"What would it take? A lot! He protects himself, he's scared, he's not ready to open up."

"It's a lion's den at Beaubourg," Blackie says, when I confront him with City-Rat's objections. "I go down there with a weapon. City-Rat goes down there like a saint. Look at the result. Sure I protect myself! Why is it always my fault? Why don't you tell him that he needs to be more sensitive to his partner? Give him the ball every so often, not steal the scene. You give him the ball, he never hands it back..."

After a month of mediation, City-Rat is finally prepared to compromise, he needs money. We meet at the *Dame Tartine* to map out a strategy, to establish the guidelines that will keep it together this time, and then everyone heads down to the *plateau*. Blackie starts out by following people. City-Rat does a Romeo and Juliet skit, pulling people from the crowd to act out the parts. His Juliet is perfect, a mischievous French girl, and his Romeo is even better. City-Rat tells Romeo to take off his jacket. And he does so. He tells him to take off his shirt, and the shirt is lying on the ground. He tells him to take off his pants, and he has his belt undone, before City-Rat stops him. "*Eh, eh, eh, doucement. Du calme, du calme.*"

As soon as Romeo has conquered Juliet, City-Rat and Blackie begin their boxing sketch. Flying high, City-Rat scissor-jumps into the "ring." But he lands improperly and his ankle buckles, a loud snap. He crumples to the cobblestones. He can't walk, his ankle is already swollen double. They stop the show, collect about 130 francs of sympathy money without even asking; the awful noise of the snapping ankle reverberates around the *plateau*. No other option: Blackie slings City-Rat over his shoulder, carries him from Beaubourg to the hospital on *Ile de la Cité*, a good half-mile, gives him the money from the hat. Exactly, down to the centime, it pays for City-Rat's crutches.

A week later, when the injury turns out to be just a sprain, City-Rat, flat broke as ever, calls Blackie up to work again. On the way down to the *plateau,* they decide that City-Rat will try and form the circle by doing his cigarette sketch. So he hops out to the middle of the circle with his crutches. "Anyone have a cigarette?" How does he smoke and hold the crutches and then fall down? He doesn't know, and as he tries to figure it out, the crowd is laughing. But by the third puff, when the cigarette begins to master the smoker, City-Rat knows it's not working. The audience looks on in horror, nervous laughter, *rires de confiance.* By the end of the cigarette, City-Rat curled up on the cobblestones, a fetus between two crutches, the audience is watching a camel being butchered, hacked apart with scimitars. City-Rat the veteran learns yet another lesson from this brutal school: pathetic on pathetic just doesn't work. He and Blackie try another sketch, but after only three minutes Blackie stops the show, can't bear to go on. "Fuck it. Nobody needs money this much. I'll *give* you a hundred francs." They leave the *plateau* to have a beer. The other street artists are mortified: no one wants to work.

A week before my appointment at the central police station, bright and early, I wait outside the *Hôtel des Impôts du 17ème,* to sign up for income tax, still hoping that somehow this will all work out. When the doors open, they accept me right away. It's the friendliest bureaucratic reception I've had in four months. The woman understands my situation, is even willing to believe I'm a writer for tax purposes. I've never earned enough, black or white, to pay taxes, and it is not the act of signing up now that is likely to change that, but with the unexpected warmth, the human connection, I can't help but feel that my luck may be changing.

From the tax office I go to get the chest X-rays and blood tests required by French law. *Contrôle sanitaire des étrangers.* The woman assures me that the tests are not really meant for Americans, but rather for Arabs and Africans.

Three days later, with the results in hand in a sealed envelope, I head off to the doctor. "Take off your shirt and shoes," the doctor is curt and business-like. I haven't seen a doctor in years, and I don't really need one now, all I need is for him to put the stamp with his name on it to certify the accuracy of the blood tests and X-rays, but he seems determined to charge full price for his expertise.

"Anything else the matter?"

"No, no, I'm fine, that should do it…"

"You're supposed to have the test for AIDS now," the doc says. I understand: either I let the hippocrate go through his routine or I'm going to be laying out an extra 400 francs for another blood test. The doctor unrolls his disease check-list and reads off the maladies.

"Entomy?"

"Yes."

"Algolagnia?"

"No."

"Cachexy?"

"Yes."

"Compassion?"

"No."

"Hope?"

"Yes."

Getting ready to say goodbye, a grind to axe, I put myself on a budget of 20 francs a day, just like the old days. Five, six hours a night sleep, rice and pasta in the stomach, showers at the American Church and the swimming pool. Drinking coffee in cafés only, scribbling away in my notebook, acidic caffeine prose, listening to the people talk, hearing voices other than my own. "The flags on the Champs Elysées are blowing the wrong way. Looks like rain," "I always told you Michel, the future is in horses." "Life is beautiful. Shall I serve you some more raspberries?" "*J'ai le bras long, Madame.*" "*C'est commode pour se gratter le cul.*"

Long walks through the warm summer nights, one hour, two hours, recalling adventures, women, meetings, kisses, good fortune and setbacks that happened on this street, this alley, in that park, reveling in the shadows of all those old buildings, the hidden details that jump out when the city has gone quiet. A man scolds the white rat on his shoulder, "*Maximilien, tu exagères.*" Maximilien, you're exaggerating. Walking down Rue de Rome, three transvestites, miniskirts, boas and stiletto heels, hands on hips, stop to watch me pass by. "Free for you honey," says the tallest one. Where *did* my heart begin to close?

I meet up with Beatrice at the brasserie on the corner of Legendre and Rome. Such pain, such tenderness, such fear. She's been away in Australia, she's learned a few lessons from watching the way her girlfriend there behaved with her man. She saw a lot of herself in that, the way she used to run off to her sister when things got bad, the way she used to sulk and be distant...

I walk her to Rue de Lévis, kiss her, lips trembling, tumbling into abandon, and then walk back. A pregnant gypsy woman stops me and asks to see my left hand. "You will live long, you are in a sad state, you are being betrayed by Jean and Georges, your bad luck and sadness will last for 18 days, there is something in your life that needs to be burned to remove the curse on you. You must be careful of the letters K, L, E, N, those are the ones that are going to cause you trouble." K, L, E, N, small wonder; how did she know? "I want you to tell me two things in which you want to succeed."

"Love..." I say.

"Two things," she says. "Work?"

"Yeah, work too."

"How much would you like to give me? I swear on the head of my unborn child, my swollen stomach and Sainte-Genevieve that what I will reveal to you is right."

"Five francs?" I say.

"50, 100 francs," she answers. I end up giving her ten francs, "*Un cadeau pour l'enfant.*" It is not enough for any more revelations.

At the *Préfecture de Police*, the mood is almost light, not at all like the state of siege six months previously when glove-wearing porkers were punching every foreign thing in sight. One of the policemen sees a woman with a baby carriage, and he requests that everyone else step out of the way so that she can pass through. Last night I spent with Beatrice, saying goodbye. If they kick me out, they kick me out.

I march up to Room 1509, fill out the usual slip and sit down in the hallway. For two hours I watch Chinese people with interpreters, Swedish models, Swiss jazz singers, Greeks and Bulgarian weight lifters march into 1509. I watch cart-loads of supplies roll one way down the hall, and then come back again. After two hours my name is called. "You must come back tomorrow," the woman informs me. "Will nine o'clock be all right? You'll be the first one in."

I just want to get it over with. "Well look, I didn't manage to get social security. But I do have an insurance card from the US." The woman considers the problem, then disappears into an office to consult with her superior. The result: they put a stamp on the heavy pink form that protects me from deportation. "*Rectification*." It looks like the most inept kind of forgery, but it gives me one more month to get my act together.

When City-Rat's ankle heals, he and Blackie get back to work. They start their show with a slow-motion warm-up, swinging canes at each other and moving out of the way. The show finishes and City-Rat makes for the bar, when Mehdi the Persian gypsy, comes for Blackie with a knife. Apparently Mehdi is displeased with the rotation of the shows. Blackie wrestles with him, knocks the knife away and tries to steer him into the corner, out of the line of sight of the Big Brother cameras that stare down on the *plateau* from the police station. This would be just the excuse the cops were looking for to shut Beaubourg street theater down for good, he thinks. Blackie clutches Mehdi around the neck, up against the wall. By now he wants to let go, but Mehdi is hanging on to a fistful of Blackie's hair. The rest of the clowns, mimes and jugglers try to separate them, but Blackie doesn't want to be separated without his hair. Finally, Nguyen, a Vietnamese magician who does an imitation Kung Fu act, manages to pry them apart. Blackie retreats to meet City-Rat at the bar, a bit shaken up, still boiling with adrenalin. He sits down and takes a deep breath to calm himself. "Good hat?" he asks.

"I don't have the hat. I thought you had it," City-Rat says. They've left the hat behind, maybe 1000 francs. City-Rat gets up in a hurry and scurries back to the *plateau*. Fifteen minutes later he returns. His face is white.

After Blackie's departure, Nguyen had started playing. As he ran around, trying to form the boundaries of the circle, Mehdi stepped in and tripped him, sending him sprawling to the cobblestones. "*Assass, attaque!*" Mehdi had set his dog on the fallen magician. The mongrel had savaged Nguyen's shins, his pants, until Mehdi jumped in too, pulled out a can of mace and thrust it into Nguyen's eye. Once, twice, three times, pushing it in, almost exploding the eyeball.

When City-Rat arrives, Nguyen is on one knee, trying to flush out his eye with water. "Is it still there? Is my eye still there?" Nguyen wants to know. The eye is swollen, a red mess, a Martian moon.

"Just keep pouring the water on it," City-Rat says.

"I'm going to kill him," Nguyen gets up and walks over very calmly to Mehdi. "I lose my eye, you lose more than that!"

Mehdi stands there, his lips gone white, trembling at what he has done. "Go ahead, hit me. Go ahead, do it," he says. He wants to be punished.

"Look," City-Rat says to Nguyen. "I think you better get to the hospital."

"Yeah, yeah, OK," Mehdi says. "I've got my car up there. I'll take you." Last City-Rat saw them that day, Mehdi had his arm around Nguyen, steering him to his car to take him to the hospital.

A month after my last appointment at the *Préfecture de Police*, I return, this time with a letter from an accountant in the United States, "proof" that I have a valid insurance policy with Blue Cross. Which I don't, actually. The woman opens the dossier calmly, checks to make sure I brought everything I was supposed to. "Taxes? Medical report? Four photos?" She examines the letterhead about the insurance company and jots down the name of the accounting company instead of Blue Cross. "We don't really need this anyway the first year," she throws out. It's summer and she can afford to be more lenient. "When you renew your permit it's going to be much stricter."

I tell her about my struggles. "Five months of mazes, and now you tell me I don't need it..."

"Well you know the French bureaucracy. It's always a bit confused. What shall I put down as your profession? *Profession Libérale*, or writer? If I put writer on it you'll be able to work." She fills out the form. I don't dare breathe. I watch the secretary type it out on a manual typewriter, rivet on the photo, put it under the seal machine and stamp it. The orange cardboard card is placed in my hand, and the woman helps me to my feet. I read the line at the bottom, right where it says, "*Profession: Ecrivain.*"

"I'm a writer!" I fall out the door, smile lighting up the police station hallway fit to get me arrested. "I'm a writer."

The headline in *Le Meilleur* announces that the French like the Americans less, find them naive, sectarian, too cocksure, too selfish, too hypocritical, not cultured enough, not discerning enough in politics, and disdainful towards the French. News! I have enough money these days to waste seven francs to find out the details. The story itself reveals how the same poll found out that the French adore America itself, and that they would, at least once, like to spend their vacations in the US. Did they really need a poll for that? Hamburger restaurants blossoming like a plague, blue jeans and neon lights, '50s haircuts and T-shirts with fractured American bromides on them, Eurodisneyland, a Mouseschwitz of their very own being built down the road in Marne la Vallée.

In the sun, now that I am legal, I walk up to one of the Pakistanis with the cardboard boxes, and plunk down my ten francs for a wind-up plastic tennis shoe toy, two shoes linked together and advancing nowhere. Calmly I wind them, place them carefully on the ground, and stomp them. Too stunned to move, the salesman just stares at the shards of blue plastic. At the *Café Costes,* across from the *Fontaine des Innocents,* the models and pretty boys pose with their dead stares. There used to be a church under their feet, an excellent burial ground, reputed for its ability, when mixed with lime, to eat the flesh off a body in nine days. "Ba-ruc, buc-buc-buc-buc-buc-buc," d, c-sharp, singing Chicken Little with its belly-full of little gift eggs to tempt the kiddies, meets the toe of a licensed Klein. The machine changes its tune, sings a haunting dhikr. The age calls for a response.

Summer. Early afternoon. City-Rat and Blackie are surrounded by a huge crowd. It's like old times, the laughter rolling over Beaubourg in waves. Waiting for them to pack up, waiting for Beatrice to arrive, I sit on the steps by the Firebird Fountain, *Eglise Saint Merri* looming overhead. In a daze, I pat my pocket to make sure the card is still there. Patrols of uniformed police walk slowly around looking for terrorists. Plainclothesmen drift through the crowd looking for pick-pockets. An old lady, kind soul, spreads some stale bread around for the pigeons. They fly zigzagging away, their little pigeon brains scrambled by the hallucinogens, to shit down on lovers arm in arm, hormones racing in the warm air. Some Arab kids play tennis, using a metal crowd control barrier for a net. It is 391823666 seconds before the year 2000. Josef Klein, the biggest midget in Paris, is feeling fine once again. In the fountain I look over the sculptures. The nozzles spray a fine summer curtain of mist over the bird of fire, the skull, the spinning snake, the hippocampus, the elephant, the hat and what may or may not be a sea cucumber. What's this? No! Not possible. I begin to laugh crazily. The sound echoes off the church, off the tourists, off the police station. The rest of the pigeons fly off, a tremendous beating of wings. The old woman clears her throat angrily. Someone ran off with the heart! Vandalism? Maybe that day in winter when it froze in mid-beat, it cracked and had to be removed. No, it's probably just in the shop for repair. Not a symbol of anything....

Rest in peace Madame Lacombe.

THE END

Paris, August 9, 2013

WORLD OF MIDGETS

ABOUT THE AUTHOR

Jeff Gross is an adventurer, traveler, and filmmaker who collaborated with Roman Polanski on several screenplays, including *Frantic* and *Bitter Moon*. He lives in Paris along with his two children, wife and mentally disturbed cocker spaniel, Bodhi.

www.ingramcontent.com/pod-product-compliance
Lightning Source LLC
Chambersburg PA
CBHW071250250626
47163CB00002B/405